THE SCRYING OF

VIOLET YARDLEY

SALLY-ANNE SMITH

ISBN: 9781798414736

Imprint: Independently published

Printed in Poland

For Sarah

Chapter one

If one thing was certain in this world it was that there would be hell to pay for this.

Joseph Davenport cursed under his breath as the grandfather clock in the entrance hall struck six, the solemn toll of the bells pealing out through the wide-open doors of Ty Mawr and echoing around the tree-lined courtyard that surrounded him. The sun had already set, turning the sky to onyx as his foot landed on the bottom step, the path ahead barely illuminated by the oil filled lanterns that dominated the entrance to the house.

'Master Joseph, where on earth have you been? The whole family is waiting in the dining room for you! Again!'

He glanced up at the silhouetted figure and hurriedly began unfastening the buttons on his grey woollen coat as he ran up the stone steps two at a time to the entrance where Agnes Morgan stood waiting for him. Freshly embroidered tea-towel folded delicately in one hand, her flustered cheeks a shocking shade of pink in the lamplight she took a step backwards as he dodged past her, scowling as he threw a sly wink in her direction. Anyone else might have been offended at such a gesture. They might also have assumed that she took a step backwards out of deference, though nothing could have been further from the truth. It was simple self-preservation. Nothing more, nothing less. That had been a hard lesson to learn as she had watched him grow. When Joseph Davenport was focused, he didn't necessarily see the big picture and that included everything and everyone around him. He wasn't ignorant, not by any stretch of the imagination. He was more, blinkered, she'd surmised. Too busy focussing on his own goals, selfless though they were, to pay heed to the world.

She threw her arm out, grabbing his riding hat off his head as he passed, tutting in exasperation as he dashed into the entrance hall and made his way towards the large mirror that rested above the fireplace where he finally came to a halt. Leaning forward over the flames he rested his hands on the mantelpiece and drew in a deep breath, watching the fire pulse in retaliation against the draft from the open doorway, its warmth soothing the chill in his bones, the grandfather clock ticking behind him warning of his increasing indiscretion.

'Don't just stand there, dithering child!'

'Of course, sorry.' He took off his gloves and tucked them under his arm, vigorously rubbing his hands together to bring them back to life. Looking up into the mirror he fixed his gaze on Agnes's reflection.

'Ride back took a little longer than expected. There were gypsies on the main road, so we had to take a detour. Thomas insisted upon it, though I doubt they'd have been any bother. It's a shame their reputation rather precedes them, don't you think?' *She wasn't with them.* He kept his eyes fixed on Agnes's, the observation left unsaid.

'Gypsies?' Agnes all but shrieked, her eyes widening, her fingers clutching Joseph's hat so tightly she was on the verge of crushing it. He couldn't help but smile. Dear, sweet Aggy. Always so dramatic.

'And we know enough of them to know they are good people who pose no threat to us whatsoever. You know you shouldn't believe everything you hear from the local gossips, Aggy. They'd have half the village hung, drawn and quartered if they had their way, guilty or not.'

'And you must stop calling me Aggy. If your father hears you being so familiar with the staff...'

'It won't make the slightest bit of difference.' Joseph returned to the mirror and started ruffling his hair.

'It's too informal.' Agnes protested. 'You know that as well as I do.'

'How can it possibly be too informal? You're not staff, you're family! More so than anyone in there. Aside from Amelia that is. The rest by blood I suppose, though that counts for little. In my eyes anyway.' He nodded towards the closed door that led to the dining room, the silence leaking from it almost palpable.

'Master Joseph, you hold your tongue! And remember, it won't be you that gets punished!'

'I'm sorry.' Joseph said hurriedly. 'You know how my mouth rushes away with me.' He stared at her reflection, his fingers fumbling with the bottle green cravat that lay in a tangled mess around his collar. 'Truly, I am sorry.' Agnes huffed and walked over to him, grabbing hold of his arm and turning him to face her.

'Well, just you mind your mouth in future. If I lose my job, I lose my home here and I've got no place to go, not now Robert and the children are…' She cut the sentence short, reaching up to slap Joseph's hands away from his tie. 'And let me do that, you're getting nowhere fast.' She deftly began rearranging the cravat, bringing the ends back together and re-creating the hefty knot that lay between the two edges of his collared shirt. When she was done, she whipped the cloth from her apron and held it to her face, the crinkling of her eyes betraying the expression of disgust beneath.

'The stench on you, lad! You smell more like a horse than that old nag out back!'

'That's because I've been riding a horse all day!' Joseph grinned impishly as he leaned forward and whispered in her ear.

'Cheeky pup!' Agnes lifted the cloth and playfully swatted him around the head. 'You really should go and change. Into proper dinner attire. Let young Gwilym help you. It'll only take two minutes!'

Agnes gestured towards Joseph's steward, a tall sandy haired boy who waited silently and patiently close by, his hands clasped together in front of him. Joseph shook his head as he shrugged off his coat and handed it to Gwilym. Gwilym took a step back, his expression pained.

'Mrs Morgan is right, sir. You are a tad putrid.'

'Is that so? How awful.' Joseph feigned an air of concern. 'Thank you for taking my coat, Gil.' Gwilym sighed and shook his head as Joseph walked away from him. 'Getting changed, Agnes, will make me later still for dinner and will earn me no favours I'm sure. I imagine I've annoyed everyone enough already this evening. God forbid I should force them to wait so long they are forced to eat Cook's parsnip soup when it's cold. It's bad enough hot.' He jumped backwards, narrowly avoiding the towel that Agnes whipped out at him in retribution a second time.

'And that's enough of that!' she hissed through tightened lips, all the while fighting to suppress a smile. 'Besides, I prepared the menu today. And what with it being your birthday and all…' She smiled when Joseph's eyes lit up. 'Silly boy. What, did you think I'd forgotten? I have something for you.' She reached into her apron and pulled out a silver watch, its chain slipping like silk down over the side of her hand. 'Every fine upstanding gentleman should have a pocket watch, don't you think?' Joseph stared dumbfounded at the timepiece.

'Aggy, you can't give me this. It's worth far too much. Isn't there someone in your own family…?'

'Not since my son died, Master Joseph, as well you know.' Agnes said, matter of fact. She looked down at the watch that still lay in her hand. 'So now, are you going to take it? Or are you going to offend me and refuse it?' She pushed her hand further forward and watched as Joseph gently took the watch from her palm, staring at it for the briefest of moments before wrapping her in a fierce embrace.

'Now you just stop that! Going, trying to make me all maudlin! I'll have none of that nonsense!' She pulled back and stared at him through glistening eyes, taking in every feature. 'Look just like your mother when you smile, you do. Her eyes used to twinkle, just like yours.' She reached up and re-straightened his cravat. 'She'd be very proud of you today, boy. Don't you forget that. Now, go get your dinner. There's roast beef and apricot Charlotte.'

'Thank you… Aggy.' Joseph whispered in her ear.

'That's quite alright, my boy Joe.' Agnes whispered back. She kissed the tips of her fingers, tapped him on the nose and disappeared into the depths of the house, leaving him to face whatever lay on the other side of the door alone.

*****

All eyes were on him the moment he entered the dining room, only one pair warm and welcoming. Amelia. He made his way around the table briefly greeting each guest in turn before he finally collapsed into his chair next to her.

'Oh Joe! You smell utterly rancid!' Amelia laughed as she threw her arms round him. 'Happy birthday brother!'

'You're late. The family have been waiting.' Amelia whipped back around to face front and stared down at the table her hands falling into her lap, as though it were she rather than her brother who had been castigated. Joseph looked up from her towards his father. Edwin Davenport's usually sallow face was red and blotchy, probably a result of the copious amounts of sherry he'd undoubtedly consumed prior to sitting to eat. He glared at his son as he grabbed his napkin, shaking it out with a vigour that was more akin to aggression before he laid it flatly on his lap, his eyes running around the table as his guests silently did the same, as though they had been waiting for their cue.

'Please, accept my apologies sir, everyone. I had intended to be back a good while ago. I've been re-training one of the horses for a while now and I took him out for his first proper ride today. I got a little over-enthusiastic I'm afraid and went further than intended and then on the way back I…'

'I think that's enough conversation for now Joseph. Let's get on with dinner, shall we? I'm sure Kitchen would like to go home at some point this evening.'

'Of course, sir. Again, I apologise.' He picked up his soup spoon and stared at the bowl in front of him that was devoid of steam, the contents of which seemed to have developed some form of skin. 'Aggy assured me there wouldn't be soup.' He leaned in towards Amelia as everyone else began eating. Amelia glanced sideways and shrugged then looked back to her own bowl.

'It could have been worse.' She whispered. 'It could have been parsnip.'

*****

They were well into their final course with Edwin Davenport halfway through his second glass of madeira before conversation resumed. There were, Joseph had come to realise, certain discussion points that were always more likely to awaken Edwin from his sombre state than others and it was a constant source of relief to both himself and Amelia that their wider family knew their father so well. One simple observation from his aunt about the grounds that

6

Edwin had so lovingly created for his late wife was all it took to bring warmth back to the room.

The rare displays of affection that followed were a phenomenon that only occurred when he was inebriated and feeling sociable. Such responsibilities had been their mother's role as far as Edwin was concerned, and both children knew his attempt for what it was, a drunken stab at filling the gap that she had left. It was only Amelia who embraced it, still at an age where she was desperate for affection from the one parent that remained alive.

Joseph watched as she beguiled those who sat with them. She was the image of their mother, an observation that toyed with his emotions, nostalgia and sadness warring to become the dominant reaction. When she spoke however, she was all Amelia. Unlike their mother who was soft and gentle and unassuming she was all sharp, but not cruel, wit. Where Amelia was, laughter always followed.

'I would like you to play for our guests Amelia. They should see what a fine accomplished young lady you have become.' He scraped the last of his dessert from his bowl and glanced over at their aunt Beatrice who sat anxiously at the other end of the table. 'I do believe sister, that one day soon she will make someone a fine wife.' He devoured the Charlotte and emptied his glass in one mouthful. 'I suggest we retire to the sitting room. For port, I think. Gentlemen, I have a fine selection of cigars that one of my contacts acquired recently from the Americas. I think you'll find yourselves pleasantly surprised.' He stood, opening his arms wide. 'Amelia, please show our guests to the sitting room.' Amelia nodded politely, rising from her seat and weaving her way past their guests towards the door. 'And Joseph, if you could remain behind for a moment. I would like to speak with you in private.'

7

'Of course, father.' Joseph frowned questioningly at Amelia who subtly shook her head in response as she made through the door and out of sight, the rest of the family trailing behind her.

It had to have been less than a minute but it felt like a lifetime before his father turned to speak to him, still failing to make eye contact even though they were alone, focussing instead on the plates on the oak dresser that adorned the long wall of the dining room and the portrait of his recently deceased wife that hung alongside it.

'Joseph.' He mused softly. 'You ride every day and you are gone for hours but I have no idea where you go. I have never known where you go.' Joseph took a sip of water to ease his suddenly parched mouth.

'Where I go? Father, there is no one place that I go. There are so many bridle-paths around here. Sometimes I head along the river, sometimes to the mountains. When the weather is more favourable, I…'

'You need to stay away from the mountains.' Edwin interrupted without apology.

'Stay away, father? I'm sorry, I don't understand.'

'The mountains.' Edwin repeated slowly, his tone all frustration, his words slurred. 'You are forbidden to ride there. It really is very simple.' He moved to stand, slowly making his way to the door before finally making eye contact with his son. 'Joseph, I have received word that the witches are back, and I am warning you now boy, if you know what is good for you, you will stay away.' Before Joseph had had chance to gather a response his father had already left the room. It was probably best that his father had left so quickly, Joseph surmised, winking at Gwilym who now stood in the empty doorway. Because at least this way, he didn't need to hide his smile.

Chapter two

By the time Joseph made his way into the parlour his father had already taken up position in the winged chair that had once been Joseph's mother's nightly domain. According to his aunt, his mother had declared it to be a chair for all seasons, it being equal distance between the fireplace and the French doors that led out onto the summer terrace. Nowadays it was more akin to a slowly disintegrating shrine, its burgundy cover almost threadbare in places.

Joseph cast his eye over the edges of the arms which were particularly worn, a conclusion to his father's absentmindedly running his fingers across them every night, placing his hands where she had once placed hers, as though he were reacquainting himself with her once more. It would probably never be re-covered Joseph thought. Not in his father's lifetime at least. With a glass of port in one hand and a cigar in the other, Edwin's gaze flickered between his daughter, who entranced the family as she played Chopin's Nocturne at the piano, and the small wisp of smoke that trailed perfectly upwards towards the ceiling from his cigar.

He looked up as his son entered the room and Joseph instantly felt the weight of his father's stare like a millstone around his neck as he turned and closed the door, his fingers shaking as he fumbled with the handle. He took a deep breath, forced his shoulders to relax and when he turned back to the room, he made a point of not returning Edwin's gaze. Instead he made his way over to the still open bottle of port that stood on top of the drinks cabinet, only pausing to refuse the cigar offered to him as he always did. He didn't much care for the taste or the smell, though he would never have admitted it. Better to seem bored or unimpressed than repulsed, the latter sentiment likely to initiate some form of disparaging remark about lack of maturity or sophistication. As he poured the ruby red liquid into a small crystal glass his father looked back to his sister and Joseph became persona non-grata once more. People were so easy to fool. More so if they wanted to be.

Not long after his mother had died Aggy had told him that if you smiled on the outside you could convince yourself that you were happy. It wasn't true, Joseph had come to realise. For small relatively insignificant matters perhaps, but not for affairs of the heart. He was no less sad on the inside than he had been before but behaving in such a way did at least mean that you could deceive those around you. Make them leave you in peace. The lesson had been invaluable. He turned around lazily, emulating his sister's beaming smile as she peered up from the piano, her fingers still flying across the keys. That reaction at least was genuine, but the false serenity of his conduct still failed to dampen the jittery sensation that toyed with his nerves and set his body to thought of flight.

He chose to sit next to his aunt, knowing that here was where conversation was least likely to occur. Still dressed in mourning attire, Aunt Beatrice always seemed to be on the verge of tears whenever she looked at Amelia or himself though whether she was lamenting their loss or her own was unclear. Either way, as raw as her grief was Joseph always found himself begrudging the sombre atmosphere she instilled in the house every time she visited, ripping open wounds that were on the verge of healing as she wandered the corridors in sorrowful silence, the small cotton loop sewn into her lace handkerchief cutting into her chubby right index finger as she reached up from time to time to dab the corners of her eyes.

As callous and selfish as it was, Joseph found that her current wordless state met his needs perfectly. He needed to focus, if only so he could concentrate on stifling every urge he felt to fidget, fearfully aware that if he pressed on the stem of the glass that lay between thumb and forefinger any harder it would shatter into a million pieces, would alert his father to his true state of mind.

He watched Amelia play with unseeing eyes, clapping appreciatively at the end of each piece, though had he been asked he wouldn't have been able to identify any of the passages that she had chosen to entertain the family with. As she sorted through the scores in front of her, he looked out of the window from the corner of his eye. The wind was picking up now, raging down the chimney all bluster and force and making the trees that surrounded the terrace twist and bend in the light of the full moon. Bright as a thousand candles it lit up the clouds that rolled across it, the wind sending them barrelling away at speed. Seconds later the first drops of rain tapped against the window. Perfect. Joseph furrowed his brow in mock concern.

'I don't wish to alarm, but it would seem as though the weather is becoming increasingly inclement.' He said, his eyes now fixed on the window, his voice loud enough that it rose above the lilting tones of the Irish ballad Amelia now played. 'The tracks away from the house are already barely passable in places and with extra rainfall I fear you might find yourself unable to leave until the flooding subsides.' One of his identical twin uncles, who was completely indiscernible from the other, got up to look out of the window. He nodded stoically, hands clasped behind his back as he stared out at the gathering storm.

'I agree.' He said thoughtfully. 'We should call for the carriages. I leave for London in the morning. I can't afford to be stranded in the middle of nowhere.'

He looked over at Edwin who stared back, brow raised as if he invited the prospect of a row. 'As much as I enjoy coming back here.' His uncle qualified, his face reddening. Charles, Joseph concluded. It had to be Charles. Robert, the second twin, who was now smirking in the corner, wouldn't have given offending Edwin a second thought. Edwin reached over and clumsily grabbed a small bell from the top of the drinks cabinet and Joseph watched in satisfied silence as the house was consumed by a flurry of activity. It was only a matter of minutes later that Edwin Davenport, flanked by his two children, was bidding farewell to their extended family from the porch, the sound of hooves on gravel practically drowning out the last of the birthday wishes that were called out as the coaches rolled away.

His father had two routines. The first routine, which was rarely adopted and which involved remaining relatively sober, was to bathe, make notes in his journal, about what Joseph and Amelia had no idea, and then read by candlelight until the words tired his eyes and he allowed them to drift shut. With routine number one he was typically awake until the small hours and sleep was minimal and hard fought for, which, Joseph suspected, had led to the creation of the second routine. The latter procedure, which he followed most nights, found its roots in excessive alcohol consumption. Here there was no bath, no writing and no reading. There was just the deep sleep through which Edwin seemed better able to find the oblivion he craved. To be able to hide from the real world longer than his sober body would allow. Sometimes, when he had drunk too much, he would roll straight into bed fully clothed where he would remain until the staff bought him breakfast. Joseph couldn't begin to imagine the secrets that were whispered behind closed doors and he was more than happy to remain oblivious. His opinion of his father was tainted enough already.

Once his father and Amelia had retired to their own quarters he hurried back to his room. He threw on a thick woollen jumper that was as black as bitumen and stared at the clock on the mantelpiece, allowing another quarter of an hour to pass before he made to leave, slipping silently from his room, deftly negotiating each floorboard just as he had done throughout his childhood when he had snuck down to the kitchen to grab midnight treats from the pantry for himself and Gwilym. Aggy had only caught him once. The scolding he could still remember word for word. What if, she'd said. What if his father had caught him? Surely, he was already familiar enough with his father's belt? And then she'd escorted him back to his room, sneaking back with a tea towel full of treats minutes later. The next day she had pointed out a more inconspicuous route in passing conversation. He never got caught again.

He slipped through the front door, holding it firmly so the wind wouldn't pull it from his grasp and when he was assured that it was secure, he ran to the back of the house and towards the stables and the track that would lead him away from the house and into the hills.

In the flickering light of the moon stood Gwilym, accompanied by two horses, fully tacked and braying softly at the prospect of a night run. Joseph felt his shoulders sag with relief even though Gwilym had never let him down to date. But then, Gil always knew what needed to be done. Taking a deep breath, he pulled his gloves from his pocket and slipped them on as he walked over to his horse. Berkeley whickered softly, stepping forward as Joseph reached for the reigns, allowing the horse to nuzzle against his shoulder as he made sure his tack was fitted securely. Gwilym stared at him thoughtfully.

'Do you know what you're doing?'

'I do. When did you hear?' Joseph said, not looking up.

'When I was at the market this afternoon.' There was a long and awkward pause. 'No-one has actually seen her you know. It might not be them.'

'I'm damned near certain that it is. I'm sure I recognised one of the lads I saw earlier. Not that I said so at the time. For obvious reasons.' He peered over Berkeley, watching as Gwilym walked round to stand beside him.

13

'Soon as I found out I knew what was coming. I knew we'd be there before sunrise.'

'Then you won't need to question me further, will you Gil?' Gwilym sighed and smiled sympathetically, something Joseph hated. Especially since his mother had passed.

'It's not my intention to interrogate you, Joe. You know your own mind. Or, you do most of the time, at least. This worries me though. The repercussions…'

'I understand the repercussions. I'm not stupid.' Joseph felt the tension in his voice, heard the rise in his pitch.

'I'm worried for you. You're my friend. And you're not…'

'Going to find out anything standing here.' Joseph interrupted, instantly silencing his friend.

He slipped his foot into his stirrup and launched himself up onto Berkeley's back, waiting only seconds for Gwilym to mount his own horse before he spun his horse around and made his way down to the fields that surrounded the house and the mountains beyond, watching as they flickered in and out of view in the moonlight. The rains never did come after all, Joseph realised, unable to stop the smile spreading across his face. How long had he waited for this? Everything would fall into place now, he was certain. Everything would get better. There was no alternative.

The smell of the bonfire hit him first, then the flickering light its flames created and then the sound of violins and drums and singing and laughter that blended together into a haphazard cacophony. He bought the horse to a sudden stop, Gwilym pulling up just behind him and together they jumped down from their mounts, tied them to the nearest tree and began to circumnavigate the base of the mountain, towards the commotion that seemed to elicit warmth even on a damp autumnal night. The sound of singing got louder, the laughter more raucous.

They finally reached the edge of the camp, the fire raging as someone threw wooden crates onto it, sending plumes of smoke and sparks into the air. The cheering grew louder, the singing reaching a crescendo and he could hear the clinking of bottles. Of course, they would be celebrating. It was Violet's birthday too. He cast an eye over the residents of the encampment, willing her to appear, silently praying that he not have gotten this wrong.

It could have been a few minutes, it could have been an hour that had passed before a lone figure stood up off a log near the fire. Her back was to him, but he would recognise her anywhere. Even in silhouette he knew the shape of her shoulders, her hips, the way her hair fell down her back in dark ringlets that begged to be played with. He heard rather than felt her name whisper past his lips and froze as she turned to stare out into the darkness, her eyes pointed fixedly at the spot where he lay and had he not been hidden in shadow, he would have sworn that she was staring straight at him. So this was what it was like to be paralysed by your own emotions. Joseph had often read of characters in horror stories who had been rendered immobile by fear or shock and until this moment he hadn't been able to fathom how the mind could take control of the body in such a way. But now...

They flinched in unison when two of her friends ran up behind her, grabbing an arm each and dragging her away from the edge of the fire towards the tents. He slowly exhaled and rolled on to his back, his hands clasped across his chest and it took a moment to understand that the feeling in his chest was nothing more complicated than unadulterated happiness. Joseph turned his head sideways to stare at Gwilym for a second then turned his eyes back to the stars

15

that were conspiring to appear before him. There could be no denying it now. She was here. Violet had come home.

Chapter three

'Get a move on, Violet Yardley! I swear if I have to wait any longer, I shall burst!'

Edie Hammond spun round and stared back at her friend, eyes wild as she dragged her forwards, weaving left and right through the revellers who had gathered together to celebrate in her honour. 'You must be beside yourself with excitement!' She dropped Violet's hand and clasped her own together with a resounding clap as they came to a grinding halt outside the large domed tent that was the beating heart of the camp. 'Well, go on then!' Edie nodded towards the entrance.

Violet craned her head forward and nervously peered into the tent. Barely a day had passed since they had arrived but in that short time the space under the canvas had quickly been transformed into a home. Rugs and cushions and oil lanterns that warmed the enclosure even on the most inclement of evenings were scattered everywhere. The small round table where they ate and socialised and met with clients was already positioned in the centre of the enclosure as it always had been and ever would be, the chest that held herbs and potions for remedies, tarot cards and the crystal ball no more than an arm's length away. Not disturbing the natural rhythm of a consultation was crucial. The spirits, when asked for guidance, expected undivided attention. Nothing less would suffice.

The atmosphere within the tent however, was a stark contrast to the norm. The usual hubbub of activity was gone. Conversation, which typically consisted of three high-pitched voices that blended into a stream of nonsense when they weren't working, calm and prophetic when they were, was little more than a series of whispered sentiments. The women, who had come to be known as the coven, fell silent when they spotted her, making the hairs on the back of her neck bristle in reply as she regarded each of them in turn.

There was no coven in actuality. Not that it was ever disputed in public. Better to embrace the epithet and reap the rewards financially. Within private confines however, they were simply family. It was true that they did not conform to societal standards, but that did not make them demonic. They were, Violet thought, closer to the earth and its inhabitants than those who bowed to their alternative gods. They lived alongside nature and those who roamed this world - past and present. They fed and nurtured and healed using the bounties from the soil beneath their feet. They listened and learned and advised using a knowledge and awareness that could only have been acquired from those who had left this life and now they stood, shoulder to shoulder, in this candle lit space, all eyes focused on her expectantly.

'What's all this?' Violet's lips curled up into a coy smile.

'What's all this?' Her mother playfully rolled her eyes. 'As if you don't already know.'

'Happy birthday, Vi. Your night is finally here.' Edie whispered into her ear. Violet took a deep, shuddering breath, tried to suppress the rising sense of dread that taunted her from within the darkest recesses of her mind. What if, when all of this was over, he had not come to her? What if he were not her chosen path? She was certain she had felt his physical presence beside her earlier, even though he had chosen not to make himself known. That was hardly a surprise, given the way that she had left. But, what if...

'Come and open your gifts.' Another voice now from the darker recesses of the tent. It was deep and warm and solid and for all of that there was the notion that laughter was never far away. Alfie Banes stepped out into the light, his flame red hair a mass of unruly curls, his shirt slipping from the waistband

18

of his trousers and snagging in his braces, his grin as wild as the wolf from which his name was borne.

'Alfie?' Violet stammered. 'I… I thought…'

'Ladies only? I know.' He moved further into the centre of the tent to stand behind her mother. 'I'll only take up a moment of your time. I appreciate that you have more pressing matters to attend to.'

'Lord knows, anyone would think you have as much riding on tonight as she does!' Constance Yardley glanced sideways at Alfie and smiled teasingly.

'Mother!' Violet exclaimed, horrified. 'Please!'

'She's right, leave the poor boy alone.' Aunt Flossie giggled softly as she reached forward and patted Alfie on his reddening cheeks.

'Boy? He's a grown man!' Constance protested. 'And he knows I mean no harm. Don't you, Alfie?'

'Of course, ma'am.' Alfie nodded politely in response, though his gaze never strayed from Violet's face, his blue eyes narrowing, measuring her response. 'I have something for you.' He walked over to the table and grabbed a parcel that was bound in rough sackcloth, the material held in place with the same string she used to bind small bags of herbs for customers. 'It's quite heavy. Be careful.'

Violet held out her arms and attempted to wait patiently, a childlike grin spreading across her face. Even with the warning, the weight of the parcel was a surprise. The ladies of the coven gasped as her reflexes kicked in and she tightly wrapped her arms around it pulling it back towards her as the bundle came close to crashing on the floor.

'Oh! Heavier than I expected, certainly!' She laughed nervously as she began to fumble with the cloth, unable to look at Alfie and the mortified expression he no doubt wore.

'It might be easier if I put it back on the table. I didn't really think through this properly.' Alfie laughed awkwardly. 'Here, let me.' He moved to take the parcel back, stopping as Violet stepped backwards.

'I can do it myself, thank you Alfie.' Violet smiled sweetly, but the warning tone was there in her voice. It was commonplace for her to be treated as weak or inferior by male members of the public. Not that that was right. That was just how it was and sometimes it was just easier to play the game. But not here. Not among her kin. Here there was no task that she was too small or too weak for. She could chop wood alongside the men, work the machine that sharpened tools and blades and mend pots and pans as well as any tinman and she had worked hard to prove it. Constance, her mother, had insisted that she did and it was something she prided herself on. Sometimes to the point of rudeness she realised belatedly.

Unable to find the words to apologise she made her way to the table at the centre of the tent and placed the package down onto its highly polished surface, her fingers reaching for the string that held the fabric in place. The knots were dispatched in seconds allowing the hessian cover to fall away.

'Alfie!' Violet turned to glance back at him momentarily. 'It's beautiful!'

'It's an apothecary cabinet.' He shrugged, his cheeks reddening all over again. 'But you already know that. Oh, these come with it.' He pulled a small muslin bag from his pocket and handed it to her. 'I've made some labels, but I chose not to fix them in place. That way you can decide how you'd like to use the chest and label it as you see fit.'

'You must have been working on this for an age.' Violet sighed wistfully, opening and closing each of the small drawers one by one. 'I wish I could use it. Properly I mean. If I could just get back into the market. This would serve me perfectly.'

'Turns out you can.' Alfie smiled.

'What do you mean, Alfie?' Constance said as all five ladies in the room turned to face him.

'I popped into town this afternoon to get a few bits and bobs for the horses. Things aren't so good. Turns out the gentleman who ran the chemists, what was his name?'

'Tom Lewis?' Flossie said. Alfie nodded.

'That's him. Died a while ago now apparently. Not surprising given the amount of opium he was getting through…'

'Alfie, don't talk ill of the dead!' Edie chastised him, her voice wavering, her eyes roaming the room nervously. 'You never know who's listening.'

'He's only telling the truth.' Constance conceded, waving her hand at Edie dismissively. 'Go on, Alfie.'

'Yes, sorry Ma'am, of course.' Alfie fumbled nervously with his cap. 'Well, after he died his son took over, but I hear he's been upping the prices. People on your average wage can't afford them anymore. There've been quite a few deaths that people are saying could have been avoided if he had been as charitable as his father.'

'That's awful.' Violet whispered. 'Who has been taken? Do we know?' Alfie stared down at his cap.

'Agnes Driscoll's two children and her husband. That was the only name I recognised.'

'Aggy's entire family?' Constance gasped, her hands flying to her face as Alfie nodded.

'She's moved into the big house now apparently. Has a home there for life they say.'

'So she should. Raised those kids she has.' Aunt Flossie said indignantly.

'As did Josephine, until she was taken.' Constance chastised her sister. 'You will not speak ill of the children's mother. She was devoted to them. And she was very good to us.' Flossie's face softened.

'True enough, sister. May she find her chosen path in peace.'

'I should write to Aggy.' Violet looked to her mother. 'What do you think?'

'I think that would be lovely. Send her my best wishes too. Tell her we're thinking of her.'

'I will.' She turned back to Alfie. 'I'm sorry, here we are talking about Aggy and paying no attention to all the work you've put into this chest. It's wonderful Alfie, really it is. Thank you so much.'

'You're welcome, Vi. Actually, I thought perhaps we could ride into the town together tomorrow, get some things to fill it and head to the market. They've even got the old stall waiting for us. We could open up for a couple of hours and you can see for yourself how much the mood has changed. I've a few things to attend to early on but I'll be free mid-morning onwards? If you'd like to accompany me, that is?'

Accompany me? The words somehow seemed very formal, especially coming as they did from Alfie's lips. Butterflies tumbled over each other in her stomach as Violet nodded in acquiescence. He was her friend, after all. And that would stay true, no matter what came next.

'I'd like that Alfie. Thank you.'

'But for now, you need to leave.' Constance said as she made her way towards the far end of tent. 'There are important matters to attend to. '

'Of course, Ma'am.' Alfie bowed, a brief informal gesture and regarded Violet one last time before he turned to make his way out of the tent. 'Good night, Vi. And happy birthday. I wish for you everything you wish for yourself.'

'Everything you wish for yourself.' Aunt Ruby muttered sarcastically under her breath. 'Everything he wishes for himself, more like! Impudent pup!'.

Violet watched in mournful silence as Alfie left, grateful that he most likely hadn't heard what her aunt has said as he walked through the opening and out of sight. That wasn't to say that her aunt was wrong. Lord knows they had talked about it often enough, she and the Coven. It was one of the few occasions where she had prayed that the ladies of the coven were wrong. Because what they thought he wished for and what she wished for herself were undoubtedly very different things.

Chapter four

Violet stood wordlessly at the table, running her fingers over the smooth surfaces of the apothecary chest as she watched Edie reach up and pull the tarpaulin door down, chasing out the light from the bonfire. She watched as her best friend darted around the tent, lighting candle after candle, dashing between them like a kitten chasing its own tail. She watched her mother and Flossie as they gathered at the furthest point away from her, hastily preparing for the ritual as they had countless times before and she watched as they looked back and watched her in reply. Aunt Ruby joined them, all bustle and excitement, as ever blissfully unaware of the tension that pervaded the area. Maybe they were all unaware, Violet thought. Maybe the only tension in the room existed within her. After all, it was only her life, her fate, that was on the line.

The rich heavy aroma of mistletoe and mugwort invaded her senses. Mistletoe to ward off evil spirits, imperative when the veil between the worlds was so thin and mugwort to sharpen the senses. Make the apprentice more open to the messages being sent to them through the void. Not that the ladies of the coven thought that the additional help was necessary. To be born on Samhain meant that you were more likely to have an affinity with the otherworld than those born at any other time. She would most likely be, they had declared, more powerful than the rest of the coven put together, once trained. Violet could find no comfort in such a declaration. What point was there in asking for guidance as to one's future if one's future was already being planned elsewhere? If one didn't like the answers they received, how comforting would it be that the messages received were clear and strong? Didn't less room for ambiguity just make things worse?

'Violet? Did you hear me? It's time.' Violet looked over to where her mother, aunts and Edie stood waiting in a hazy huddle, each with their hands clasped together and resting against the pinafores of their skirts.

'I'm sorry, what did you say?' Violet shook her head, waking herself from the trance she had placed herself in.

'Come here girl, it's time.' Her mother laughed. 'Dear god, what is the matter with you?' Violet inched her way towards the ladies of the coven, trying to block out the leaden feeling in her limbs that betrayed her hesitancy. Like a lamb to the slaughter. They were stood behind two chairs, Violet noticed. Deep mahogany with delicately carved high backs, legs that had been turned into ornate twists and wicker seats, these were specifically for client readings. But then of course, tonight she was the client. A small table was placed next to the chairs, containing nothing more than a candle and the scroll that would guide proceedings. The smell of mistletoe and mugwort was stronger now, the familiar scent that usually calmed now the source of her greatest unease.

'Why are there two chairs?' Violet asked.

'You didn't think I'd have you do this alone did you?'

'But that's not common practice.' Constance smiled.

'Common practice does not include my daughter. And besides, I am as keen to see your future as you are.'

'Maybe more so.' Violet grimaced.

'Come, it will not be so bad.' Constance beckoned her over. 'Come. Sit with me.' Ruby and Flossie took a step backwards as mother and daughter came to sit side by side in the chairs, so close their knees rested against each other's. 'Before we begin, I have a gift for you.' Constance reached into the pocket of her apron and held out her hand, waiting for Violet to do the same. Violet peeked down and smiled.

'You're giving me Nana's necklace?'

'The pendant is made of Celestite.' Constance said as Violet picked it up and held it to the light. The bright blue oval stone glistened from within its ornate silver mounting of twisted vines.

'Such a beautiful colour. I never tire of looking at it.' Violet said. 'I remember Nana wearing this when I was a child.' Constance laughed.

'What? What did I say now?' Violet said, looking up from the pendant indignantly.

'Nothing, my darling. I simply find it hard to accept that you are no longer a child. You are a woman now and yet I still see the precocious four-year-old who used to drape herself in worn out blankets and declare that one day she would be a princess.' Violet rolled her eyes playfully and turned back to the pendant. The blue reminded her of his eyes. All sparkles and warmth. The world darkened further still.

'You are not worried child surely?' Flossie asked. 'You have witnessed this ceremony a thousand times.'

'Perhaps, but I was never the one whose fate hung in the balance before.' Flossie raised her handkerchief to her lips as Ruby began to laugh.

'That's a tad dramatic isn't it?'

'I don't think so.' Violet frowned, her voice all cold and sharp edges.

'What makes you so ill at ease?' Constance said softly. Violet cast her eyes around the room.

'What if…' She took a deep breath and let the words flow. 'What if the things that I see are not the things that I wish for? What if the things I see disappoint me? Am I to embrace a life or a person that leaves me cold because the spirits desire that it be so?' Constance stilled for a moment, watching the way her daughter held onto the pendant and then it was as if everything became clear. She took Violet's hands into her own.

'My darling Violet, it may well be that the things that you see are not the things that you wish for. The imagination is such a powerful force. It allows us to dream of a world that cannot be matched by reality. It leaves us disappointed when we are forced to see that our dreams are nothing more than falsehoods and impossibilities. You need to open your mind and your heart to the possibilities that lay in front of you. Sometimes they may even exceed the confines of your imagination. If you let them.' Constance took the pendant from Violet and placed it around her neck. 'Sometimes, Violet…' She placed a finger under her daughter's chin, forced her look her in the eye. 'Sometimes you need to say goodbye to the dream. Do you understand?'

'I understand.' Violet said, though the words barely came out as a whisper. She looked up at the ladies that surrounded her, all warmth and smiles and anticipation.

'It is time.' Constance said turning to Ruby. 'Sister, please remove the veil from the mirror.'

Chapter five

Violet had sat and observed the ladies of the coven conversing with the spirits through the mirror for as long as she could remember. She had listened to the enchantments and mouthed along as the clients requested assistance from those who had passed and, as much as she had warned herself against it, had closed her eyes and imagined this very evening and the moment that his face appeared within the confines of the frame.

Now that that moment had come, now that she knew the impossibility of her situation it took all the strength she could muster not to plead with her mother to put an end to it, this rite of passage that foreshadowed her destiny and hers alone. Drumming her fingers on her lap, she tracked the heavy black and ivory damask fabric as it slid away from the gilt edges of the mirror into Flossie's arms and stared into the black abyss in front of her, casting her eyes over her muted reflection. Crafted from a single sheet of onyx, unlike its painted cheaper cousins, the mirror was polished to a high gleam. Cheap replicas, the sisters had opined, were for charlatans. They were not for those that truly had the gift.

'You understand what is about to happen?' Constance spoke to her softly, taking her hand. Violet nodded.

'You need to answer aloud Violet.' Constance reminded her.

'I know. Mother, you know that I know.'

'Then you will also know of the intricacies of the ritual. You may not have summoned the spirits yet, but they hear you Violet. They hear you and they sense your temperament. They will not stand for insubordination. No

28

matter how powerful you may become you will always be a lesser and you will show them the respect they command, or this will not end well for you.'

Violet winced. She had witnessed such an outcome herself. An aging female customer who had entered the tent all bluster and cynicism. By the time she had fled the tent the spirits had forced her to witness her own bloody death as punishment for her arrogance. None of it was true, but that was of little consequence. The woman never left her house again, leaving this world an empty shell, her passing unnoticed by all that had known and loved her at one time or another.

'I apologise.' Violet said, her voice barely a whisper. 'I beg forgiveness of those beyond the veil.' Constance nodded in approval.

'Then I will ask the question again. Do you understand what you will see tonight Violet?'

'Yes. Tonight, I will learn of the path that is intended for me.' She turned to look back at the mirror. This was a practice that went back over centuries, the idea that on the first full moon after one's eighteenth birthday one could summon the face of the person they were to marry. If no face appeared, as had happened with her aunts, then there would be no marriage. The face would be replaced by a skull, meaning that one would leave this world without ever finding true love. For most women, this was a stark warning of the harsh life of a spinster that was to follow. For Violet, and for the other female members of her family however, it was a call to service. A sign that they would form part of the next generation of soothsayers which was the highest honour one could have bestowed upon them. Constance handed her a small, battered scroll of parchment.

'Here is the enchantment. You are required to read this aloud. I will read with you in order that I may see what you see. Once we have read the enchantment, I will help you seek the state in which the spirits will become apparent to you. As you see, so you need to speak. Your aunts will work to depict that which you see before you, so it is important that you provide as much detail as possible. Do you understand?'

'I understand.' Violet said. She snuck a glimpse at Ruby who stood alert beside the mirror, pad of parchment and charcoal in hand, ready to sketch as Violet furnished her with as much information as she could provide.

'Then let us begin.' Constance smiled and squeezed her daughter's hand. 'Turn to the mirror darling.' Violet turned and stared into the mirror, taking one last look at the hazy image of the girl who was about to change into something unknown. Something knowing.

'Read the words now child.' Flossie's voice floated towards her from somewhere in the dark recesses of the tent. She would be sat at the writer's desk, Violet imagined, quill already dipped in ink, waiting to transcribe whatever was dictated to her. Violet looked down at the scroll, sliding away the thin red strip of ribbon that held it in place and unfurled the parchment, keeping a firm grip on each end so that it didn't fold back in on itself. She glanced over at her mother and Edie in turn then focused her attention back on the incantation as she and her mother repeated the words aloud as one.

'Mirror of souls, I call to thee,

Remove the veil that I might see,

Send spirits forth, reveal their light,

Let darkness fade within their sight.

Mother of souls I pray of thee,

Pull down the veil, confide in me,

My one truth path, my life revealed,

In stories told and silence sealed.

So mote it be.'

'The spirits are here for you, Violet.' Flossie said quietly. 'Can you feel them sister?'

'I feel them sister, but how can this be so?' Constance's voice raised up in pitch as she turned to look for Flossie. 'Vi hasn't even moved to talk to them yet.'

'They have clearly been waiting for her arrival. They are here and they are clearly upset.' Flossie said warily. 'Perhaps she is stronger than even we foresaw. Focus Violet. What do you see?'

'I cannot see anything.' Violet stammered. 'But I can hear them. There are so many voices. It's like they're fighting for my attention. Mother, there are too many people talking at the same time. I can't make sense of anything.'

'Flo.' Constance interrupted. 'We need to stop this. She needs to learn how to focus. How to see…'

'There is no time Connie. Do you not hear them? The spirits will not wait.'

'I do hear them sister.' Constance shifted towards Flossie, her voice agitated. 'But without training, how will she know how to decipher what is good and what is…'

'It would seem that she is not to be afforded that luxury.' Flossie cut in. 'And if the child is truly as powerful as we believe her to be, she will see well enough and she will know what to do. Violet, what appears in front of you girl?'

'I see me. Just me.' The tent fell silent as Violet peered closer at her own image 'No, wait, it's changing.'

'What do you see child. Tell me that I may draw it.' Ruby's voice, by the side of her now. Violet squinted in the dim light.

'My hair. It's getting shorter. Lighter. Still brown, but lighter.' She stared, lips parted. 'It's above my collar now. And it's straight. No hint of a wave or a curl. My fringe rests just over my eyes. I look awful!' She giggled nervously.

'Enough of the vanity!' Flossie shouted. 'What do you see child?'

'I'm telling you!' Violet shouted in exasperation, aware of the scratching of charcoal against parchment. Furious movements across the page. She squeezed her mother's hand tighter.

'What do you see now, Violet?' Ruby asked again, her voice calmer, more sedate. Violet took a deep breath, aware that Edie was whimpering in the corner. She would calm her later. Edie was always quick to panic.

'My face.' Violet said. 'It's changing shape. It's longer. My chin is sharper, my cheekbones more prominent. My eyes slightly narrower. My skin is becoming paler. The person I am becoming knows nothing of working the land. I no longer look weathered.' She leaned in towards the mirror. 'I see him so clearly. So much so it is as if he is here in this very room. It's as though I can actually feel his presence. But I have no idea who this person is....'

'This is too much.' Constance interjected. 'The spirits are too strong for her.'

'Sshhh!' Ruby said. 'Connie, you can assist in controlling this. All is well.'

'No, this is beyond my ability Ruby. Something is gravely wrong.' Constance whispered, eyes wide as the candles placed around the edges of the tent flickered and died. 'Sister, we must put an end to this.'

'Not now. Not when we are so close. And you know as well as I do, the spirits will not take well to being silenced.' Ruby glanced up from her sketch, the charcoal between her fingers still fluttering across the page. 'Violet, tell Flossie of his temperament.' Ruby asked as she continued drawing.

'He looks…gentle.' Violet pondered. 'He smiles, though it is a secretive smile. He is… looking at me?'

'No, this is your reflection, his movements are merely your own. He cannot see you.'

'That is not how it feels. The way he stares. He does not look at me as though he were a mirror of myself. He seems like a person in his own right. It feels as though he is looking straight through me. As though he were staring into my very soul.'

'Does he scare you child?' Constance asked. Violet shook her head.

'No, he does not scare me, but his expression. It's as if he knows me. He knows every inch of me. He knows every thought and emotion. And yet I do not know him. I know nothing of him.'

'I need more detail.' Flossie looked up from her pad. 'You need to tell me more'

'Wait, aunt.' Violet leaned further forward. 'Something is happening. There is someone behind him. Mother, your reflection.' Constance leaned forward.

'I don't understand.' Constance watched in confusion as her own reflection shifted forward and came to a stop just behind the stranger.

'Mother what's happening?' Constance shook her head.

'I don't know Vi. I…' Her voice broke off as her own reflection began to evolve. Dark hair became blonde, twisted up into plaits, made by invisible hands that pinned the braids around her ears. Her cheeks grew thinner, her skin turned as grey as stone, her collarbones, once covered by flesh sharpened to blades. Her eyes changed from brown to blue. Celestite blue. Constance gasped. 'Josephine?'

Violet stared at the mirror, held her breath as Josephine Davenport floated to the front of the mirror. In contrast to the boy she appeared beside hers was a face riddled by torment. Tears streaming from wild eyes, mouth wide though her screams were silent.

'She sees me.' Constance whispered. 'By all that is holy, she sees me.'

'You must end this!' Flossie jumped up from her seat, her voice tight with panic. 'Connie, end this now!'

'No, she was my friend and she is in need! I cannot turn her away!' She turned back to the spirit embedded within the mirror. 'I see you Josephine. I see you. Tell me what you want of me.' The wraith pulled back from the centre of the mirror.

'What's happening to her?' Violet asked urgently. 'She's fading away!' Constance shook her head.

'No, she's…she's changing. Heavens preserve us. Something is gravely wrong. Ruby…'

Ruby dropped the paper and charcoal and dashed forward, pulling the heavy cloth from the ground, sweeping it up in a wide arc to cover the mirror and break the link through the veil but it was too late. The reflection that was Josephine began to mutate, skin melting away, flesh falling from her face into the palms of her hands, blood dripping through her fingers until all that was left was a bare skull, it's eye sockets black caverns, and yet for all that it still seemed to stare at Violet and Constance as it propelled itself towards the mirror. The blanket slid down the front of the mirror seconds before it shattered into a million pieces and Ruby threw her arms up to shield her face as the cries that had been held within the sheet of onyx were released, piercing the air as the room plunged into darkness.

Chapter six

Hands clasped firmly behind his back, Joseph stood and stared out of the window towards the mountains that bordered the edge of their land. Autumn was stretching out much longer than he could remember, he thought. There was a chill in the air at night now, though it was not overly bitter, and a cool mist in the early morning that hung low in the valley obscuring the rivers and pathways. By day however, as soon as the sun rose, the panorama was as cloudless as the welkin of summer, the deep azure sky making the colours of the season seem more vibrant than ever. The bracken that blanketed the mountain had turned to rust, the trees to flame; a final show of defiance in their cyclical dance of self-destruction, paving the way for the bleak harshness of winter.

He imagined that a life lived outdoors was not yet a harsh one. The thought comforted him as he watched a single trail of smoke spiral up into the air in the distance. Given his way he would have been out riding, enjoying the last of the season's warmth as soon as the sun had risen. He might even, he supposed, have unwittingly found himself at the camp. His father had gone to great lengths to ensure that he couldn't, as he had done for several weeks now, creating work just so he could keep his son occupied. If it hadn't been so conspicuous it would have been utterly genius.

He listened to the house staff filing out through the door behind him, his skin prickling in a room that was overly warm. The fire had been lit though there was no need of it, most likely based on memories of one rogue season that had been uncharacteristically cold. It made the work required to light it, the fuel required to maintain it seem like such a waste. Still, no-one dared question his father's commands. He begrudgingly turned back to the large walnut writing desk that dominated the room, it's leather bound centre strewn with piles of paperwork still to be completed. Now, as he began to take over the estate, he would increasingly find himself restrained by more pressing administrative matters. There were financial accounts to become acquainted with, gardens and livestock to ready for winter. He wondered how the staff took his commands with such good grace, lord knows they had been working the land and caring for the livestock for years before he was born. Maybe they felt his discomfort, he thought. They must have thought him a cretin. He certainly saw himself as a fraudster.

His mother had always said that she could never see him as a man who would be confined to the suffocating lifestyle of the landed gentry. He would be an explorer she had predicted, her smile stretching from ear to ear as she rocked back and forth on the swing that hung from the tallest oak in the grounds, her toes pointing to the sky. Or he would be a physician or an academic. He would be someone who would bring good to the world rather than starve it of its bounties, unlike the family business which took everything and gave nothing in return. The memory made the world seem a little darker still.

'You asked to see me, sir?' There was a gentle bang on the door and Joseph looked up to find Agnes watching him expectantly.

'Yes. Come in Agnes. Close the door behind you.'

'Is something wrong, sir?'

'Just close the door please, Agnes.' Joseph sighed wearily.

'Of course, apologies, sir.' Agnes hurried to close the door behind her, shutting out the rest of the world before she turned back to face him, her cheeks ruddy, her hands bright red as she rubbed them fiercely.

'You look positively frozen.'

'I was up at the allotment when you called for me. Just getting in the last of the veg.'

'I heard. Where is your coat?'

'Gave up the ghost last year. Seamstress said it was more stitches than material.' Agnes smiled as she blew on her hands.

'Well then you should have a new one! Why has it not been arranged? You cannot work outside without proper clothing.'

'I'm not asking your family to clothe me, Joe.' Agnes said softly. 'Unlike so many these days I have a job, food on my plate and a roof over my head. There is much to be grateful for, and besides, no-one ever died from a little fresh air.'

'Perhaps, but if you got ill because you weren't properly attired. I won't see you being mistreated, Aggy. I'll make sure the housekeeper gets you a new one next time she's in town. Please, come sit by the fire for a while.' Joseph gestured to the high-backed chairs that sat nearest the hearth.

'Thank you for your concern, but I have chores to be getting on with.'

'Sit.' Joseph said again, this time more sternly. Agnes sighed and moved to one of the chairs. 'I've saved you some tea and Welshcakes.' He raised a hand to silence her before she had even had a chance to open her lips. 'I know. They're not meant for you. Still, here they are. Eat. I insist.'

'If cook knew…' Agnes chuckled.

'I would tell her myself, but I fear the repercussions.' Joseph said slyly as he handed her a cup of tea.

'Did you call me in here for a reason? Aside from the tea and the cakes I mean? Not that I'm not grateful.'

'I did, yes.' Joseph walked back to the bureau and the pile of correspondence lying on top of it.' This came for you today. Hand delivered.' He picked up a small white envelope.

'For me?' Agnes shook her head, confused. 'I can't imagine who would write to me now. I only recently received a note from my sister, and you know how infrequent they are. Unless, perhaps something is wrong. I do hope the family are well.' She fretted as Joseph ran his finger along the top of the envelope before he looked back at her. 'Dolly usually takes care of my mail for me Joe, you know I can't -'

'I know.' Joseph said quickly to prevent her embarrassment.

That Aggy couldn't read was a secret between only them. When he was four, she had been instructed by his father to tutor him, but it had soon become apparent that she couldn't recognise the words written on the page any more than he could. How humiliating that had been for her, when he had realised and yet so horrified was he when she had suggested that she be replaced, he'd taken it upon himself to learn how to read without help. So many nights spent in front of the fireplace struggling to grasp the strange symbols and shapes lain out in front of him and all of it a waste of time and a continual source of frustration. Still, he refused to let Aggy confess her illiteracy. When Aggy had let slip her secret to Dolly, one of the chamber maids, they were both relieved when the maid took it upon herself to teach Joseph, insisting that Agnes stay and learn alongside the boy.

Agnes didn't get very far, not that she seemed particularly bothered. There were always more important things to be doing with her time than sitting and reading she'd said, although in recent years she admitted there was pleasure to be had from listening to Joseph as he recanted the works of Dickens and Bronte. It was Mill on the Floss by Elliot that truly caught his attention. He would liken himself to Tom Tulliver. Not his character as such, but his desire to do the right thing by his family and friends. And now, still he read to her. Still keen to do right by those he loved. Agnes wondered if he really knew how proud of him she was, resolving to tell him more often. It was, after all, unlikely that he would hear the same sentiment elsewhere.

She watched as Joseph grabbed a small brass letter opener from the desk and slid it into the top leaf of the envelope, slicing upwards and opening the envelope in one swift movement before he absentmindedly dropped the blade and gingerly pulled out a small folded sheet of paper

'Who is it from, Joe?' Joseph moved silently back to the chair opposite hers and sat down, his eyes scanning the page fleetingly, his fingers trailing softly over the words held there.

'Joe. What's wrong? Is it my sister? The children?'

'Wrong? There's nothing wrong. Sorry, Aggy. I didn't mean to worry you.' Joseph looked to Agnes, cleared his throat and went back to the letter.

'Dearest Aggy.

I hope that this brief note finds you well. Before continuing I feel I must apologise to you for leaving without saying goodbye. You are as close to me as any of my own family and I would be so very upset if I thought that you had been offended by my sudden departure. Events rather overtook us and it was imperative that we leave as soon as possible. I pray that you will forgive me for not telling you so in advance.

Our circumstances have changed recently and I find myself living once more in the foothills of the mountains. Whether this is a blessing or a curse has yet to be discovered, but I understand that the fates have decreed that it be this way and so I have returned albeit with some trepidation.

Since returning I have heard the most terrible news, that is, the sad passing of Robert and your children. Mother and I were so very sorry to hear this Aggy. I pray that you have comfort in reflecting on the short time you were allowed to share your heart with them. Please know that you are very much in mine and my family's thoughts and if you should ever feel the need to talk or to share your grief, know that there will always be a place for you in our home, night or day, no matter the hour.

I pray our paths will cross soon. Mother and I very much look forward to seeing you again. With great fondness,

Violet Yardley.'

Joseph looked up at Agnes fleetingly before returning to stare at the paper in his hands.

'Oh, Joe, I'm sorry. If I'd had any inkling that it had come from Violet, I'd never have asked you to read it.'

'Do not trouble yourself. I already knew Aggy. I recognised her handwriting.'

'Then you should have said.'

'To what end? That I might be left in peace?'

'I could at least have prevented old wounds being re-opened.'

'They have never healed.' Joseph said, his voice barely a whisper. 'Besides, perhaps this is a good thing.' Agnes frowned as she took the letter and its accompanying envelope and slipped it into the pocket of her pinafore.

'I'm sorry Joe, I don't follow you.'

Joseph pushed himself up from the chair and walked back to the window. Back to where the world outside was rich and vibrant and where the small spindle of smoke continued to drift upwards, a single slash of white against a brilliant blue sky.

'Maybe she has the answers we seek. Maybe she can put an end to all this mess. She feels comfortable enough to write to you here. Perhaps if I went to see her. Maybe she would speak to me.'

'You know you can't do that. Your father…'

'Does not need to know.' Joseph spun round to face her. 'You won't tell, will you Aggy?' Agnes sighed and looked away.

'You know very well that I wouldn't. But these things have a way of getting out. There are no secrets around here. Not for long anyway.'

'Well, maybe by the time it's out we will have good news. Maybe this cloud that hangs over us all can finally be eradicated.'

'You would still give all of this up for her.' Agnes sighed. 'Even now.'

'No amount of time will ever change that Aggy.'

'Then you must go.' Agnes conceded as she got up from her chair leaving the tea and the cakes virtually untouched. 'I'll make sure no-one knows. Go and find the answers you need. But be gentle Joe. Remember, yours was not the only heart broken.' She walked over to the window and followed his gaze towards the camp. 'If nothing else, I pray you find peace. I pray you both find peace. Now, go.'

Chapter seven

The brightness of the skies had been misleading. Though the sun still beat down on the earth with the same vitality it had done over the summer months there was a subtle chill now that without doubt heralded the start of autumn. The air was perfumed by the smell of log fires burning, burnished leaves crackled underfoot and the ground was strewn with conkers, all waiting to be collected by children who would surreptitiously soak them in vinegar and bake them until they had created a weapon that would be unbeatable. Joseph found himself smiling at the memory. How many times had Gwilym declared him to be a cheat for doing the same? He couldn't remember now. How simple life had been then.

He drew the biting air deep into his lungs as he made his way down to the river, basking in the leaves that fluttered around him and the repetitive song of the sparrows as they fluttered to the ground over and over again to seek out seeds and grains to sustain them over the winter months. Behind him the sheepdogs had begun barking in their enclosure. No matter. If he were spotted, he could simply say he was checking the state of the land near the river's edge. His father knew that the groundsmen had been working there for weeks, attempting to create a series of log structures that would re-channel the river to prevent flooding over the winter. Now that maintenance of the land was his responsibility, it was only right that he inspect the results.

Water began to seep up from the ground around the soles of his boots as he finally made it to the edge of the river, though with minimal rainfall over the summer it had transformed into more of a babbling stream, the water glistening as it trickled over the rocks and stones that lay in its path. It took a fraction of a second to spot the boulder trail that he, his sister and his mother had used to traverse the river when they had gone out in search of adventure and without pausing for thought he jumped down onto the first of them and began moving swiftly from stone to stone, a process honed over years, each jump and landing as precise as the last.

It seemed like only seconds had passed before he had reached the other side of the river. With both feet back on solid land he reached down and flicked the splashes of mud from his trousers before turning back to face the house. All flint stone and ivy, it dominated the landscape from where he stood, a home that could have been created in a nightmare rather than in one's dreams. But maybe that was just the way he saw it. Maybe he wasn't looking at the house but rather at the tainted memories of the life that he now led there. Everything was darker, now that his mother had gone. The sound of distant laughter fought for his attention and he turned around to look at the path behind him that would steer him towards the mountains edge and the camp beyond. He wedged his foot into a crevice in the bank and launched himself up onto the pathway, each step taking him further from the house he loathed and closer to everything he had dreamt of coming to know as home.

*****

'In stories told and silence sealed. So mote it be...'

Violet let the last words linger on her lips before she allowed her eyes to flicker open, slowly focussing on the rippling reflection that rushed up to meet her, her fingers gripping tightly to the edges of the wooden pail. The sisters would be waiting for the water, she knew. They could wait a little while longer.

The face that met her now was thinner and paler than usual which was no surprise given that her appetite and her ability to sleep had become almost non-existent in the weeks that had passed since the scrying. Now the night hours were consumed by the apparitions that had lived, albeit briefly, the entire event unfolding scene by scene in her mind's eye like a macabre play. She had not been alone. The ladies of the coven had not slept either. They had waited and spoken in whispers once she had retired for the night. In the dimmest of candlelight, they had tried to read the cards and the Ouija board. They had held seances, openly begged with the dead for answers, but all had been in vain. They may have spoken in whispers through the witching hour, but their voices had still been as clear as crystal and it was clear that her mother and her aunts were scared.

'Josephine, please.' Violet implored. 'Please speak to me. Help me to understand! I don't know what you want me to do! Should we leave? Are we in danger here? Have we angered you perhaps? The man who was with you. Is this the man I am destined to marry? You are clearly distressed but I don't know how best to help you. Please make yourself known to me...'

'Vi?' Violet gasped at the sound of his voice, pushing herself up and away from the pail and wincing as the hinge sliced cleanly through the palm of her hand before the bucket upturned itself, emptying its contents on the ground around her and soaking the hems of her skirt. Of all the moments to choose! Violet's heart raced. Oh gods, what if he had heard her?

'I am so sorry Vi! I didn't mean to startle you! I just, I heard your voice and I...oh, you're hurt.' Violet lifted her injured hand to her chest and shook her head dismissively, avoiding looking down at the cut that made her hand throb as though it had a pulse all its own.

'Please don't trouble yourself, sir. I'll tend to it back at the camp.'

'Don't call me sir, Vi. Here, let me help. It is my doing after all.' Joseph walked over to her, removing the handkerchief from his top pocket and held his hand out, his eyes locked on hers. 'May I?'

He must have noticed her hesitancy Violet thought. Must have seen that split second when she was weighing up her options before she finally acquiesced, gently placing her injured hand palm up in his and watching in silence as he gently dabbed the cloth over the cut before folding the material into a bandage.

'I watched my mother do this too many times to forget.' He smiled as he wrapped the bandage around her hand. 'Of course, I was normally on the receiving end.' The memory turned his smile into something more wistful. 'I heard you talking to someone.' Joseph scanned the area as he spoke. 'Is there someone here with you?'

'No!' Violet replied too quickly, silently praising the powers that be that he had not heard her calling his mother's name. 'I was just practicing. The summoning ritual. I am to take up a more prominent role within the coven.'

'I see.' Joseph nodded thoughtfully. 'Aggy got your letter this morning. She was pleased to hear from you.'

'And you came all the way here to tell me that?'

'Well, no. That wasn't my main reason for coming.'

'Then why are you here, Joe?' Violet took her hand back as soon as Joseph had finished tying the bandage.

'I wanted to see you Vi. You've been back for weeks I know, but father has been keeping me busy with taking over the management of the estate.'

'I daresay he has.' Violet said derisively.

'You left without saying goodbye.' The words tumbled from Joseph's lips, unbidden. 'I told you I loved you and just left.'

'You know why I left.' Violet grimaced.

46

'Please Vi, my mother had just died. My father...'

'Accused us of killing her Joe!' Violet turned and grabbed the empty pail from the ground. 'He said we had placed a curse on her. He said that my mother was a murderer. He called for us all to be hung!'

'He was grieving Vi. I know what he did was wrong but, he wasn't thinking straight. Mother's illness and her death, it all happened so quickly.'

'So am I to believe he's thinking straight now?' She shook her head when Joseph looked away. 'I didn't think so.'

'He needed someone to blame. He still does. We're still looking for answers, even now.' Violet froze.

'Do you believe that we cursed her, Joe?' Joseph reached up and rubbed his face vigorously.

'No, but I find myself so confused lately.'

'What is there to be confused about? You either think me capable of murder or you don't.'

'Do I believe you could take a life in cold blood? No, of course not. But it's not as simple as that.' Violet watched as Joseph took the pail from her and walked over to the pond to refill it.

'What do you mean?'

'What do I mean? Vi, I don't know where to begin. I don't even know what to say to you.'

'It is easy to speak the truth Joe.' Violet said slowly. 'Maybe you struggle to find the right words because you hate the thought of lying. And maybe the truth is simply that you don't trust me.'

'Don't trust you? I love you Violet. If I didn't trust you I wouldn't be here now, risking everything.'

'You're risking everything? What, will father banish you to your room without supper if he finds you've sought me out?' Violet snorted. 'I know you think you love me, but you love the idea of me Joe. You love the idea of getting away from that house, you love the idea of living the life that I do but you do not love me.'

'That's not true!'

'If you loved me, you would not think me capable of murdering Josephine.' She looked down at the re-filled pail as he placed it in front of her. 'I think you should go now. I don't think we have anything more to say to each other. Thank you for your assistance earlier.'

'Violet, please, I need your help. You said you love me. Was that a lie?'

'No, that was the truth. I loved you Joe.'

'Loved?' Joseph took a step back, flinching at her use of the past tense. 'So you do not love me anymore?'

'What difference does it make, whether I love you or not? The point is I stopped liking you.' Violet's gaze met his. 'I stopped respecting you the minute you allowed your father to launch his drunken tirades upon my family.'

'No!' Joseph barked, his fists clenched at his sides. 'You will not lay that accusation at my door! I would never have allowed my father to hurt you or anyone else in your family. Do you know how I fought against him for you? How I had to physically restrain him from coming out here to kill you all himself? He is a broken man Vi, he needed someone to blame!'

'And now here we are, and you are asking me for help? Not friendship, not forgiveness, Joe. Help. I cannot imagine that there is much that you do not have a member of staff for and I cannot imagine that there are many things that you would seek from me and me alone. So, I have to assume that you come to me for a cure. And if you believed that what your family suffered from was a commonplace ailment, I know you would not be here with me. You would be seeking more conventional means. Which means I have to conclude that you come looking here for a cure to something you believe only I can control. Because you think it existed.' Violet closed her eyes and whispered under her breath. 'Because you think that either I or my mother killed Josephine.' Joseph sighed, reaching up with one hand to pinch the bridge of his nose and wincing as though he were bothered by an unspoken pain.

'I don't, Vi. Honestly, I don't. Please, if you would just let me explain! I need you!'

'No, Joseph.' Violet said softly. 'You don't need me. You need something I cannot give you because you choose to believe the lie. Now please leave. You are not welcome here.'

'Vi…'

'I said goodbye, Joseph.' She bit her lip fiercely, willed her eyes to stop smarting as she picked up the pail, ignoring the water that spilled over the top and began to make her way back to the camp. It took all her strength to not turn back.

Chapter eight

'I'm still not convinced that this is a good idea.' Violet bounced lightly from one foot to the other, her hair, a mass of damp curls, dancing in time to the movement of her feet as she stood underneath the stone archway at the entrance to the town market. With the crowds gathering she wrapped her hands into her shawl and kept her gaze focused on Alfie as he hoisted his wooden cylindrical knife sharpener onto the trestle table that would be their makeshift stall for the next few hours.

'Well, it's too late to change your mind now.' Alfie smiled. 'Constance is long gone, the horse and trap with her so best make the day worthwhile if you ask me.' He looked over towards the group of locals that observed in silence before turning back to her. 'You will find no animosity here, Violet. I wouldn't bring you here if I thought that was the case. You trust me, don't you?'

Violet nodded without thinking. Alfie's loyalty was something that could never be called into question. He was someone she had faith in, even when she didn't have faith in herself, though he had barely spoken to her since the scrying. One good thing to have come out of this already was that it had nurtured some kind of interaction between them again, even if she got the feeling that her mother had pushed Alfie into it. True, things still weren't as cordial as they had been, but given time maybe all that would change. The world already felt like too empty a place.

A week had passed since her confrontation with Joe. Seven drawn out days and sleepless nights spent regretting her outburst and speculating about what he had been trying and failing to say. Her mother had always bemoaned the fact that she never could keep her lips sealed. Could never allow people the time they needed to articulate their own feelings. And it was true. It was her greatest fault. Peppering others' words and thoughts with her own worries and doubts, the words spilling out of her before she gained any semblance of control. And to what end this time? That she would never know what he had really come to say now? That she would never get a right of reply? The thought left her feeling cheated.

She shook herself out of her reverie and watched intently as Alfie placed the apothecary chest onto the table. It was nearly full now, a satisfying conclusion to hours of careful methodical preparation, each label engraved with due diligence by Edie who had always had better penmanship than she. Only two boxes remained empty, but it would not stay that way for much longer. She turned to glance over at the chemists which was situated directly across from her. The gas lantern which was mounted on the wall was still lit from the night before casting out a warm flickering light against the murky autumn dawn which to anyone else or under any other circumstances would most likely have seemed welcoming. The butterflies in her stomach began to flutter, an erratic uncoordinated dance that quickened her breath and made her pulse race. She gnawed on her bottom lip as people entered and left the building, most turning to stare at her fixedly.

'You truly believe we are welcome here?' She raised her eyebrows, her expression disbelieving.

'Perhaps not in the chemist, after all, you'd be competition, but as for the rest of us? We've never been more pleased to see you.' Violet spun round at the sensation of an unidentified hand coming to rest on her upper arm, its warmth seeping through her shawl and into her bones.

'Mrs Rees!' Violet's hand came to rest on the old woman's unconsciously, squeezing her fingertips lightly. 'It is so good to see you! Do you still have your stall here?' The old woman laughed.

'Vi, I've been stood here behind you since the minute you arrived! Here, take this, you look utterly frozen!' She raised her free hand to Violet, in it a steaming mug of tea. 'And you just pay heed to young Alfie. Your family are welcome here.' Eirlys Rees watched out of the corner of her eye as two women made their way into the market. They slowed for a moment, glancing across surreptitiously as they passed, pausing only briefly to nod in Eirlys's direction. Eirlys Rees shook her head slowly.

'Your leaving here was a disaster.' She said quietly.

'Their expression says different.'

'They are not here to judge you, silly girl.' Eirlys replied. 'Nor are they here to gossip. They are not angered by your presence. They welcome it. If you weren't welcome, you'd have been told as much by now, believe you me.'

'And yet they walk past as if I did not exist?'

'People here feel they have to be careful Violet. If they had their way, they would be coming over here in droves. But they cannot afford to behave in such a way. Jobs are scarce here now. The Davenport estate is one of the only employers left standing and that man has eyes everywhere. If you only knew how much they need your help.'

'But they cannot risk losing their livelihoods.' Violet watched as people passed the stall, glancing sideways, never slowing.

'It's a sorry business all this, aye.' Eirlys continued. 'When old man Davenport lost his wife, he took it hard he did.' Violet whirled round to face Eirlys.

'Please, Mrs Rees, you must know that my family, we would never have harmed her.'

'How many times have I told you to call me Eirlys? And I know child. We all know.' Eirlys glanced back at her stall briefly to check for customers or, more likely Violet thought, eavesdroppers. 'The thing is Violet, people can say and think some awful things when they have lost someone they love.'

'Grief can make people do the most inhuman things...' Violet's insides curdled. She looked up as Eirlys continued talking.

'Old man Davenport took to the drink awful bad. Those that work at the estate say they're surprised he's still standing. It's the children who've had it hardest, mind. Weren't even given a chance to grieve themselves, see. They've just been left to clear up after him.' Violet stilled, schooling her features as Alfie observed her from a distance, his expression as wary as it was on the night of the scrying.

'I'm sorry for their loss, I truly am, but we were forced to flee as though we were criminals! Our lives were turned upside down!' Eirlys shook her head sadly and looked out of the market towards the town, her thoughts seemingly a million miles away.

'There has been too much loss.' She said. 'There has been too much loss and too much anger. It must stop.' She closed her eyes and took a deep breath. 'And if you don't stop hiding in the woodwork Gladys Evans, I swear to god I will drag you over by yur with my bare 'ands!' she shrieked suddenly.

Violet joined with a dozen other stares as they watched a small timid figure emerge from behind a small stall laden with oil lanterns and candles. Eyes narrowed she tightened her shawl and scurried over to where Eirlys stood.

'Eirlys Rees, I suggest you hold your tongue and stop making a show of yourself!' Gladys hissed through gritted teeth. 'Unless you want word spreading back.'

'I've got nothing to hide and neither have you!' Eirlys shouted in reply. 'My Thomas is gone, your Arthur is gone and I'm telling you now, there's a good chance they might still be alive if we hadn't stood by and done nothing while that man ran these folks out of town. Their deaths might not have been our doing, but we listened to the drunken rantings of a madman and said nothing and we have all paid the price!'

'And there are more stand to lose their jobs still.' A man who Violet didn't recognise came to stand next to Gladys Evans. 'I need that job Mrs Rees. My family will not survive without it.'

'And if you fall ill Mr Richards? What then? You think he'll help?' Eirlys nodded towards the chemist.' You know full well that Vi and her family are needed if the town is to survive this depression. Now, isn't it time we all started to stand up for what is right? Haven't we lost enough to see how blind we have been?' Violet watched in silence, her hand reaching out and tightly gripping Alfie's as the crowd that had gathered around them began to nod in assent. 'Right then. Anwen, you were asking whether I'd seen Vi yesterday as I recall?' There was an awkward moment that seemed to drag on for eternity before a familiar face peered out from the crowd.

'Mrs Madog!' Violet smiled. 'How are you?' Anwen Madog smiled apprehensively.

'I am well, girl.' She peered around her from side to side before she moved closer to the table where Violet and Alfie stood. 'You used to prepare an ointment.'

'For your husband. To help him with his breathing.' Anwen nodded.

'He's awful bad again, Miss Yardley. There are so few staff on the estate now he's working twice the hours for no more money. Plain exhausted he is. And his chest is so tight, he can barely draw breath when he comes home.'

'I'll happily prepare the remedy again for you. And please, call me Vi. Just, Vi.' Violet looked at the medicine chest and glanced over at the chemist before she turned back to the queue that was now forming behind Anwen. 'There are ingredients that I need to purchase. But I could come to your home with the preparation this evening if it would please you?' Anwen smiled again, her shoulders drooping as though a burden had been lifted.

'It would please me greatly, Vi. How much do I owe you?'

'No change to before.' Violet replied as though the answer were obvious. 'It is the same compound after all.'

'Bless you child.' Anwen turned to look at the queue gathering behind her and her smile widened further. 'Eirlys Rees,' she laughed, 'I think you've finally used your mouth for good. There may be redemption for you yet!' She shook her head and laughed as she made her way into the main market and Violet turned to the next customer.

'Here, let me do that.' Alfie said. 'I'll make a list and we can deliver everything this evening. In the meantime, you need to get to the chemist. Do you have the money?' Violet nodded and held up her small leather pouch.

'I only need laudanum and eucalyptus. Shouldn't be more than a few minutes. Thank you for making me come, Alfie.'

'I told you we would be welcome, didn't I? I see now that that might have been an understatement.' Alfie laughed gently. 'Now go, let's make a start on putting everything right that has gone wrong.'

Chapter nine

The sharp metallic peal of the bell which hung over the door sliced the air as Violet slipped through the entrance to the chemist though it was doubtful that the chimes would have been heard given the level of noise inside the building.

Customers stood in rows three deep, their impatience a living, breathing entity, their mutterings of dissatisfaction instantly piquing her curiosity though she did not show it. There was a game to be played here after all, if she was to be seen as the pharmacists equal. While it galled her to pretend to be anything other than she was, being dispassionate and business-like was the only way she would ensure acceptance among the crowd in which she now stood. She quietly closed the door behind her, allowing herself a moment to stop and take in the building and the atmosphere within it, allowing old memories to awaken, not all of them pleasant.

Very little had changed inside the shop which surprised her. Before his death, Berwyn Lewis had been a fiercely traditional man who had publicly fought against the alterations his son, Charles, had tried to force upon him in the name of profit. Violet had imagined his passing would have afforded Charles, who was also a physician to those in the area who could afford it, the opportunity to carry out the modifications he had desired for so long but for the most part everything looked the same.

At the back of the shop there was a deep mahogany wall to wall cabinet. Each shelf was adorned with glass jars and bottles in a variety of colours and shapes and sizes. There was everything from camphor to chamomile to medicinal leeches that writhed around and over each other in fluid movements leaving her transfixed and repulsed in equal measure. She had never found the courage to purchase or use them in her work.

There were a few more of the fanciful products that Berwyn despised Violet noticed as she took in the detail. The solid glass cabinets which were also used as counters were now laden with a cornucopia of items one needed in everyday life, or at least customers were led to believe they did. Stacks of perfumed soap, cosmetics, packets of tobacco and children's toys were all arranged in neat columns, waiting to be purchased by those who could afford such luxuries. And there was someone new behind the counter now. A thin wiry boy who ran around wordlessly, his face reddened by the exertion he employed in his need to meet the demands of the clients who waited for attention. Two people behind the counter but only one serving, Violet observed. Whilst the young apprentice dashed from shelf to shelf, Charles Lewis was attending solely to the needs of one customer and by his expression looked to have been doing so for some time. So, this was the cause of the crowd, Violet realised as she watched the levels of agitation within the confines of the chemist reach fever pitch.

'Some of us have homes to go to you know!' Someone shouted out from the middle of the crowd.

'Just like his father that one. Apple never falls far from the tree.' A woman in front of her muttered under her breath as she tightened the shawl wrapped around her shoulders. Violet looked back to the man behind the counter. Charles Lewis raised his hands at the crowd, his expression pained, pleading for their patience as he leaned forward towards his customer again, his voice ringing out loud and clear against the protestations of the room.

'There is nothing else I can suggest sir. You must understand, I have worked through the night and read umpteen journals on the matter. I have scoured through the medical encyclopaedia we hold in store and I have spoken to colleagues in London and all are as stumped as I am. I don't know what more

I can say! So please, I have many customers waiting. If you would move aside…'

'Is it money? Is that it? Do you want more money?' The man at the counter leaned forward, his voice tight with frustration. 'You know that I can meet your demands.'

'Forgive me, but this has nothing to do with money.' The chemist replied. 'Do you not think that I would rather keep my reputation intact? This speaks as much to my inadequacy as it does to your discomfort and for that I apologise but there is nothing else I can do. Now please sir, move aside!'

'Excuse me Mr Lewis, is there something wrong? Perhaps I might be of assistance?'

Violet called out over the head of the crowd, the words tumbling from her lips before she'd even given herself time to consider the consequences. As if they were one body, everyone turned at the sound of her voice and it wasn't without mirth that she was able to pinpoint the exact moment that each and every person present recognised her.

She wasn't sure if it was surprise or courtesy that instigated the mass reaction as one by one they stood aside, but what she did know was that there was a small part of her that revelled in the notion that she was the catalyst for a show of deference usually meant for those in a higher class than she could ever aspire to. She kept her lips sealed, her shoulders high and proud as the fissure in the room deepened, giving her clear view of the counter and of Joseph Davenport his hands still gripping to the glass cabinet as he stared at her, his flushed cheeks a stark contrast to the black scarf he wore tightly around his neck. Though the sight of him knocked the wind out of her, she did not back down. Did not allow the smile to leave her lips.

'Your assistance is not required here Miss Yardley.' Charles Lewis's lilting Welsh tones pulled her out of her trance. She glanced at Joseph for a second and then back to Charles Lewis whose expression was decidedly colder. Eirlys was right. Here she was competition. His current temperament therefore should be of no surprise. And yet it was. Hadn't they been friends prior to her departure? If they had been, all that had certainly changed now. And yet she could feel nothing for despair for the decline in his character. How tragic it was that greed could change a person so.

'Are you sure?' She said, cultivating a tone in her voice that was devoid of emotion. 'Perhaps there is some combination of compounds that I might offer by way…'

'You are too generous.' Charles cut in with more of a snarl than a smile, his tone derisory to its very core. 'But simple herbal compounds would be ineffective here and a waste of money to boot.'

'I sense that your more sophisticated scientific methods have also been of little use thus far?' Charles eyes narrowed.

'Miss Yardley.' He said wearily. 'Is there something in particular you seek? I have a shop full of customers waiting to be served. Or are you just here to cause further damage to this community?'

'Please do not speak to Miss Yardley with such disrespect.' Joseph turned to look at the chemist. 'She was kind enough to offer her assistance. Surely gratitude would be a more appropriate response?'

'Of course.' Charles simpered, his tone drenched in false courteousness as he spoke through gritted teeth. 'Miss Yardley was there something of particular import you were inquiring about?'

'I would be happy to wait in line, Mr Lewis.' Violet said.

'No, I insist. Consider it, an apology.'

'I am most grateful.' Violet stared at the glass jars behind Charles, fixedly avoiding Joseph who watched her intently.

'I need eucalyptus oil. A small bottle if you would be so kind. And two ounces of laudanum. I find I have many simple compounds to produce.' She kept her eyes on Charles, ignored the fevered whisperings that surrounded her.

'Of course. That will be three shillings.' Charles turned to pull a jar down from the shelf behind him.

'Three shillings?' Violet tilted her head in confusion. 'But that is twice the usual price, sir!'

'We are in a recession Miss Yardley. Everything is more expensive.'

'Perhaps, but this is extortion!' The chemist shrugged casually.

'I have one shilling and sixpence.' Violet said quietly, her hands wrapped tightly around her purse. That is all the money I have Mr Lewis.'

'Then I am afraid I cannot help you.'

'I will fulfil the balance Mr Lewis. You may put it on the estate's account.' Joseph leaned on the counter and stared at Charles, his expression challenging. Charles took a step backwards, his eyes never leaving Joseph's.

'I would need your father's authorisation for that sir. As head of the estate he would need to approve such an expense.' Joseph shook his head.

'It is common knowledge that I oversee the estate now. My authorisation is all you need as you well know. Unless you would like me to take my custom elsewhere which I would be more than happy to do.'

'But, this is the only chemist in town.' Charles began to bluster, the blood draining from his face.

'And I have transport. There is another chemist situated in the next town over from here and I am led to believe that he has chosen not to inflate his prices as you have, sir.' Joseph replied blithely. He smiled sideways at Violet. 'So, can I confirm that you are able to complete Miss Yardley's order?' Charles smiled, a derisive leer that made Violet's skin crawl.

'Happy to oblige.' He bowed abruptly and turned to take the jar from the shelf as his apprentice came to assist him, a large bottle of eucalyptus oil in hand. Joseph moved to stand next to Violet.

'Whilst I'm grateful for your assistance, you should know that I cannot accept your charity Mr Davenport.'

'Very well, Miss Yardley.' Joseph replied. 'Do not see this as charitable. See it as an investment. Anything that knocks Charles Lewis off his throne is a worthy cause. The man has been bleeding these people dry of late as I'm sure you've heard.'

'Indeed I have, sir.' She glanced around the room at the eyes still fixed on her. 'You may not be aware yet that I have re-established my own stall in the market. In fact, I have already begun taking orders for treatments. There will be no changes to the prices. Of that you can be assured.' Joseph nodded approvingly as customers began to file from the building towards the market gates.

'Please consider this an apology as well, Vi. When I came to your home the other day, the things I said…'

'There is no need to apologise.' Violet spoke softly. 'If anything, I should be apologising to you. I did not allow you to speak and for that, I am truly sorry.'

'No, I did not choose my words well, but then I always tend to get rather tongue tied when I am around you. If you would just grant me a moment of your time. There's something I need to speak to you about. Perhaps after you have collected your purchase?'

'Of course.' She stopped and looked at him more closely. There were red rings around his eyes and now the heat had seeped from his cheeks his complexion was almost grey. 'You look tired. Has something happened at the house?'

'You could say that.' Joseph said wearily and Violet couldn't help but think of Edwin. Perhaps Eirlys had understated the seriousness of his condition. 'Perhaps we could take a turn around the castle grounds?'

'I'll need to tell Alfie, but that should be fine.' Violet looked up as Charles Lewis walked around the counter and handed her a large brown paper bag.

'I have included an extra half ounce of laudanum in here. By way of an apology.' He said, though the statement was directed more at Joseph than herself.

'Thank you, Mr Lewis. I appreciate the gesture.' She handed Charles the contents of her purse and turned back to Joseph. 'Do you need anything, Joseph?' Joseph looked to Charles who waited beside them.

'No, thank you. I will return another time when you are less busy.' He turned his back to Charles, dismissing him without another thought. 'And thank you Violet. I promise I won't take up too much of your time.'

'I think you need to come with me sir.'

'Gil!' Violet squealed with delight as Gwilym came through the door to stand beside them. 'You look well! It is so good to see you!' Gwilym quickly removed his cap and bowed stiffly.

'It is good to see you too miss, and I'm sorry to interrupt but, Joe, there is something you need to attend to.'

'Why, Gil, you are positively shaking! What on earth is wrong?' Gwilym looked from Joseph to Violet and back again cautiously.

'It's alright Gil.' Joseph said. 'Violet can be party to whatever it is you have to say.' Gwilym turned to walk towards the exit and stopped, his hand resting on the door handle.

'Sir, it's your father. You need to come now. There is something gravely wrong.'

Chapter ten

'I don't understand - Is father unwell? Why have you not bought the carriage round?' Joseph held the door open for Violet, allowing her to pass through. He fixed his grey woollen bowler hat in place as he followed a step behind her, out onto the street and into view of the market and the town beyond.

'There is no need for the carriage, sir, he is here. Well, he's round by the chapel. And he is not unwell as such, he is more, out of sorts.' Joseph grimaced. A quick glance around at passers-by told him that the locals already knew. They were staring at him now as they had at his mother's funeral. Pity that rolled towards him in suffocating waves all sideways glances and condolatory smiles.

'Out of sorts?' Violet looked at Joseph and Gwilym.

'*Out of sorts.*' Gwilym repeated slowly, emphasising each word.

'He is drunk, Violet. Again.' Joseph said. He turned his back to the wall and fell back against it with a resounding thud that echoed through his chest. 'He is drunk again.'

'Oh. I see. I'm sorry.' She cast a glance over the road towards the stall. A long queue had formed and both Eirlys and Alfie were taking orders, Eirlys's own stall having been entirely abandoned, though by her expression she seemed not to care. Alfie was all smiles, jotting something down on a small sheet of paper when he glanced up and spotted her, his gaze running from her and then to Gwilym and finally, Joseph. He murmured his thanks to his customer, the smile slowly falling from his face. It was an expression she hadn't seen, she realised, since the night they had fled town. The same night that Violet and her mother had travelled to Ty Mawr to pass on their condolences and had instead found themselves hastily retreating from the house, Edwin Davenport's hounds hard at their heels as Edwin watched from the top of the steps and warned them to never return. That he would see them hung if they didn't leave before sunrise.

She recalled the flurry of activity around her as the camp packed up their lives into their wagons and how she had found herself in Alfie's arms as she'd admitted her feelings for Joseph. And she had told him of Joseph's betrayal. How he had failed to defend her even as Edwin had accused them both of murder and Alfie had listened wordlessly, offering neither judgment or reproach and when she had finished talking, he had held her fiercely, promised her that he would never let Joseph harm her again. That he would kill him first.

It was to her great surprise and relief that Alfie did not move from the stall now. Nor however did he return to serving the line of customers that vied for his attention. He simply folded his arms and continued to observe from afar. Violet could feel the full weight of his stare upon her as she turned back to Joseph and Gwilym, the bag of medication bouncing against her hip as she wrapped her arms around herself against the chill.

'How bad is he?' Joseph asked.

'I tried to quieten him, but it was of no use. He refused to come back to the cart. Said he had unfinished business. Looks like he dragged himself through every muddy ditch he set his eyes on the way here. He still has a bottle with him, well, the remnants anyway. The police are keeping an eye on him. I'm worried he might end up being arrested if we don't address this quickly. I have asked that Constable Harris wait while I fetch you, but his patience will only last for so long I'm sure.'

'Of course. Thank you Gwilym.' Joseph turned back to Violet.

'We will have to postpone our stroll, I think.' He smiled a thin, hollow smile.

'Of course, Joe.'

'I could visit you at the camp perhaps, if you think I would be welcome there? Or here in the market, whichever you would prefer.'

'Either would be acceptable, but I wonder if I might walk with you now? If I could just speak with your father. Maybe I could help him.' Violet looked at Joseph pensively.

'I wouldn't advise that Violet. He's very angry.' Gwilym shook his head.

'And most of that anger is directed at me and my family, Gil.'

'Which is precisely why I think it's a bad idea.'

'But perhaps if we could talk, I could help him to understand. Maybe it would be a way of easing his distress.'

'No, Vi.' Joseph moved to stand next to Gwilym. 'Please don't misunderstand me. I know you've done nothing wrong, but my father isn't thinking straight. If anything were to happen to you, I would never forgive myself. When father is drunk, he can be, violent. I would not wish that upon you.'

'Joe, there is nothing your father can do or say that will injure me, you have my word. This dispute began with us. Perhaps we should be the ones to put an end to it.' Joseph watched her for a moment, taking time to measure her words and trying to dispute their logic, silently cursing to himself when he was unable to find a flaw.

'Very well, but if he becomes overly agitated, please, promise me that you will remove yourself and get as far away as you can.'

'I promise.' She turned to Gwilym, deliberately blocking Alfie from view, knowing that at least this way she could remain immune to his judgement a while longer. 'Now, where is Mr Davenport at, Gil?'

*****

Violet could hear raised voices before the church had even come into view. There was a crowd rapidly gathering, the carriages that normally flowed in a steady stream brought to an abrupt halt by bystanders who filled the road, defiantly ignoring the protestations of the footmen who had stepped down from their coaches and pleaded with them to move.

Most who watched and listened to Edwin Davenport did so with unfettered disdain. Some had even begun to heckle him, mocking him for his slurred speech and his staggered movements and they shook their heads in reference to him when they spotted her moving amongst them. It was a show of solidarity, she supposed, but their expressions were inviting, almost compelling in their fervour. Were they were waiting for her to align herself with them? To whip the crowd up into a greater frenzy? She focused on the ground beneath her feet as she moved forward. Was this vindication? If it was it bought little comfort.

The old man's utterances were mostly unintelligible, but the sound of his voice brought to mind a time when every word he had uttered in this very same place had been clear as a bell, his anger implacable. She and Alfie had snuck into town the morning after the camp had been dismantled to pick up a few things for the journey east only to find Edwin stood where he stood now, calling for the ladies of the coven to be found and tried for murder.

'They behave as false gods and we have permitted it, even though we know the wrongness of such practices. They placed a curse on my wife that no man of faith or repute could dispel. We are men of honour! Surely it falls upon us to ensure the safety of our loved ones? I do not care what the law says, they should be tried and convicted as witches! There can only be one outcome!' The memory turned Violet's blood to ice. Still she moved forward, following behind Joseph and Gwilym as they wormed their way to the front of the crowd, eventually reaching the walled forecourt that surrounded the Methodist church.

There was nothing grand or imposing about it, Violet thought. It was a simple white building that could have tricked a passer into believing it was someone's home rather than a place of worship if they didn't stop to look more closely. Two large stained windows adorned the upper half of the building, between them a plain wooden cross which was displayed within an arched inset at the church's centre. Large pillars supported a comparatively plain porch that sheltered two imposing wooden doors, in front of which stood Edwin Davenport.

Gone was the robust, distinguished gentleman, who'd a presence that exuded a higher status than those around him. In his place stood a hollow shell of a man. His face, gaunt and unshaven he swayed gently from side to side, a near empty bottle in one hand. His clothes were sodden from the waist down and he shivered violently in the cold morning air.

'He must have been up drinking all night. Strange that I didn't hear him.' Joseph muttered, more to himself than those around him as he stepped out from the crowd. His father spotted him immediately.

'Ah, Joseph, my son, my heir and my biggest disappointment!' He squinted focussing in on Violet. 'And I see you have found your witch!' He raised his bottle in acknowledgment.

'Father, please, you are not well.' Joseph raised a hand and reached to take hold of his father, grabbing hold of empty air as Edwin reeled backwards, his arms flying out from his sides to save himself from falling over. The elder man began to laugh hysterically.

'Nearly came a cropper!' He giggled to himself and raised his finger to his lips to shush the baying crowd as Joseph turned to Gwilym.

'Gwilym, will you fetch the cart please?'

'Of course. Are you sure you don't need me here?'

'What I need is to get him away from here.' Gwilym nodded and instantly broke into a sprint, apologising as he cut through the crowd. Edwin watched the boy disappear around the corner before he spun round on his heels unsteadily to look at Violet.

'Do you know what they used to do to witches, Miss Yardley? They burned them at the stake! What do you say to that?'

'I say it is a tragedy that so many innocent lives have been lost in such a brutal way.' Violet replied, all eyes now on her. 'I should also like to add that I am not a witch though I have often been portrayed as one. It would be a lie to say that it has not worked in my favour financially at times but ultimately it is not true. Nor do I consider myself a god as you have previously suggested. I do not consider myself to have any divine power, sir.'

'You think that their deaths were brutal?' Edwin nodded thoughtfully. 'I fear none were as brutal as the death of Josephine, Miss Yardley. Do you know how she suffered? Has Joseph told you? Has he told you how she screamed with the pain? How she begged me to end her life for her? I wonder if your mother has any idea how much Josephine endured before she finally departed from this world.' Violet sighed wearily as the crowd fell silent.

'I do not claim that any one party has superiority over the other when it comes to suffering, Mr Davenport. My family and I held Josephine in the highest regard. Her passing was a tragedy, but I must say to you now that whilst I sympathise with your loss, I will not allow my family to be scapegoated over the death of your wife.'

'You were named after her.' Edwin turned back to Joseph, widening his eyes as he struggled to focus.

'I know father. But please, why don't we get you home in the warm? Perhaps then we could talk?'

'You were named after her and yet you covet those that killed her. The girl has bewitched you. I see it in your expression. You cannot fool me boy!' He turned to lean his shoulder against the stone pillar beside him. 'No matter, it will not be for much longer. I will bring decorum back to my family.'

'By behaving in this manner? Forgive me, but I see nothing that indicates any sense of propriety here.' Violet scowled as she moved to stand next to Joseph.

'Impudent pup!' Edwin lurched forward to grab her. 'It is about time someone taught you a lesson!' The crowd gasped as Joseph shot towards his father, pinning his arms behind his back.

'Do not touch her. I swear if you harm her in any way…'

'You'll kill me?' Edwin mused. 'You are doing her dirty work for her now perhaps?' Violet took another step forward.

'I would not wish to see you come to harm sir, rather, I would wish you well. I would also wish that your children had someone who is fit to father them, but the sad truth of the matter is you seem to be hell bent on destroying not only your own life but your family's too.'

'Lies!' Edwin spat. 'How dare you judge me, witch!'

'I have no expectations of you sir, and therefore I do not judge you.' Violet said. 'You are answerable only to your children and to the memory of your wife and it seems to me you have failed on both counts.' Edwin paled and fell still against Joseph's grasp.

'No. That is not true. I loved her. I would never fail her. '

'Vi, step back and hold your tongue!' Strong hands wrapped around the tops of Violet's arms, pulling her backwards. She started and spun round to face Alfie, his cheeks reddened with rage. 'What do you think you are doing, girl? Have you lost your mind?' Violet pulled her arms from his grasp.

'Do not put your hands on me Alfie Banes. I think perhaps it is you who has lost his mind. And you do not need to be so overly dramatic. Someone needs to put an end to all this hostility for everyone's sakes and I mean to do so now, without any interference from you!'

'And you think behaving in such a hostile manner yourself is the way to go about it?'

'It was not my intention to be hostile.' Violet snapped, even though she knew she had allowed her own pride, her own need for retribution to override any promises she had made to Joseph. 'I'm simply telling him the truth. He needs to know how much damage he has caused. He could still put it right if he had the inclination which he clearly does not!'

'Vi, please, no more.' Violet looked back as Joseph dropped to the floor beside his father. Edwin had now fallen to his knees, his body trembling as he placed his hands on the ground to balance himself.

'She is gone, child.' He looked up at Joseph disbelievingly. 'She is gone!'

'I know.' Joseph said. Edwin looked down at the floor and lifted his hands to brush the grit from them. He ran his palms over his sodden trousers and slowly, hesitantly, lifted his eyes to take in the rows of faces that silently observed him.

'Dear god, what have I done?'

'You are grieving.' Violet said softly.

'Do not speak to me, witch! I do not need your sympathy!' Edwin looked to her. 'I need you to stay away from my family. I need you to lift the curse.' Joseph exhaled slowly.

'Father, there is no curse.'

'Yes, there is.' Edwin protested. 'There is no other way to explain…'

'Stop, father. Please.' The old man fell silent then. 'Let me help you up. Gwilym is here with the cart.' Edwin gripped onto Joseph's arm fiercely as his pulled himself up off the floor.

'Take me home, son.' He murmured, his eyelids fluttering. 'I am so tired.'

'I know.' Joseph beckoned Gwilym forward and the two of them half carried, half dragged Edwin into the waiting cart.

'There's only room for the two of you sir.' Gwilym said, his reverential tone back now that they were in public view. 'I'll make my own way back shortly.'

'Thank you Gwilym.' Joseph glanced over at Violet, his expression apologetic before he turned and climbed up into the cart. He gently placed a large blanket over his father's lap and moments later they were making their way along the narrow road that led to the castle nearby, Edwin's head resting on Joseph's shoulder. Without slowing they turned the sharp corner and disappeared from view, the sound of hooves on cobbled stones the only indication of their ever having been there at all. As soon as they had gone the crowd began to disperse.

'Why did you do that? Put yourself in danger like that?' Alfie stared at Violet in disbelief.

'I was not in any danger. And besides, what did you say earlier? About putting things right?'

'Not by getting yourself killed!'

'You're being overly dramatic Alfie. Again. The man has lost his wife and can no longer think straight such is his pain. I thought if I could help…'

'Violet, if I might have a word?' Alfie watched hesitantly as Gwilym appeared at Violet's side.

'Of course. What is it Gwilym?'

'I'm sorry to be so forward, but I must ask a favour of you.'

'Do you not think that that house has asked enough of Violet? If you had any decency you might leave us in peace.'

'Alfie, please. Gwilym is my friend.' Violet placed her hand on Alfie's arm, silencing him instantly. 'What is it, Gil?'

'There is something I need your assistance with.'

'Of course. Tell me, is it the same reason why Joseph came to the camp?'

'Joseph came to the camp?' Alfie snapped. 'When was this? Why did you not tell anyone?'

'It was a few days ago' Violet glared at Alfie. 'And I did not tell anyone because there was nothing to tell and even if there had been it would have been nobody else's business.' Ignoring Alfie's scowl, she turned back to Gwilym.

'He said he needed help then, but I confess I didn't give him the opportunity to explain why. Is it the same matter?' Gwilym shrugged.

'Possibly Vi, I couldn't say for certain.' He paused for a moment, and eyed Alfie nervously 'I was wondering if you might pop by the house tonight?'

'Pop by the house? Have you lost your senses?' Alfie flared up again. 'Can you imagine what would happen if she were caught trespassing?'

'Alfie, please!' Violet snapped, her patience finally worn through. 'Stay out of this!'

'You cannot be contemplating agreeing to his request?' Alfie's mouth fell open as he looked at Gwilym and Violet incredulously. 'Violet, this is the most ridiculous thing I've ever heard!' He threw his arms up in exasperation and for the first time in her life Violet found herself flinching away from him. 'You might as well hand yourself to old man Davenport on a plate! He'll see you put away for life if he catches you on his property, or worse!'

'Gwilym is my friend and he has asked for my help.' Violet snapped through gritted teeth. 'And if you are truly my friend you will help not hinder me.'

'You're a fool if you think this will end well. I don't know what else to say. I give up.' Alfie shook his head and walked away, leaving Violet and Gwilym to an awkward silence.

'I'm sorry.' Gwilym grimaced. 'I would have waited to ask if I had known it would cause so much trouble.'

'No matter. Alfie will calm down.' Violet waved her hand dismissively. 'What is the reason for my coming to the house Gil? Alfie was right after all, I would be walking into the lion's den.'

'I... If you could bring your medicine cabinet with you, I would be most grateful' Gwilym said awkwardly, his cap a tightened twist in his hands. Violet frowned.

'I'm not sure that Mr Davenport would be particularly receptive to anything I have to offer Gil, but if you think I can be of help...'

'Thank you.' Gwilym unfurled his hat and placed it back on his head. 'And Vi, this news is to go no further.'

'Of course, but why me? Why do you need me?'

'Because maybe you can provide the answer.' Gwilym shrugged. Violet looked down at the battered paper bag in her hands for a moment.

'Please promise me that this has nothing to do with this damned curse? You are not seeking me out to remove something that never existed in the first place?'

'No, Vi. I promise you. I just, I don't know where else to go for help. I trust you more than anyone one else. And I know that you are the best at what you do.'

'Very well, Gil. Yes, I'll be there.' Gwilym broke into a grin.

'Thank you Vi! I'll meet you on the path by the stables at half past nine? Old Mr Davenport should have retired by then. I'll bring a maid's uniform with me for you to change into. Better safe than sorry.'

'You've been planning this for a while I take it?' Violet chuckled.

'Since I heard you was back.' Gwilym confessed.

'So it would seem. Nine thirty it is then.' She turned to walk away and then spun back to face Gwilym. 'I hope you've thought of everything though,

Gil. Because if we get caught, I'm not sure who Mr Davenport will kill first, me or you.'

'He'd kill me first.' Gwilym laughed. 'I imagine he would probably want to torture you a bit before he finishes you off.'

'Well then, let's hope we do not get caught.' She said goodbye and made her way back to Alfie and the stall, ignoring the eyes that were still on her, one singular thought spinning through her mind.

'What on earth are you doing?'

Chapter eleven

'I don't understand why we are walking when we have a perfectly good carriage at our disposal. Nor do I understand why you are insisting that we whisper when it is obvious that no-one in the house would be able to hear us unless we were shouting at each other.'

'Because I don't want to wake the dogs. If Mr Davenport is disturbed, then all of this will have been for nothing.' Violet said softly, her patience tissue-thin as they made their way down the track to the house, the oil lantern from the front of their carriage barely illuminating the path in front of them.

'Then perhaps it would be for the best if the dogs were disturbed.' Alfie muttered under his breath as he walked ahead. Violet glared at his back.

'If you didn't want to come you should have left me at the crossroads.'

'I promised your mother I would make sure you were safe while you did your rounds and that's exactly what I'm doing. I don't appreciate having to keep this from her though, Vi. She doesn't deserve this.'

Violet ignored his protestations as she pulled her fob watch from her pocket and aimed it towards the lamp. The clock that nestled within the silver casing was just visible, the fine black metal hands and dials standing out in stark contrast against the silver background. When she had been regularly late for their meetings, Joseph had bought it for her. The watch hadn't made her any more punctual. The thought made her smile.

'It is just gone nine o'clock.' She looked up at Alfie as she picked up speed and made her way past him. 'It will take us ten minutes to walk to the stables, maybe a short while longer. So, if we could pick up the pace a bit? Unless you have any objections?'

'Unless I have any objections?' Alfie smirked. 'Why would you even waste your breath on such a question?'

'I was being polite.' Violet said. 'I could have just ordered you to take me there, but it is not within my nature to do so.'

'Asking for my opinion implies that I'm doing this willingly. Which I am not.' He moved ahead of her, letting the silence surround them once more.

Within minutes they came to a small fork in the road. To her right, Violet could see the lights of the house flickering through the trees and she couldn't help but look up at Edwin's window. As if it had been timed to coincide with her arrival the light spluttered and faded into darkness. She cast her gaze to the front of the house where the light in Joseph's room glowed brightly, casting light out onto the gravel driveway below.

'Why are you doing this Vi? After everything he put you through. After everything he put us all through. Haven't you been hurt enough?'

'Do you think I haven't thought about that, Alfie?' She said, her eyes never leaving the window. 'Do you think I haven't churned this over and over in my mind?' She finally turned to face him, the light from the lantern casting shadows across her face. 'Joe didn't run us out of town.' she said finally.

'He didn't defend you though, did he?' Alfie snapped back. 'He didn't support you when his father came for you.'

'Is that really the case though? I'd always thought it was, but something he said at the camp the other day makes me question whether that's true or not. Don't get me wrong, his father behaved abominably, but were we right to accuse Joe in such a way? I really don't have the answer to that.'

'Why did he come to the camp?'

'To ask for help.'

'And so here you are…'

'Please don't be angry with me Alfie.' Violet sighed.

'I'm not angry Vi, I just don't understand. Please, just tell me, what does he have that I don't?' He placed the wooden case and the lamp down on the track, plunging them both into darkness and Violet guessed that it was more for his benefit than hers, that she might not see his face while he finally confessed his innermost secrets to her.

'It isn't like that.' Violet whispered.

'Then what is it like? I mean, I know I've never been totally honest with you where my feelings are concerned. I've never just walked up to you and told you that I loved you. I've never been one to make a song and dance over anything, not really. But I thought you knew how much I cared for you. I thought you saw how loyal I was to you. God, I would lay my life down for you, Vi. Looking back, I realise I should have said something sooner, but I knew that the scrying ritual was coming and I told myself that fate would deal me a good hand. But it wasn't me that you saw, was it? It was him. It was always going to be him.'

'It wasn't him.' Violet said. 'The face that I saw. It wasn't him. I don't know who it was.'

'What? I don't understand.'

'Neither do I.' She walked up to stand next to Alfie. 'If I'm honest, I thought it would be you too Alfie. And you are wrong if you believe that I was unaware of your intentions. I knew how you felt, and I knew what you wished for.'

'So, tell me. How would you have felt? If it had been me?' Violet paused for a moment.

'Sad, because I know I could never love you the way you deserve to be loved. Scared at the thought of losing your friendship if I were to reject you. Angry, because I would have felt that fate was creating a future for me over which I had no control.'

'Then there is no chance?' Alfie asked, a thin flicker of hope still residing in his voice. 'Vi, some people can waste their whole lifetime waiting to be loved and never find what they are looking for. I know you do not feel for me what I feel for you, but maybe that would change in time. I would rather have half of you than nothing at all...'

'Alfie, no. You should be with someone who can give you their all. You deserve nothing less. I'm sorry, but I will never be that person.'

'Sorry, am I interrupting? I can come back.' Violet and Alfie turned as Gwilym appeared at the fork in the road, the lantern that he held aloft gently swinging from side to side, creating a circle of light that danced across the trees surrounding them.

'Could you please Gil?'

'No, there is no need.' Alfie interrupted. 'It's probably a good job you arrived when you did. You've undoubtedly prevented me from making a bigger fool of myself than I already have.

'That's not true, Alfie.' Violet protested.

'Do you want me to wait at the crossroads?' Alfie turned to Gwilym, ignoring Violet's objection.

'There is no need for you to wait out here in the cold. I can bring Violet back to the camp.'

'And what am I to tell your mother, Violet? She will ask where you are, I'm sure.'

'Just tell her that I am with someone who needs my assistance and that I'll return as soon as I am assured of their wellbeing. That is the truth, isn't it?'

'Very well. I'll see you back at the camp.'

There was something different in the way he looked at her, Violet thought as Alfie glanced at her briefly before he turned to walk back down the path and the change in him was as clear to Violet as the beating of her own heart. He held his shoulders high, his gait strong and determined and he did not look back as he so often used to. He was saying more than goodbye she realised, surprised at how much the thought made her heart heavy.

'Are you well?' Gwilym's voice pulled her from her reverie.

'I am well.' She replied. 'Now, if you would be so kind as to show me the way, I believe I have spells to create and miracles to perform.' She forced a smile as she picked up her apothecary cabinet and followed him down the path to the stables and a past she thought she had left behind.

Chapter twelve

'Here we are.'

Gwilym came to a halt by the entrance to the stables. 'I've already lit a couple of lamps in there, so you should be able to see your way around. Oh, and I've placed a uniform in the end stall. I'll wait out here for you while you change but call me if you need anything.'

Without giving herself time to reconsider she made her way to the end stall and pulled the door shut, eyeing the uniform that was hung up in front of her as she unlaced her own garments, throwing them into an unceremonious heap on the floor. Trying to ignore the winter chill that danced over her skin she nimbly slipped into the long black dress and white apron and once it was fastened, she placed a matching white cap on her head, fixing it in place with one of her hairpins. She took a deep breath, smoothed the apron down, collected her case and walked out to meet Gwilym.

'Well, don't you look a picture.' Gwilym mocked gently. 'Perhaps you were made for a life of servitude after all.' Violet glared at him.

'Say that again Mr Lewis and it will be you in need of medication.' When he laughed, she couldn't help but follow suit.

They followed the track from the stables, past the now barren allotments before slipping through a side gate that led to the back door. Gwilym placed a single quieting finger on his lips as he slowly worked the handle and eased the door that led to the kitchen open. He peered in and when he was assured that the room was vacant, he held it open, ushering Violet in and following behind, closing the door as gently as he had opened it and swiftly moving past her to a large wooden butcher's table that stood in the centre of the room.

'I thought it best if it appeared as though you were going somewhere with purpose. Just in case any of the other staff are around or, god forbid, the family are still awake.' He said furtively.

'You really think that could happen? The family might still be up and about I mean?'

'It's doubtful, but just in case. This is usually Aggy's last task of the day.' He pointed to a large ceramic wash jug on the table. 'I'll fill it with hot water and it will need to be taken upstairs. No-one would be surprised to see a new member of staff if they did come across you. Given old man Davenport's behaviour recently…well, let's just say there are more new household members than there are old.'

'And my case?'

'I'll bring it up.'

'Very well.' Violet glanced around the room. 'Does Aggy know that I'm here? I would have liked to have seen her.'

'She does, but I suggested she take the evening off. She did ask me to give you this though.' He pulled a slim white envelope out of his pocket. 'Her words, my handwriting. Wiser to read it when you get home I reckon.' Violet slipped the letter into the pocket of her apron, saying nothing as Alfie walked to the stove and picked up a kettle of steaming water. He filled the jug in one fluid motion and placed the empty kettle on a cast iron trivet on the table before he turned to pick up Violet's case.

'Please be careful Gil.' Violet warned him. 'It is packed full of glass jars and bottles and some of the contents are very expensive to replace.'

'I'll bear that in mind Miss Yardley. Believe me, I would rather incur old Mr Davenport's wrath than yours any day of the week.' He grinned as he lifted the case and once she had collected the jug beckoned for her to follow.

They made their way into the main entrance where the fire continued to glow in the hearth. It was as though time had stood still Violet thought. Every painting, every sculpture still placed as it had been when Josephine Davenport had put it there. And there were ghosts in every corner. Voices that echoed memories long buried away and replayed past horrors for those who had had the misfortune to witness them first hand. The house had held an air of warm congeniality before but now, even as the fires burned it seemed a cold, soulless place. Violet looked up at the portrait of Josephine that hung next to the fireplace. How heartbroken she would be if she knew. She thought back to the reflection in the mirror. Maybe she did know. Maybe it had been her who had led Violet to this very point in time. She unconsciously curtseyed in deference before she followed Gwilym, trying not to spill the contents of the jug as she turned away from the main entrance and up the stairs that led to the bedrooms.

'Wait here one moment.' Gwilym placed her case next to her, knocked on Joseph's door and without waiting for permission he let himself in.

'You cannot be serious?' Violet turned towards the barely open door at the sound of Joseph's voice. 'Gwilym, I am in no fit state to see her now.'

'You went to her for help, didn't you?'

'Yes, but…'

'Now she is here to help. Do not turn her away, Joe. She has put herself at risk to come here. And you need her.' The room fell silent.

This was a mistake. Mentally kicking herself Violet stood at the entrance to Joseph's room and contemplated her next move, trying to figure out the quickest way to get out of the house undetected as Gwilym reappeared. Without a word he collected her cabinet from the floor and beckoned her in.

Where the rest of the house was comfortably warm, Joseph's room felt like a furnace. The fire was stacked high with large oak logs that blasted heat into the room with a violent roar. There were candles placed haphazardly around the room, the writing desk strewn with books, some of which were classic fiction but most appeared to be medical encyclopaedia which lay open to create a state of total disarray. Violet walked further into the room, placing the jug on a chest of drawers and stopped when she noticed the figure in the bed. Joseph lay on his side, his face grey and beaded with sweat. His nightshirt, damp to the point of near transparency, clung to the sinewy muscles beneath as they spasmed erratically. Joseph watched her nervously, his breathing slowing as the convulsions began to subside.

'And so now you know the truth of it.' He said in short quiet bursts. 'I did not call your here for my father, I called you here because I need your help.' He closed his eyes as though he could hide from her. 'I'm dying, Violet.'

'No, that cannot be true.' Violet made her way over to the bed, taking Joseph's hands in her own. His skin was cold, his fingers contorted in such a way that he must have been in agony Violet thought. Gwilym moved to stand at the end of the bed.

'We've tried everything Vi, but nothing has worked. The pharmacist is completely stumped.' Violet thought back to the conversation in the chemists. 'There is nothing else I can suggest sir' So was that it? Charles Lewis knew and just intended to walk away? Leave Joseph to die without further intervention? She shook her head in disbelief.

'Tell me, what are the symptoms Gil?' Gwilym stared blankly at his friend as if he had already resigned himself to his loss.

'Fever, muscle cramps, he complains of stomach pain a fair bit.' He moved to the books on the bureau and started piling them into stacks. 'This seems to happen in cycles. He'll be fine for a couple of weeks and then he has another bad night like this. They seem to be increasing in frequency though.'

Think, Violet, think. She took her hand back from Joseph, her fingers shaking as she ran them back and forth across her forehead, her mind tumbling through a maze of illnesses and disorders and treatments.

'I need you to clear the table, Gil. And open the window a notch. The air in here is stifling and won't be doing Joe an ounce of good.' She sprang from the floor and grabbed hold of the wooden chest as Gwilym created a workspace for her and as soon as he was done, she placed the chest on the table and threw the lid open.

'Fetch me some whiskey and some honey.' She said, her eyes never leaving the contents of the cabinet in front of her. 'Quick as you can please, Gil.' She was vaguely aware of him dashing from the room as she pulled a small granite pestle and mortar from the cabinet, lining up a series of jars and bottles next to it before she grabbed a set of small measuring spoons and pipettes. Light. She needed more light. She moved from one corner of the room to the next, Joseph's eyes following her every move as she transferred as many candles as she could onto the table and then sat back down and began to work.

By the time Gwilym had reappeared Violet was combining plants and liquids and compounds in ways she never had before, confident that if nothing else they would not contraindicate each other rendering the final product useless. Whether the mixture would produce the desired outcome was unknown, even to her. She muttered her thanks as Gwilym put the whiskey, honey and a crystal tumbler on the table in front of her and began to pour differing amounts of each ingredient into the glass and when she was satisfied she made her way back over to Joseph, choosing to sit beside him so she could administer the remedy more easily. Joseph stared at her wide-eyed.

'You are wearing a maid's outfit.'

'I know. The lengths I'll go to to play witch.' She moved aside slightly as Gwilym helped Joseph into an upright position. Joseph sighed and leant back against the pillows then turned his head to look at the glass apprehensively as Violet leaned forward, swirling the grey-green contents.

'What is that?'

'This is a mix of plants and minerals that I hope will at least counteract the symptoms, even if it not the final cure itself.' She said. 'I'll explain more later. For now, I just need you to drink.' Joseph leaned forward and stared into the glass uncertainly. 'I've added whiskey and honey to soften the taste. It's not as bad as it first appears, I promise. Please, just drink it. For me, Joe.' He hesitantly leaned forward and put his lips to the edge of the tumbler, his eyes wary, never leaving hers as he consumed its contents and when the glass was empty, he fell back against the pillows and closed his eyes.

'Christ, that's vile.'

'I said I'd softened the taste, not that I'd created an elixir.' She smiled as Joseph half-opened one eye.

'When do you have to leave?' He murmured, taking hold of her hand and weaving his fingers between hers.

'Not yet.' Violet said, defying the warning bells that rang in her head. 'I'll stay and make sure that the tincture has taken effect.'

'I see. So then, even if it does work, I suppose I'll have to pretend that it hasn't.'

'Well then I suppose I'll just have to prepare another one and maybe next time I won't sweeten it.' Joseph smiled and Violet watched as the tension slowly eased from his body, his muscles relaxing as he sank into the mattress. She let go of his hand and went back to the table to write up detailed notes, trying and failing to keep her eye on the page as Gwilym helped Joseph change his nightclothes and when Gwilym was finished she returned to Joseph's side.

'My father said that you were a witch.' Joseph whispered. 'And while your heart and your soul are pure, I fear he may be right.' Unable to find a single thing to say in reply, Violet watched as his breathing slowed and he fell into a deep sleep.

Chapter thirteen

Violet's life had been one of perpetual migration, moving between towns and villages with a certainty and regularity one might only observe in the rise and fall of the moon or the ebb and flow of the tide. Each relocation bought with it its own idiosyncrasies. It might be a change in climate or geography or possibly the disposition of the locals, some of whom were warm and welcoming, others more hostile. For all of that though, there was an underlying continuity. The heaviness of the covers that engulfed her as she lay in her makeshift bed that was little more than a few hastily assembled crates, the smell of incense that filled the tent and the sounds of birds in song as the sun rose. All these things, as nomadic as she was, she knew to be persistent and true.

It was that awareness of continuity that exacerbated the wrongness that she felt now. Though she were not blanketed she felt warm and content. There was no birdsong either, just a stillness that tried to lull her back to her dreams.

'Violet, wake up, lovely girl.' Soft footsteps behind her, creaking floorboards, an unfamiliar voice pulled her back from her slumber to a state of near waking. 'Gwilym, how on earth did you allow this to happen?' There was a gentle tap on her arm which roused her further still, alerted her to the hand she held tightly in her own. Gwilym? Confusion fogged her thoughts, left her with a growing sense of anxiety.

'I'm sorry!' Gil's voice now, all harsh whispers and protestations. 'It took an age for the medication to work and then he kept waking up and the pain just took him as soon as he opened his eyes. At one point, we weren't even sure if…' Gwilym took a deep heavy breath, shuddering as he exhaled. 'We were so tired…'

'Nonetheless, you should have woken me. I appreciate that you were trying to do right by Joe and I'm glad that he is improved, but if his lordship catches her in here, we'll all be for the high jump!'

A warm hand shook Violet's arm lightly. 'Vi, come on my love, you need to leave before someone spots you.' Aggy, Violet realised. Oh, dear god what had she done? She kept her eyes tightly shut, blocking out the presence of those in the room with her, shame burrowing into every nerve and fibre at the thought of her indiscretion. What if this became public? It wouldn't take long for word to spread and oh, how excited, how frenzied, the gossip would be. The exiled witch spending the night in the company of the gentleman whose mother she had been accused of murdering. Whether they believed the accusation to be true or not would be of little consequence. To walk alone with a potential suitor in daylight was frowned upon, but this? Spending the night in the bedroom of a man to whom she was not betrothed? She slowly pushed herself upright, blinking wildly to remove the sleep from her eyes, Joseph's fingers still tightly interwoven with hers. One quick glance at him told her that he was still soundly asleep, his skin now restored to a healthier pink, his fever seemingly abated, at least for now.

'Violet, I am truly sorry. I have behaved so stupidly!' Violet shook her head.

'This is as much my fault as yours Gil. If I had thought this through properly, I could have prepared another dose and gone home. We knew the treatment was working, albeit slowly. There was no need for me to have stayed.'

'Need and want are very different beasts and speak to very different hearts.' Aggy said softly. 'Come, Gwilym has been charged with taking me into town. You will travel with me.'

'At this time?' Gwilym frowned.

'Yes, at this time child! We have guests arriving today as much as you'd like to forget I'm sure.'

'Guests, Aggy?' Everyone turned as Joseph spoke.

'You are awake.' Violet smiled.

'How could one not wake in all this commotion?' He mumbled, his gaze following Violet's to the place where their hands met. He tightened his grasp for the briefest of moments before he let go of her, slowly dragging his hands back to place them in his lap. 'Who's coming today?' He asked again.

'The Parnells, as well you know.' Aggy replied. Joseph scowled and closed his eyes.

'The Parnells?' Violet looked over at Aggy and back to Joseph who still had his eyes shut tight.

'They are no-one of any import.' Joseph said with an air of resignation.

'I wouldn't let your father or the Parnells hear you say that.' Agnes snorted.

'I thought I had convinced my father to change his mind. He said he was rethinking the visit.' Joseph said.

'And you believed him?' Agnes fussed around him, straightening his bedding and fluffing his pillows 'Besides which, your father has plans and I don't think your wants or wishes form part of them, do you?'

'What is his plan?' Violet asked.

'Doomed to failure with any luck.' Gwilym muttered under his breath.

'And you need to button your lip Gwilym Lewis. You're in enough trouble as it is.' Aggy rubbed her hands together, calling everyone to action. 'Vi, I assume you have your own clothes somewhere?'

'I left them in the stable.' Her cheeks reddened as Aggy's eyes widened. 'It was the only place I could change! There was nothing untoward about it!'

'Of course not.' Aggy fussed. 'Very well. Gwilym, collect Vi's belongings and get the cart ready for town. We will escort Vi back to the camp on our way.'

'Yes, ma'am.' Gwilym mouthed a silent apology to Violet and fled the room.

'Thank you, Gil.' Violet whispered after him. 'And thank you, Aggy. I am truly grateful.' She stood and moved to the table to reassemble the contents of the medicine case, allowing Agnes to take her place at Joseph's side. Agnes's expression instantly softened, Violet noticed, taking on a maternal air as she leaned over and ruffled his hair tenderly before resting her hand against his cheek.

'Try to sleep for a while longer. Gwilym will arrange your clothing when he returns.'

Joseph nodded, his head sinking back further into the pillow where he agitated the feathers within it. Such a small gesture but it caught at something in Violet's heart. Forced her to acknowledge the facts as they lay themselves bare before her. That she wanted to be where Aggy sat. That she wanted it to be her hand that rested upon his cheek. That in all the time that she had been away, nothing had changed. That her heart was still his. And that knowing the truth scared her more than she would ever be able to say. She buried the thought away and turned back to the case, gently placing the bottles into their specified compartments, ensuring that each was matched to its corresponding label, affording the task more concentration that was actually required so desperate was she to avoid following her train of thought to its logical conclusion.

'You will not get out of bed and start rummaging through those blessed books the minute I leave?' Aggy said as she straightened his covers. 'You will stay here and rest?'

'I will.' Joseph looked over to table as Violet pulled the two leaves of the medicine chest together. 'Let me just say goodbye to Vi before she goes.'

'Of course. I'll wait for you outside.' Agnes followed Gwilym out of the door leaving Joseph and Violet alone.

'You look much better, Joe.' Violet said, running her fingers along the leather handle at the top of the case. 'Last night, I was so anxious for you.'

'You thought I would die?' Joseph frowned.

'For a time, yes.' Violet's voice quietened to a whisper. 'Nothing would abate the symptoms. They kept returning and you were so distressed. And then all I could think was that you came to me for help and that I was going to fail you.'

'You could never fail me Vi.' Joseph said as he turned in the bed to face her. 'And I have to say, I cannot remember a time when I woke feeling this rested.' He raised his head slightly and manoeuvred his arm so that it lay underneath the pillow before he placed his head back down. 'I feel it would require minimal effort, even for those with the laziest of imaginations to know how this has come to pass.'

'I am glad that I was able to help.' Violet flushed bright red as she picked the chest up off the table. 'I must go, before I get everyone in trouble, but, if you require my services again, please, just send for me. Or perhaps Gil could pick something up and bring it back here? It would certainly be less controversial.'

'I'll send for you.' Joseph smiled, allowing himself a brief moment to watch her as she slipped silently out the room before his eyes fluttered shut.

*****

The curtains at old man Davenport's window were still closed. Violet let out a sigh of relief and walked hurriedly along the back path that circled the house, making her way towards the stables where Gwilym waited for her. She glanced over towards the carriage house where three of the land-workers were cleaning the formal carriage, their arms a flurry of movement, their breath vast clouds of steam such was the speed with which they worked.

'The Parnells get the fancy carriage.' Gwilym answered her unspoken question.

'They seem to be of greater importance than Joe implies.' Violet said thoughtfully.

'They like to think they are.' Gwilym snorted. He gingerly took the medicine chest from her, lifting his other arm to reveal a tan leather carpet bag. 'Your clothes are in here. They're not packed very well I'm afraid. Can't say as I've had to fold ladies' garments before.'

'It doesn't matter.' Violet shrugged. 'I'm just grateful you did it in the first place. I'll return your bag to you as soon as I can.' She ran her eyes over the luggage. 'It really is quite lovely, Gil. Are you sure you want to lend it to me?'

'So, you approve of it?' Gwilym asked.

'I do. Who wouldn't?' Violet smiled.

'Then you may keep it, if you'd like? I have several of them. I make them from the leather the upholsterers can't use to re-seat carriages. And from scraps from the tannery and worn out equipment from the stables. When I get the opportunity, I sell them at the market. Doesn't happen very often unfortunately but it does bring extra money into the house.'

'You made this? Gil, I had no idea you were so talented! Are you sure you would not rather sell it than give it to me?' Gwilym shook his head.

'Consider it an apology. I could have gotten you into a lot of trouble.'

'And I you.' Violet smiled conspiratorially and looked back at the bag. 'You know, if you want me to put some of your merchandise on my stall, I would be more than happy to oblige.'

'You would? Vi, that would be fantastic.'

'Just drop some of the bags down next time you're at the market.' Gwilym bowed his head, his expression formal and business-like, although it only lasted a matter of seconds.

'I will, thank you, Vi. And thank you for agreeing to help last night. I don't know what I would have done without your support. I truly don't know if he would have survived the night.'

'He is our friend.' Violet said. 'And we do what we can for our friends do we not?'

'Even if we run the risk of being burned at the stake?' Violet laughed and peered up at Joseph's window as Gwilym placed her luggage on the floor of the cart. When he was done, she took his hand and climbed into the cart.

'Yes, Gil.' She sighed. 'Even then.'

Chapter fourteen

'We'll just be a few moments before we set off. Gwilym, we need to take Angharad and Winnie back into town. They'll be out now. They're just finishing up in the kitchen.' Aggy walked along the side of the cart and climbed up to sit at the front next to Gwilym before she turned to face Violet. 'Do you have something warm to wrap around yourself, Vi? I can see you shivering from here.' Violet nodded silently and opened the leather holdall that Gwilym had placed at her feet pulling out the shawl that was rolled up at the top and throwing around her shoulders. Aggy was right. There was a bitter chill in the wind this morning that heralded the true onset of winter. She looked back at the house and the smoke spiralling up from the chimneys and couldn't help buy wonder, how much time would come to pass before she no longer thought of the warmth inside Ty Mawr and compared it to the bitter air that she would wake up to for the foreseeable future? Spring suddenly seemed a lifetime away.

'Ah, here they are now.' Violet looked up as two girls ran from the house towards the cart. The first girl, her red hair a mass of unruly curls launched herself from the gravel path, one foot then the other landing with a resounding thud. She stopped, her mouth falling open when she came face to face with Violet, lurching forward as the second girl slammed into her.

'Careful, Winnie, what on earth are you doing? Oh!' The girl who was still hidden from view, Angharad presumably, called out. Her face appeared over Winnie's shoulder and Violet watched in contained amusement as the two girls froze where they stood.

'Don't just stand there, girls!' Agnes whirled round a second time. 'We have places to be!'

'Sorry!' Winnie moved into the cart and took the seat facing Violet, allowing Angharad to climb up and sit beside her, making the cart rock from side to side as she dropped down onto the seat with an enthusiasm that was less than necessary. Violet nodded in greeting and the girls mirrored her gesture, their lips pursed as if they shared an unspoken joke. Violet sighed inwardly. Social politics was a nightmare at the best of times, but this early in the day? It was not a minefield she cared to even attempt to cross. The horse began a slow plod forwards, bringing the carriage to life and Violet watched as Winnie looked out over the fields and then back to her, her stare questioning, her lips curled into a tight smile.

'Are you well Miss Yardley? We'd heard you were back of course, but I must say, we hadn't anticipated seeing you so soon, and here of all places, at this ungodly hour.'

'I'm quite well, thank you.' Violet replied, watching the girls as their eyes travelled upwards, fixing on a spot above her head. She reached up, her hand finding the waitress's cap that now lay askew at the side of her head and the strands of hair that had slipped down to frame her face. She must look as though she were in total disarray she realised. Might as well reveal her indiscretions now. They were stamped over her for all to see anyway.

'I'm telling you now girls, if the pair of you have any wits about you, you'll be keeping your lips sealed too. What happens in those four walls is nothing to do with the likes of us.'

'I was just inquiring after Ms Yardley's health.' Winnie protested.

'Looking for something to gossip about was what you was doing!' Agnes shrieked harshly. 'Now just you listen to me. If word gets out it'll be the two of you out on your ear, I'll make sure of that. So, you bear that in mind when you get home.' Violet sighed quietly to herself as the two girls turned as one to glare at her.

'How is your mother, Violet?' Grateful for the distraction, she turned sideways so she could see Agnes more clearly.

'She is well, thank you. She looks forward to seeing you very much.'

'And I her.' Agnes smiled. 'I have a day to do as I please towards the end of the week. I'll get word to her. Perhaps she would like to meet at the tea rooms? I seem to recall she had a particular fondness for the scones there.' Violet laughed.

'You remember correctly.' She leaned further forward so she could speak in confidence.

'Mother and I, we are truly sorry for your loss.' She said softly, placing her hand on Agnes's shoulder.

'Thank you, pet.' Agnes reached to pat Violet's hand but kept her eyes fixed front. 'It was a very sorry business, aye, but mercifully they did not pass the infection on to my nephew and niece. My sister still watches them both like a hawk though, waiting for the first sneeze or the merest hint of a fever. Not that they would be able to afford anything in the way of a cure.'

'God forbid it should ever happen, but you must know, if you need me, you would not need to pay me Aggy. I would not see your family suffer.' At that Agnes did smile.

'You are a kind soul, Violet Yardley. Did Gwilym pass you the letter?' Violet reached down and patted the pocket of the apron she still wore.

'Yes, I have it.' Agnes nodded.

'I hope it will explain everything.' Agnes said. 'The times are changing here, Violet. They are changing in ways no-one imagined. Everything seems darker, I think. But there are some things that remain constant. You must never forget that.'

'I won't.' Violet said hurriedly, the unread letter suddenly burning a hole in her pocket as the cart picked up speed and turned away from the house.

'Woah!' The horse and cart came to a sudden stop, sending Violet lurching forward. She threw her arms out, grabbing the wooden door and somehow managed to halt the momentum that carried her body forward, only just stopping herself from landing in Angharad's lap. The girls opposite her squealed in horror as the horse reared up on its hind legs, threatening to tip the cart onto its side sending them all flying into the mud beneath them as Gwilym leapt from the front bench and lunged for the horse's reins. He pulled down hard on the leather straps, bringing the horse to an abrupt standstill, his voice conspicuously calm in the sea of chaos that surrounded him. As the girls clung to each other and cried and Agnes gripped on to Violet's hand fiercely, Gwilym whispered in soft tones until the horse was calm, the buggy thankfully still upright. He breathed out heavily, resting his head against the horse for a moment before he turned and stormed towards the cart that had appeared out of the morning mist.

'Stupid reckless imbecile!' Gwilym called out to a woman who was climbing down from a trap in front of them, her face obscured by a long flowing hood. Are you trying to get us all killed? These roads are not designed for that kind of speed! Oh, Mrs Yardley!' Gwilym faltered and came to a standstill as Constance Yardley pulled down the hood to reveal her face. 'I'm so sorry! If I had known it was you I should never...'

'…have spoken to me that way? I can't see why not. It was thoroughly deserved. I was travelling far too fast. I'm sorry, Gwilym, but I am here on an urgent matter. Violet, is she with you?'

'She's here with me.' Aggy stepped down from the coach and rushed to greet Constance. 'I was just saying to Violet I hoped to see you soon. I hadn't realised how soon that would be.'

'Aggy. It is so good to see you.' Constance wrapped her friend's hands in her own.

'Good lord, Connie, you are positively shaking! Come, sit here for a moment.' Constance shook her head as Agnes tried to lead her back to the coach.

'No, I am quite well, thank you. I just needed to make sure…When Violet didn't come home I…'

'You didn't know she was here?'

'No, I did not.' Constance turned to face her daughter, her expression thunderous. 'I was led to believe that she was with a sick child. That she could not leave her side. That her parents feared they would lose her in the night.'

'I assume Alfie told you I was here.' Violet asked as she stepped down from the cart.

'He did, eventually.' Constance said. 'How could you put him in this position Violet? It was only this morning when he found out you hadn't come home that he told me that he'd bought you here and, more to the point, what had gone on between you and old man Davenport in town yesterday. Do you know how scared he is? He waits at home now fretting that he has unwittingly become an accomplice to your arrest or worse still, your death and it's taken all of my strength to stop the men of the camp coming down here and taking the house by storm! This will not do, Violet! It will not do!'

'I'm sorry!' Violet protested. 'Joe needed my help. He was ill. You would not have had me turn him away surely?'

'Of course not, but neither would I have agreed to you behaving in such a reckless and foolish manner. Do you realise the danger you put yourself in? How do you think Alfie would have felt if your scheming had gone wrong? It was wrong of you to put that burden on him. And to make him lie to us like that? It is unforgivable Violet.'

'I know.' Violet said, more softly this time. 'I'll apologise to him when I see him, I promise.'

'What on earth are you wearing?' Violet looked down at the battered maid's outfit.

'It was necessary.' She stuttered. 'To avoid being recognised.'

'I see.' Constance gave her a withering look. 'Violet, gather your belongings and get in the trap please.'

'Yes, mother.' Violet dashed back to the cart where her bags now lay haphazardly on the floor and tried to quell the rising panic at the sight of the medicine case which had been flung from one side of the carriage to the other. Doing her best to ignore the smug expressions on the girls faces she grabbed both bags and made her way back to her own cart, clambering in and waiting attentively as her mother said her farewells to Agnes, eventually climbing into the cart beside her.

'Not a word, Violet.' She muttered under her breath. 'I don't want to hear a single word. Do you understand?' Violet nodded hurriedly. 'Good. Then let's go home. You have people you need to apologise to.'

*****

When they arrived back at the camp Violet found Edie and Alfie sat on one of the logs that surrounded the fire though the fire had long gone out now. As soon as she spotted the cart Edie leapt up from the makeshift seat and ran towards Violet, flinging her arms around her before her feet had barely hit the floor.

'Vi, I have been so scared! Are you well?' Violet pulled back from her friend's grip and took her hands on her own.

'I'm fine. Don't worry Edie.'

'That was such a dangerous thing to do, Vi! But so romantic!' Edie swooned.

'He was sick, Edie. It was not romantic. Not in the slightest!'

'And is he well now?'

'He is improved but I wouldn't say he is well.'

'Vi, I'm sorry.' Violet turned to face Alfie. He looked exhausted, shaming her even further.

'No, I am the one who needs to apologise Alfie. I promise I will never do anything like that again.' Alfie nodded and smiled as they reached out their hands at the same time, a simple handshake that would normally be able to right all wrongs. Violet wasn't sure if it would be so simple this time.

'We have to go. Alfie is taking me into town!' Edie squealed. 'I want to visit the castle and take tea at the tea-rooms and see the birds in the market!' Alfie laughed.

'I'm not sure my wages extend to tea in the tea rooms.' He said as though someone had firmly lodged a plum in his mouth. 'You may have to settle for Welshcakes from the market.'

'I have money too! We'll have plenty between us. Please, let's go, I can't wait any longer! Bye Violet, see you soon!'

Violet smiled as Edie grabbed Alfie's arm and dragged him towards the cart. 'Times are changing, Violet.' Agnes's words twisted and turned in her mind as she watched Alfie and Edie set off in the cart towards town. Perhaps they were, she thought. But maybe sometimes it was for the better.

She was relieved when, instead of interrogating her the moment they set foot in the tent her mother sent away to wash and change. They were not, she said, servants to the man who had turned their lives to chaos and they would not dress as such. Violet dropped down onto her makeshift bed and lifted the letter from the pocket of her apron, pulling her shawl tighter around herself before tearing a small hole at the corner of the envelope and sliding her forefinger along its top edge. Inside, was a sheet of paper that had been wrapped around a postcard. She placed the postcard on her lap and delicately unfolded the letter.

Dearest Violet,

I know that in writing to you I am interfering in matters in which I have no business but I think it is of utmost importance that I disclose to you the full facts regarding the Davenport family and the current situation that Joseph finds himself in.

It may well seem that after the death of his mother Joseph took upon a course of action that supported his father's appalling behaviour towards you and yours. This is untrue. The truth is that Joe confronted his father on several occasions though his protestations were ignored, indeed, he carries the scars of his perceived betrayal. He still fights for you now.

You also know now that Joseph is ill. His symptoms are the same as mother's and so it is only natural that one might link the two. I'm not suggesting that there is still a belief in this so-called curse. We all know that it is nothing more than a story made up by a man consumed, but when Joe is in pain all causes that may carry a cure become plausible, no matter how illogical. He may say things or act in ways that are against his nature. So please, I beg of you, see him through new eyes. He fears death but not as much as we fear losing him. Help him. I know that you can. Maybe together you can shed a little light on the world.

I apologise if my interference offends you. This note is sent with the best of intentions and I hope you will keep my confidence after reading its contents. I found the enclosed card in the dustbin in Joseph's room just after you left and felt that you would want to know of its existence. I pray that I am right.

With warmest regards,

Agnes.

Violet folded the letter and lifted the card from her lap. It was a Valentines card. A picture of a couple, bedecked in the finest garments sat atop a smiling crescent moon, the woman's dress covered in fresh roses, the gentleman on whose lap she sat smiling down at her adoringly. 'To My Valentine' was written in the top left corner, above it a single heart. Violet smiled as she turned the card over. The missive on the back was short and simple and undeniably written by Joseph.

Look in thy glass and tell the face thou viewest,
Now is the time that face should form another.

The words instantly took Violet back to another place and time when she and Joseph had sat at the edge of the camp, away from the rest of the family and she had told him of the scrying to come. He had quoted these words to her then. Shakespeare, he had said. The sonnet in its entirety had had a greater meaning. It was a plea to the viewer of the mirror to look not at themselves but at the lives they should create. Given the context of their conversation, it was apt that he should end his recital where he did. Perhaps, he had said, the face in the mirror would be his and the lives she would create would be theirs. He had stolen a kiss and run back down the side of the hill towards home like a child caught with his hand in the sweet jar his arms flailing around him to help him maintain his balance. Nothing since had made her laugh as she had then. The image still made her smile now.

Violet put both the letter and the card back into the envelope, holding them tightly to her chest for a moment before she lay the envelope under her pillow. She would read them again tonight by candlelight, deal with the workings of her heart when none could encroach upon her. Before then, there were more important things to address. She had to get to the market because people were banking on her, but more importantly she had to contend with her mother, the sisters and their interrogations and as much as it pained her, she knew that aside from Joseph's condition, all she would be able to offer them was a beautiful web of lies.

Chapter fifteen

The sun seemed to have taken its last breath and succumbed to the onslaught of winter, forcing a particular greyness onto the landscape that left one with a sense of mourning for days passed. The summits of the hills that surrounded the town were now subsumed by clouds and though the grass was still green it had lost its vibrancy as the light had suffocated. Saturated by rain, the grey stone buildings in the town had taken on a darker hue, seeming to close in not just on themselves, but on the people that walked the streets between them, stifling the everyday conversation that usually filled the air.

The vendors who were normally positioned at the entrance to the market had moved their stalls further into the gateway to avoid getting wet, but the move still wasn't enough to enable Violet to ignore the cold air that gnawed at her. It was at this time of year, when everything was sodden, that life under canvas was at its most challenging. Waterproof covers shielded the tents from the majority of the bad weather, but they did not prevent the damp from seeping in from the ground up. There was however a brief respite when, for one glorious moment each morning, she dressed hurriedly in the clothes that her mother had warmed for her in front of the stove. The heat from the garments warmed her bones, made her aching body droop in a state of near total relaxation, but the moment soon passed as winter claimed them for its own. Memories of the warmth of Joe's room, of the fire that burned fiercely there did not dissipate, instead they strengthened, coming back every morning to remind her of a luxury that she would never truly know. For the first time in her life she found herself genuinely envying those who had unwittingly been born into wealth.

Violet hated this time of year. Preparations for the coming yuletide season only served to highlight the difference between the rich and the poor.

More so since the recession had begun to bite which made the festive season seem uglier than usual. While the affluent wandered from shop to shop buying luxury foodstuffs and baubles and trinkets, the disadvantaged queued in a solemn line in front of her, giving her what little money they had simply to ensure that their loved ones would be well, would live to see the new year. Christmas to them was a burden they could not afford and yet they fawned over her with gratitude, thanking her for her return as though she were a deity. Their reaction towards her felt like a hypocrite. Because when all was said and done, whose money would she be spending when purchasing gifts for her own family? Though she smiled warmly as she stood behind the table, she could barely look them in the eye.

'Why don't you go and get us some soup and bread before your face actually turns to stone?' Violet turned back from the queue to face Alfie. He glanced over at her briefly as he handed a customer change, the last of a long queue that had been waiting for him when he had arrived. His was also a trade that made a substantial profit at this time of year with domestic staff clamouring to ensure that their masters would be appropriately equipped with the sharpest of blades as they stood at the head of the table and for one day a year only, carved elaborate birds for their families to consume. What a show it all was. What a facade.

'Vi, are you listening to me, or have you actually frozen to the spot?' At that Violet did smile.

'I'm sorry Alfie, I was miles away. What did you say?'

'Go and get us something to eat, will you?' He nodded towards the stalls that were buried in the market as he sharpened a carving knife on his whetstone. 'Get me a bowl of cawl? And some bread. And if you've enough change, maybe a couple of Welshcakes. I'm starving.'

'Yes. Of course.' Violet said. 'Will you…'

'Look after the stall? Naturally.' Violet took a few coins out of her money belt, unfastened it from her hips and handed it to Alfie as she made her way out from behind the table and into the cavernous hall that held the main market. The stone slabs inside were as wet and slippery as those on the street but at least in here there was some respite from the bitter air of winter. Stalls dotted the area, selling everything from freshly carved joints of meat to cheap ornaments and household goods. Stretched out along the walls, farmer's wives stood in front of over-sized wicker baskets that were laden with vegetables while the farmers themselves stood close by, guarding stalls from which they sold fresh milk, their handcarts bedecked with urns and tin pails that customers could carry their produce home in.

Everything that one would need to run a home could be found here and now that Christmas approached it was busier than ever, creating a fevered excitement that made the vendors shout a little louder and made everything seem slightly more desperate than usual, as if the shoppers were being warned that time was running out, even though there were a good few weeks to go before the festivities would truly begin. While the gentry who perused the streets were near silent, the hubbub in the market more than made up for it.

Violet made her way to a small stall at the far side of the market and joined the queue. This cart was more colourful than most, adorned as it was with glitter and cheap Christmas tree decorations. The few tables and chairs that surrounded it were occupied by weary shoppers. Their baskets full to the brim they sat and watched, disengaging themselves from the furore that surrounded them, the calm eye in the middle of the storm.

'Alfie said that I would find you here.' Violet spun round to find Gwilym stood inches from her. He lifted his cap and bowed, his smile wide. Three weeks had passed and in all that time there had been no word from Ty Bryn. Three weeks since she had received the letter and the card enclosed within it. Both were starting to look worn at the edges, she had read and re-read them so many times. Three weeks not knowing if he were well, if he needed her. She fixed her face into a smile and bowed her head in greeting. Held back the questions she wanted to pepper Gwilym with.

'How are you this hideous morning, Miss Yardley?'

'I am well, thank you, Gil. It feels as though it has been an age since I last saw you. Are you well?'

'I am well, and you are right, it has certainly been an age.' He said wearily. 'We have been away for the past few weeks, in the north of the country. There is an estate up there that provides the facilities for grouse shooting which I'm to understand has become the popular pastime of the landed gentry.' He raised his eyebrows, his expression mocking. 'Old man Davenport thinks that he might be able to use some of his land to create a similar business here, though I've no idea why. The lay of the land is totally inappropriate. The only good thing to have come out of the trip is that the old man has ceased his excessive drinking which has made everyone's lives a little easier.' Violet turned briefly to the market vendor, placing her order before she looked back to Gwilym making a conscious effort to school the tone of her voice.

'And did you all travel north?'

'No, just me, the old man, Mr Parnell and Joe, who was so bored I can't begin to tell you. It is not his thing as you know but he was required there for any dealings that might have taken place, not that any did. One blessing is that Miss Parnell stayed behind, though I am to understand that that was a complete disaster.'

'Miss Parnell?' Violet took possession of her order, passing it back to Gwilym to hold while she fished a selection of coins from her pocket and paid the vendor.

'Mr Parnell's daughter.' Gwilym explained, leaning forward to speak quietly into Violet's ear. 'And she is ghastly. They live in London for part of the year so you can imagine how she has to lower her standards in order to survive in this apparently primitive country of ours. I've never heard anyone whine and complain as much as she does. When we returned home, Amelia was in a dreadful state. Miss Parnell had taken it upon herself to rearrange parts of the house while we were gone. Said something about how the decor would be laughed at by those who frequented the same social circles as her in town. She took down the picture of Mrs Davenport in the hall.'

'You're not serious!' Violet cried. 'How could she possibly imagine such behaviour would be appropriate?' Gwilym shrugged.

'I am as mystified as you are, Vi. You can't begin to imagine how angry the old man and Joe were when they returned. The painting she'd replaced it with was very promptly removed and Mrs Davenport returned to her rightful place. Miss Parnell took to her room sobbing for the rest of the day.'

'Maybe she was just trying to help. Insensitive as she was.'

'Perhaps.' Gwilym conceded. 'But she is too impetuous. She is unaware of the ability she has to offend those around her. Too much talking and not enough listening if you ask me.' He handed the food parcels back to Violet and she held them close, relishing their warmth as they made their way back through the market towards the stall where Alfie stood waiting. He rubbed his hands together with enthusiasm before he grabbed hold of one of the containers of cawl, a chunky soup that was packed with chunks of lamb and vegetables.

'How much longer will the Parnells remain in town?' Violet asked as she passed Alfie the rest of his food.

'The stay looks to be an extended one. At least they certainly show no signs of going home. I can only pray that their departure is sooner rather than later. Actually, while I have your attention there's something I need to ask you…'

'Careful…' Alfie, muttered ominously. Violet and Gwilym looked up towards the path that led to the centre of town.

'Christ, are they done already?' Gwilym cursed as Edwin Davenport walked towards them with another gentleman. Mr Parnell, Violet guessed. He was of a comparable age and stature, their faces similarly joyous, their arms animated as they walked towards the market. They were reliving past tales Violet supposed given the ferocity of their laughter as they pointed out particular locations. After what felt like a lifetime, Joseph came into view behind them, walking with a girl Violet thought was the prettiest she had ever seen.

The first thing Violet noticed were her gloves which were the purest white, a stark contrast to the dark grey sleeve of Joseph's coat where she clung, her fingers wrapped tightly around his arm. Her head turning from side to side she took in her locale with wide enthusiastic eyes and everything about her screamed that she was not from around here. That she was in some way better than here. She carried herself with a notion of class that could only have been acquired from good breeding, walking with an air of confidence that made heads turn, her smile all ease and delight. Her enthusiasm was every bit as excessive as her father but there was a delicacy to it that softened the edges, making her seem more graceful, somehow.

Her platinum hair was curled into barrels and tucked neatly within the confines of a dark purple fanchon, her skin pale and smooth save for the slight pinking of her cheeks in the cold air and her bustle coat which virtually touched the floor opened slightly as she walked to reveal the vibrant purple silk dress she wore underneath. She was everything that Violet was not. The thought hit her like a blow to the stomach, leaving her breathless. Joseph walked alongside her, lips unmoving, but then, even if he'd had something to say, Violet thought, it was unlikely that he would get to express it, such was the speed with which her mouth moved.

'Am I to take it that this is Miss Parnell?' Violet inquired, her eyes never leaving the woman as she drew nearer.

'One and the same.' Gwilym confirmed miserably. 'Looks like a peacock, wouldn't you say?'

'Gwilym, that is mean!' Violet scolded him, hiding her laughter behind mittened fingers. Was it wrong to take a disliking to someone on sight alone? Of course, it was. She had experienced the same prejudice all her life and knew how much it hurt. So why did that awareness not change the way that she felt now? It was an avenue she chose not to explore.

'I had better go.' Gwilym said. 'I just wanted to ask, you said you would sell some of my bags. I have some free time tomorrow morning, so I was wondering if I could bring some down?'

'Of course.' Violet said. 'We'll be here fairly early so just pop down whenever you're ready.'

'I'm afraid that isn't possible.' Alfie walked over to stand behind Violet.

'Oh, I apologise.' Gwilym stammered. 'Violet had offered and I...'

'I am still offering!' Violet turned on Alfie, her brow furrowed. 'Why on earth are you saying no? Gil is our friend!'

'I know he is our friend Vi. And I'm not saying no to selling his bags. I'm saying no because we won't be here tomorrow and I would rather he avoided a wasted journey.'

'What do you mean, we won't be here tomorrow?'

'There is to be a party.' Alfie sighed. 'Back at the camp. It was supposed to have been a surprise belated celebration for your birthday. Make up for the last attempt. No exploding mirrors, no hysteria.'

'Oh. I had no idea.' Violet's cheeks reddened.

'I believe that's how surprises work.' Alfie turned to Gwilym. 'I'm sorry Gil, I should have explained myself more clearly. I would have if I had been given half a chance.' He glared at Violet, those his expression was playful. 'If you could come down here the day after tomorrow, Vi and I will quite happily make space for your bags. And seeing as the party is no longer a secret, if you would like to attend tomorrow evening you would be more than welcome. I believe Aggy has been invited. Perhaps you could travel together? If you can get away from the house that is?'

'I'll be there!' Gwilym grinned. 'God knows, I could do with letting my hair down a bit after the last few weeks. Thank you for the invite.'

'We'll be lighting the fire as soon as the sun sets.' Alfie said. 'You're welcome at any time.'

'Thank you. Until tomorrow evening then.' Gwilym dashed across the road to where the rest of the party stood waiting, the irritation on old man Davenport's face a stark contrast to Joseph's which was all light and warmth. His eyes not leaving hers, Joseph turned to whisper something in Calissa's ear and as soon as she had released her hold on him, he made his way across to the stall without looking back.

'Mr Davenport, you are looking well.'

'Indeed, I have never felt better Miss Yardley. Which is in no small part down to you. I haven't had the opportunity to thank you before, but I do so now. I am very grateful for your assistance.'

'Do you appreciate how much danger you put her in?' Alfie scowled at Joseph.

'Alfie, do not stick your nose in where it is not wanted!' Violet protested as Joseph raised his hands in placation.

'No, Alfie is right. As grateful as I am, I know I shouldn't have come to ask for your help in the first place. Neither should Gil for that matter. It was, remiss of me, of us, and for that I apologise.'

'I chose to come to you. I wasn't coerced into it. I have a mind of my own though you seem not to see it, either of you! It was my lack of judgment that put me in such a precarious position, no-one else's so if you don't mind, I'd like to consider this matter closed!' Her face pinched, Violet balled her hands into fists to mask their shaking as she waited expectantly for both Alfie and Joseph had apologise and only when they had did she continue, taking a deep calming breath before she turned back to Joseph.

'I understand you have been visiting new pastures, sir?'

'We're reverting back to sir, Miss Yardley?' Joseph shrugged casually. 'Very well. To answer your question, yes, we have indeed been away from the house for a while. A waste of time in all honesty but it was pleasant to escape for a while. Even so, I am happy to return. There are some things that I have missed in my absence.' He flashed her a coy grin as he reached into his pocket.

'I wanted to reimburse you for the medication you provided.' He reached forwards, placing four shillings in her hand, his touch lingering longer than was necessary, not long enough.

'This is far too much money.' Violet protested. 'I did not spend anywhere near this amount on the treatments I prepared for you.'

'Christmas is coming. I thought perhaps if I funded your stall for the season we might, between us, be able to offer a free service. What do you think?'

'I think that would be extremely generous. I'm sure the folk of this town would be very grateful for your contribution.'

'Please, do not tell anyone of my involvement. It would just be embarrassing.' Joseph said. 'But I think it only right that we do what we can to help, especially at this time of year.'

'And I would be more than happy to assist you in your endeavours.' Violet smiled. 'I believe your guest is waiting for you.' Joseph peered over his shoulder. Gone was the demure face that Violet had admired such a short time before. Calissa Parnell's character had changed from contented to bitter, her scowl corrupting her beauty entirely. Edwin turned back to her, muttering something behind a raised hand and Miss Parnell nodded in understanding. 'That's the witch. It was she and her mother who cursed the family.' It took little imagination to guess what he was saying to the woman who stared at her now. He would be tearing her character apart, safe in the knowledge there was no way she would be able to defend herself.

'If looks could kill.' Joseph muttered. 'I had better return to my guest. It was a pleasure to see you again, Miss Yardley. I hope we will meet again soon.'

'Indeed, sir. Please pass on my best to your father.' She smiled demurely and curtseyed, grateful for the raucous laugh that Joseph bellowed in response.

'But that I could, Miss Yardley! His reaction would provide humorous relief for us all I think!' He doffed his hat to Violet and Alfie before he made his way back across the road, studiously avoiding his father's gaze. Violet smiled politely as Miss Parnell re-took possession of Joseph's arm, taking time to look over her shoulder and glower in reply as they walked away. If looks could kill, indeed. It was at that moment that Violet couldn't help but wish that such a thing might be achievable, and that Miss Parnell might be suddenly confronted with a mirror.

Chapter sixteen

'It is not appropriate for you to wear your hair down Violet. You are no longer a child.' Violet grimaced, glancing at the pins that adorned the table next to the stove.

'Please, mother! I really do not want all this fuss. It's not as if we are being seen in society, is it? And I would rather enjoy myself than sit poker straight the entire evening for fear that my hair might come apart. Please? For me?'

'You can put my hair up Mrs Yardley! My mother never has time and you do it so well!' Constance Yardley sighed relentingly and ushered Edie into the chair in front of her immediately getting to work, separating the girl's long black hair into several strands. One by one she wrapped them around her finger, rolling them up and pinning them in place so deftly you could easily imagine her being able to carry out the task with her eyes closed.

'Do you like the dress then Vi?' Flossie looked up from where she stood next to the stove. 'One of the dressmakers in town allowed us to borrow a pattern. When your mother said it was for you, she couldn't wait to hand it over. Gave us the cloth to make it 'n' all! Said it was one of the most fashionable designs she had. Seems to me, you're quite the local hero.'

'I don't know about that.' Violet grabbed hold of the edges of her skirt and swirled it around her legs. The material was a course ivory linen which was peppered with pastel coloured flowers, the skirt itself ruched at the hips, leading down to a series of ruffles that repeated until the skirt reached the floor. The dress had a high buttoned neck, the waist was so tightly fitted she barely had room to breathe and it was not until she had seen herself in the mirror that she had realised how she had transformed from a skinny child to a woman, all curves and contours. Perhaps they were not as different after all, her and Miss Parnell she realised. Perhaps if she wore dresses of the finest silk, her hair pinned into the perfect chignon, she would be more than a match for the girl who was born with everything.

'I like the dress very much.' Violet said, returning to stare at herself in the mirror again. 'I know I have thanked you already, but I truly am grateful. You have all worked so hard to make this for me.'

'You are welcome, child.' Aunt Ruby murmured as she pored over the medicine books that were piled high at the corner of the tent. They had taken it in turns to look for a cure for Joseph's condition since she had returned from the house but one problem still remained. How could one find a cure if one could not even diagnose the condition?

She returned to her own corner of the tent and sat on her bed, leafing through the symptoms that she had noted while she was at Joseph's house. She had to be missing something, but then, gone was the notion that there were only so many physical ailments in this world. New diseases were being discovered and new treatments created all the time. And that being the case maybe she was no longer the best at what she did.

The sisters had taught her everything she needed to know in order to recreate traditional herbal medicines and granted that had gotten her a long way in her career. But there was so much more out there now. Real scientific research was taking over which would probably have a greater chance of providing the answers she needed. She placed the notes back into the bag that Alfie had given her. Maybe there was a way. There was a newly opened institute in Cardiff which would she would be able to visit over the course of a couple of days. If she could convince someone to accompany her and then successfully gain access to the resources there. If those that guarded such a resource would agree to allowing her entry.

'Your mother is ready for you. Just a ribbon to tie your hair back, I promise.' Edie peered her head round the curtain that created a makeshift wall, her hair perfectly coiffed to within an inch of its life.

'Well, come here and let me see!' Edie strutted into Violet's makeshift quarters and slowly spun round on the balls of her feet.

'What do you think? Do you think everyone at the party will approve?' Violet smiled.

'Do you seek the approval of everyone at the party, or do you seek Alfie's?' Edie's cheeks flushed bright red.

'Violet Yardley, what on earth do you mean?'

'Oh, come now Edie. You've had your heart set on Alfie for as long as I can remember.'

'I have not!'

'Edie…' Violet said wearily. 'I have eyes. I can see what's going on around me. Besides which you talk about him all the time. How you feel is out there for everyone to see.'

'You must hate me.' Edie pouted.

'What? Edie, no!' Violet moved a pile of charcoal sketches from her bed, picture upon picture of the face that had appeared in the mirror, each one an attempt to keep his image fresh in her memory. 'Come sit next to me.' Edie took the pictures from Violet's hand and stared at them as she dropped down next to Violet. 'Why do you imagine I would hate you?'

'Because it's always been the two of you, hasn't it? It's always been Vi and Alfie. Everyone expects it.'

'They do? Did they not think to ask me? Edie, I love Alfie as though he is my brother. I have never been in love with him and I never will be. There could never be anything but friendship between us. You of all people must know that.'

'I know that he feels a great deal more for you than simple friendship.'

'I think maybe he thought he did.' Violet said. 'And I won't lie to you, we did talk about it. But Edie, I have watched him these past few weeks and I have seen the way he is with you. His heart is yours for the taking and you deserve all the happiness that I know will come your way. You are two of the people that I love most in the world. That you might find each other, believe me, nothing would make me happier.'.

'You are not just saying that to save my feelings?'

'No, you have my word.'

'Thank you, Vi. That means a great deal to me.' Violet grabbed hold of Edie's hand and squeezed it warmly.

'You do not need to thank me. I'm just telling the truth. Come on, let's finish getting ready. I suspect that when Alfie sets his eyes on you, I may be the last remaining spinster in the camp.'

*****

'Aggy is not here yet. Or Gwilym.' Violet said as she dropped down onto a hay bale next to her mother.

'I know. I do hope she comes.' Constance stared at the path that led to the camp as though she were willing Agnes to appear on it. 'I missed meeting her in town today. I was held up by every passer-by that came my way and by the time

I arrived at the teashop she had already gone. I hope she's not offended. That she doesn't think I reneged on our promise to meet.'

'She would never think that of you.' Violet reassured her. 'She's probably just running late. Besides, Gwilym also had an invite so I'm sure he would have reminded her if she'd forgotten.'

'You are right.' Constance agreed. 'I'll apologise to her when she arrives. I had no idea how much of a trial it would be to get from one end of town to the other. When you said we had been welcomed back I had no idea to what extent!' Violet laughed.

'Being popular is a strange concept to grasp, isn't it?'

'Violet, come and dance! I need you to show Alfie what to do, he's terrible!' Edie called out.

'Do you mind?' Violet turned to her mother 'I can stay if you'd rather?'

'No.' Constance smiled. 'Go and dance. It is nice to hear you laugh so, and I am content to sit here by the fire and listen to the music.' Violet leaned forward and kissed her mother on the cheek.

'No-one ever had a mother as wonderful as you.' She leapt from the hay bale and ran around the fire to join her friends, the sound of horse's hooves in the distance catching her attention.

'I think they're here!' She called back to her mother, keeping her focus on the track that was dimly lit by the fire as a shadowed figure came into view. There was no horse and trap, just a single stallion, the rider slumped over in the saddle, their head bobbing with the rhythm of the horse's slow steps forward, its gait measured and gentle. The horse came to a gradual stop and Joseph lifted his head and took in his surroundings immediately spotting Violet in the crowd. The music died away, plunging the camp into silence as Joseph climbed down from his mount, his movements unsteady, his face shimmering in the light of the fire.

'Violet, I, I had nowhere else to go. I'm sorry.' He took a deep rattling breath, his hand slipping from Berkeley's reins as his eyes rolled backwards and he fell to the floor, the sodden mud beneath him cushioning his fall. Violet was aware of a chorus of gasps around her as Constance ran through the crowds and knelt beside him, placing her fingers on the inside of his wrist to feel his pulse.

'Alfie, I need you to place Joseph on Violet's bed please, away from prying eyes. And then take care of the horse, will you? Make sure it's tied up properly and fed and watered.'

'Of course, Ma'am.' With his father's help Alfie carried Joseph's limp body into the tent, making a beeline for the back of the tent as Violet followed in behind them and ran to the medicine chest. How was this possible when he had looked so well yesterday? Unless it had all been pretense? She pulled her notebook out of the case and began to lay out all the ingredients that she had combined before.

'Are these the same symptoms?' Ruby asked quietly as she walked up behind her.

'I think so.' Violet looked up at her aunt. 'He was nowhere near this bad before though. He never lost consciousness. And I don't recall ever seeing Josephine in this state, so is it the same thing? Does he suffer from the same condition? I cannot answer that question!' She began to mix the same compounds. 'Dear god, what if I am wrong? What if I am treating the wrong thing? What if I make the problem worse?'

'You can only go by what you know, my love' Ruby said softly. 'Treat the symptoms as before and if he wakes and shows anything different then we will adapt accordingly.' Ruby moved to place her hand on Violet's shoulder.

'You were correct in your treatment before, I am sure you will be correct this time as well. Have a little faith in yourself. I'll go and see if your mother requires any assistance.'

By the time she had mixed the compound together, her mother had removed the damp clothes from Joseph's top half and covered him in blankets to ward of the chill in the tent while Alfie built up the fire in the stove.

'Did you know about this?' her mother asked as Violet walked into the small enclosed area.

'Did I know about what?'

'This.' Constance pulled back the blankets and stood aside so that Violet could get a clearer view of Joseph. He was still unconscious and lying on his front, the candlelight dancing on the beads of sweat that coated his fevered skin. Scars ran the length of back which, though they were healed, were still angry and red. They could not have been there long. Violet dropped to his side and ran her finger along one of the marks.

'He has been beaten. Violet, I'll ask you again. Did you know about this child?'

'This happened because of me.' Violet whispered. 'He defended me, and this was his punishment.' Violet heard her mother gasp but did not turn to look at her. 'Josephine would be heartbroken if she knew'

'Do you think she doesn't know?'

'So perhaps she was warning me to stay away from him. So that Joe might not be punished further.'

'Perhaps.' Constance replied. 'We can think about that later. First, let's ensure that he is well, shall we? Here, help me turn him.'

Between the two of them they moved him onto his back and Violet whispered her thanks to the gods when he finally opened his eyes.

'Violet?' He gripped on to her arm fiercely. 'I'm sorry. I had to come here…'

'I know. I'm glad you came.' Violet said softly. 'Here, drink this. Same as before.' She placed her hand behind his head and raised him slightly so that he could sip from the glass.

'I don't know what to do.' He whispered, his eyes dropping. 'Tell me what to do.'

'Ask me again when you are well. We will find the answer together.' She lowered his head and pulled the blankets further up around him as Alfie burst into the tent.

'Now is not a good time Alfie.' Constance peered up from Violet's notes.

'I know ma'am and I'm sorry for interrupting, but I think you need to hear this.'

'Alfie, what is it? You are as white as a ghost!' Alfie ran his hands across his face awkwardly, glancing over at Joseph who had lost consciousness once more.

'Two of the boys have just come back from the police station. They've been held there for questioning all afternoon.'

'What? Why?' Constance stood up and moved to stand next to Violet.

'It's Aggy. They found her on the road this afternoon.' Alfie said quietly, keeping his eyes on Joseph. 'I'm sorry to have to tell you this, but Aggy is dead. Ma'am, she's been murdered.'

Chapter seventeen

Violet's father had taken his own life when she was only three years old so she had no recollection of him. She could call his image to mind if she wanted to, she supposed, but that was only because she had seen photographs of him. To be able to afford photographs of one's family was a rare thing in their community but the ladies of the coven had been given such a gift by a local photographer for whom they had provided treatments and who, as part of his payment and because he believed them to be a fascinating source of inspiration, had offered to provide photographs of the members of the camp.

In most of the pictures, which had been taken before his conscription her father could be seen sitting and smiling with the rest of the camp, Constance sitting steadfastly by his side, their hands clasped tightly together. And then, against her mother's wishes he had chosen to sign up for the army after hearing tales from those that had returned from Crimea, saying that he had wanted to play his part, to fight for his country and to fight for a safe world for his infant daughter to grow in. In the final two images that were taken of him he was still standing with her mother, but he now wore the red and black uniform of the fusiliers, his expression hard and determined, as though he were already steeled for war. According to her mother these final images had been taken just before he left to join his battalion. He'd never smiled again.

They knew little of his life there, except that he had fought at the Battle of the Great Redan, one of the bloodiest battles to have taken place during the conflict and they only knew that because of the medal he had received. When he returned, he was little more than a ghost. He had, her mother had said, never been able to get over the fact that he had survived and his comrades had not. What he had seen was never discussed but the sisters had sometimes talked about the nightmares he had endured night after night, the screams that had rocked the camp and made the other residents doubt his sanity. Over time they grew to fear him, a reaction which was understandable given his increasingly erratic behaviour, and then one day he had simply disappeared. They found his body some weeks later. That was all Violet knew. It was all her mother wanted her to know and Violet never asked.

There was a certain amount of emotion attached to the images she kept stored away in her memory, but it was more of a nostalgic sadness. A what might have been rather than a real sense of loss and she had never mourned his passing because there was nothing truly tangible for her to mourn. She had certainly never experienced the pain that she knew Joseph had felt when he had lost his mother. Or indeed how he felt now. How did one even begin to relate to someone who had lost so much? How could one even begin to find words that would provide some consolation? She silently prayed that when she saw him, her heart would know what to do. All these things danced through her mind as she woke.

Save for the sound of Aunt Flossie's gentle snoring the tent was silent. There was no sound of movement, none of the usual hubbub that came with the dawn. The peacefulness was soothing and unsettling all at once. She peeled her eyes open slowly, their lids heavy from the lack of sleep. Light was beginning to seep in from underneath the hems of the heavy canvas shelter which meant that dawn had come and gone. There would be no trip to the market today she supposed, hoping that Gil was not still planning to meet her there as they had previously agreed. Did anyone even know that Joe wasn't home? If anyone would know it would be Gil surely. He would have seen that Joe's bed hadn't been slept in. And he would know to come here surely? She hadn't stopped to think about how Joe's family would react if they knew where he had gone, it had been so frenetic last night. The thought of old man Davenport turning up sent a shiver down her spine. No. Even if he knew he wouldn't stoop so low as to come here to the camp. Would he?

She dragged herself from her mother's bed and picked up her dressing gown. Stifling a yawn, she wrapped it around herself, pulling the cord tight around her waist and pulled her hair out from the high collar, allowing it to drape down her back. Her mother was still with Joe, she guessed. They had taken it in turns through the early hours of the morning, one staying to administer his medication as he needed it, the other retreating to the opposite side of the tent for much needed rest. The lack of scurrying around now made her hopeful that the treatment had worked. She moved round the bed and pulled back the drape that separated her mother's private space from the rest of the tent. In the middle of the tent, at the table where the sisters met with their clients sat Joseph.

He was leaning back in one of the chairs, holding a mug in both hands, clearly relishing the warmth that emanated from it when she caught his eye. He smiled, but it was a mask, Violet thought, because his eyes portrayed something else entirely. They spoke of sadness and exhaustion and fear. She had seen the same expression in her mother often enough to know the truth behind it, as much as she wished she hadn't.

'Good morning Violet. I seem to be going out my way to ruin your reputation, don't I?' Violet looked down at her nightwear.

'I would argue that I have very little reputation left to ruin.' She took a seat opposite him as he poured her a cup of tea. The tent was cosier than usual, a consequence of the sisters heaping wood onto the fire through the night so Joseph wouldn't get cold. It was an association that was becoming harder to ignore. That where Joseph was, warmth followed. She watched his hands move as he poured milk into her cup. It was the most mundane of tasks and yet it felt more intimate than anything she had ever experienced. Certainly, it was more intimate than the dizzy-headed romantic notions that Edie conjured up on a daily basis because this was real and Joseph was real and she knew the workings of his heart. And, as much as she tried to deny it, of her own.

'How are you feeling?' Violet asked.

'I feel as though Berkeley threw me off and dragged me all the way here by the ankle.' Joseph winced as he moved to pick up his own cup of tea and reclined in his chair. 'But this is the first time I have been ill since you came to the house. It took a few days to fully recover whilst we were first away in the north but since then all has been well. Until last night, that is.' He took a sip of his tea, his fingers shaking as he put the cup back on the saucer.

'You are still in pain?' Joseph nodded.

'Yes, but it is not just my body that ails me.' He stared away looking at the flames that still danced in the fire. 'It is my mind. I feel as though it is not my own. It seems to have splintered into a thousand tiny pieces and I feel as though I cannot get a true grasp on anything.

'You are exhausted, Joe.' Violet offered. 'So much has happened.'

'Perhaps. I cannot help but feel that you must consider me such a pathetic imbecile.'

'You cannot be serious? Joe, you're one of the strongest people I know.'

'I appreciate the sentiment Vi, but I think we both know that's just not true.' Joseph shook his head as Violet placed her own cup down.

'Look at me.' She took a long drawn out breath, waited for him to turn back to her. 'I don't mean to embarrass you, but you should know, I saw the marks on your back and moreover, I know how you got them. Please don't ask me how I know, but I do. It was because of me, wasn't it?' Violet leaned further forward. 'Don't you see it, Joe? To stand up for someone like that? To not back down, even when you are forced to endure such retaliation? You are so brave.'

'I was not being brave Vi, I was doing what needed to be done.'

'You may see it like that if you wish but I see someone who fought for me when I could not defend myself. I see someone who is selfless and loyal and as brave than any I have known before.'

'Perhaps if I had done something earlier, you might not have left.' He glanced at her briefly and turned back to the fire, the flames flickering across his face. 'But that is done now. You are back, and all is well.'

'All is well.' Violet agreed, even though deep down she knew it was a lie. 'But I do have one question. Why did you come here? We agreed, if you needed me…'

'You would come to the house again?' Joseph interrupted. 'I had to get out, Vi. The staff are besides themselves, not surprisingly. Amelia was hysterical and nothing could placate her. Father was pacing the house like a lunatic, trying to play everything down, though I see he feels the loss keenly. Aggy was after all another connection to mother was she not? And Calissa was beyond insensitive. I think she sets out to antagonise. No-one could be that heartless naturally.' Violet shook her head wordlessly.

'I understand and I sympathise with your current condition, Amelia.' Joseph raised the pitch of his voice mockingly. 'To lose such a well-trained member of staff can be so tiresome. But in time you will find a suitable replacement and it will be as though she never existed. Amelia fled to her room which led to another row and Calissa flounced off to her quarters in tears again. The noise was unbearable. And then I could feel my temperature rising, the pain returning and, I just had to get away.' He stopped, glancing around the tent inquisitively. 'Where is my jacket?'

'It's hung up over there.' Violet pointed to a wooden rail and watched in silence as Joseph made his way over to the coat, burying his fingers into the pockets.

'Oh, dear god, I have lost it.' His face paled.

'Lost what?'

'My watch, I had a silver pocket watch. I know I bought it with me.' He ran his fingers through his hair in exasperation. 'I cannot afford to lose it!'

'Oh! No, please, don't worry yourself, Joe. It's here, see?' Violet leapt from her chair and walked over to the table in the corner where she mixed her medicines. 'It was hanging out of your pocket when you arrived. I put it inside the chest to keep it safe.' Joseph closed his eyes and put his hand over his heart, willing his body to calm.

'Here.' When he opened his eyes, she was no more than a breath away, the pocket watch in her palm. 'This must be very important to you.' Joseph nodded as he took the watch from her.

'Aggy gave it to me for my birthday.' He flipped the watch over and looked at the inscription on the back. 'Charles Arthur Morgan.' He whispered. 'Her father. She said that now that her son was gone, I was the most deserving of it. She said I was like another son in all but name and in truth, she was like a second mother.' He looked up from the watch. 'Please, don't misunderstand me. I'm not saying that my mother could ever be replaced. But Aggy…'

'You loved her.'

'They slit her throat.' Joseph's fingers wrapped tightly around the trinket. 'They took her possessions and they slit her throat and they left her in the ditch to die alone. Can you believe anyone could be that callous? I had to identify the body as her family are not local. Have you ever seen a dead body?' Violet shook her head. 'I have seen two now and it is a surreal experience. It is as though someone is there and not there at the same time. Does that make sense?' He furrowed his brow as he spoke. 'You find yourself in a situation where you are standing beside someone you have known your entire life and you are talking to them and half expecting them to reciprocate in some way even though you know in your heart of hearts they cannot. Deep down, you know that that voice, that soul is lost to you forever. That what you are looking at is nothing more than a shell. It is the most painful realisation, Violet. I pray that you never experience such pain, though I know that it waits for us all at some point in our lives.'

'Joe, I'm so sorry.' Violet reached up to brush away the tears that streaked her face and she thought about Josephine and the mirror and wondered how she might tell him that death was not so final. Tell him that his mother had reached out to her. Such a revelation might make her seem like a lunatic, but then maybe, maybe it would ease his grief.

'I have not told the rest of the family how she died.' Joseph interrupted her thoughts. 'I thought if I could save Amelia from further pain. They think her heart took her.'

'Then I am glad that you have told me.' Violet said. 'No-one should have to carry such a burden alone. And thank you for trusting me.'

'You are not angry that I have inflicted it on you?' Joseph closed his eyes, as if to shut out the world. 'I feel as though my family has troubled you enough over recent times.'

'We are friends. I would not have you carry this alone.'

'I don't know what I would do without you.' Joseph took a step forward so they were only inches apart. 'I pray that I will never have to find out.'

'I pray for the same.' Violet moved a step closer, wrapped his hand in her own. 'As long as I have breath in my body Joseph Davenport, you will never be alone.' She whispered as he finally allowed the grief to take him.

It could have been minutes, it could have been hours later that Constance made her presence known. Dressed in black from top to toe, she appeared as a silhouette at the entrance to the tent and softly cleared her throat to get their attention. When Violet looked to her mother, she found no anger at finding her daughter in such a compromising position, no sign of any retribution to come. Instead, she found understanding and empathy and it dawned on her that it wasn't just Joe's family who mourned because her mother too had lost a friend.

'It is time to get ready.' Constance said softly. 'We have calls to make. Violet, perhaps you would like me to do your hair now?'

Chapter eighteen

'Are you respectable?'

'I am, come in.' Violet stifled a yawn that made her eyes water as Constance pulled the makeshift door to one side. She wiped the tears away as her mother slipped through the narrow gap and turned to fix the blanket back in place, her black skirt swirling around her legs as though she were in the centre of the storm. Only when she was assured of their privacy did she reach out across the small enclosed space, handing Violet a bundle of neatly folded pale purple linen.

'The sisters collected this from town for you yesterday.'

'For me? I don't understand.' Violet frowned as she unfolded the material. 'I was given a new dress for my birthday. Why would I need another one?'

'They never gave me a specific reason, Vi. Just said they thought you would need it. They ordered it last week apparently. First, I've heard of it.'

'What do you mean? Did they know that I would need this today specifically? What else do they know? Have they seen something?'

'Good lord child' Constance laughed. 'I came in here with a gift for you. I anticipated surprise, gratitude certainly, but not an interrogation!'

'I'm sorry, I'm grateful, truly I am, but I don't understand. Why would they think I needed it? Do you think they foresaw Aggy's death?' Constance shrugged.

'I cannot say Vi, and neither would they even if they did know. As much as they might want to.'

'But they would not see someone they know harmed, surely?'

'Having the sight does not mean you are gifted with the authority to change the future, child. To do so would be to become god-like and that is not why we bear the gifts that we do. We cannot change the destiny of others, we can simply navigate a path towards the best version of ourselves in the hope that our own fate is a bearable one.' Constance gestured towards the garment in Violet's hands. 'This dress does not have a bustled petticoat with it. The sisters did not think you would want it.' She said as Violet ran her hand over the dress. 'You're lucky that crinolines are no longer the height of fashion. I only wore them on a couple of occasions and I was relieved that it was that way. Impossible to breath in, impossible to move in and society expected you to dance in such a contraption? Most women fainted at some point or another during the evening, the restrictions on their breathing were so great.'

'When did you wear such dresses?' Violet looked up at her mother.

'When your aunts and I returned to the family home.'

'You didn't mind going back there? Even though grandfather had put you in the workhouse?'

'We all begrudged him a little at first, I won't lie. But he was a widow and had no clue as to what to do with us. We were still too young to be sent out to work and he couldn't afford to stay at home and look after us, nor did he have anyone to take care of us being an only child himself. Over time I suppose we all came to see it for what it was.'

'So you forgave him?'

'Yes.' Constance mused. 'I suppose we did. Anyway, eventually I met your father and we moved into the camp and papa found himself a new wife. When our stepmother's parents died, they amassed quite a fortune and he was always keen to show off his new-found wealth whenever we visited so balls were a must. We didn't go there often. Our choice of lifestyle wasn't exactly approved of. But that isn't the point I'm trying to make, Violet. My point is that it was at such a gathering that I realised how lucky we are in this life of ours. We may not have the glitter and the glamour of the well-heeled, but we have a freedom that they will never experience or understand and for that reason alone I think we are richer. Wouldn't you agree?' Violet smiled at her mother knowingly.

'Joseph is a friend, mother.' She whispered, conscious that he sat on the other side of the divide. 'I have seen my fate in the mirror and as confused as I am about it, I know I can be certain that Joseph is destined to be no more than a friend. I don't expect the glitter and the glamour that comes with his life or his social circles. And, if I'm being honest, I would not want it even if it were offered to me.'

Constance stared at her daughter for a while, measuring her response but, in the end, she said nothing. Instead she simply nodded and took the dress back. With sure and steady hands, she gathered together the material, holding it so the neck of the dress was open in front of her. Violet stood, dropping the blanket that she had held around her shoulders as her mother placed the dress over her head, the heavy material instantly sliding into place. There were at least a dozen simple onyx buttons that fixed the tight bodice into place, the sleeves, collar and the hem of the dress all adorned with simple strips of black velvet. A dress for half mourning. She ran her fingers over the velvet on the cuff, her eyes meeting her mother's as she fixed the last button at her collar. The sisters must have known about Aggy, or at least that someone close would lose their life. Why else would they have acquired mourning garments for her? Either way, they must have kept it from her mother. They had to have done. Her mother was as surprised as she was last night. There had been no acting on her part.

'I've been sitting with Aggy this morning.' Constance said, as if she were joining the conversation. She sat Violet down on the bed and began working on her hair. 'Two of the girls from the house bought down her favourite dress and I have fixed her hair, in case she should receive visitors prior to the funeral.' Violet whirled round, her hair slipping through Constance's fingers.

'You saw her?'

'Yes. I saw her. As did the maids. And they were quite distressed, as you can imagine. The sight of her was quite of shock.' Violet turned back around as her mother began brushing her hair. 'You do not seem to have much to say on the subject Vi. I take it you already know of her condition? You know how she died?'

'Yes. Joe told me a while ago. He doesn't want Amelia to know.'

'I see.' Constance began lifting Violet's hair into pleats, fixing them in place with pins that lay haphazardly on the bed. 'The undertaker informed us of the situation when we arrived. He wanted to warn us of her condition so we wouldn't be overly distressed, but that still didn't prepare us for what we saw. The collar of her dress covers her wounds, but there is some bruising on her face that cannot be masked, even with cosmetics. Mourners will assume that they are the result of the fall I suppose, but how the lad intends to keep this a secret is beyond me.'

'Please, Joseph doesn't want her passing to be linked to something so brutal. It's irrational, I know, but he doesn't want her memory tainted like that.'

'I understand that more than most child, believe me. When your father…' Constance continued working on Violet's hair, leaving the thought hanging mid-air. 'Don't worry, we will not break Joseph's confidence, though he must know that word of her death and the reason why will be public soon enough. And I would have thought the police will be keen to interview as many people as they can. If I'm honest I'm surprised they aren't already up here dragging everyone into the station.'

'He was simply trying to save his sister from further distress.'

'Yes, well, I doubt that peace will remain in place for long. You know how these things get out.' Constance said as she fixed the final pin in Violet's hair and opened the small trunk at the end of Violet's bed. 'Now, I think you should wear your black hat and gloves. Do you agree?'

*****

When Violet entered the main area of the tent, Joseph and Alfie were already waiting for her and it was to her surprise that they were engaged in a conversation that by its tone seemed almost cordial. They spoke in hushed voices, both rising to their feet as she entered the room in a display of etiquette that seemed bizarrely out of place within the confines of the tent.

'Our roles appear to have reversed.' Joseph cast an eye over his own attire and looked back to Violet. 'I seem to belong in this tent more than you do, Miss Yardley.' He wore a thick navy jumper that looked familiar and black trousers that had clearly seen better days. The boots at least were his own. In his arms he was carrying a linen duffle bag that held the remainder of the clothes that he had arrived in.

'I think we both know that that would never be the case Mr Davenport, no matter our attire.' Violet snorted. 'Where did you get the clothes?'

'Alfie.' Constance said as she grabbed her hat from the table. Violet's jaw dropped.

'Alfie?'

'What?' Alfie shot back. 'I'm a nice person!'

'Paragon of virtue is what you are, lad.' Constance laughed. 'Is the carriage ready?'

'It is ma'am, but I'm unsure as to what to do with your horse Joseph.'

'Leave him here.' Joseph said. 'This is his last working year. He'll be put out to pasture come the spring and I sense that he would be happier here with you, Violet. He seems to prefer you to the rest of us.'

'You are gifting him to me? No, Joseph, this is too much!'

'Nonsense. You'd also be doing me a favour. I don't think I could take the constant whinnying and sulking he'd undoubtedly put us all through if he thought he wasn't getting enough attention. He'd make our lives a misery.'

'Our old nag won't be fit for pulling the cart much longer.' Constance conceded. 'Do you think he would do well with that?'

'He's pulled the coaches for years, ma'am.' Joseph said proudly. 'He really is well trained, he's just a little demanding at times. Vi seems to know how to appease him though.' Violet looked to her mother, seeking her approval before she responded.

'I promise, we will take good care of him. Thank you, Joe, I do have a soft spot for him. He is such a magnificent creature.'

'I can't imagine anyone who could take better care of him, Vi.'

'Well, now that's sorted,' Constance spoke through the pins she held between her lips as she fixed her hat in place. 'shall we get you home?'

*****

The carriage was in near silence for most of the journey. Violet watched, transfixed as Joseph's state of near calm began to evaporate leaving his jaw clenched, his shoulders taut and fixed as though they were carved in stone.

Whilst Alfie steered the cart her mother sat beside him and stared across the valley, her gaze focussing on a seemingly random point in the distance. It was only the gentle tapping of her gloved hands on her handbag that betrayed her alleged calmness.

'What your mother said to you. Back at the tent.' Joseph leaned forward and finally spoke as they turned into the long drive that led to the house. 'She was right, you know. Your life is so much richer than my own, Violet. Never covet the life I lead. I would never want to see you restrained. And yet, somewhat selfishly on my part, I still wish…' He fell back in his seat, leaving the sentence hanging. So he had heard. Violet's cheeks pinkened. But what had he heard? Had he heard her say she did not covet his life or that she did not desire a life with him? The thought filled her with dread because when it came to the latter nothing could have been further from the truth. Better that he hear that truth, surely?

'So do I.' Violet spoke softly so her mother wouldn't hear. Joseph nodded in understanding.

'When I arrived last night. There was a celebration going on.'

'It was a belated birthday celebration.'

'No! Oh, Vi, I'm so sorry!' Violet shook her head dismissively.

'Do not fret. There will be other birthdays and there will be other parties. Believe me, it is not a huge disaster.'

'You have taken part in the scrying. You would have done it on your birthday. On our birthday. How on earth did I forget?' Joseph turned to look at her, his eyes wide. Whoever had said the eyes were the window to the soul had definitely been on to something. Damn the optimism that blossomed across his face! Violet cursed silently. Damn him, damn the stranger and damn the mirror!

'It is not something I wish to discuss.' Violet said curtly.

'Oh. I understand. Of course. As you wish.' Joseph turned away and though he said nothing else Violet could feel his eyes on her long after they had stopped talking. When he finally looked away she stole a glance at his expression. He and her mother sat like bookends now, back to back, their postures rigid they stared out at the countryside around them, but Violet could find nothing serene in either of them. Whilst her mother continued to drum on her handbag, Joseph ran his fingers along his lips, his thoughts seemingly a thousand miles away, his expression one of resignation. Perhaps he had gotten the answers he sought without the need to discuss it further. Violet prayed that that was the case, even if it wasn't the answer she had wanted to give him.

Chapter nineteen

It was probably because she had been engaged in a game of cat and mouse with Edwin Davenport the last time she was at Ty Mawr that Violet couldn't help but stare up into the windows of the old manor, looking for signs of life as the cart circled drive at the front of the drive. To think it had been only a few short weeks since she'd last been here. Strange that something that had happened so recently felt like a lifetime ago. So much had changed and yet everything looked the same on the outside.

The cart had barely come to a stop when the doors flew open and Gwilym emerged from the house, running down the steps towards them two at a time. He was as pale as a ghost, and Violet could pinpoint the moment when he had to physically stop himself from embracing his master the way one would a brother as Joseph climbed down from the cart.

'It is such a relief to see you sir. I'm so sorry I couldn't get to you last night. Things were so chaotic here, it didn't feel right to leave. Are you well?' Gwilym pored over every detail of Joseph's face, studiously looking for signs of his illness.

'I am for the most part.' Joseph brushed his hands over his trousers. 'Gil, calm yourself. And please, dispose of the formalities, we are among friends. You do not need to keep up the pretence out here.'

'Of course. Sorry.' Gwilym turned to bow at the rest of the travelling party who remained in the cart. 'Good morning Ma'am, Alfie, Miss Yardley.'

'Call me Vi, Gil, please.' Violet smiled. 'Did you not hear what Joe just said?'

'Vi. Yes. Again, very sorry. I trust you are all well?'

'We are all well.' Joseph moved to reassure his friend. 'I'm going to assume from your current state that my absence has been noted?'

'They sent one of the maids up to your room this morning when you didn't show up to breakfast and she informed your father that your bed hadn't been slept in, stupid girl. Your father called me to the dining room, demanded I tell him everything. I did say that my opinion was nothing more than guesswork, but it fell on deaf ears.' Gwilym's cheeks pinkened. 'I'm so sorry, Joe. He said if I didn't tell him what was going on, I'd be out on my ear.'

'The truth was going to come out eventually.' Joseph reached out to pat Gwilym on the arm. 'I wouldn't be surprised if he already knew and simply wanted you to confirm his suspicions. I'm just sorry you had to face him. It should have been me he confronted, not you.' He looked towards the house. 'So, the Parnells know about my, condition?'

'They do.'

'And how did they react?'

'With great concern, but they were very sympathetic. The whole situation was quite bizarre if I'm honest.' Gwilym said. 'Your father was furious at first, knowing that you've been seeking help from Vi and her family an' all. But then the strangest thing happened.'

'What do you mean?'

'Calissa. She came to your defence. And Vi's. It really was quite astonishing, the way she stood up for you all. And once she had spoken up her father stood to defend her. Between the two of them they seem to silence your father completely. By the time they had finished talking he was almost contrite.'

'Calissa did that?'

'She did. And for what it's worth she sounded utterly genuine in her response. I mean, you know I have little time for her, but what she did really was quite astounding.'

'Well, then I suppose I must thank her.' Joseph murmured, staring up at the open door.

'I suppose you should.' Gwilym echoed. 'Also, your father has requested the pleasure of Violet and her mother's company.'

'Now?' Joseph frowned.

'The family are gathered in the drawing room waiting for you. Your father heard the horse pulling up and sent me out here.'

So, the sisters did know. Violet looked down at the dress they had acquired for her. And if they knew this, then what else did they know? The notion that fate was uncontrollable suddenly seemed weak and unjustifiable.

'He doesn't get to request anything. Not after the way he has treated Vi and her family.' Joseph all but growled.

'Perhaps that is so, Joseph. But we have done nothing wrong and we have nothing to hide. Refusing his invitation would imply otherwise.' Constance countered. 'Gwilym, please take us to Mr Davenport. We would be glad to meet with him.'

'You don't have to agree to it, Ma'am.' Joseph turned and rested his arm on the side of the cart. 'There's every chance he's just doing this for show. To impress his guests.'

'I'm aware of that Joseph and believe me, if I didn't wish to meet with him I wouldn't. I, more than most, know how your father is when he is angry, indeed I have lived with the fear of it these past twelve months, but it sounds as though he may dance to a different tune these days, even if the tune is not of his own making. I should be very interested to see how he is changed in his attitude towards my family.'

'I have to say, I agree with Joseph. I really don't like the sound of this. Not after what happened in the market.' Alfie said as he jumped down from the cart and moved to stand beside Violet. Constance stared at the two boys undeterred.

'Well, then we shall enter the house under advisement gentlemen. I thank you both for your concern, but I am not intimidated by your father Joseph, nor am I prepared to flee like a coward. So, if you please?'

'As you wish, Ma'am.' Joseph shook his head and sighed as he held out his hand and waited for Constance to take it, helping her and then Violet down from the cart before he made towards the steps, Gwilym counselling him as he walked.

That Violet was using the main entrance, intended for residents and welcome guests was incongruent with everything she had come to know of the Davenport family and how they felt about her and her kin. She took her place beside her mother, the sound of their heeled boots crunching on the gravel as they walked speedily towards the house and as Constance gathered up her skirts Violet followed suit as they began to ascend the steps. Would that she could be any place but here right now. The notion that her status had changed to that of a welcome guest did nothing to abate her anxiety and she couldn't help but feel relieved when Joseph slowed his own pace until they caught up and positioned himself between them.

'Good god, I wonder if the girl would jump into Aggy's grave as quickly.' Joseph muttered angrily. Constance and Violet looked up the steps to the entrance to where Winnie stood waiting for them, her hands flattened against her apron, her posture rigid. Petrified, even. Of what, Violet could only imagine.

'Don't be angry with her, child.' Constance said. 'Your father would have insisted that there be someone to take over Aggy's duties and by the look on her face, I get the distinct impression that she would rather be anywhere else but here right now.'

One glance at Winnie and Violet knew that what her mother had observed was true. Gone was the bubbly maid that had leapt into the cart beside her in the early hours of the morning. The girl that stood in front of them now looked pale and exhausted, the rims of her eyes, the tip of her nose reddened by crying. This was not a girl that relished her new position. This was a girl who mourned no less than the rest of them. For all the antagonistic talk and glances the last time they had met, Violet could not help but feel sorry for her.

When they reached the door Winnie stood aside, her head bowed.

'Good morning, Sir.' She whispered and curtsied, her eyes never leaving the floor. Joseph made his way through the entrance without so much as a glance in her direction.

'Joseph…' Constance said, with a cautionary tone that made him stop in his tracks. 'The girl has wished you a good morning.' Joseph sighed heavily and turned back to face the maid whose gaze hadn't lifted from the floor.

'Yes, I'm sorry. Winnie, that was rude of me. I apologise. Are you well?'

'I am sir, thank you.'

'You are here to replace Aggy?' Winnie nodded, raising her head as Joseph peered down to catch her eye. 'Well, I'm sure you will do well in the role.'

'I will do my absolute best to make her proud of me, sir. She taught me a great many things and I promise I won't let her down.' She lowered her gaze back to the floor. 'Sorry. She always said I talk too much. I promise, I will try to stop sir.'

'Nonsense. The last thing we need around here is more silence.' He removed his hat and passed it to her. 'And I'm sure that she would be proud of you. I'm sorry I ignored you. It just feels, strange, you being here and not her.'

'No, please don't apologise, I understand, sir. It is no less strange for me I can assure you.'

'Well then we will start again, yes?'

'Very well, sir.' Winnie curtsied again. 'Your father…'

'Is waiting for us. I know.' He shrugged off his coat, not waiting for Gwilym to assist him and handed it to Winnie. 'There is nothing for you to do this morning, seeing as my room is already made. Perhaps you would like to take the time to sit with Aggy a while?' Winnie's eyes widened in surprise.

'You wouldn't mind?'

'I'm suggesting it Winnie. Why would I mind? I would actually be rather grateful if you did. I would go myself, but I fear that is not possible.'

'Of course. Sorry, that was stupid of me. Yes, I would very much like to see her.'

'She needs flowers.' Constance said softly

'She liked yellow roses, Ma'am. I used to bring her bunches of them from my mother's garden. For her room. But they're out of season now.' Winnie pulled a handkerchief and dabbed at her eyes.

'Go round to the back of the house, Winnie. To my mother's glasshouse. It's full of winter flowers. There's bound to be something in there you can make a bouquet with.' Joseph said softly.

'That sounds perfect.' Constance reached out and rubbed Winnie's arm soothingly. 'Joseph, I don't think we should keep your father waiting any longer, do you?'

'Do you not want me to take your coats, Ma'am?' Winnie stepped forward to assist her.

'No, dear.' Constance said, already walking away, closely following behind Joseph as he walked down the hall. 'I shouldn't imagine we'll be here very long. There really isn't much to say.' She smiled sideways at Violet. 'An apology,' she whispered, 'is only one word after all.'

*****

Though she knew that they had not done anything wrong Violet still couldn't help but feel as though they were dead men walking when they entered the sitting room, forming an orderly line behind Joseph. Violet glanced over his shoulder and looked around the room, taking in each resident in turn, all fixed in position as though they were characters in a play, unspeaking, waiting for the scene to begin. Waiting for the final members of the cast to arrive.

Edwin Davenport stood in front of the fireplace, his elbow resting on the mantelpiece, master of all he surveyed. Mr Parnell was sat in an armchair directly in front of him, both men turning to face the doorway as one as Joseph entered. Calissa Parnell and Amelia sat in chairs adjacent to each other in the bay of the window. Whilst Amelia sat with her hands folded neatly in her lap and stared out of the window, Calissa seemed to be busying herself by embroidering a small square of fabric. Even from a distance Violet could spot the intricacy of her handiwork, all dark purple flowers and delicate green leaves.

She raised her eyes slowly, smiling when she spotted Joseph and placed her needlework in her lap.

'Violet, you are here!' Amelia ran across the room and pulled Violet into a warm embrace that would have pulled Violet off her feet had she not steeled herself. She shook her head slowly as Joseph moved forward to assist her and he stopped instantly, his expression warming for the first time since they had arrived. Whilst there was little love lost between Joseph and his father, the bond between him and his sister was clearly evident in the way he watched her now. At least he had that, Violet thought. He was not truly alone.

'It is good to see you, Amelia. You have grown into a fine young woman.' Violet smiled.

'Where are your manners, child?' Violet felt Amelia flinch in her arms as Edwin Davenport bellowed from where he stood. 'Have you taken leave of your senses?' Amelia pulled back immediately as though she had burned her hands in the fire.

'I'm sorry, father.' She said hurriedly, though her voice could barely be heard. There was something about her demeanour, the way she trembled, never lifting her gaze that triggered the desire to protect her Violet realised, and she could see it in Joseph's expression as strongly as she felt it in her own heart. How could Edwin not see how his children looked at him? How did he not realise that they didn't see a loving father? They saw a monster.

'Mr Davenport.' Calissa sighed as she placed her needlework on the small table beside her chair. 'The gypsy girl is clearly her friend and when our children are grieving it is a relief to know that there is someone with whom they can find comfort is it not?'

'There is also a need for ladies to display a certain measure of decorum, Miss Parnell.' Edwin blustered.

148

'Indeed. But there are times when such rules can be relaxed, don't you agree? Especially when one is in one's own home.' Calissa rose from her seat and walked over to where Violet stood. Her hair was simply parted in the middle and braided to form an elaborate bun which hung loosely at the nape of her neck, loose strands twisted into curls that caressed her cheekbones. Her skin was as smooth as porcelain, her cheeks flushed pink from the warmth in the room, unlike her own, Violet thought, which were dry and ruddy, a consequence of living and working in the cold air of winter. Calissa wore a simple pale pink dress with a princess line that enhanced her décolletage, the skirt draping down in pleats to a small train that gave one the impression that she was floating rather than walking so delicate was she in her approach. When she reached Violet, she smiled warmly and curtsied.

'I have not had the opportunity to make your acquaintance before.'

'My apologies.' Joseph said awkwardly. 'Miss Yardley, this is Miss Parnell.' The blond girl smiled.

'I am pleased to finally meet you.' Calissa said as Violet curtsied in reply.

'And I you, Miss Parnell. Are you enjoying your stay?'

'Why, yes, thank you. I do so enjoy the countryside around this area, but at the same time I find myself missing London society dreadfully which is where we have not long arrived from. Have you visited the city, Miss Yardley?' Violet shook her head. 'It is an entirely different world, I must say. Such fine buildings, such beautiful exhibitions and exquisite restaurants. I think you would enjoy it immensely.' Calissa glanced at her father who stared at her expectantly. 'But, this place has its charm too and I do so enjoy meeting up with old friends and family. I take it this is your mother?' Calissa curtsied again as Constance did the same.

'It is a pleasure to meet you.' Constance said. 'I understand that you and Joseph have all but grown up together?'

'Yes, but, how did you know?'

'Josephine.' Constance replied simply and for a brief moment it felt as though all the air had been sucked out of the room. 'I used to meet with her frequently when I last lived here, indeed I feel as if I know you and your father as well as I know Joseph and his family, if only by reputation.' Violet glanced at her mother wondering what else she knew that she had never shared.

'It is true that Josephine was always chattering to someone about something.' Mr Parnell said nostalgically. 'She had everyone in her confidence and she was in theirs. I often thought she could charm the birds from the trees if she put her mind to it.'

'I fancy she probably did when you weren't looking.' Constance smiled as she looked over to where Edwin stood. 'And you, Mr Davenport, are you well?' It seemed to take an age for Edwin to pull himself out of his trance and Violet wondered where he had gone at the sound of his wife's name.

'I am well, Mrs Yardley.' Edwin finally replied, still staring at the fireplace as if he wasn't quite ready to return to reality.

'Mr Davenport has something he wishes to say to you, Mrs Yardley. Isn't that right, Mr Davenport?'

'Well, then perhaps if you stopped interrupting, he might actually be able to get around to saying it.' Mr Parnell turned and glared at his daughter.

'Quite.' Edwin frowned, his eyes meeting Constance's for the first time since she had arrived, his discomfort rolling off him in waves. 'I'm sorry, would you like to sit?'

'Thank you, but we must be on our way presently.'

'Of course.' Edwin cleared his throat. 'Mrs Yardley. I have asked you to come here today... I need to apologise to you, but I assume that you have already guessed as much.' Edwin turned away from the fireplace, clasping his hands together behind his back as he walked towards the window. 'When Josephine died, I found myself in a very dark place and I lashed out at those that did not deserve it, my own children included. I have lain accusations at your door that I know were unfounded and in doing so I put your livelihoods and your welfare under threat. I know now that I was utterly wrong and I hope that you will find it in your heart to forgive me. Constance stepped around Joseph and walked forward into the silence, her eyes never leaving Edwin.

'I know the loss that you have felt, Mr Davenport, and I understand that that loss can take your soul to the darkest of places. I have visited many of those places myself, indeed when Violet's father passed, I thought I would never see the light again and I was so very angry. But that anger did pass in time, even though I sometimes prayed that it wouldn't. It became a perverse source of comfort, such was its familiarity.' Edwin turned to face her, his brow rising and it was clear that Constance had hit a nerve. 'You know that Josephine was a good friend to me and I would never have seen her harmed. I only wish I could have helped her for all our sakes.' She turned back to glance at Violet and Alfie momentarily. 'On behalf of my family, I accept your apology, Mr Davenport. I hope that we can now move on knowing that there is no longer such a poisonous animosity between us?'

'Then we are agreed that this is the end of the matter?' Edwin looked to Constance, waiting for her agreement as though they had reached the end of lengthy business discussions, nothing about his tone even remotely suggesting remorse. Nothing to suggest he regretted the distress he had put the camp through and Violet found herself baulking at the sheer arrogance of the man. Constance pursed her lips for a moment before she spoke.

'We are agreed, sir. I would very much like to put this behind us.'

'I am pleased you feel the same way. And whilst you are here, I should like to thank you for helping Joseph.'

'Indeed! Joseph is such a dear friend to me. I would be heartbroken were anything to happen to him.' Calissa smiled at Joseph as though he were the only person in the room and Violet watched intrigued as Amelia rolled her eyes. 'Which reminds me.' Calissa continued. 'Miss Yardley, there is a pleasant little tearoom in town. I was wondering if you would like to take tea there? Tomorrow afternoon perhaps?'

'Oh!' Violet felt her cheeks flush red. 'I'm dreadfully sorry, but I work on the stall until sunset Miss Parnell.'

'But surely your friend here can take your place for an hour? You would not mind, would you?'

'I would not mind at all.' Alfie broke into a conspiratorial smile.

'Oh, I am so pleased! I have so missed having a female companion! Amelia is alright I suppose but she is still a child, and there are some things that a woman needs to discuss with someone her own age, don't you agree?'

'Calissa, you cannot simply drag Violet away from her work. She is such a help to the community!' Joseph interrupted, the blood draining from his face leaving him looking pale and exhausted.

'It will only be for an hour, Joseph. Do not fret so! I'll come for you at three!' Calissa said excitedly, clapping her hands together like an enthusiastic schoolchild.

'Very well, Miss Parnell. I look forward to it.'

'And on that note,' Constance interrupted, making her way back to the door, 'I think we should take our leave. Violet, Alfie are you ready?' Violet curtsied as she followed her mother and Alfie out of the door.

'I'll see you to the carriage!' Joseph ran out after them.

'No, please stay indoor Joseph, it is cold outside and you have no jacket on.' Constance turned to face him as she reached the threshold.

'As you say.' Joseph conceded. 'Perhaps I'll see you in town again soon, Vi?'

'Perhaps.' Violet said as she took Alfie's arm, the two of them walking back down the steps to the waiting carriage. She climbed back into the carriage, sliding up to her mother who pulled a blanket over the pair of them and turned back to wave at Joseph and Gwilym who stood together on the front steps to the house.

'Well. That was a turn up for the books!' Constance said the smile spreading across her face. 'If only Aggy had been here to see it. I'll tell her later. I intend to sit with her tonight.' She tucked the blanket around their legs sealing them in. 'Now, let us go home. I believe you and Alfie have a stall to open.' Violet nodded in agreement though nothing could have been further from her mind. She needed peace, not the chaos of the marketplace. Needed time to think. Because she was starting to question everything. Not least her own heart.

Chapter twenty

'You know you don't need to come with me, Vi. What with everything that happened last night and you working the stall all day, you must be exhausted. Really, I would be happy to drop you at the camp and come back.'

'No!' Violet protested as she jumped up into the cart beside her mother, the last of a long list of remedies safely delivered. 'I won't have you sit in there all night alone. I can't imagine it's the safest place to be.'

'Society may be on the decline, but I think the majority of folk still have respect for the dead and those mourning them.' Constance glanced over at her as they made their way through the town's narrow streets, the wheels of the cart ricocheting off the cobblestones beneath them.

'The majority is not everyone. And wouldn't you prefer company? Sitting there alone all night would be quite daunting I think.'

'I'm going to sit and watch over my friend, not the body of Frankenstein. Good lord child, you really do let your imagination get the best of you sometimes.' Constance laughed under her breath as she steered the horse and cart off the main road and down a small side street. Several of the houses were already in darkness which was not surprising given how many of the town's residents were still tied to the land in some way. Light, she knew, would return to the cottages before dawn as workers strived to make it to the fields in time to see the sun rise, ready to reap the rewards of winters bounty and earn themselves a wage in the process.

The street lamps flickered and danced against the rising winds and the rain that had begun to fall in heavy drops as Violet jumped from the cart and pulled open the large metal gate that guarded the entrance to the carpenter's yard. Strange that they would keep the deceased here if they had no formal home to return to and yet this was how it was. The bodies lay cooling in one room while craftsmen prepared their final resting place in another.

Violet closed the gate once the horse and cart had made their way through and headed towards a row of small stone sheds that had been erected next to the main warehouse. Now that they were away from the tightly knit maze of streets that made up the centre of town the wind seemed to take on a greater ferocity, barrelling down from the mountain and whistling around the outbuildings. Her mother hopped down from the front of the cart and tied the horse to the metal railings that surrounded the property.

'Do you think she'll be alright out here? The storm seems to be worsening.' Violet ruffled the old cob's mane.

'I think she's seen a lot worse than this don't you?' Constance grabbed a small black bag from the footwell of the cart, loosening the strings that held it shut tight and grabbed a handful of carrot chunks that the horse devoured within seconds. 'See, if she was upset, she'd have turned her nose up. Wouldn't you girl?'

'I suppose.' Violet agreed 'Doesn't mean I don't worry about her though.' She pulled the heavy blanket that they had used to keep themselves warm on their rounds from the seat of the cart and followed her mother towards the only shed that was lit, a flickering warm glow emanating from the small single window at the front of the building. Shaking off the rain that had already begun to soak through her thick woollen cape she ran past Constance and grabbed at the door, pulling up the stiff metal latch that held it tightly shut. The lock released with a dull click.

'A business transaction? That is what this is to be reduced to? Surely it has to be worth something more than that?' Joseph's voice. Violet's hand froze on the latch and she turned back to look to her mother for guidance.

'It's rude to eavesdrop, Vi.'

'I know but I don't want to interrupt.'

'We're already here so he's going to be interrupted. Just make yourself known!' Constance reached around her and rapped her knuckles against the door.

'Well, he certainly knows we're here now.' Violet grimaced and slowly pushed the door open. Inside the light glowed more fiercely, casting shadows across the stone walls and creating dark caverns in all four corners of the building. This was not a place to enter unaccompanied, less still to sit with the dead, Violet thought. Overactive imagination or not.

There was a series of small stone steps in front of her which led down to an uneven flagstone floor. The slabs were fractured in several places, allowing grass to grow up between the cracks, making the space seem strangely ethereal. Tall white church candles were affixed to brass candlesticks around the small enclosure and there were chairs of different sizes and designs along each wall, many of which were in a state of total dilapidation. In the centre of the room there was a large wooden table on which Aggy's coffin lay. It was surrounded by dozens of irises and calla lilies that seemed to bask in the candlelight bringing welcome colour into the monochrome room and filling the void with the most delicate perfume. Winnie's tribute was glorious, Violet thought. No less than a woman like Aggy deserved.

Joseph stood next to the table, his arms wide apart he leaned against the side of the coffin. He was back in his own clothing, wearing a black suit and his thick grey woollen coat that was now embellished with a simple black band on the upper arm of one sleeve. He stood as still as a statue and stared at her across the dark void, his face a perfect picture of dismay as his fingers wrapped tightly around the edges of the coffin.

'Violet, Mrs Yardley, when did you arrive?' he said apprehensively as he turned and stooped into an awkwardly formal bow that seemed completely superfluous given the events of the last few days. Still, Violet and Constance curtsied in reply as though they knew no other way.

'This very second.' Violet said. 'I'm sorry if we startled you. We did not think anyone would be here.'

'Aggy's family are on their way now.' Joseph glanced over his shoulder at the coffin. 'The local vicar stayed here last night with her but he was called away. I didn't want her to be left alone.'

'Of course. Would you like us to leave? We would not wish to intrude.' Violet glanced around the room.

'There is no-one else here Violet. I was talking to Aggy.' Joseph said sheepishly.

'It must be quite strange, her not arguing back.' Constance leaned over Violet's shoulder.

'Mother!' Violet stared at her, horrified. 'How can you say such a thing?'

'With great ease! And if Aggy were alive she would have laughed along with me!' She placed both hands on Violet's shoulders and manoeuvred her down the steps. 'We are here to sit alongside Aggy before she makes her final journey, Violet. Her life was beset by sadness and her passing a tragedy, but she was a woman full of heart and spirit and joy. Do not let this journey be a sorrowful one. Let it be a fond farewell. Convention, be damned.'

'You are right.' Joseph conceded. 'She would hate to be the cause of upset. It just feels very wrong to be showing any display of humour. It feels, unseemly.'

'Because that is what society has taught us. But we know Aggy best. We know how our beloved friend would wish to be remembered as she leaves us for her final destination? So, come, let us sit and we will share tales and we will say goodbye the best way we know how. And we will make her smile.'

*****

Several hours passed before the laughter faded away. Joseph, Violet and Constance had chosen to sit in a row along the wall, sharing the blankets that Constance had brought with her, and to Violet's surprise it was Joseph who had taken centre stage, treating the evening like a confession and sharing the times when Aggy had covered up for his and Violet's wrongdoings. He spoke of how she'd hidden antiques that had been broken through his perpetual clumsiness; of how she had begged for the local farmer's forgiveness when he and Violet had been caught scrumping; of how she had discovered him deliberately ruining the parsnip soup that had been destined for the table that evening by throwing in handfuls of salt and finally he told of how Aggy had whisked Violet out of the house from under his father's nose just a few weeks ago and as he told each tale they took a sip of brandy from his hip flask and raised the small canteen in her honour as the night hours passed by and the candles dwindled away to nothing.

'I had no idea you two had gotten into so much trouble together.' Constance smiled as she peered over at Joseph. 'And there was me and your mother talking about what a good influence you were on each other. Shows how little we knew.'

Violet wasn't sure how much time had passed before her mother fell into a fitful slumber, her head resting on her upturned hand, her section of the blanket wrapped firmly around her from neck to ankle.

'You were angry. When we arrived.' Violet said quietly as she made sure her mother was securely tucked in. Joseph leaned forward and rested his elbows on his knees, his eyes fixed on the coffin.

'Just another ridiculous plan by my father. You know how he is. But, I managed to persuade him not to go ahead with his plans for the grouse shooting enterprise so I hope I can do the same for this too.'

'I thought you said you had control of the family business now?'

'I do, to an extent. But he still likes to be involved in other matters. As long as it doesn't involve the tedious day to day running of the estate, that is. I think he would lose his mind if he had nothing to attend to.'

'Surely it's good that he has re-found his enthusiasm? It shows that his health is improving and that news alone must be welcome?'

'Of course.' Joseph agreed. 'But when he and Mr Parnell are together, they formulate the most irrational of schemes and expect the rest of us to fall in line with them. Father is looking in all the wrong places if he wishes to revamp the estate and Mr Parnell often has sound advice, but not all the time. I think sometimes he focuses on how he can best serve himself and his family rather than his friend. Not that that should be a surprise to anyone. I'm sure we would all do the same...'

'I would argue that few are truly selfless when it comes to financial affairs. Especially if they wish to be successful. Your father is quite lucky in that regard.' Violet suggested. 'He is fortunate that you are there to guide him.' Joseph sat back in his chair and scoffed.

'And who is there to guide me?'

'We all are, Joe. Your sister, your aunts and your uncles, your friends. Me.' Violet reached over and lay her hand on top of his, feeling the warmth of his gloved hand beneath her own as he entwined his fingers with hers. 'And our lives will not always be easy. There will be love and laughter and hope but there will also be trials and losses and sadness. But, in that too, I think we are lucky.'

'We are?' Joseph looked at her sceptically.

'We are.' Violet smiled. 'Because it means that we have lived to fight another day.'

'This, I am prepared to concede.' Joseph said, running his thumb lightly over Violet's hand. 'I am to travel with the coffin tomorrow, back to Aggy's family home and I'll be staying there for a few nights until the funeral has been held. There is a small coaching inn near the church, I understand. They have reserved a room there for me. I have offered to pay for the service but the family have refused. I worry that I may have offended them. Her brother said he was quite capable of looking after his own. As though I had deemed him inadequate in some way.'

'I'm sure they know that your offer came from a kind place, Joe.' Violet said.

'I hope so. Still, I am unsure as to what to say to them when they arrive.'

'You simply tell them what she meant to you. I'm sure those are the most important words they could possibly imagine hearing.' She took a sip from Joseph's hip flask and handed it back to him. 'And speaking of knowing what to say, I am meeting with Miss Parnell this afternoon.' Even in the dim light Violet could see Joseph's shoulders stiffen.

'If you are going to ask me why she should extend such an invite, then I'm afraid I cannot offer you a rational explanation.' Joseph admitted. 'I have heard her say often enough how she misses female company. Perhaps that genuinely is the reason for her invite.'

'Perhaps. But I doubt very much that we have anything in common. I have no idea what to say to her.'

'Just be you. That's all you need to do.' At that, Joseph let go of Violet's hand. He reached into his pocket and found the top for the hip flask and with nimble fingers he screwed it into place before putting the flask back in his pocket. 'Just remember.' He said softly. 'She has a mouth like a foghorn and little control of the words that come flying from it. So, pay no heed to whatever she says, because the majority of her truths are hers and hers alone.'

'Very well.' Violet watched as Joseph leaned forward again, resting back on his knees in ponderous silence. Perhaps he was not simply annoyed by Calissa's presence after all she thought. There was something else, an edge to his tone that went much deeper. She leant back against the chair then and closed her eyes and hoped that whatever Calissa had said to rile Joseph so much, she kept it to herself when they met.

Chapter twenty-one

Having three people standing behind the stall did not work.

It was probably because Violet and Alfie had worked together for near on two years that they moved as sparring partners might, able to anticipate every move the other was about to make from the simplest of gestures and they could spend the entire day dancing around each other and not make contact once. It was something Violet hadn't even considered until now because it had happened so naturally.

The same could not be said when Edie was added to the mix. It was all graceless collisions and apologies and awkward laughter when what one really wanted to do was scream. Having had such a minimal amount of sleep probably didn't help. Her patience was paper thin, Violet realised, given the way she had overreacted when she had spilt lavender oil on to her cape as Edie had bumped into her for the umpteenth time. Edie had apologised but from the look on her face, Violet wasn't sure that she had meant it. Which made her wonder if the accident had not been an accident at all.

Out of the corner of her eye she watched Edie disappear into the crowds, a long strip of paper in her hand containing the lunch orders for every stall holder in their section of the market and couldn't help but pat herself on the back. The assigned task had to have afforded her fifteen minutes at least. Half an hour if she was lucky. Fingers crossed it was particularly busy. She leant back against the wall, breathing out slowly, her eyes closed as she counted to ten.

'That was a bit unnecessary, wasn't it?' Violet opened her eyes to find Alfie staring at her.

'No! It wasn't!' Violet pouted and stamped her foot in frustration. 'I love her dearly, Alfie, but why is she insisting on coming down here and getting in the way like this? She's causing chaos!'

'You cannot be serious? Alfie laughed. 'You really need to start paying more attention to what's going on around you, Vi. Lord, if I can pick up on it…'

'What exactly do you mean by that?' Violet crossed her arms defensively. 'Edie hasn't said or done anything out of the ordinary! There's been nothing to pick up on!'

'Really? You haven't noticed the one-track conversations? The never-ending questions? Constantly trying to help you and prove herself useful. Violet, don't you see it?'

'See what?'

'Miss Parnell!' Alfie said, raising his hands towards the heavens in frustration. 'Miss Parnell, Violet! Think about it! When did Edie announce that she was keen to come and help?'

'Yesterday afternoon, why?'

'What had you been talking about before that?' Miss Parnell, Violet realised. They had talked about the trip to the tea shop while they had been preparing the vegetables for dinner, Alfie sitting idly by. He had not gotten away with it for long.

'But Edie didn't say anything particularly out of the ordinary.'

'She said she thought it was odd that a perfect stranger should turn up in a town and demand that someone become their particular companion without a thought for anyone else's feelings. She said Miss Parnell sounded wholly untrustworthy and that her serpent's tongue was more likely to be hiding a dark heart rather than a bumbling brain.'

'She said that?'

'She did. Clearly, you weren't paying attention. Don't you see it? She's jealous Vi! The two of you have been together since you were babes. And now this woman turns up out of nowhere and demands your attention and suddenly here you are leaving the stall to take afternoon tea with her, all airs and graces and fancy dresses!' Violet looked down at the cape and the dress beneath it.

'Fancy dresses that smell like a burnt-out lavender field.' She grumbled under her breath.

'I wonder why?' Alfie snorted, his voice riddled with sarcasm.' Makes you seem a little less desirable as a companion, does it not?'

'But this is all quite ridiculous! Edie knows how I feel about her! She is more a sister to me than a friend!'

'Does she Vi? On what do you base that? This Calissa Parnell seems to have turned your head pretty quickly. Perhaps you see her as a way into the Davenport household, I don't know…'

'Alfie, that's a ridiculous thing to say!'

'Ridiculous, is it? Your feelings for Joseph are clear for everyone to see. Perhaps you think if you become her particular companion then old man Davenport will come to see you in a new light, maybe even come to approve of you and see you as worthy enough to take the family name.'

'Miss Parnell asked me! I did not suggest this arrangement!' Violet protested, her cheeks reddening with rage. 'And I have no desire to seek old man Davenport's approval nor do I covet his family name to such an extent that I would reject my own kin!'

'You do not covet it to such an extent? So, you do covet it?' Alfie stared at her, eyebrows raised, his expression victorious.

164

'I…no, I…'

'What are we talking about?' Edie appeared at the side of the stall, a selection of paper bags in her hands.

'I was just teasing her.' Alfie said, quickly filling the silence. 'She's been dropping everything. A right clumsy mare, if you ask me.'

'Well, if you need me to help.' Edie checked the contents of the remaining bags and handed one to Violet. 'They didn't have any cheese left so I got you one of those pies you like.' Violet took the bag and inhaled the aroma that came from it.

'Wonderful, thank you. This is certainly better than anything I'll get in that snooty old tea shop this afternoon.' She deliberately averted her eyes, ignoring the knowing smile that was etched into Alfie's face. 'Only a best friend would know what to do in the event that the cheese ran out.'

'Only a best friend would.' Edie said haughtily as she sat down beside Violet and began to consume her own lunch.

'Tell me, would a best friend also know how to get lavender oil out of a cloak? So that that cloak didn't like a public convenience?' Edie shrugged and looked away.

'It's possible, but I wouldn't raise my hopes. Best friends are only human, after all.' She took bite of her roll that was filled with scraps of hot roast lamb. 'But I suppose they would at least try to help. After all, no-one wants to smell like a public convenience.'

*****

The afternoon hours seemed to pass in relative peace. Violet and Alfie regained their natural rhythm as Edie sat in the corner of the stall working on Violet's cloak and Violet was relieved when Edie successfully managed to at least remove the oil stain from the front of her cloak. Though the unsightly mark had gone there was no denying the strength of the lavender aroma that still emanated from the gown. Violet bit her lip and said nothing, focussing instead on taking every opportunity to huddle up and gossip with Edie. To make her understand that it was obligation that was taking her away, not choice. To put a smile back on her friend's face. She was relieved when Edie finally capitulated, because whether Edie knew it or not, her friendship was everything.

'Everyone to attention please! Her ladyship has arrived!' The girls looked up as Gwilym pulled the Clarence carriage up alongside them. He smiled sympathetically as he leapt down from his seat and ran back to open the door, holding out a gloved hand to support Calissa as she stepped down on to the street. She wore a similar design to the purple gown and coat that Violet had first spotted her in, all layers and embellishments but this outfit was a deep emerald green that made her hair, a mass of pale blonde ringlets stand out in stark contrast against the hue of her attire.

'She is beautiful.' Edie conceded.

'It's all superficial.' Alfie countered. 'I'd imagine she's fairly plain underneath the layers of make-up. And her nose would be better placed on a pig.'

'Alfie, stop!' Violet hid her laughter behind her hand as Calissa made her way over to them.

'Miss Yardley! I trust I find you well?' Calissa Parnell smiled and curtsied as she reached the stall. 'And you...' She narrowed her eyes and regarded Alfie. 'You were at the house yesterday. I didn't catch your name.'

'Alfie, Miss. A pleasure to see you again, I'm sure.' Calissa nodded her approval as Alfie bowed, glancing over his shoulder towards Edie.

'Miss Parnell, this is Miss Edie Hammond. Edie curtsied, her expression more closed as she assessed the intruder.

'Miss Hammond! Well, aren't you a treasure!' Calissa exclaimed in a voice that was too old, too pompous for her years. 'Your face is a little mousey, I suppose, but you are pretty enough. And your hair is glorious. Like an unkempt mane that one might see on a wild cat.'

'Shall we make our way to the tea shop?' Violet cut in before Edie could reply, her hands wrapping around her waist length hair defensively as Alfie spun her round and engaged her in conversation.

'You can scream at me when they've gone.' Violet heard him mutter under his breath as Violet moved around the table to stand next to Calissa.

'Gwilym will accompany us until we are seated and after that he has a list of errands to attend to so our time will be our own to talk about whatever we please. It is such a chore to know that you are being watched I find.' Violet nodded, conceding the point though she had no idea what it would be like to be escorted anywhere by anyone except for friends and family. Gwilym wordlessly chaperoned them to their destination, taking his instruction to return in an hour with a simple bow before he made his way from the cafe. The subtle shake of his head was not unnoticed as he disappeared through the exit.

They had only been sat for what seemed like seconds before a waitress appeared in front of them, a stark contrast to the service that Violet was used to. It was a flagrant reminder of the difference in their statuses and what type of treatment they could expect because of it, Violet realised. Calissa in her finery would not be expected to wait for anything or anyone. Violet by comparison would be expected to take her rightful place in the queue and she would be expected to wait with grace as the Calissas of the world took their place in front of her. Calissa barked an order and scarcely any time had passed before a steaming pot of tea was placed between them.

'No, no. I am quite happy to pour.' Violet looked up as Calissa dismissed the waitress with an enthusiastic flap of her hand as though she were shooing away an irritating dog.

'As you please, Miss.' The waitress moved away from the table as Calissa lifted the tea strainer and picked up the pot. With a surprising efficiency, she began to pour tea into Violet's cup.

'I do so like to pour my own tea when I come to these places, don't you?' Calissa giggled, looking over the steam that seeped out from the spout. 'What am I saying? Of course, you wouldn't! It must be a relief to you that you are not the one serving!' Violet smiled fixedly. So, this was what Joseph meant when he talked about her brain not engaging with her mouth.

'I have to say, it is not something I have even stopped to contemplate.' Violet admitted as the waitress returned with a three-tiered selection of sandwiches and cakes.

'Really? Doesn't everyone aspire to obtain the unobtainable? Perhaps not. I thought it was natural for everyone to assume the grass is greener on the other side?'

'I don't think that is always the case, Miss Parnell. For my part, I wish for no other life or family than my own. I perceive no shortcomings in them and I do not aspire to anything that exists outside of my social sphere. I find all the pleasures and the comfort I need quite close to home.'

'Indeed. Then perhaps it is just me.' Calissa said thoughtfully as she picked up a small pot of milk adding a splash to each cup. 'I must confess that since I have come to know of your existence I have listened to many tales of the work that you do for the community and the danger that you have put yourself in and I find myself full of admiration for you, Miss Yardley. It makes my own existence rather dull and tiresome, I fear.'

'I'm sure that's not true at all. I would imagine that there are a variety of charitable ventures that you could contribute towards. Do you have a local church perhaps? I'm sure they would appreciate your time. There are so many people in great need of assistance.' Calissa seemed to take time to consider the proposal, tapping her finger against her bottom lip as she stared at Violet.

'That would be an option, I suppose, though I imagine my father would argue otherwise. I am an only child, you see, my sisters both having passed, the latter taking my mother with her. Papa is frightfully protective. It's a wonder that he has allowed me to meet with you today, but we have heard so many wonderful things about your family.'

'Is that so?'

'From Joseph and Gwilym mainly.'

'I see.' Violet said, choosing not to explore a path that she knew would lead to her undoing. 'I understand that you are to thank for elder Mr Davenport's change of heart?'

'I didn't really do a great deal. Please, help yourself.' Calissa gestured towards the cake stand, taking a small sponge cake for her own plate. 'When Gwilym explained what you had done to help dear Joseph it seemed like someone had to stand up for you.'

'I can't claim to have done anything particularly valiant.' Violet said cagily.

'Miss Yardley, I think we both know that that is not the case.' Calissa smiled. 'You went out of your way to ensure his health and for that I am truly grateful. Joseph is so dear to me.' Violet swallowed the urge to declare that until her recent appearance, Joseph had never so much as uttered her name out loud.

'So, the two of you have been friends since infancy?' She asked instead. 'Do you visit frequently?' She watched as Calissa took a delicate bite of her cake and followed suit with the scone that she had chosen, mimicking her companion's behaviour and consciously fighting the desire to devour the small confectionery treat in one mouthful. Her mother was right. The cake was delicious.

'We visit much less frequently than we used to.' Calissa dabbed her napkin at the corners of her mouth. 'When we lived nearer, we spent a great deal of time here, if we weren't in London of course. But the death of my mother's parents meant we were required to move to their estate so my father could better manage the land. Since then it has just been the two of us, residing in a house that is far too big for our needs.'

'I'm sorry to hear that.' Violet said, finding that she actually meant it.

'Life it what it is, Miss Yardley. And things are improving. More recently, my father has found an estate manager that he can trust in his absence and so we are now better able to pay visits to those we have neglected for too long which means we get to visit town far more frequently. And visit the Davenport family of course.'

'This must please you greatly.'

'Oh, yes! When I think of how ill Joseph has been and I had no idea. The thought of losing him leaves me utterly panicked as you can imagine.' Calissa leaned forward as if she were about to expose a long-hidden family scandal. 'I disguise it well Miss Yardley, but in private I can be awfully pushy. It's my biggest fault! I very often speak without thinking and I seem to offend people without the slightest awareness that I have done so! Can you imagine that?'

'No, I cannot.' Violet said, dabbing at her own mouth with her napkins as she struggled to keep the smile from her face.

'Joseph is one of the few people I know who sees all of this and still chooses to be my friend and as such he matters a great deal to me. Which reminds me, I have requested the attendance of my own physician. I appreciate that you have worked hard to keep Joseph well, but I am hopeful that he will be able to provide a long-term cure for whatever ails him.'

'Oh, are you saying that Joseph no longer needs my assistance, Miss Parnell?' Violet fought to quell the rising panic that welled up inside her.

'I am saying just that.' Calissa replied. 'Which is a wonderful thing, don't you agree? You cannot be a servant to the Davenports and be my companion. I wouldn't hear of it! From now on you will visit the house as a welcome guest and not as an employee. Won't that be better?' Violet nodded absentmindedly.

'When does the new physician arrive?'

'He intends to arrive in a few days. Which reminds me. I have even more exciting news! There is to be a ball!'

'A ball?' Violet's eyes widened.

'Yes! It took a little persuading, but Mr Davenport has agreed. It has been more than a year since dear Josephine's passing and whilst I appreciate that Amelia cannot indulge in the dancing and the frivolity while she is still in half mourning, I do think she should be allowed to re-enter society, don't you agree?'

'I suppose…' Violet said hesitantly.

'It is to be held at the town hall. Mr Davenport has agreed that your family should be invited as guests of honour. It is nothing in comparison to the distress that his actions have put you through, but we hope that such a public declaration will go some way to righting the wrongs that you have all endured.' Violet placed her cup down as it began to slip from her fingers.

'You want us to attend as guests of honour?'

'We would be thrilled if you would. And as my particular friend I should be very happy if you would come to Ty Mawr so we can prepare for the event together. You may choose from any of my gowns. I have bought far too many with me and I would suggest that we are roughly the same size?'

'Perhaps, but…'

'Then I'll hear no more about it. I have the perfect dress for you. It may need taking out at the waist a little, but you will look so beautiful in it! Plus, it will be an opportunity for you to meet Dr Tremaine. He can be a bit of an old fusspot at times, but he really is very good at his job. I am keen that you provide him with as much information as you can about Joseph's condition so that he may best know how to treat it.' Violet sighed inwardly. Of course, she must attend. If there was something she could do to permanently improve Joe's health. Her own treatments would only last so long. That much she knew having witnessed Josephine's demise. Even if it meant…she left the potential consequences hanging. No, there would still be a way to see him. She would find a way.

'We would be glad to attend. Thank you for you the invite.' Calissa clasped her hands together and beamed at Violet.

'I am so pleased! I have taken it upon myself to oversee the planning, having attended so many functions in town, though I do not have nearly enough time to do it justice. Ten days! Can you imagine? Everything has been arranged though. From the music to the flowers. You must listen!' Violet lifted a small sandwich from the stand. Cheese. She smiled and took a bite as Calissa launched into a monologue that would take up the rest of the hour. It was not the incessant rambling that gnawed at her now though, it was the knowledge that her one tie to Joseph had been inexorably cut and there was nothing she could do about it.

Chapter twenty-two

'I simply cannot wear this, Miss Parnell!'

Violet stared at herself in the full-length mirror that stood in the corner of Calissa Parnell's room and tried to conceal her horror behind her hands. 'My mother will be furious if she catches me in this dress. It is far too revealing!'

'It is fashionable, Miss Yardley! Everyone in town wears something similar. Besides, I thought your mother believed in the advancement of women?'

'She believes in girls achieving their potential and being seen as man's equal. She certainly would not agree with them flaunting their bodies as though they were on sale at a cattle market!' Calissa chuckled as she walked over to stand behind Violet.

'I can assure you, you do not look as though you are a potential purchase at a cattle market and anyone who says otherwise would have to be a complete imbecile!'

Violet glanced at Calissa's reflection in the mirror then turned back to look at herself more closely. The rich scarlet dress was stunning, that she couldn't deny, and whilst there was something about the colour that was scandalous enough by itself, it was the cut of the dress that had taken her breath away.

Gone was the expanse of material that normally covered her from neck to shoulder to wrist. Now her décolletage was not only on display, it drew the observer's attention, a thin strip of gold silk at the top of the corset emphasising her honey-toned skin in ways she could never have imagined possible. Two rows of red silk roses formed a set of straps that hung just below her shoulders, their detail so precise you could almost believe them to be real and the bodice and skirt had been cut in such a way they seemed to change the shape of her body, flattering her curves and cinching in her waist so as to make it look miniscule. The boots that she wore added inches to her height, which only compounded the overall effect but as much as she looked like a woman in her prime, Violet still couldn't help but feel like a child playing dress up.

Her hair at least was something she was pleased with and she was grateful that Winnie had gone to great lengths to perfect it for her. It was delicately pinned back from her face, falling into a river of smooth dark brown curls that cascaded her back, the raised crown decorated with a band of cream and red rosebuds. Pulled away from her face as it was it made her almond eyes seem bigger and brighter than ever. Around her neck she wore a simple string of pearls that belonged to her mother.

Her jewellery was a stark contrast to the web of rubies and diamonds that Calissa had chosen to wear with a pale pink gown that seemed almost conservative in comparison to her own. Where the material of Violet's dress was simple however, Calissa's dress was decorated with fine lace around her bustline that flowed into delicate sleeves that veiled her upper arms. The same lace covered the lower sections of the dress, shimmering every time she moved as hundreds of sequins and gemstones glistened like frost caught in the early morning sun, making her look like the Snow Queen made flesh.

'Do you not trust me?' Calissa said in frustration waking her from her reverie. 'Winnie, what do you think of Miss Parnell?' Winnie spun round, her lips peppered with spare hair grips. She hurriedly pulled them from her mouth as she eyed Violet from top to bottom.

'I think she looks very handsome, Miss.' she replied in a heartbeat, her tone so factual that Violet knew the maid was speaking nothing but the truth.

'You also know my family, Winnie. Albeit minimally.' Violet smiled. 'Don't you think my mother will be slighted vexed by my appearance?'

'Not at all, miss. If I may be so bold, I think you will turn a lot of heads this evening. You look very fine indeed.' Violet felt her skin flush.

'Well, that is in no small part down to you Winnie.'

'It was my pleasure, miss.' The maid curtsied but the gesture didn't sit well. After all, dresses and pretence aside, weren't she and Winnie the same? She bit her lip to stop herself from begging Winnie never to bow or curtsey before her again, silently cursing herself for not having the courage to side with her own in front of Calissa.

They turned in unison when there was a knock at the door. Winnie hurried over, pulling the door open a fraction.

'Are Miss Parnell and Vi...I mean, Miss Yardley ready? The rest of the party are ready to leave.'

'We are!' Calissa called out. Winnie pulled the door open a little wider and Gwilym peered in, casting an eye over the room until his gaze finally fell on Violet.

'Do you not think she looks fine, Gwilym?' Calissa chirped and Violet could hear the unspoken subtext that followed. 'For a commoner, that is?' Gwilym's face flushed bright red, his mouth opening and closing like a fish out of water struggling for air.

'I think she looks very fine.' He stammered.

'And you do not think that the dress lessens her character?'

'Miss Parnell!' Violet protested as Calissa laughed again.

'You are right. I'm sorry, Gwilym. That was unfair of me. You and Violet are friends. I should not have put you in such a position.' Gwilym bowed silently, as Calissa and Violet made their way to the door, Gwilym winking at Violet when Calissa had passed.

'You look lovely.' He whispered.

'Thank you.' Violet mimed as she passed him. She decided not to ask why he muttered 'God, help us all' under his breath to Winnie as he and the maid followed them down the stairs.

Her nerves were beginning to get the better of her. Violet reached out for the balustrade to steady herself, gauging each step one at a time as Calissa drifted down the stairs in front of her all poise and delicacy. Amelia was already waiting at the bottom of the stairs with the three gentlemen of the house. Edwin Davenport was quietly conversing with Calissa's father whilst Joseph leant back against the far wall, studiously running his gloved fingers over his top hat as though he were keen to avoid any kind of social interaction. He wore a black dress suit with a crisp white shirt and black bow tie, the tie the only sign that he was still in mourning for his mother and he looked as if he had been groomed to within an inch of his life. He looked, stifled, Violet thought, his expression a mask, his frustration coming from him in waves.

She had always thought him to be handsome but, dressed as he was, and even though he was scowling, there was something about him that simply took her breath away. Maybe it was precisely because he was scowling, she surmised. He wasn't all false airs and graces and he wasn't out to impress anyone or garner their favour. He was just, Joe. It did not seem appropriate to call him beautiful, but it was the only word she could summon that even began to adequately describe what she saw when she looked at him. He was simply beautiful. He looked up lazily and Violet could have sworn that she had physically felt the moment when he had spotted her. He propelled himself away from the wall, his eyes turning to flame as he watched her descend and she whispered a silent prayer of thanks when her feet finally made contact with solid ground. Still, she was painfully aware of the way his eyes never left her as she moved to stand next to his sister and when she returned his gaze it seemed for a moment as though there was no-one in the room save for the two of them.

'Violet, you look absolutely perfect!' Amelia gushed, severing the silent tie between them. 'I should say you look every bit as handsome as Princess Helena, wouldn't you Joseph?'

'I would indeed.' Joseph forced a smile onto his face for his sister. 'Miss Parnell, Miss Yardley, you both look delightful.' Calissa bowed her head in appreciation and turned to Amelia, expectantly.

'And what do you think of this dress, Amelia?' Amelia let her head fall to one side as she assessed Calissa's gown.

'It is quite exquisite, Miss Parnell. But then you never wear anything that is less than exquisite.' Amelia conceded though the enthusiasm had clearly evaporated from her voice. 'I am forced to continue half mourning so had no choice but to wear this drab old thing again.'

'You still look lovely.' Violet said. Amelia looked down at her plain purple gown.

'It doesn't matter either way. I can't imagine that I would ever look as magnificent as you.'

'Magnificent?' Violet laughed. You make me sound like a battleship!'

'I take it all this tittle tattle means that we are ready to depart?' Edwin Davenport called over as Winnie helped both ladies into their capes.

'We are ready sir.' Calissa replied.

'Very good.' We have two coaches. 'Calissa, you will travel with your father and I. Joseph, please escort your sister and Miss Yardley to the town hall.'

'But why can I not travel with Joseph and Violet?' Calissa frowned. 'It seems very unfair that they all get to travel together and I have to travel with you! Besides which, Miss Yardley is my companion. We should travel together!'

'Here we go.' Gwilym whispered in Violet's ear as Clarissa's father rounded on her.

'It is not appropriate. Now you will travel with me or you will stay behind and we will celebrate without you. What is it to be?' Calissa glanced over at Joseph who studiously turned away avoiding making eye contact with her as she moved to stand beside her father.

'You are right. I apologise. Joseph, Miss Parnell, I will meet you inside the great hall.' Intrigued by her sudden conciliatory tone, Violet watched as Calissa led the charge from the house, leaping into the first carriage and leaning out of the half open window before it pulled away. 'Do not start dancing without me!' Before Violet had found a suitable response, the carriage had disappeared from sight.

*****

'How are you?' Violet sat next to Joseph as his sister sprawled out on the seat opposite them. 'It feels as though an age has passed since we last spoke.'

'Three weeks' Joseph said abruptly as he watched the house disappear into the trees. 'And I am well, thank you.'

'I am pleased to hear it. Tell me, did Aggy's funeral go well?' Joseph turned away from the window for the first time since the coach had left Ty Mawr.

'It went very well. Aggy's family were far more generous with me than they needed to be.'

'Why would they not be generous with you? You did nothing wrong Joe. If anything, you went out of your way to help them.'

'They have lost another family member and that would not have been the case had she not been here working for me.'

'That is not your fault.'

'It was me that begged her to stay though, Vi. When her family passed. It was me that offered her a room under our roof because I couldn't bear the thought of her leaving. If I hadn't done that she would have been long gone and away from that blessed path. I may not have put the knife to her throat, but....' Joseph muttered, watching his sister as she stared out of the window, blissfully unaware of the conversation unfolding around her. 'What are you pouting about now, Amelia? You have to wear the dress so I don't know why you're still sulking.'

'Because I'm not allowed to dance either! You heard what Calissa said. All three of you will be dancing and my friends will be able to play games and I have to sit there like a statue while you have all the fun! It simply isn't fair!'

'I could sit with you if you like? I'm sure I don't know half the dances anyway!'

'No!' Amelia looked horrified at the suggestion. 'I insist you allow Joe to dance with you! I should think you would be the most handsome couple there.'

'Amelia, you shouldn't say such things.' Joseph turned and snapped, turning the atmosphere inside the carriage to ice in an instant.

'What? I was only saying!' She flounced back in her seat, folding her arms against her chest as she pulled a face at Joseph. Her brother stared at her for a while before he turned to look back out of the window.

'Amelia didn't mean any harm, Joe.' Violet searched his face for signs of illness. 'Are you sure you're well?' When he said nothing, she reached out to touch his arm lightly. 'Joe?'

'I have already told you once that I am well!' Joseph snapped as he moved her hand away and shifted further along the seat, so far from her that he was nestled up against the wall of the carriage. Resting his elbow on the window ledge he closed his eyes and lowered his head guiding his fingers to the bridge of his nose.

'I'm sorry, Amelia.' He looked up as Violet rose and moved to the other side of the carriage to sit next to his sister. 'Vi, I'm sorry. I had no right to speak to you like that. I have a lot on my mind. Not that that is a sufficient excuse.'

'Is it still the business?' Violet asked.

'You could say that.'

'Anything we can help with? Sometimes a problem shared is a problem halved.' Amelia leant forward and grabbed hold of her brother's hand and Joseph smiled awkwardly as he squeezed her fingers.

'If only it were that simple.' He looked over at Violet. 'Truly, I am sorry Vi. And I should tell you now, before you get whisked away by a thousand possible suitors, you look truly beautiful.' Violet smiled coyly.

'Why, thank you Joe. For that I might even allow you to sign my dance card.'

Amelia sat back and stared out of window as they travelled down the hill away from Ty Mawr, the street lamps that flickered in the town below beginning to peek through the tree-lined track as Violet and Joseph stared at each other in companionable silence.

'See?' She giggled smugly to herself. 'You'll be the most handsome couple on the floor.'

,

Chapter twenty-three

Violet could hear the melody of a familiar waltz before she had even stepped out of the carriage and the sound thrilled her to her core. She had learned to dance when she was quite young, her mother teaching her the steps to the waltz, the polka and the quadrille to name a few but where privileged girls were afforded proper classes, she had practiced at the camp, dancing along to an impromptu orchestra that consisted of fiddles and flutes and whistles and an old bodhran that one of the camp had bought back from Ireland years before.

Her musical knowledge came from regular trips to concert halls as they travelled from town to town. Not that they had ever sat in the auditorium with the regular attendees. They were instead confined to the back of the theatre, near an open stage door and her mother had danced with her and helped her practice until they could dance no more. 'If you had been borne into another family.' her mother had said wistfully. 'You could have been so accomplished.' Violet could never imagine wanting any other family than one she had been borne into, but that didn't mean she had never dreamt of attending an occasion such as this. And now it was here. With their cloaks secured away at the entrance she, along with Calissa and Amelia, made their way to join the gentlemen in their party.

'Joseph, you must escort Miss Yardley into the building. This is your ball and she is your guest of honour after all. I will follow with my father and Amelia, you can walk alongside Mr Davenport.'

'She certainly seems to have it all worked out, doesn't she?' Violet muttered as Joseph moved to stand next to her.

'You have no idea.' Joseph held out his arm and watched as Violet tightly wrapped her fingers into the crook of his elbow. 'Shall we?' he whispered as they turned to face the stairs that led to the ballroom.

'Wait, I haven't to attach my dance card to my wrist.' Violet protested.

'All in good time.' Joseph took the card from her. 'Let me add my name to the card first, otherwise I might never get a look in.' Violet looked at him suspiciously as they began to ascend the stairs.

'I think the illness may be taking you. You're clearly delirious.'

'I think you may be the one who's delirious.' Joseph grinned.

'I could go back to the camp, prepare a treatment now if you'd like?'

'As long as you promise to take me with you.' Joseph sighed, his eyes wandering to the balcony that surrounded them. 'Look up, Violet. Look at what's going on around you. Do you see how many people are staring at you?'

'Because I'm with you, clearly.'

'No, they are staring at you because you are the most beautiful woman in the room. Not just in appearance but in heart and soul. You are glorious, Violet.' They came to a stop and waited for their names to be called before they entered the hall, Violet spotting her mother as soon as she entered the building. To resounding applause, they made their way into the room, Joseph walking her over to where Constance stood alongside Alfie.

'I have to greet the guests for a while.' Joseph said. 'I'll be back for my two dances.'

'Wait!' Violet called after him. 'You still have my card!'

'I know!' Joseph looked over his shoulder and smiled as he slipped her dance card into his pocket and threaded himself back into the crowds.

*****

'Did you ever imagine that we would invited to something this grand? In this town of all places?'

184

'In all of my wildest dreams? No!' Violet laughed as Alfie spun her around the floor. This at least, dancing the polka with Alfie was familiar territory. With every step and spin she felt her muscles relaxing back into a state of near normality.

'You look very dapper, Alfie. Where did you get the suit?'

'Joseph. He wanted to make sure your mother had someone to accompany her so he leant me one of his suits.'

'That was nice.'

'It was.' Alfie conceded. 'But if I'm honest, I was glad to get out of the camp. With Edie gone off with her mother to visit family and you here it would have been horrifically dull. The place isn't the same when the three of us aren't together'

'You're missing Edie.' Violet smiled slyly, trying keep her voice even.

'Perhaps. And do not even think of interrogating me, Violet Yardley.'

'What? Edie is my friend, and as such I have every right to question your intentions towards her.'

'I enjoy her company a great deal, and I believe she feels the same way. Is that what you want to hear?'

'She makes you happy.'

'Very much so. And that is all you need and have a right to know, so enough. Are you having a good time? This is in your honour after all?'

'I'm starting to feel a little frazzled, truth be told.' Violet confessed. An understatement if ever there was one. The balls of her feet were starting to ache now, but then that was what you got, she supposed, if you spent hours being passed from one potential suitor to another, all by Calissa's design.

'You think this is really a public apology and nothing more?'

'I think it's an attempt to garner public support.' Violet said. 'But if it makes Joe and Amelia's lives easier then I have no complaints. Besides, they're also raising funds for the needy so a great deal of good can come out of this evening.'

'Not if you're name is Joseph Davenport by the looks of things.' Alfie stared across the dance floor, nodding towards the far side of the room.

'What do you mean?' As the dance slowed down and drew to a close, Violet followed Alfie's eyeline and turned to find Joseph. It took a fraction of a second for her to spot him. He was stood at one end of the head table with Edwin, Calissa and her father stood at the other and Joseph was looking anywhere but directly at them. Violet watched intrigued as Edwin placed his hand on Joseph's shoulder and muttered something into his son's ear then walked away to stand next to Calissa and her father, the two men talking briefly before Edwin picked up a fork and began tapping the side of his glass.

'Ladies and gentlemen, if I might have a moment of your time…' The ballroom came to a standstill.

'This is a night for celebrating all that is good about the land around us and the people that live here. It is a time for reconciliation and it is a time for building bridges and for re-establishing friendships.' Edwin laughed awkwardly. 'It is no secret when I say that I have recently been made all too aware of my own shortcomings. I have seen how life can take you from a state of bliss to bleak hopelessness in the simple passing of a heartbeat and I have seen how that loss can impact upon an entire community if it is not confronted. This evenings fundraiser will help to ease the same pressures for those in our society who do not have the luxuries that we in this hall enjoy. Over the past few weeks, my son, Joseph, my colleague, and good friend, Mr John Parnell and

I, have been in discussions with local businesses who are represented in this room tonight to create a series of opportunities for the residents of this area which we hope will help to return prosperity to this area. At the same time, the funds from this evening's event will also go towards the provision of food, clothing and medical help for those in need. I understand that so far we have raised in excess of five hundred pounds, so, from the bottom of our hearts, we thank you!' He raised his glass in salutation as the crowd erupted into applause.

'Joseph, come here, son! Don't be so shy!' Edwin called over the noise. Violet watched as Joseph slowly walked out of the shadows over to stand next to his father, his face thunderous.

'What's going on? Why the animosity?' Alfie murmured into Violet's ear.

'I have no idea.' Violet said, her voice barely a whisper as Joseph squinted against the light, finally spotting in the crowd and Violet barely caught the words that slipped silently from his lips before he turned away from her.

'I'm sorry.'

'Calissa, would you join us, dear?' Edwin smiled as Calissa moved to stand next to her father and Violet was dimly aware of Alfie placing his gloved hand on her shoulder as waiters began to appear with trays bedecked with flutes of champagne. They wove through the crowds, breaking off from a single line and spilling out into the furthest corners of the hall, handing glasses to everyone they passed.

'No.' Alfie whispered. 'This must be a joke. Vi...'

'Not now, Alfie. Please.' Violet stood transfixed, unable to look away from the spectacle unfolding before her eyes as Alfie politely took a glass for himself and Violet from a passing butler.

'The son of a bitch. He's planned this down to the last detail.' Alfie glared at Edwin. 'This is beyond cruel. Vi, let's go. What do you say? You don't need to be here.'

'No. I'm not leaving'

'Please Vi. Don't do this to yourself.' When he was met with a wall of silence Alfie sighed and let his hand fall away from her. 'Then I'm sorry. I cannot stand here and watch him humiliate you like this.'

'Go if you must.' Violet felt rather than saw Alfie leave her side, felt the vacuum open up behind her and she was suddenly alone in the crowd, surrounded by strangers who clamoured to get a view of the Davenports and the Parnells, their chattering reaching fever pitch.

Before Edwin Davenport had even started talking, she knew. She knew from the way that Calissa looked at Joe. She knew from the way he looked at her and looked away and she knew from the increasingly excited hum that filled the hall. She knew and there was no way to stop herself from knowing.

'In keeping with all the other good news this evening. I should tell you that there is one more relationship that has been recently forged that has bought a warmth to my heart. The Davenports and the Parnells have been friends for as long as I care to remember and now it would seem as though we are to become family! It gives me great pleasure to announce that my son Joseph and Calissa are engaged to be married!' Smiling, he turned to face Calissa. 'Calissa, I know you will bring much joy to our family, as a wife, as a daughter and as a sister to Amelia and we welcome you with open arms.' He turned and raised his glass towards the crowds that gathered around them. 'So, please, join me in congratulating them. To Joseph and Calissa!'

'Joseph and Calissa!' The sentiment echoed around the ballroom as the crowd raised their glasses simultaneously. Violet sipped her champagne and watched on in silence, unable to speak or move or even begin to process the maelstrom of activity that whirled around her as Calissa smiled softly and leaned into Joseph raising her eyes towards his so their faces were only inches apart.

'Are you not going to kiss the bride-to-be?' A lone voice sounded above the heads of the gathered crowds. Joseph looked to the sea of smiling faces, his expression one of unfettered dismay as he turned his back to Violet and faced Calissa. If she was disappointed that he chose to ignore the way her face was raised to meet his, kissing her gloved hand instead she hid it well, even as their audience voiced their disappointment. Their protestations they fell on deaf ears, because Joseph's attention was already diverted elsewhere.

Amelia rose from her seat and walked towards him. She smiled a wan smile as she pecked Calissa on the cheek and reached up to whisper in her brother's ear. Joseph froze as she glowered at him for a second and turned and walked back to her seat and did not look at her brother again. If he had looked upset before, it had taken a single comment from his sister to break him, Violet thought. As the crowd began to congratulate the couple, Joseph's eyes never left Amelia.

*****

'Why has he done this?' Alfie said as Violet made her way over to the edge of the hall and sat in the chair next to her mother.

'Why not? He has made no such promise to me, nor did I expect him to. We are friends and nothing else, Alfie. Have I not made that perfectly clear all along?'

'You have tried to. Not that anyone has ever believed you. But even then, even if you were telling the truth, this makes no sense. He does not care for her, Vi! Any fool can see that he despises her.'

'Then that is for him to endure.'

'Would you like to leave now?' Constance leant over and whispered in Violet's ear.

'Please.' Violet's voice wavered at the understanding in her mother's tone.

'A wise decision. Alfie, fetch the coach please.' Constance stood to collect her bag from the table behind her.

'Yes, of course Ma'am.'

'Don't be long, Alfie.'

'No ma'am. I'll meet you directly outside.' Alfie fled from the hall, apologising as he cut a path through the crowds.

'Miss Yardley, you are not leaving?' Violet whirled around to face Calissa and Joseph. She glanced down at their intertwined hands, somehow managing to summon an expression of happiness as Joseph watched her apprehensively.

'I'm afraid we must. I am quite exhausted and I have insisted that Violet accompany me.' Constance smiled, taking a step forward to stand beside Violet. 'But before we leave, I must congratulate you, of course! I confess, I did not expect such joyous news!'

'Thank you, ma'am, we are very happy! I must apologise to you though, Violet. I have been keeping this secret from you for so long and I have nearly told you so many times. You and Joe are such good friends and I so dearly wanted us to be able to share our good news with you, but father insisted that we announce it formally. We didn't even tell Amelia for fear that she would blabber!'

'Do not upset yourself Miss Parnell.' Violet reached forward and rubbed Calissa's arm soothingly. I understand that there are certain traditions that need to be adhered to. And I wish you and Joseph all the best. Seeing the two of you standing here together, it is blindingly obvious how perfect a match you are.' She feigned a smile, though it was so rigid it would have been surprising if it had been seen as anything other than false. There was some satisfaction at least in the way Joseph flinched at her words and Violet bit her lip because if she continued talking now, she knew that she would never stop. She would make a fool of herself and ruin everything. So she stood by quietly as Calissa beamed, leaning into Joseph, oblivious to the barbs in her comment.

'Oh, that is so sweet! Isn't it, Joe?'

'Indeed. Thank you, Violet.'

'And now, if you don't mind, I don't want to keep Alfie waiting.' Violet moved to pick up her bag.

'Of course!' Calissa said hurriedly. 'But there is one more thing. I have someone I'd like you to meet.'

'It is a little late for introductions, don't you think, Miss Parnell? Besides, Alfie will be waiting for us. We really must be on our way.' Violet glanced backwards as she gathered her belongings.

'It will be brief, Miss Yardley, I promise you. Where is he? Ah!' Calissa turned to beckon a gentleman who stood not far behind her.

'Miss Yardley. This is my physician, William Tremaine.' Violet turned to face the stranger that waited behind her. He bowed enthusiastically and smiled as he peered up at her, his eyes twinkling.

'Miss Yardley. I have been trying to make your acquaintance for the better part of the evening! It is good to finally meet you at last.'

'I…' Violet turned to look at her mother and then back to the stranger that stood in front of her.

'Are you alright, Violet? You've gone quite pale! Would you like to sit down perhaps?' Joseph watched her uncertainly, his body tight as though he were preparing to catch her should she fall.

'I am quite well, Joseph, thank you. I apologise Doctor Tremaine. It has been a very long day. My wits appear to have abandoned me somewhat.' She curtsied belatedly, her mother following suit behind her. 'It is a pleasure to meet you finally, sir. Am I to understand you arrived recently?'

'This very evening, Miss Yardley. I have been on the road for most of the day so I can fully appreciate your current state and I totally sympathise.'

'I understand you are to become Joseph's physician?'

'That I am.'

'I confess that I am relieved you have arrived. It is very comforting to know that I am leaving Joseph in safe hands.'

'Leaving me in safe hands? What on earth are you talking about?' Joseph frowned and stared at Violet in confusion.

'We spoke about this at dinner the other evening. Doctor Tremaine will be your physician now, darling. And I'm sure that he will find a cure for what ails you in no time.' Calissa patted Joseph's arm soothingly.

'We discussed nothing of the sort and I have not agreed to anything as you seem to imply. Violet has treated me very successfully.' Joseph blustered, his cheeks reddening as Calissa glanced at William Tremaine and subtly shook her head, a despairing look briefly stealing her smile away.

'Doctor Tremaine has a proper medical background.' Violet looked to him, her expression hardened. 'So, you will not need to seek out my assistance any longer, Joseph.'

'But I am content with the treatment you have provided, Miss Yardley.'

'But it has always been common knowledge that the treatments I have prepared have been temporary solutions at best. I strongly suggest you refer to Doctor Tremaine from now on. Besides which your fiancée informs me that Doctor Tremaine works for her family so you very much fall under that remit now. And I understand he is very knowledgeable. Is that not so Doctor?' William Tremaine smiled awkwardly, glancing between Joseph and Violet.

'I like to think I do my job well, Miss Yardley, though I would appreciate meeting with you at some point? I believe we have much to discuss, and I am intrigued with regards to your own methods of treatment for different conditions. I would be interested to hear about more traditional techniques. Perhaps we could meet soon?'

'I'd be most happy to Doctor Tremaine. You will find me on the stall in the market most days. Miss Parnell knows where to find me.'

'Of course! I would be happy to advise you William. I should show you the town at the same time perhaps. But, enough now. We have held you up long enough I feel.' Calissa wrapped her hand around Joseph's arm, briefly glancing up when he sighed heavily and looked away. 'I hope you enjoyed this evening?'

'Very much so, Miss Parnell. And thank you for the invite. Until we meet again then.'

Violet fixed a smile onto her face, curtsied her farewell and ignored the pounding of her heart as she took hold of her mother's arm and walked hurriedly towards the exit. In a matter of minutes, the world had turned on its head. She thought of Joseph as she slipped on her cape, of the man he was becoming, of the husband he would become for Calissa and she thought of Doctor Tremaine, the man who had come to cut the last tie between them as she retreated into the cold night air and hastily made her way towards the carriage, glancing up at Alfie and smiling her thanks as he held the door open for her, his face devoid of emotion. She leapt in unceremoniously, her mother climbing up to sit beside her as Alfie slammed the door shut and ran to the seat at the front of the coach. Within seconds they were pulling away.

'Violet!' Violet glanced back as Joseph appeared in the doorway, his face panicked. Alfie slowed the coach.

'You want me to stop?' He called out over the hooves as they clattered against the cobbles.

'No.' Violet shouted in reply, shaking her head. 'Do not stop Alfie. There is nothing to be said.'

'As you wish.'

'It's him, isn't it?' Constance squeezed her hand as the carriage barrelled around the corner and away from the hall. Violet nodded in reply, her breath hitching in her throat as another piece of the puzzle fell into place, this time in the form of William Tremaine, the apparition in the mirror.

Chapter twenty-four

'You're sure you don't mind me leaving early?' Violet looked up at Alfie as he balanced on the table fixing bows of holly and mistletoe to the front of their stall.

'Not in the slightest. You must be exhausted.'

'It's true I didn't sleep a great deal last night.'

'Which is hardly surprising.' Edie blew into her mittens to try to keep the chill at bay. 'Vi, you have no idea how sorry I am.'

'What on earth for?'

'As soon as I got back and your mother told me, I insisted she bring me down here, but I should have been there last night when you got home. I am so sorry.' Violet couldn't help but smile.

'My darling friend, you were visiting your family! And besides, what is there to say? There's no great scandal here.'

'No great scandal?' Edie's hands dropped into her lap. 'You cannot be serious! Joseph Davenport has treated you abominably!'

'How? He has offered nothing but friendship.' Violet felt the lie seeping through her bones as Edie turned puce with rage.

'He has done nothing of the sort! Since we have returned his every word and deed has suggested a desire to court you. And all that time, he was considering the hand of another? His behaviour has been callous and wicked!'

'In his defence, and you of all people should know that I am not keen to defend him, from the way he behaved last night I don't think he'd been considering anything of the sort. Seems to me, this is an arranged marriage.'

Alfie jumped down from the edge of the stall and dusted off his hands. 'Don't get me wrong, I agree he's behaved badly, but I don't think this is a union he wants. Which reminds me, the banns have been read out in church apparently, so I assume Miss Parnell does not wish for a long engagement.'

'Enough.' Violet said firmly. 'I don't want to talk about this anymore.' She handed her purse over to Edie. 'I'll see you back at the camp.'

'Miss Yardley?' Violet spun round at the sound of her name. 'You said it would be convenient to see you here?' William Tremaine bowed and smiled at Violet. 'I hope I am not interrupting?'

'No! Not at all!' Violet curtsied. 'Doctor Tremaine, this is Mr Banes.'

'Mr Banes? I believe I saw you at the ball briefly last night, but I did not have the pleasure of being introduced.'

'Is that so? Then I am pleased to make your acquaintance now, sir.' Alfie bowed graciously.

'This is Miss Hammond.' Violet said as Edie stood and hastily curtsied, her eyes never leaving William Tremaine's face as she took in every detail.

'Miss Hammond.' William bowed.

'Doctor Tremaine! 'Edie exclaimed, her mouth dropping open. 'It is good to finally meet you, sir!' William tilted his head to one side, his confusion apparent.

'You have been anticipating my appearance, Miss Hammond?'

'I was just telling Miss Hammond about the ball last night and informed her of your arrival.' Violet fired Edie a warning look.

'Violet and I discuss everything!' Edie blustered as Alfie frowned at both of them. 'Did you enjoy the ball, sir?'

'Indeed, though I did not get the chance to dance as much as I would have liked.'

'Then let us hope that there will be more social events in the future so that we can resolve the issue.'

'I very much hope that that is the case, Miss Hammond.' William bowed his head and turned back to Violet. 'I was hoping you might have had an opportunity to think about a convenient time when we could meet?'

'I confess I haven't, sorry. Tell me, do you have plans that I might be able to fit around?'

'Not particularly.' William confessed. 'I'll be going into Cardiff tomorrow. There is a university opened there recently and I want to make use of the library. But I will be free the day after tomorrow if that is useful?'

'You are going to the library?' Violet echoed.

'I am. There are some fine sections on the sciences I am led to believe.' William paused for a moment and watched Violet pensively. 'Would you like to accompany me?' Violet hadn't even asked Edie for help in the market before she was already nodding. But then of course she would help. She would be running the stall with Alfie. Alone together all day. Wild horses wouldn't have prevented her from saying yes.

'I would like that very much, sir. Recently I have become keen to expand my knowledge beyond traditional herbal remedies. And to do that I need-'

'Books!' William exclaimed. 'Well, then this is perfect!'

'It would certainly seem so.' Violet grinned. 'Come, I'll walk with you back to your cart and we can arrange a convenient time before I head home.'

'Oh, you are leaving? I could take you home if you'd like?'

'No, thank you, sir. I would prefer to walk. It affords me much needed time to think.'

'I couldn't agree more. When I am at home, I very often take myself down to the sea when I find myself bogged down by the intricacies of life. It is humbling to realise that one is part of a bigger picture, I think.'

'I could not have said it more perfectly myself. I'll just gather my things.' Violet walked back to where Edie sat waiting for her, looking every inch like a champagne bottle that was about to explode.

'Why didn't you tell me earlier? It's him, isn't it?'

'I didn't get the chance and yes, it would certainly seem that way.' Violet said as Edie handed her her shawl. 'Calissa Parnell said her physician was coming but, I swear my chin must have hit the floor when I saw him. I'll see you at the camp later, explain then. Bye Alfie!' She wrapped her shawl around the tops of her arms as she dodged around him and led William away from the stall and into the night.

*****

The small puddles beneath her feet had already begun to turn to ice, each one cracking under the weight of her step and releasing the water that still flowed beneath its shell. Violet walked in slow, rhythmic steps, pulling the grips from her hair one at a time, allowing her hair to drift down around her face and her mind to wander away from the here and now and back to the night of the scrying. Two appearances in the same mirror. It was an occasion that had never arisen before and the night had ended with more questions than answers, but maybe if one searched thoroughly enough…

Perhaps, Violet thought, there was no connection between the appearance of William Tremaine and Josephine at all. Perhaps the simple truth was that in seeing William she had seen the face of the man she was to marry, though that thought didn't sit well with her. Perhaps, she supposed, Josephine had merely seized the opportunity to warn her of the risk she believed her family faced at the hands of Edwin Davenport and that given the intervention by the Parnell family that risk was no longer real. It could even have been that Josephine had been warning Violet to stay away from Joseph because she believed Calissa to be a better match for her son, though, knowing Josephine as she had and knowing how well Josephine had known her son, the probability of that being the case seemed implausible. Or maybe that was just how she chose to see it.

'Violet!' Violet gasped as the pounding of hooves rolled out of the silence. She took a step back as Joseph brought Sterling, a beautiful dapple-grey mare, to a halt alongside her.

'Joe! What are you doing here? What on earth is wrong?'

'What's wrong? What are you doing walking home alone?'

'I'm sorry?'

'Of all the foolish things to do!' Joseph jumped down from his horse, his chest rising and falling as he fought to catch his breath.

'Do not use that tone on me, Joseph Davenport.'

'Do you honestly expect me to remain quiet when I see you behaving in such a ridiculous manner? These paths are dangerous, Violet!'

'Sir, I am a grown woman, sir and you will treat me as such!'

'Then behave like one!''

'How dare you.' Violet turned and began to walk away, heading further into the darkness. 'I have walked this path many times before.'

'So had Aggy!' Joseph shouted, stopping Violet in her tracks. She turned back to him, allowing him to catch up.

'So had Aggy.' He breathed out slowly as he wrapped his fingers around Sterling's reins and leant against the mare's neck. 'God, Vi. If you had seen her. Seen what they did to her. When Tremaine came into the stables and said that you were walking back to the camp, the thought that you were out here alone…Please, just let me walk with you. Let me make sure that you are safe.'

Violet sighed and considered his proposal. He was right. Of course, he was. Aggy's killer was still out there and she had made herself vulnerable to the same threat. Choosing to walk home alone on the same path had been stupid beyond belief, her only defence that she had been too tired to think logically and as much as she wanted to reject his proposal now doing so meant choosing to consciously put herself in danger.

'Very well. I accept your offer. Thank you, Joe.' She turned and continued walking, listening to the sound of Sterling's hooves as he plodded along in a slow undulating rhythm beside her.

'You're still calling me Joe at least. I suppose one should be grateful for small mercies.' He shrank back, his thin smile fading when Violet turned and glared at him. 'Talk to me, Vi.'

'I'm not sure that there is anything left to talk about.'

'Nonsense, there is everything to talk about.'

'I think you're mistaken.' Joseph sped up and moved to stand in front of her. 'Vi, please.' He stepped from left to right, countering her every attempt to pass him.

'Let me through.' Violet growled.

'No. Talk to me.'

'Very well!' Violet stopped and clasped her hands together in front of her with a piercing clap. 'What would you like to talk about?'

'What happened yesterday evening. At the ball.' Joseph watched her intently as Violet began to laugh.

'What happened at the ball…' She drew the words out, slowly and deliberately, tapping her forefinger on her lips. 'What is there to say that isn't already known? You are getting married. To Miss Parnell. Perhaps you wish me to congratulate you again? Is that it?'

'Don't be petulant.' Joseph said tiredly.

'I will behave as petulantly as I damn well please Joseph Davenport!' Violet moved closer until her face was only inches from his. 'How dare you! How dare you come to me while you plan your wedding to someone else!' She ducked under his arm, storming ahead as Joseph cursed and tied Sterling to a tree, one eye fixed on her as she disappeared off the main track and onto a side path that led through the woods and into the camp. As soon as the horse was secure, he broke into a sprint to catch up with her before she disappeared into the night and Violet scowled as he reappeared beside her and continued unabated, all the while fighting to catch his breath.

'I did not plan this Vi, nor do I want to be a part of it! My father sees this as the perfect transaction, a way of securing the financial assets of both families for future generations. He has given me no choice in the matter! He has all but drunk away our fortune!' Violet stopped and turned to look at him. That at least she could believe. That it would be down to Joseph to once more get his family out of the mess his father had created. Joseph leaned down, looking Violet directly in the eye, willing her to understand. 'If I don't marry Calissa we could lose everything, and I cannot stand aside and watch Amelia being forced from her home. She's already lost her mother.' Violet felt the ice around her heart fracture a little.

'I assume that this was the deal you were talking to Aggy about? In the carpenter's yard?'

'So, you heard?'

'A little. Not enough to know what you were referring to. It doesn't matter anymore, though does it?' Violet sighed tiredly. 'You should go home, Joe.'

'Let me see you home safely first.'

'We're not so far from the camp that I can't run the rest of the way, though I doubt Aggy's attackers are still hanging around. Besides, your fiancée will be waiting for you. You should go to her.'

'What? No! I have no desire to be near her! I love you Violet. I have never made a secret of it!'

'You cannot say such things Joe. You cannot play with my feelings like this. Please, go home!' Violet grabbed hold of the edges of her shawl and wrapped it tightly around herself as she ploughed forward.

'I cannot tell the truth? Look at me, Violet!' He grabbed hold of her arm and spun her around to face him so that they were no more than a breath apart. 'I love you and I know you love me.'

'What does it matter whether I love you or not? You are with someone else now.'

'I will always be yours.' There was a brief stillness before his lips found hers and his hands were in her hair and he was pulling her towards him as though he could meld them as one soul, if that wasn't what they already were.

'Tell me I am wrong to kiss you.' Joseph pulled back, his breathing laboured. 'Tell me that you do not love me and I will never come near you again.'

'Joe, please, don't do this.' Violet lowered her gaze.

'No, you don't get to hide from me, Violet Yardley." He gently caught her chin between thumb and forefinger, guiding her face back to his. 'Look at me and tell me that you don't love me.'

'You know that I can't.' Violet whispered. Joseph exhaled and leaned forward more tentatively this time, slowly brushing his lips against hers over and over again, each kiss slightly longer, slightly deeper than the last, forcing her body to respond as though it was no longer her own, every move a physical compulsion that left rational thought lagging far behind. He tasted of sweet port and the cigars that she knew he hated so much. Her heart sank. Once again, he had capitulated in order to keep peace in his family, to avoid his father's derision. He would even go as far as to marry someone else. She slowly, reluctantly pulled her lips from his.

'We can't do this.' Violet whispered as Joseph rested his forehead on hers, his eyes still closed. 'Someone might see us.'

'I don't care.' Joseph murmured. 'The whole damned world could burn around us and I would not care.' He inhaled sharply as Violet kissed him again.

'All the time that I was away, I would lie in my bed at night and think of the last words that you said to me. That you loved me. I would lie there and wonder if you still felt the same and then when I came back and I knew that you did, I was so happy. Finding out what you did for me made me love you more. I hadn't even thought that was possible.'

'And now?' Joseph said as he placed his finger under her chin, lifting her lips to his.

'Now, I have lost you anyway.'

'You will never lose me.'

'You are getting married,. I have already lost you.'

'It is just a contract. A slip of paper and nothing more.'

'It is greater than anything we will ever have between us.'

'No, nothing will ever surpass us, Vi. No-one will ever love you the way I love you.'

'What use are feelings when they must be denied.' Violet smiled sadly. 'You know that we cannot do this again, Joe. It wouldn't be fair to Calissa or you or me.'

'What are you saying?' Joseph took a step back.

'I'm saying I will always be your friend Joe. I will never turn you away. But I have to find a life beyond us. For both our sakes'

'You have to find someone who is eligible you mean?'

'Marriage isn't the answer to everything Joe.'

'You should spend some time with my father. I'm sure he could convince you otherwise.' He leaned forward and kissed her forehead. 'I should take you home. Before I run away with you.' Violet chuckled softly and reached for his hand and tried to ignore the spark that took flared up in her mind. We could run away...

'I think there's been enough scandal for one day, don't you?' she said as they began to wander through the trees and along the muddy track back to the camp.

'Since we are being open and honest, tell me about the scrying.'

'Very well.' Violet said apprehensively. 'What would you like to know?'

'Did you see someone? Because after the way you reacted the other day, it led me to think that if you had, you weren't pleased?'

'I did see someone, though I can't say I was pleased or displeased, given that I didn't know them.'

'Didn't… So, you do now?'

'I know of him.'

'And you're not going to tell me who it is, are you?' Violet couldn't help but hear the bitterness in Joseph's voice.

'No.' She said simply. 'I don't think that would benefit anyone, do you?'

'I suppose.' Joseph conceded. 'But if someone came along who swept you off your feet, you would marry him?'

'Do you think someone will come along and sweep me off my feet, Mr Davenport?'

'I do, Miss Yardley' Joseph said. 'And I know that when that happens, he will be the luckiest man on earth and I by comparison will know what it is to have one's heart truly broken. When will I see you again?'

'Tomorrow, as it happens. Dr Tremaine and I are travelling into Cardiff. We will be leaving from Ty Mawr to visit the university. To the library more specifically. I said I would help him remember? Now he is your physician it seems only right that I provide him with as much information as possible.'

'But I haven't agreed to his being my physician.'

'He's the best chance you've got a finding a cure,' Violet shrugged. 'and he seems honourable enough.' They stopped as they reached the edge of the camp. 'Thank you for walking me home. I'll see you in the morning.'

'Until tomorrow, Miss Yardley.' Joseph lifted Violet's hand and kissed the back of it gently.

'Go now. Before you catch your death.'

'Right now, death would be a sweet release.' Joseph smiled sadly. 'Given that hell seems to have taken up residence on earth. I love you, Violet Yardley.' He walked back down the path and away from her, turning to wave before he disappeared into the darkness.

'Hell is indeed residing among us.' Violet whispered as she turned and made her way back to the camp. 'And we are all mourners.'

Chapter twenty-five

'You know, I can't decide if you're telling the truth when it comes to Joseph or if you're a glutton for punishment.' Alfie mused as he bought the horse and cart to a slow stop on the drive at Ty Mawr. 'You say you are nothing more than friends and, though you appeared distressed at first, you've reacted to news of his impending marriage as if you truly are nothing more than friends. But the way the two of you've behaved around each other since we returned? Anyone who had seen you would say you were far more than acquaintances.'

'You are still looking for scandal where this is none.' Violet rolled her eyes and tried not to protest too much.

'We have known each other since we were children. There is very little you can hide from me, Vi. Even your reaction now speaks volumes.'

'I am hiding nothing from you now!' Violet looked up from the bag she'd been pretending to rummage through in order to avoid eye contact. 'Yes, I was surprised when the engagement was announced. I certainly didn't imagine Joe would keep something so important from me. Maybe he thought he was sparing my feelings, I can't say for certain. But what I can tell you is that I have known that we could never be anything more than friends since the camp returned here. Even the blessed mirror knew that! That doesn't mean that I don't care for him. I would be lying if I said I didn't. But he will never be more than an acquaintance.'

The lie burned on Violet's tongue, but what other option was there? What would the truth achieve? She had thought of nothing else as she had retired for the night, every trail of reasoning leading her to the same conclusion. If it were her, if her family's lives were on the line, she wouldn't hesitate to do the same thing as much as it would hurt them both. So, the ugly truth of the matter was that they had no choice but to accept the consequences. And maybe in time, the lies she told herself and her family and friends would become the truth.

'You can compose an admirable yarn that provides you with some comfort if you wish but it is nothing more than that.' Alfie watched her impassively. 'I see you Violet. I see every emotion and I know whether it is real or false. I hear how you feel by the tone of your voice and I know when you are lying. Even now your face is bright red. You have been found out and it mortifies you.'

'My face is red because I'm cold! And my voice is like this because I'm losing my patience! Now, are you going to help me down or not?'

'Like I said, if it helps you to lie to yourself. I just hope you know what you're doing.' Alfie grumbled as he jumped down from the cart, the doors to the house opening behind him. He hastily made his way round to Violet, helping her down from her seat as Gwilym came down the steps towards them.

'Good morning! Hope you're ready for your trip into town?'

'Good morning Gil, I certainly am!' Violet took her bag from Alfie. 'Do you like my bag?' Alfie smiled, taking in the small leather holdall.

'Well that looks like some fine craftsmanship.'

'I acquired it locally.' Violet teased him.

'Well, whoever made it is certainly talented.' He winked playfully as he ruffled Berkeley's mane. 'Go on up into the house. I've just got to go get the carriage. We have an hour to get to the station or we don't get to go at all.'

'The train station? We are catching the train?'

'Of course! It would take us six hours to get there and six hours to get back if we travelled the entire way by coach. Didn't Doctor Tremaine tell you?'

'He didn't.' Violet searched her bag for her purse. 'Not that he's to blame. I didn't even stop to think how we would get there. Gil, I don't think I have enough for a ticket.'

'Already paid for by Old Man Davenport as decreed by Miss Parnell. You're doing this for his son after all.' Gwilym wandered off towards the coach house. 'You'll have to let yourself in, mind. Winnie is otherwise engaged. Something to do with a hat. Don't ask me.' The ever-needy Miss Parnell. Violet smiled to herself.

'Of course. Thanks for dropping me over, Alfie, I'll see you this evening?'

'Don't be too late. We've got work in the morning and I don't want to have to drag myself out of bed to come and find you.' Alfie jumped back up into the carriage and fired a warning look at her. 'So what time should I head back here do you think?'

'I have no clue.' Violet shrugged. 'Any ideas on train times, Gil?'

'We'll make sure she gets home.' Gwilym called back as he headed towards the stables. 'Save you a journey.'

'There. Now you don't need to worry about losing out on your beauty sleep. Have fun with Edie today!' Violet smiled sweetly as she made her way towards the stairs, not bothering to wait for a response. Whatever Alfie was going to say next was probably not going to have been pleasant and certainly wouldn't have been something she would have wanted aired in public.

*****

When she opened the door to the house and made her way into the hall, she found William Tremaine sat by the fireplace reading a letter, his brow furrowed, though whether he was angered or worried by the note was unclear. He looked up as she entered, his dour expression melting away as he stood and bowed swiftly, folding the slip of paper as she closed the door.

'Doctor Tremaine, how are you this morning? I hope I didn't disturb you?' Violet eyed the letter in his hand.

'Miss Yardley, you find me very well indeed and eager to learn!' William smiled. He waved the missive between thumb and forefinger. 'This is just a note from my mother. As soon as I leave town for a few days she seems to find herself under the weather. I fancy that it is not a coincidence.'

'Are you the only child?'

'The youngest, and therefore destined to be the baby of the family forever, I fear. I am also the only physician in the family and she knows how to use it to best advantage.' William looked at the small bag that Violet carried. 'You do not have any literature with you?'

'Everything I need is in here.' Violet patted the side of the bag, her hand thudding against the hard covers of the books inside.

'Apologies, I am used to working with much larger tomes. The world of medicine can be a tad cumbersome when it comes to research.'

'Well, there are larger botanical encyclopaedia.' Violet smiled. 'But the basic properties of the ingredients we use are contained within the books I have bought with me. My family have used the same remedies for generations with extremely good results and so we continue to use them until this day. As for Joseph specifically, the final design for his treatment is also written down, though the process is already committed to memory.' She pulled out the notes she had taken on the first night that she had come to the house. 'I did wonder if I should bring my medicine case with me, but I decided against it. Perhaps I should have done so?'

'Another time, if you would? I would be very keen to understand the methods you apply in developing your treatments. Especially those you have developed for Mr Davenport.'

'Of course. Are you ready to leave? Gwilym was just fetching the coach.'

'I'm ready.' William reached for his briefcase and bowler hat. 'We're just waiting for the rest of the party.'

'Rest of the party?'

'I believe Doctor Tremaine is referring to me.' Violet turned around as Joseph made his way down the stairs, his broad smile knowing and secretive. 'Miss Yardley, you're looking well.'

'I am well sir.' She said falteringly, her cheeks flushing as she looked between Joseph and William. 'You are coming into Cardiff with us today?'

'We all are!' Calissa appeared directly behind Joseph, bouncing down the stairs on the balls of her feet and looking down on the gathering below her as if she owned the world. 'When William told Joseph about your jaunt into town today, Joseph insisted that we come along too. While the two of you make use of the library, Joe and I will visit the town. I haven't been there since we were small children and I am keen to see how much it has changed in that time. I'm also hoping to find our wedding rings there. There is, I understand a shopping arcade newly opened so we might be lucky!' She landed on the bottom step and placed her hands on Joseph's shoulders. 'I saw a very beautiful three carat ring in London and I wish for something similar.'

'How wonderful!' Violet fixed a smile on her face, her anticipation for the day ahead already waning.

'How unnecessary.' Joseph muttered under his breath as he moved a step forward, out of Calissa's reach. 'Did I hear you screaming at Winnie, Calissa?

You sounded most vexed a while ago.' Joseph turned to look up at her. 'I could hear you from my room.'

'Silly girl has no idea about fashion!' Calissa tutted as she walked around Joseph and over to the mirror above the fireplace. She tutted again as she delicately manoeuvred her hat. 'I told her the hat needed to be pinned at an angle. She's utterly clueless. Elizabeth and Penelope would make me a laughing stock if they saw me looking like this. There.' She moved the hat until she was satisfied, although if asked, Violet would have had to admit that she could see no change in Calissa's appearance whatsoever.

'I wonder, Mr Davenport if you would happen to have a protractor about your person that we might gauge the angle of the hat upon Miss Parnell's head. After all, we would not want to face the ridicule of the Ladies of London, should they happen to be in town.'

'And I will thank you not to be facetious!' Calissa whirled on William, ignoring the sniggers around her. 'One does not spend a fortune on clothing only to have one's maid dress them as a clown!'

'Of course. I apologise.' William bowed his head in atonement though his smirk did not diminish at his being rebuked. 'Now that your hat is fixed correctly to your head are you ready to leave, Miss Parnell?' Calissa took one last look in the mirror.

'I believe I am, Doctor Tremaine.' She dashed over and grabbed William's arm, wrapping her hand around the crook of his elbow. 'Come, let us escape the dull confines of this god-awful place, even if it is just for a few blessed hours.'

'Do you think I am dressed to look like an academic?' Violet asked Joseph as they followed William and Calissa out of the door and towards the waiting carriage. He shrugged as he took her leather bag, staying close to her side as they made their way down the steps.

'I don't know. What does an academic look like?'

I have no idea, that's why I'm asking you!' Violet whispered through gritted teeth.

'Sorry I'm as in the dark as you are. Vi, I manage the estate here. I've never set foot in a university.' He slowed down as they reached the coach. 'For what it's worth, I can say with some certainty that if you were going to be herding cows, you would be completely overdressed. Does that help?' Violet gave him a withering look.

'No. It doesn't.' She took back her bag and playfully slammed it into his arm. 'And if you don't be careful, Joseph Davenport, you will have more than one condition that requires medical treatment.'

*****

The engine that pulled the carriages was a beast, there was no denying it. To see one from a distance, gracefully slipping across the countryside leaving a trail of clouds in its wake was one thing. From a distance, it was a thing of beauty. To stand before it and feel the brutal force that emanated from it as the staff readied it for departure was another entirely. The thought that she was placing her life in the hands of a machine over which she had no control could not be ignored.

'You would like to see how the engine works. To assure yourself of its safety.' William came and stood next to her, raising his voice so he could be heard over the hustle and bustle.

'You noticed.' Violet looked from the train to William.

'You have done nothing but stare at the train since we arrived a good half an hour ago.' William smiled. 'And yours is an expression I see in myself so often. To gain understanding is to equip oneself with the ability to make informed decisions, even if that decision is something as simple as whether or not one should board a train.'

'You see through me all too easily.' Violet conceded. 'I find myself on very unfamiliar territory and it unsettles me greatly. Perhaps I am not as brave as I have always believed myself to be.' William nodded towards the engine compartment. 'Come. We still have fifteen minutes.' We will find all the answers you need. Mr Davenport, I believe we are able to board now.' He began steering Violet towards the engine. 'Shall we meet you and Calissa in the carriage?'

'Of course.' Joseph replied; his eyes fixed on William's outspread hand where it made contact with Violet's lower back. 'Unless you would also like to look at the engine, Calissa?'

'Pfft, I couldn't imagine anything drearier.' Calissa said dismissively. 'Can we just get inside the carriage please, Joe. It's far too cold to be standing around out here.' William smiled, seemingly unaware of the indignant glares that Joseph was directing at him and whilst Violet did not enjoy seeing it in Joe, there was something about Calissa's reaction that was particularly satisfying as she looked over her shoulder briefly and smiled coldly as she boarded the train. It was a callous gesture, Violet thought. But then, wasn't everything callous these days?

With her questions answered and her nerves eased, Violet fought to keep her hands and her feet still as the train slowly built up speed and began to cut a swift and violent path through the Welsh Marches. To travel by horse and cart was a relatively peaceful experience even if the ruts in the road causes one to ricochet around in the cab somewhat. But this… Though the ride was smoother it was noisier, the continuous pulse of the wheels on the track adding a strange sense of urgency. She placed her hands against the window as the countryside slipped by, the sheep in the fields scattering as the train's whistle blew, piercing the air with sudden bursts of noise that only added to the feverish atmosphere of the journey.

'I am glad you are able to come along with William today, Miss Yardley.' Violet pulled herself away from the view and looked over at Calissa who sat opposite her.

'It's my pleasure, Miss Parnell. As I said this other day, If I can be of any help.'

'You are such a good friend. Isn't she Joe?'

'She is indeed.' Joseph muttered from his behind his newspaper. Calissa flicked her eyes upwards in mock indignation.

'I am almost certain that, between the two of you, you will find something to battle whatever it is ails my dear Joseph.' She paused, glancing out of the window. 'But at the same time, I wonder if perhaps we are being cruel, allowing you insight into such a prosperous world that will ultimately be denied you.'

'Calissa!' Joseph dropped his paper onto his lap, the edges curling where his hands balled into fists. 'What a cruel thing to say!' Calissa's mouth fell wide in surprise.

'What? I do not say it to upset. Far from it! Do you not think it is cruel to show someone what they cannot have? We are after all members of particular social spheres, are we not? We reside in one and Violet resides in another and there can be no denying that there are opportunities available to us that most people in Violet's sphere would not dream of aspiring to. I wonder if perhaps

Miss Yardley would be left begrudging of that which she cannot obtain when she has to return to her own life.'

'You may rest at ease, Miss Parnell.' Violet smiled, genuinely amused by the slight. 'Contrary to your opinion, and as I have already stated, I find that I consider myself richer rather than poorer for having experiences such as these. In knowing both spheres I find myself more appreciative than those who choose to not to explore beyond the station that is afforded them. I know what is to be missed and what isn't.'

'And you do not think luxuries such as these are to be missed?'

'Not at all.' Violet stared back out of the window. 'One can enjoy the beauty of the world around them whether one is on a train or on the back of a milk cart and one does not need the latest fashions to meet someone and fall in love. Nor do they need a luxurious mansion to feel the warmth that only a family can provide.'

'Is that so?' Calissa watched her guardedly.

'You would, however, draw the line at the angle of your hat I assume, Miss Yardley.' Joseph winked and smiled at Violet before he lifted his paper and brought the conversation to a close before Calissa could draw breath. Violet turned back to the window and chewed on her lip to stop herself from laughing as the train surged forward. This was going to be a very, long journey.

Chapter twenty-six

'I must apologise, Doctor Tremaine. I imagine we would have made much more progress than we have if I were able to focus on the task in hand more readily, but I find myself utterly distracted by this building.' Violet whispered as she glanced over at William, who sat studiously poring over a range of medical encyclopaedia, writing a series of notes as he flicked between the pages, his wire-framed spectacles perched on the end of his nose.

She wasn't quite sure what she had expected when she had been told about the library, but in her mind's eye she had created a simple, modest stone construction that was functional in nature. Never in her wildest imaginings had she expected to find a structure that was almost spiritual by design. Ornate semi-circular windows at the top of the library drew one's eye to the domed ceiling which was embroidered by the most elaborate architrave that travelled the length of the ceiling until it reached a wall of glass, the light that seeped through it making dust motes sparkle where they fluttered. It was a new building but it smelt of old books, lending a familiarity to the environment and it was as though she had finally found a place outside of her own world that afforded her a level of peace she had always thought unattainable elsewhere.

'This is a fine building.' William said as he unscrewed the top of his fountain pen. He handed the casing to her, smiling his thanks before he reached into the side of his briefcase and retrieved a small bottle of ink. Violet watched in comfortable silence as he drew ink into a small dropper and refilled the barrel of the pen, meticulously ensuring that not a drop was spilt, his movements sure and steady. Only when he had screwed the top of the pen firmly back in place did he look up, removing his glasses as he did so. 'I remember the first time I saw the library in Cambridge and I can say with some certainty that my reaction was identical to yours. It is rare to find somewhere so, gratifying I think.'

'It truly is.' Violet said as she took in the rows of books and the students around them. Some sat alone, others in small groups, whispering amongst themselves, all equally keen to learn whether it was from each other or the books they held. 'But my being overawed by this place does not solve our issue.'

'Do not judge yourself so harshly.' William said. 'Using your list of symptoms, I have, I think, established a relatively exhaustive list of potential conditions that may be the underlying cause of Mr Davenport's current state.'

'You have?'

'I have. Given that you have first-hand experience, it would seem prudent that we go through the list one by one. By a simple process of elimination, I think we should be able to find the answer. What do you say?'

'I say read your list, sir.'

'Very well.' He replaced the glasses and Violet couldn't help but smile as he wriggled his nose until they were in position. There was something utterly disarming about the gesture that made Violet feel utterly relaxed in William's company. But not so much that... She silently cursed Joseph.

'The first possible cause I think we can eliminate fairly quickly. I have not known Mr Davenport long, but long enough to assess his character, I believe. Nonetheless, you have spoken to a suggested fragmentation of his mind, so...' He looked up at Violet. 'Is there any possibility that Mr Davenport may have contracted syphilis?'

'Dr Tremaine!' Violet whispered harshly, casting her eyes around the room to see if there was anyone in earshot. William held his hands up in surrender.

'I didn't think so, but it would be remiss of me not to consider the possibility. Public and private personas can often make for uncomfortable bed fellows.'

'Well, I can assure you that that is not the case here. No, there is no way that Joe has behaved in a manner that would put him at risk of such a disease. In public or in private.'

'As I said, I didn't imagine it to be the case.' William removed the lid of his pen and struck a line through the first row of writing.

'There are a variety of options available to us now, each of which has its flaws. I will go through my list one by one and give you the reasons as to why I feel each does not apply here. Please, interject at any time if you disagree with my assessment.'

'Very well.' Violet leaned forward as William cast his eye over the list.

'Firstly, tuberculosis or as it's more commonly known, consumption. Mr Davenport displays a few of the symptoms associated with the condition, namely fever and fatigue and confusion. However, given the cyclical nature of his condition, plus there are no signs of dramatic weight loss I am inclined to rule this out. Do you agree?'

'I agree.'

'Very good.' William drew another line across the page. 'Scarlet fever - You say there is no rash?'

'No. No rash.' Violet shook her head and breathed out through pursed lips, relieved that the current line of questioning did not extend any further.

'Then we can eliminate scarlet fever. Typhoid, a common disease and again several symptoms present, temperature, muscular aches, confusion and stomach pain but again it is degenerative in nature, so I think we can rule this out. Do you agree?'

'I do.' Violet watched as two more lines were struck through.

'Which brings me to my two main areas of interest. There is a condition known as periodic fever syndrome. Hereditary in nature rather than being infection borne it might explain why this condition has only been experienced by Mr Davenport and his mother rather than the wider family. Assuming they alone are susceptible to it. Certainly an argument for, however, it is cyclical in nature and morbidity rate is nearly non-existent. In addition, this is a condition most likely to be experienced during childhood, so for that reason I think we are forced to limit ourselves to our final option.'

'Which is?'

'Pleurisy.'

'Pleurisy?' Violet frowned.

'It is an inflammation of the lungs...'

'I know what pleurisy is, Dr Tremaine.' Violet interrupted.

'I apologise. I don't mean to offend Miss Yardley. Clearly you are well-read in these matters.'

'It is necessary for us to have at least a basic awareness of the human condition and the diseases that ail it. We are not all hocus pocus.' Violet waggled her fingers in the air. 'If anything, I'm a trifle embarrassed that I failed to diagnose the condition myself, if that is what we are dealing with.'

'Sometimes, when it is a close acquaintance it's hard to see the wood for the trees.' He turned back to the open book in front of him. 'Given that we know pleurisy is the result of an undiagnosed infection and manifests in ways you have observed in Mr Davenport, I would suggest that the treatments you have provided have certainly treated the symptoms with a great deal of success…'

'But not the underlying cause.'

'Exactly. It would also explain Mrs Davenport's death, despite your attempts to treat her. Do you know if Joseph was in contact with her?'

'Frequently. So was my mother, Joseph's father and of course, Old Dr Lewis, though he has long since passed on. The cause of his death, I am unsure of, though there were rumours of excessive opium consumption. Even so, I'd be surprised that he didn't pick up on something so obvious.'

'Age often takes the best of us, Miss Yardley.' William said sadly. 'That Joseph had contact with the deceased certainly bolsters my argument further. And without seeing the results of an autopsy to refute the argument, there is always the possibility that Dr Lewis died as a result of the same infection. As for the others, maybe luck was on their side.'

'So, what do you propose we now? If we have an underlying infection that we do not know the source of?'

'I attended a series of lectures in London recently on the treatment of infections during the American civil war.' William said softly. 'Some of the injuries, you wouldn't believe. But even then, it wasn't necessarily the severity of the injury that killed but the infection that set in thereafter. It was during that time that physicians began to use metals to fight infection. And with great success.'

'They used metals?'

'Bromine being the most widely used. Mortality due to secondary infection dropped at a staggering rate. Since then it has become more widely used in society. I would suggest that we try something similar here.'

'You can obtain this metal? What did you call it?'

'Bromine. And yes, it is possible for me to obtain it, though it will take a couple of weeks at least. These compounds are not cheap and certainly not what one wants to keep on their person. In large amounts metals can be extremely toxic. They should therefore be kept under extremely safe conditions. I would have to employ a courier to ensure the materials were delivered securely'

'So, in the meantime?'

'In the meantime, we can investigate further as to the possible root of the infection. And if you would advise me as to the treatments you have administered, should the need arise we can use those same methods until we are able to provide a more substantial solution.'

'Of course.' Violet said earnestly.

'I can see the relief on your face, Miss Yardley. Mr Davenport is a good friend.' Violet smiled as she brought him to mind.

'He is. Our mothers were acquaintances and so we spent a good deal of time in each other's company. Much like Miss Parnell, I suppose.' Violet closed her bag. 'I confess, this has been a huge weight on my shoulders. To have your friend's wellbeing in your hands is not a situation I would recommend to anyone.'

'Indeed. I have found it is better to stay away from friends and family and recommend them to another physician rather than to take on the responsibility myself. The stakes are too high, the pressure too great for one to be able to make rational decisions. Especially if one is looking at a worst-case scenario.' He frowned and looked around the library.

'And if I'm not mistaken, your stomach has been rumbling now for the past two hours?' Violet's cheeks flushed bright red.

'You could hear that?'

'I imagine half of Cardiff could hear that.' He chuckled as he whispered. 'I spotted a barrow boy selling roasted chestnuts as we were walking here earlier. Perhaps we could buy something from him and sit in the park? We've an hour before we meet Miss Parnell and Mr Davenport at the station. Does that sound agreeable to you?'

'It sounds perfect.' Violet said as she stood to remove her coat from the back of her chair, heartened by the knowledge that a potential cure had been found and scared that doing so had rendered her surplus. But then maybe it was better this way. After all, wasn't it her who had said she and Joseph had needed to distance themselves from each other? So, she had gotten what she wanted. Hadn't she?

Chapter twenty-seven

'The day after tomorrow is Christmas, Miss Yardley and I have to confess I have no idea where the past few weeks have gone.' William Tremaine held out his arm for Violet to hold on to as they made their way down the steps from the library.

'Time certainly seems to be running away with the best of us at the moment.' Violet accepted sadly. 'I assume you will be staying with the Parnells and the Davenports?'

'I shall. I understand it will be a celebration like no other. At least, Miss Parnell has promoted it to be as such. There is to be an extended family gathering, partly to celebrate Christmas, but I think the main focus of the day will be to congratulate Miss Parnell and Mr Davenport on their engagement before Miss Parnell goes into confinement until the day itself.'

'That all sounds delightful.' Violet said, concocting an enthusiasm that jarred against her true feelings.

'You would like to take my place?' The physician glanced sideways as they made their way towards the park. 'Because I'm sure that could be arranged.'

'I'm sorry, I already have plans.' Violet smiled with a fake sweetness that made William laugh out loud.

'Thought you might. If only I could boast the same. Ah, there's the stall.' They made their way over to the barrow boy and purchased two cones of roasted chestnuts, continuing into the city before they settled down onto a bench that stood in the grounds of Cardiff castle, the high stone wall behind them affording them some shelter from the bitter winds of winter.

'So, what do you do at Christmas, Miss Yardley?'

'Aside from the annual rituals of drinking goat's blood and human sacrifice?' Violet said innocently, making William laugh raucously again. 'I don't think we are different to any other family although our celebrations will be utterly plain in comparison to those to be held at Ty Mawr, I'm sure. You will probably have an elaborate meal which runs over several courses while we will have a hog roast and my mother will purchase candies and fruits and cakes for dessert. You will drink fine wines and ports and brandies and listen to piano recitals, we will have ales and meads and there will be singing and dancing around the fire which often goes on until the early hours of the morning.'

'It sounds like a great deal of fun.' William mused. 'I find myself quite envious.'

'I am sure Christmas with the Parnells will be equally entertaining.' Violet giggled. 'But if you find yourself in need of escape and you are able to get away you would be welcome to join us. When we were last in town many of the locals did come along in the evening and we have invited them again this year. Just remember to wrap up warm. And be prepared to sing and to dance for they will be plenty of both.'

'I will bear that in mind. And thank you for the offer, it is much appreciated. I have to say I'm surprised that you are still so congenial towards the local community. Miss Parnell told me about some of the difficulties you have faced. I have experienced similar myself. Charges of assuming a divine status from those who wish to find their fate in God alone, as though I am seeking to defy nature in some way. Such accusations are unpleasant when one's only aim is to help the afflicted.'

'Better to be associated with God than the devil I would argue.' Violet peeled open a chestnut, allowing it to cool between her fingers before she took a bite. 'Besides, it was only a handful of people who protested against us and that was more because they feared losing their livelihoods than they feared us. I can understand why they behaved the way they did. They were simply protecting their own as we all would.'

'That's very magnanimous of you, nonetheless.' They sat in silence for a while, listening to the carol singers practising inside the castle as they finished their late lunch. 'Now would be a perfect time for some of that mead, if you happened to have some on you.'

'Oh, I do not carry it on me, Doctor Tremaine. Like this bromine of yours, in the wrong hands I fear it could do irreparable damage. Perhaps I could interest you in a cup of tea on the train? I sense our hour is nearly up.'

'Seeing as tea is all that is available, I suppose it will have to do.' William said half-heartedly. 'Perhaps we may even indulge in a slice of the rather dubious looking fruit cake that the buffet had to offer.'

'Why, Doctor Tremaine.' Violet laughed. 'If you believe you can survive that, maybe you are strong enough to survive the camp ale!'

*****

The train was already in the station, the passengers waiting to board when Violet and William made their way out onto the platform.

'Doctor Tremaine! Miss Yardley!' Violet caught sight of a gloved hand waving above the heads of the crowd.

'I wonder who that could be.' William said sarcastically.

'Indeed.' Violet rolled her eyes as they wove through the masses that had gathered, making their way towards the spot where Joseph and Calissa stood waiting to board the train. As Calissa continued to gesticulate frantically, Joseph stood with one hand on the door handle seemingly eager to make his escape, his expression which appeared impassive at first glance, only betrayed by the slight narrowing of his eyes as he watched Violet and William approach.

'Poor Joseph.' William lamented. 'I'm surprised that he wasn't too scared to suffer a relapse once Miss Parnell had arrived. I certainly can't foresee him finding the courage to be sick once they're married. Imagine the havoc that would play on her social calendar!'

'Stop it, she'll hear you!' Violet coughed lightly to muffle her laugh.

'She is my client, Miss Yardley. That doesn't mean that I have to like her. Calissa Parnell can be very importunate at times. Especially of those she deems to be below her, which by my reckoning is most people she meets. The fact that she has chosen you to be her particular companion is quite a compliment if I do say so myself. Just, be cautious, Miss Yardley. People are not always what they seem.'

'And Miss Parnell would fit into that category?'

'Possibly. Although, by the thunderous expression on Mr Davenport's face, the same could be said of him, I think. One could almost consider him capable of murder. But then he has just spent the day in the company of Miss Parnell.' William smiled. 'I could be wrong though. Perhaps he is simply jealous of our chestnuts. It is so difficult to tell.'

'William, stop!' Violet exclaimed as she glanced over Joseph. He was right, though. Murderous was the only way she could describe Joseph's countenance now. Violet glanced at William warily as they finally managed to squeeze through the crowd to where Joseph and Calissa stood.

'I thought you were studying Doctor Tremaine, not enjoying a day out.' Calissa eyed the physician suspiciously as Joseph opened the door. 'My family are not paying you to have fun.' She chastised the physician as she boarded the train.

'One can study and enjoy oneself, Miss Parnell. They are not mutually exclusive concepts. Indeed, I have very much enjoyed today.' William collapsed down onto the seat as soon as they arrived at their compartment. 'What about you, Miss Yardley?'

'I've had a thoroughly enjoyable day, Doctor Tremaine. Thank you for bringing me.'

'It has been my pleasure. You have helped me tremendously. In fact, I can say with some certainty that I would not have found Pupil's Pharmacopeia if it hadn't been for you.'

'Being short can have its advantages, I suppose.' Violet said. 'Although, I fear my knees may be bruised in the morning.'

'You have been crawling around on your hands and knees?' Calissa cried in disgust. 'How demeaning!'

'More dynamic I would say, Miss Parnell' William retorted, silencing Calissa immediately, though she did not lose the expression of disdain. 'Actually, while I was signing the book out, I did take the opportunity to obtain this for you.' He pulled a small scroll of paper out of his briefcase. 'It's a copy of the periodic table.'

'William, you are too kind!'

'Well, you seemed particularly interested in learning all the elements so I thought you might find it useful. I confess I did not go as far as to think about where you might display it which was rather short-sighted of me.'

'I have a table I can lay it on.' Violet rolled out the parchment and stared at the table detailed within. 'This really is very generous. Thank you.'

'You are most welcome. So, Miss Parnell, Mr Davenport, how has your day been?'

'Joe is sulking, I think.' Calissa giggled.

'I am not sulking, Calissa, I just don't happen to agree with the price you are prepared to pay for wedding bands when you could have the same thing for a fraction of the cost.'

'You cannot put too high a price on love, my darling.' Calissa said coyly, pouting as he turned to look out of the window.

'Should love have a price on it at all?' Joseph said, looking out of the window as the train pulled out of the station, leaving the burgeoning city behind them. Violet looked across to him as the sky slowly began to darken, their eyes meeting in the reflections they created in the window.

'No.' She mouthed as William read through his notes and Calissa trawled through her handbag, seemingly oblivious to the despondency in Joseph's voice. 'True love has no price on it.'

*****

'Would you like me to drive you home, Miss Parnell?' William offered as he climbed out of the back of the carriage, holding out his hand so Calissa could climb down after him. 'I would be more than happy to assist and I must admit that I am keen to see this camp of yours.'

'There is no need, thank you, Doctor Tremaine. I have already said that I'll accompany Gwilym into town so he can spend Christmas with his family. I would be more than happy to drop Miss Yardley off first.' Joseph briefly glanced at William as he passed Calissa her bag.

'As you wish.' William bowed. 'Then perhaps I may see you the day after tomorrow, Miss Yardley.'

'You would be very welcome!' Violet smiled and waved as Gwilym set the coach back in motion.

'You said you would drop me off first.' Violet looked to Joseph as the coach turned towards town instead of the camp.

'I know, but I couldn't have said otherwise back there could I? Besides, Vi, we need to talk.'

'If you want to discuss what happened last night, then please say nothing. What we did was wrong.' Joseph's face fell.

'A sentiment which I will never agree with and it saddens me that you feel that way, but no. This is not related to last night. I will tell you soon enough.' Violet nodded and sat back, looking in any direction other than at Joseph. How easy it was to build lie upon lie.

With Gwilym waving from the door of his family home Joseph moved to the front of the coach, jumping up to grab the reigns that hung loosely over the wooden footrest.

'Aren't you coming up here?' Joseph turned to Violet. 'I can't very well talk to you while you're seated behind me and I don't particularly fancy having to speak so loudly that the rest of the world knows our business.'

'Of course.' Violet stepped down from the carriage and climbed up into the front with Joseph, dropping her bag into the footwell and pulling her skirts into the small cab as the horse began to move slowly forward. Joseph pulled gently on one side of the reins, steering the coach on to the track that led to the camp, before he reached inside the top pocket of his thick winter coat and pulled out a small red velvet box.

'I want you to have this.' Joseph placed the parcel in the palm of Violet's hand.

'What is it?'

'My mother's engagement ring.'

'No.' Violet shook her head. 'Joe, I can't take this.'

'I want you to have it.'

'But…'

'Please, allow me to explain.' Joseph slowed the cart, guiding the horse onto a grass verge by the side of the track. When they came to a stop, he turned to face Violet, his eyes never leaving the gift she held in the palm of her hand. 'My mother always said that when the time came, she would have me pass on this ring to my betrothed. It belonged to her mother and her mother before that. When she died, it was put aside for safekeeping until of course when the marriage was arranged and my father insisted that Calissa be given the ring.'

'Then surely that is what should happen?'

'No. Mother always said I would give it to the girl that I wished to marry and it would be a symbol of luck for us, for our lives together as it had been for generations before. She said it would be as though fate itself had thrown together the circumstances in which the next bearer had been chosen.' He looked up at Violet. 'I cannot give that ring to Calissa. I do not love her and I will not dishonour my mother's memory in such a way. The ring was to be yours and I will not give it to anyone else. I would rather throw it in the river first.'

'What about Amelia?'

'Amelia has no interest in it. Besides which it was always destined for my bride. She helped me to steal it in fact. Just to prevent Calissa from getting her hands on it. Father has half the staff turning the house upside down looking for it as we speak. Calissa of course is blissfully unaware and I think even if she knew about the ring she wouldn't want it. It wouldn't fit in with her precious friends in London. She'd probably lose it at the first opportunity.' Joseph said bitterly.

'Surely they'll recognise it if they see me wearing it.'

'I have attached it to a chain. Here.' He took the box from her, gently removing the lid before he lifted the chain up with one finger, the ring dangling on the end though it was too dark to make out the detail of either. 'Will you wear it then? I would just like to know that it is with someone who will appreciate it. I want it to be worn by the person I had chosen for it, even if it is hidden away.

'I'll wear it.' Violet said softly. Joseph let out a sigh of relief as she leaned forward so that he could lift the necklace over her head, letting the chain slip through his fingers as it settled around Violet's collar.

'You know, I didn't mean it.' The words slipped from Violet's mouth before she'd had time to consider them.

'I know.' Joseph replied, as if her statement required no qualification. 'And thank you, for accepting the ring. Just knowing it is with its rightful owner means the world to me. Even if I cannot be.' He turned to pick the reigns back up and guided the horse back onto the track.

'It's him, isn't it.' Joseph's voice punctured the silence as Violet toyed with the ring, sliding it along the chain.

'What do you mean?'

'The doctor. Tremaine. It was him that you saw during the scrying, wasn't it?'

'Why do you say that?'

'The way you look at him.' Joseph said thoughtfully. 'You meet a lot of people, doing the job you do. I've seen the way you interact with them and I've seen the way you interact with him. It's different. You're more, inquisitive. Less formal. You're relaxed in a way that suggests you already know him, though I know you've never met him until now. Which means you must…'

'…know of him.' Violet finished his sentence. 'You're quite the detective' Violet said, letting ring and chain hide itself away beneath the bodice of her dress.

'So, I'm right?'

'Yes.'

'He certainly seems respectable.' Joseph shrugged noncommittally

'I cannot say that I know him particularly well, but he would appear to be. I have no interest in him though. Not in that way. To suggest I did would be a falsehood.

'Maybe that will change over time.'

'I doubt it. Besides, I know the path that lies ahead for me. The camp will stay here for a while and then we will move on as we always do.'

'You will leave again?' Joseph said, his voice panicked.

'We never settle in one place for long, you know that. Well, very few of us do. There's the odd exception.'

'Then be that exception!' Joseph implored her, grabbing hold of her hand. 'Vi, you can't go away again.'

'I think it would be best for everyone concerned if I did, don't you?' Violet gently pulled her hand back and grabbed on to the edge of the cart as it rolled to a stop just outside the camp.

'You have invited Doctor Tremaine to the Yuletide celebrations here tomorrow?'

'It is an open invitation to the whole community as you well know.' Violet said sarcastically.

'Then I am also welcome?'

'Now who's being petulant?' Violet grinned. 'Besides, tomorrow is yours and Calissa's engagement party. I would have thought you'd have other priorities.'

'You'd think, wouldn't you?' Joseph jumped down from the coach and walked around to help her down.

'Thank you for bringing me home, Joe. And for the ring. I swear I will treasure it.'

'I know you will.' He took her hand as she climbed down from the coach, placing it to his lips before she had a chance to pull away.

'Merry Christmas, Violet.'

'Merry Christmas Joe.' Joseph watched as Violet wandered back into the camp, her arms wrapped around her bag. It was, he thought, the first thing that had gone right in as long as he could remember.

*****

'There are two chains around your neck.' Constance peered over at Violet who sat in a chair next to hers in front of the stove, the aunts already asleep in their beds.

'I'm sorry?'

'I can see two chains around your neck. Your grandmother's and another. What are you wearing child?'

'So much for keeping it secret.' Violet muttered to herself as she lifted the ring up into the light created by the flames that raged in front of them. Violet looked up at her mother apprehensively.

'It is Josephine's engagement ring. No, please mother, hear me out.' Violet spluttered as Constance raised her brow suspiciously. 'It was a gift Joe wanted me to have. It is not a symbol of anything. It is just a gift, I promise you.'

'Oh, good lord!' Constance exclaimed. 'Of course, it is a symbol, Violet! Why must you keep lying to me? Josephine and I were friends remember? Please do not treat me like a fool!'

'I'm sorry, it wasn't my intention to. I was just trying to say that there is no expectation on my part. That I know it is a present and nothing more.'

'So, he chose not to give it to his fiancée?' Violet's insides curdled.

'He said he it wasn't meant for her.' Constance leaned back in her chair and sighed.

'This much is true. And it is indeed a beautiful ring.' Violet held it up to the light.

'Then you know more of it than me. It's too dark for me to see it properly.' She squinted, pinching the ring between two fingers.

'Then allow me. I know this ring as if I have worn it myself, so often has it been the subject of conversation.' Constance reached forward, grasping the ring between thumb and forefinger.

'The ring itself is made of rose gold. Nicely cut I suppose, but nothing fancy or ostentatious. No, it is the gemstone that makes this ring so special.' She twirled the ring in the low light of the fire. 'Amethyst. A very beautiful stone indeed. I often admired it and Josephine always asserted that destiny was written within it. Loathe as I am to say it, I agreed with her, God rest her soul.'

'Amethyst is purple, isn't it?'

'It surely is.' Constance smiled. 'So, now do you understand why this ring was destined to be yours, Violet Rose?'

Chapter twenty-eight

'Could you put the candles out, Constance, dear?' Ruby looked up at her sister and gestured towards the circle of candles that filled the tent with light as she placed her book of prayer back into the leather chest at the end of her makeshift bed. 'So many new flames.' She sighed. 'So many losses. It is sad beyond words.'

Five more flickering lights to be exact, Violet counted to herself. One for Aggy, two for her children, one for Josephine and one for Timbo Driscoll who, until age had taken him a few months previously had been the head of the camp. Whilst his passing had been sad, he had at least been afforded a full life, Violet thought. He had reached his potential whereas the others had simply fallen by the wayside, all promise and hope torn away from them, victims of the cruellest of circumstances.

Silas Hammond, Edie's father, sat beside Violet, his usual daytime attire hidden by the long black ceremonial cloak that he now wore having been elected to replace Timbo as the head of the camp. He'd handled this first ceremony well, Violet supposed, but then he had borne witness to them since birth. What he didn't know about the camp, its traditions and the people in it wasn't worth knowing.

They knelt together in quiet contemplation as Constance began to extinguish the candles, Ruby and Flossie following behind and spraying the enclosure with the essence of niaouli and myrrh to remove any negative energy left by the spirits, a ritual they carried out every year once the celebration of the dead had been completed. The Yuletide ceremony was a coming together like no other throughout the year, the residents fasting during the day before they gathered inside the tent and incantations for the deceased were recited. It was a single point in time during which loss was acknowledged and hope embraced and it created the community that they would become in the year that followed.

Violet watched as her mother hesitated in front of her father's candle, the only one that remained lit. She wore the same conflicted expression now that she did every year. It was as if lighting the candle somehow brought his presence back into the tent and by dousing the flame, she was saying goodbye to him all over again.

'Would you like me to do that?' Constance turned at the sound of Violet's voice. She shook her head timidly and turned back to the candle and gently blew it out, regret instantly masking her features as she took a step back and gave a final swift bow to the dead before she silently made her way out of the tent, towards the camp fire that raged outside, lighting up the night sky.

'Give her a few moments to herself.' Silas gently placed his hand on Violet's arm as she got up to follow. 'Allow her some time to grieve.'

'Of course. You are right.' Violet said sadly as the sisters returned to their own areas of the tent. 'I'll pack everything away, so she doesn't have to do it herself later.'

'You're a good daughter.' Silas smiled.

'I hope so.' Violet moved to pick up the box from the floor and began placing the candles back inside, gently laying them in rows. 'I hope that I haven't disappointed them.'

'I think I can say with some certainty that you have not.' Silas rose from his knees, brushing the front of his gown. 'Your mother never shares memories of your father during the ceremony.' He said thoughtfully. 'Her loss is still so great, even after all these years. I wonder if she has ever told you about how they met?' Violet shook her head slowly.

'I know that she was in the workhouse when they met, but I know little else.' Silas nodded in understanding.

'We were living just outside London back then. Your father and I were walking into town when he spotted your mother out in the backyard. Pegging out laundry I think she was. We were supposed to move on within a day or so but your father insisted we stay where we were and Driscoll, old romantic that he was, agreed. For weeks after that your father would walk to the workhouse and pass food over the wall to feed all three of them. Every day he visited her. Looking back now I don't know how they got away with it. But they did.' Silas smiled nostalgically.

'There was only a handful of us then. My mother used to do all the fortune telling though it was a complete farce. Still, the locals used to lap it up. And then one day your mother and her sisters came to visit the camp. All three had to pretend they were going looking for work because it was the only way they could leave the workhouse. Anyway, they saw what my mother was up to and plain mocked her there on the spot. Mother was furious. Constance bragged about her and her sisters having the gift and mother demanded they prove it. That was the night of your mother's scrying. Right here in this tent, in front of everyone, your father appeared in the mirror. Driscoll got the women in the camp making your mother and her sisters their own clothes and the next day they took their uniforms back and signed themselves out of the workhouse. Your mother and father were married weeks later. Fate was what it was.'

Violet looked at Silas appraisingly. There was that word again. She reached up and ran a finger along the chain that held Josephine's ring. Fate. It was a blessing and a curse, raising expectations and delivering the most crushing of blows. No wonder her mother could not bring herself to talk about her father. No wonder that even the simple act of extinguishing a candle was so upsetting. They were more than husband and wife. They were soul-mates. The notion made the bitterness seem even more sweet.

'Mr Hammond, sorry to interrupt sir, but I wondered if I might have a word?' Violet and Silas looked up at Alfie who peeked through the entrance to the tent.'

'Oh, good lord, what has that daughter of mine done now?' He sighed heavily. 'She'll be the death of me that one.'

'Whatever it is, I'm sure it was done with good intentions.' Violet laughed as Silas made his way to the entrance. He looked over towards the fire and smiled.

'I think you should join your mother now.' He said warmly 'Solitude to mourn is important but one should never be left alone to mourn for too long.'

'Of course.' Violet grabbed her shawl and made her way out of the tent, taking a seat next to her mother in front of the fire. Clasping her mother's hand in her own they sat in contemplative silence, watching the residents take turns in rotating the hog as it cooked over the flames and Violet felt rather than heard her stomach rumble as the aroma seeped into the air around her promising a feast that was unrivalled. Roast pork, potatoes that had baked in the heat of the fire, beans with plums and candied fruits and cakes to follow. Her mouth watered at the thought. A row of flickering lights in the distance caught her attention as Edie's mother placed a cup of mead in hers and Constance's hands. So, the invite to the locals had been accepted with more than a little enthusiasm. The sight bought a smile to Violet's face.

'See?' Tillie Hammond pointed at the river of lanterns that slowly moved towards them. 'The plea for reconciliation has already been heard.' She laughed as she moved back towards the impromptu serving counter that was laden with mead and ale. 'Steel yourselves ladies. I think this may well be the party to end all parties!'

The celebrations that followed felt more like a reunion as the residents of the town and the camp came together as one once more, gorging themselves on food and drink as they sang and danced their way into the night and Violet was more than grateful for the distraction the evening provided. She had no idea how much time had passed as she grabbed her cup of mead from the table and slumped back on a hay bale next to her mother, feeling another tap on her shoulder before she had even had a chance to make herself comfortable.

'Give me a second, I just need to catch my breath.' She laughed as she whirled around to face Alfie and Edie.

'We have news.' Edie beamed, her hand wrapped tightly in Alfie's.

'Is it what I think it is?' Violet's mouth fell open as she looked from Edie to Alfie.

'It is! We are engaged!' Edie squealed, holding out her hand to reveal a delicate silver ring as Alfie put his arm around her protectively.

'Oh, this is wonderful news!' Violet jumped from her seat and wrapped her arms around them both. 'Truly, I am so happy for you I could burst!'

'We wanted to tell you before word spreads.' Alfie smiled as he glanced at Edie. 'I can imagine word spreading quite quickly.'

'As it should! Good news should always be shared! When will you be married do you think?'

'As soon as possible!' Edie said enthusiastically. 'I would become Mrs Banes tomorrow if I could.'

'You will need a dress. I'm sure the sisters would help, they are such wonderful seamstresses. And you will need flowers. I have many friends in the market who would create a beautiful bouquet for you.'

'Would you be my bridesmaid?'

'Nothing would give me greater pleasure.' Violet laughed, clasping her friend to her fiercely.

'Oh, I think someone is waiting to speak to you.' Edie peered over Violet's shoulder and Violet turned around to find Charles Lewis hovering nearby, his face flickering in and out of the darkness as the fire danced in front of him. Had he no shame? The man who could have helped so many when they were sick was now stood amongst them now as though he hadn't done a single thing wrong in his life. Violet forced a smile onto her face as she walked over to him, dragging Edie with her. They stopped directly in front of him and curtsied as one.

'Season's greetings, Mr Lewis and welcome to our little gathering, sir. Are you well?' Charles Lewis bowed stiffly.

'I am, Miss Davenport and season's greetings to you and yours. I wondered if we might be able to talk?'

'Of course.' Violet squeezed Edie's hand tightly before letting go and leading Charles away from the hubbub that surrounded the fire and towards the edge of the camp.

'Is there something wrong?'

'I won't beat around the bush, Miss Yardley.' Charles Lewis took a sip of his ale and glowered at Violet, his face all hard angles and sharp lines. 'Since your return, the number of customers I receive in my shop daily has more than halved.'

'And you think that's my fault?' Violet scoffed, her hands balling into tight fists.

'Not entirely.' Charles admitted. 'When I took over the business, I had no desire to acquaint myself with the residents of the town as my father had. I'll also admit that I used your departure to my advantage. I increased my prices safe in the knowledge that I was the sole source of medicinal aid. So, to answer your question, I am fully aware of the part that I have played in my own financial downfall. But I have a proposal which I think you will find interesting.' He nodded his appreciation as Alfie wordlessly refilled his cup and walked away. 'I would like to offer you a space in the shop.'

'You want to become partners?'

'No, the shop will still exist in my name only. At first, at least. I will have my accounts and you will have yours. I would deal with anything pharmaceutical and you would be responsible for herbal applications. Where you are unable to help or where you know that I may provide something more effective you will pass your customer on to me and I'll do the same for you if I believe a cheaper alternative is available. As part of the same agreement, I will reduce my prices back to those my father employed. What do you think, Miss Yardley? Do we have the beginnings of a deal?' Violet took a sip of her mead pensively.

'Why are you suggesting this Mr Lewis? What's in it for you?'

'I wish to restore the reputation of the shop and my family's name. I visited with my sister recently and well, let's just say it's not something I want a repeat performance of.' Charles shrugged. 'I know that reversing my own fortunes cannot happen without your assistance. I also know that you are very good at what you do. You are successful with your treatments so I know my reputation as a chemist is in safe hands and I know your popularity among the locals will ensure that they return to the store.'

'So, what's in it for me?'

'A chance to establish yourself as a serious trader, a warm place to work, a laboratory where can prepare your treatments in a more appropriate environment. Additionally, I won't charge you rent until we have established that this is a successful partnership for both of us, so you'll actually save the money you've been paying for a stall.'

'And what about Alfie?'

'He is welcome too. There is a storeroom we could adapt with minimal effort. We could combine all the services under one roof.' Violet rolled her cup across her bottom lip as she eyed Charles.

'I'll need to speak to Alfie as this is his business too. However, I am inclined to think that he would be open to the idea, especially now that winter is here. I'll get in touch over the next few days. Would that be acceptable?'

'I think that would be perfectly acceptable'. Charles at long last smiled and raised his mug in salutation, before taking a large gulp. 'I wish I could stay longer but unfortunately I have to return to work, although it looks like a fine celebration.'

'You are not working through Christmas night surely? Because you would be welcome to stay.'

'No, I am indeed working. Through choice though, not need.' Charles said animatedly. 'I have for the last few days been trawling through medical dictionaries trying to find some possible explanation for the condition that ails Joseph Davenport. All have led to failure thus far, unfortunately.'

'Then you may rest at ease because I think we have found the answer. You may have met Dr Tremaine. He arrived recently? He is the Davenport family's new physician.'

'They have a new physician? So, am I to assume that my services are no longer needed?' Charles's shoulders slumped.

'I'm sorry Mr Lewis, I didn't think.' Violet winced as Charles waved his hand dismissively.

'Please, don't concern yourself. I should not be surprised I suppose, given that neither my father or I have been able to help the family. To answer your question though, no, Miss Yardley. I have not had the good fortune to make his acquaintance yet.'

'I'm sure you will in the very near future. He will need to visit your store to place an order for certain medications. Bromine to be more specific.'

'Bromine? I don't understand. Bromine is used as a topical application for wounds. To eliminate or prevent gangrene.'

'And more recently it has been declared safe for ingestion and appears to be very successful. Dr Tremaine and I travelled to the university library in Cardiff recently and after some discussion we concluded that Mr Davenport most likely has pleurisy as a consequence of a pre-existing infection. One that is almost certainly contagious. If our assumptions are correct, I would suggest that it was Josephine Davenport who originally contracted the illness. That in itself wouldn't be a surprise given the charitable work she undertook in the asylums. Perhaps even your own father succumbed to it, given that he had regular contact with the deceased.'

'No, my father's demise was solely down to his excessive consumption of opium. I admit that I did not seek an autopsy, but I knew my father well enough to know he didn't require one. Pleurisy, you say?' Charles frowned. 'I'll admit that it was something I didn't consider. We had tried so many common treatments with Mrs Davenport it didn't even occur to me to look for the obvious, much as it embarrasses me to say it.'

'Do you know if she was treated for Pleurisy?'

'Without having her records in front of me I wouldn't be able to confirm either way. As for your assumptions regarding a pre-existing infection, well, on that front it would seem we do not think that differently. I admit I may not have spotted something as obvious as pleurisy, but I have for several days now been reading through a series of medical journals that investigate the cause and treatment of both tropical diseases and slow diseases. You see, I too have been thinking about the link to Josephine and the people she nursed, some of whom came from very distant shores. I remember marvelling at the way she cared for everyone when I returned from college.'

'So, you agree with us? In our conclusion?'

'I say there is certainly merit in it. But the use of bromine... I know how effective it was as a treatment in the war, but in times of war we take risks, Miss Yardley. Surely to use it as an oral treatment on a patient now when its efficacy is still being tested, I...I can't help but feel that to do so seems a little too ambitious.'

'Had we not exhausted all other avenues I would agree with you.' Violet sighed. 'If it helps, I assure you that Joseph will be fully informed of any proposed treatments and if he feels the risk is too great then we will of course continue to look elsewhere.'

'I'll admit I do find some comfort in that.' Dr Lewis confessed. 'I would also make sure to alert him to the risks of undergoing treatment when the root cause of his illness has not yet been diagnosed.' Charles shook his head uncertainly. 'Are you quite sure you are ready to begin treatment when there are still so many unanswered questions?'

'Indeed, we are!' Violet whirled round to find William Tremaine stood directly behind her. 'Sorry to interrupt. I should introduce myself.' He reached around to shake Charles's hand. 'I'm Dr Tremaine. It was I who completed the diagnosis, but I see you have some concerns?' Charles Lewis's cheeks flushed.

'Not concerns as such.' The usurped physician began to stutter. 'I'm just surprised that something as obvious hasn't been caught before now, though it would seem that I may have a part to play in that. I went looking for the obscure when perhaps I should have stayed closer to home.'

'It is unfortunate, but these things can happen.' William countered. 'What matters is we have the answer we seek and we can put an end to Mr Davenport's condition before it exacerbates any further. Besides which, it would also be very pleasing to see Miss Yardley and her family finally get the absolution they deserve. It is tragic, don't you think? The way they have suffered as a result of such hideous, unwarranted allegations?'

'Tragic indeed.' Charles Lewis blushed. 'To think I might have spared you such distress as well, had my father and I done our job properly.'

'You are working to do so now for which I am very grateful. Now, seeing as we are near to a conclusion why not stay and relax a little Dr Lewis? Perhaps take some time to mend a few bridges.' Charles looked around at the sea of faces that glared back at him in reply.

'Another time perhaps? I confess I am more eager to return to my study now than I was before.' Charles laughed awkwardly. 'I will continue to concentrate on the tropical diseases as a potential cause, if that does not offend you?'

'We would be poor scientists if we didn't continue to ask questions.' William laughed. 'Besides which you are simply looking for the answers that I too will be seeking in the morning. I may pop by first thing, if you don't mind. See if you have managed to establish anything?'

'You would be very welcome. Just make sure to bang the door heavily, I do enjoy a glass of port while I study. Helps to loosen the mind, I feel.'

'Well then I shall certainly bear that in mind. But enough about work, Violet, I would be greatly honoured if you would give me a guided tour of the camp? I confess my imagination has been running riot since we last spoke.'

'Of course!' Violet enthused. 'Mr Lewis, I'll come to see you in the next few days with my answer. And do try not to work too late into the night. It's Christmas. You should be relaxing!' She called back as she wove through the crowds, William following behind her.

'Christmas is a time for family.' Charles muttered, more to himself than those around him. He gazed around the throng of revellers for a friendly face, failing to find one amongst them which was no great surprise he supposed, given his recent behaviour and so he politely accepted a refill, which he drank in one sitting and began his way down the hill on unsteady legs back into town, still looking for answers.

*****

'I do feel a tad sorry for Charles.' Violet admitted. 'By the looks of it the way he has run the pharmacy has caused all manner of conflict within his family. It seems sad that anyone should be alone at Christmas.'

'He chose to go home, Violet' William reasoned with her. 'He could have stayed here if he had truly wanted to.' He smiled, doffing his hat and extending greetings to fellow revellers as they made their way through the crowd. 'He sits very much in the traditional medicine camp, doesn't he?'

'Less traditional than mine one might argue.' Violet laughed.

'Sorry, I didn't mean that to come across as a slight.' William blushed. 'No, I just meant, I imagine for example, without having even set foot in his shop that it is full of leeches to purify the blood?'

'Possibly.' Violet smiled cagily.

'I knew it. It is so frustrating to me. Medical professionals need to understand that the world is constantly moving forward. Diseases evolve and so the treatments we use need to evolve to keep up. Otherwise what would be the point?' He slowed as they rounded the fire, holding his hands out to absorb some of its warmth. 'Perhaps I should offer the hand of friendship. There may be things he can learn which will help him to advance his business.'

'I would suggest that he'd take any help that was on offer at the moment. He might say that the pharmacy is just a business but it's more than that to him and his family. It's their last link to their father. And whilst he hasn't said as such, I think perhaps he's lonelier than he'd like to admit, now he's there on his own.'

'Then we should do something to resolve that.' William turned in a slow circle and took in the entirety of the camp. 'So, this is where the magic happens.'

'I fear you may have imagined the camp to be somewhat more subversive and romantic than it actually is.' Violet laughed. 'In truth, it is nothing more than a ramshackle bunch of tents occupied by friends and family.'

'I think it is more than that.' William replied as he followed closely behind her. 'My reception here this evening, for example. I cannot recall a time when I, as a complete stranger, was greeted so warmly.'

'All are welcomed in the same way here. We have no airs and graces and we have nothing to prove to each other because we are equals.'

'Then this camp already has a place in my heart.' William held his hand to his chest. 'And it is a far cry from the hideous pretence that I have left behind.'

'Something is wrong at Ty Mawr?' Violet asked.

'Wrong is an understatement.' William came to a stop next to Violet outside of the main tent. 'They should be sitting there in hats and coats; the atmosphere is so frosty! Oh, I have an envelope for you. Two, actually.'

'Thank you.' Violet took the letters from him. It is that bad? At the house I mean?'

'Worse. Calissa and Edwin Davenport are trying to inject some humour into the evening but if you weren't aware that this was a celebration of Christmas, and of course Miss Parnell and Mr Davenport's engagement, you would think you had unwittingly wandered into a wake. I've never seen so many sour expressions in one room. They all look like they've been chewing lemons!'

'That doesn't sound particularly festive.'

'I've attended funerals that had more joviality.' William looked up at the large marquee. 'So where are we now? This looks like a circus tent.'

'This is my tent,' Violet explained. 'My mother and her sisters also live here and it's where we invite guests for readings and so on. It's also where I keep all of my herbs for making treatments. I thought it would be a good point to start the tour.' She pulled back the entrance to the tent. 'I should say, we've not long had a ceremony in here so if it smells like we have just snuffed out dozens of candles, well, it's because we've just snuffed out dozens of candles.' William laughed.

'Well, I shall take that under advisement.' He ducked as he followed her into the tent where the ladies of the coven sat staring at the flap in the tent as though they had been awaiting their arrival.

'Mother, Aunt Ruby, Aunt Flossie!' Violet exclaimed. 'Why are you not outside enjoying the celebrations?'

'Far too cold and noisy.' Flossie grumbled, her gaze fixed on William. 'I don't believe we've met?'

'Everyone, this is Dr William Tremaine. Dr Tremaine has recently come into the Davenport families employ. He is their physician now so he will be helping Joseph in future.'

'Oh, so you are the doctor who's come to save us all?' Ruby cackled.

'Aunt Ruby!' Violet turned to look at William. 'Sorry, she has no respect for anyone or anything.'

'Nonsense, her honesty is a breath of fresh air!' William said dismissively as Violet glared at her aunt. 'So, this is where you work?'

'It is.' Violet moved to the table where her case sat. 'This is where I prepare my treatments. And over here…' she walked to the table at the centre of the tent. 'This is where my mother and the sisters carry out their readings.'

'As in fortune telling?'

'Indeed, sir.' Flossie got up from her seat. 'I sense that you do not believe.' She hobbled over slowly and stood next to William, her head inclined as she assessed him. 'You are a man of science and it blinkers you to anything that doesn't exist within books.'

'Not at all true.' William rebuffed her. 'Whilst I align myself to the scientific world, I wouldn't be so ignorant as to disregard your beliefs and methods so readily.'

'Is that so?' Flossie pulled out a chair from underneath the table. 'Then take a seat, sir. I could read your palm if you'd like? Give you an insight into our, methods, as you say.'

'Am I required to cross yours with silver?' Flossie laughed.

'You are a friend of Violet's sir. I would not accept your money even if you offered it.'

'Aunt Floss! Dr Tremaine is a guest in our home!' Violet's cheeks flushed bright red. 'What on earth are you doing?'

'Do not upset yourself, Miss Yardley. I would be fascinated to hear what your aunt has to say about me.' He smiled at Violet as he sat in the chair that he had been designated while Flossie moved to sit opposite him.

'Give me your hand please, sir.' Placing her glasses at the tip of her nose, she reached out as William placed his own hand palm side up in hers.

'Now, do you see all these lines?' Flossie asked, peering over the top of her spectacles as William nodded. 'Each of these tells a tale of your future. This one here for example' She pointed to a line that begun under his little finger. 'This is your heart line. This is the one that tells me about the workings of your heart.'

'And what does the line tell you?'

'It is a long line, Dr Tremaine, but it is frayed at several points along the way. I would say that you are a stubborn individual when it comes to matters of the heart. You are a man who would love irrationally. You are a man who would change and adapt his life, sacrifice himself even, for love, if needs be.' William nodded thoughtfully.

'And what is this line?' William pointed to the long line that travelled the length of his hand, almost dividing his palm into two equal halves.

'Ah, well spotted Sir. This is the most important line in determining someone's future. This is the fate line.'

'Is that so? And what does it say?'

'You were a contradictory child, weren't you?' William stared at her warily, his eyes narrowing.

'I could be challenging I suppose. I was just very curious, I think.'

'Indeed. And your career choice. Your family disapproved.' She looked to William for confirmation. 'But I sense that they approve now.'

'Now I am able to assist them financially? Yes, I believe they now approve.' Flossie nodded thoughtfully.

'There is a fork in your fate line. So, for all your study and career choices, your path is still unclear. And there are still choices to be made. You find yourself wavering even though the path you should choose as is clear as the nose on your face.' She raised his hand, moving it towards him so he could see his palm more clearly. 'If you look closely, you'll see that one of the paths ends with a fork like symbol. This means imprisonment.'

'Imprisonment?' William looked up horrified.

'Not necessarily in the literal sense, Dr Tremaine.' Violet quickly moved to reassure him. 'It means you are likely to come across a restriction or barrier. That the road is limited in some way. It constricts you. Doesn't allow you to reach your potential.'

'I think he understands now!' Flossie cut in. 'Be quiet child!' The elder aunt shrieked at Violet before returning to William.

'You are faced with choices. Not all of which work in your favour. You have quite the dilemma in front of you.'

'My parents.' William said uncertainly. 'They wish me to return home, set up a local practice, find a nice girl and settle down. I wish for more. It has been a bone of contention for several years now.' Flossie nodded again as William smiled knowingly at Violet.

'There is much to be considered when one is contemplating the future, William and you are a strong man with a strong heart. Do not allow it to rule your head.' She placed William's hand back down on the table. 'I am tired now.' Flossie got up and made her way back to her seat by the stove. 'Violet, you may show Dr Tremaine your work another day. It is time to leave.'

'Of course.' Violet faltered. 'I can bring the case to the house if you'd like?'

'That sounds like the perfect solution.' William turned to face Violet's mother and aunts. 'It was a pleasure to meet you. And thank you for the reading. Most insightful.'

'You are welcome, sir.' Flossie said as William made his way to the entrance. 'Oh, and Dr Tremaine?'

'Yes, Ma'am?' William stopped, one foot outside the tent as Flossie looked up at him from her seat.

'The world is a big place that holds much wealth and many temptations. Bear that in mind.' She glanced between Violet and William then turned back to the fire. 'And for your sake, Dr Tremaine, choose the right path.'

'I will indeed ma'am.' Joseph bowed and turned to Violet. 'I believe I hear the opening bars of a polka Miss Yardley?' Violet chuckled.

'I believe you are correct, Dr Tremaine.'

'I confess it's not a dance I'm familiar with.'

'Then you may rest at ease.' Violet guided him from the tent. 'I can teach you everything you need to know.'

Chapter twenty-nine

'It makes no sense.'

'Hmm?' Violet peeked sideways to look at Edie who was absentmindedly playing with her hair.

'That.' Edie nodded towards the cards in Violet's hands. 'It makes no sense.' Violet looked back down at the pieces of correspondence, making a conscious effort not to screw them up there and then. Would that the situation be taken out of her control. That a sudden burst of rain might wipe away the words on the pages. Not that such an event would change the facts. Nor would it ease her nausea or the ache in her heart. 'I mean, the wedding invite, as much as it pains me to read it, I can understand it. You are friends of the family.' Violet eyed her cynically. 'Well, not friends as such.' Edie conceded. 'But I can understand that you might be invited, given your past. Asking you to be her bridesmaid? That seems utterly bizarre.'

Violet looked back at the wedding invite. An elaborate gold postcard, the words on it handcrafted in the finest script though most of them were a blur to her. She didn't care about the location or the time. Only the date stood out, emblazoned as it was in the centre of the card so that it stood out like a sore thumb. Saturday the second of January 1886. Seven days away. Seven days. Her stomach roiled again. There could be no denying it anymore.

She turned to the second piece of correspondence, a handcrafted missive from Calissa, wishing her the best for the Yuletide season and asking if she would stand alongside Amelia as one of her bridesmaids.

'It is a little strange I admit, but...'

'A little?' Edie scoffed. 'Establishing a friendship so that you might have someone to take tea with, that's one thing. But isn't there some kind of etiquette that determines who you might ask to be your bridesmaid? Surely Miss Parnell has better suited acquaintances than you?'

'Could you not find anything more insulting to say?' Alfie turned around from the front seat of the carriage. 'I'm sure that if you thought about it for a little longer…'

'Oh pish! You know exactly what I mean Alfie Barnes so stop trying to cause trouble! Vi, you two barely know each other and yet here she is asking you to participate in what will be one of the most important days of her life.' Violet sighed and placed the cards inside her bag where she could no longer see them.

'Think about it, Edie. Both of her sisters passed years ago. Most of her friends live in London so I can only assume that she has been let down at the last minute. It is an odd request though I'll grant you that.'

'And you are content to agree to it?'

'I didn't say that. But it is only one day after all and as you say, it is one of the most important days of her life. To say no would be spectacularly cruel.' The girls looked up as the cart came to a standstill.

'She will make my wedding look like a pauper's affair.' Edie grumbled.

'It is true your wedding will be nothing like hers.' Violet admitted. 'But that does not mean that your wedding is the poorer cousin. Hers may have the glamour and couture designs, but it will not have what yours will. It will not have genuine happiness and it will not have love and truth.' Violet jumped down from the carriage before Edie could question her. 'I would rather be wearing a hessian sack and be stood next to you as you marry Alfie than I would be drinking champagne and celebrating the perfect match between the higher echelons of society.

'I wouldn't say that too loudly. You could end up in a sack yet.' Edie winced. 'What is that noise?' Violet turned towards the house and the high-pitched screams that rang from it.

'That,' Violet sighed 'is Miss Parnell.'

'Really? It sounds as though someone's strangling a cat in there!'

'Alternatively, the dressmaker has arrived and they haven't quite met expectation. I should rescue them before she does any lasting damage. To think the poor girl left her family on Boxing day for this.' Violet lifted her bag from the footwell of the carriage. 'Wish me luck.'

'I think you're going to need more than luck.' Edie said as the screaming increased in volume and pitch. 'We'll be back for you at sunset.' Violet watched as the carriage sped away from the front of Ty Mawr and turned to look up at the front of the house where Joseph stood watching from his bedroom window. He looked as he had when his mother had died she thought; all notion of happiness a distant memory, though his face was, she supposed, a perfect mirror of her own expression right now. As the door opened and Winnie curtsied in anticipation she stared at Joseph for a moment longer before she made her way up the stairs wondering how in hell they had gotten here.

*****

'Miss Yardley, I am so glad you are here! Will you please explain to the dressmaker that this is not what I asked for? She does not appear to understand basic English!'

Calissa whirled on her the moment she entered her room and Violet felt herself pale at the sight in front of her, unable to breath, let alone offer

258

consolation. The pale gold bridal gown she wore was a twist on a polonaise design. Panels of cream lace swirled down from the tight bodice revealing the gold silk skirt underneath and there were trails of rose gold flowers that flowed down from the edge of the bodice to the bottom of the dress, creating a wreath of blossoms around the hem. The same flowers were affixed to a ruched panel at the top of the bodice and she wore simple pale cream gloves that left the merest hint of flesh on view where the capped sleeves ended.

'Miss Parnell, you look utterly enchanting. What on earth could possibly be the wrong with the dress?'

'There should have been more layers of lace! I'm sure I asked for more!' Calissa protested, her cheeks fuchsia pink.

'This was the pattern that we discussed ma'am.' The dressmaker stood to one side, making sure that each of the flowers was fixed securely. 'When we showed you the dresses you said that aside from minor adjustments to the sizes you required no alterations. To either design. Maybe you recall the head seamstress telling you how relieved she was? She said that had you requested anything intricate we would never have been able to deliver the order on time. Not with Christmas an' all. I have the order here with me. See?' Calissa scowled at the piece of paper that the dressmaker produced from her needlework bag and looked away.

'I am certain that I asked for more intricate layers than this. I would not have asked for anything so ordinary.'

'Ordinary?' Violet baulked. 'The dress is stunning!'

'Are you doubting me, Miss Yardley?'

'With respect, I am suggesting that you have the jitters because you want this dress to be perfect and you are worried that it is not. I can assure you that it is and you look truly beautiful.'

'Do you think so?'

'I wouldn't say it if I didn't think it.' Violet replied, grateful that this at least was something that she could be honest about. Calissa took a deep breath and returned to the mirror.

'Perhaps you are right. Perhaps I am overreacting.' She turned to the dressmaker, her bottom lip caught between her teeth. 'I apologise. I shouldn't have treated you so harshly.'

'Do not apologise ma'am. Believe me, I have heard much worse in my time.' She got up and smiled at Violet. 'And I am very pleased that you like the dress miss, as I have another one here for you. It is almost identical, save for the floral details.'

'You have one of these for me?' Violet felt her mouth fall open.

'Of course, silly!' Calissa laughed, as though the last few minutes had never happened. 'And one for Amelia as well. Amelia has already had hers fitted so will just require a final check the day before. With yours, I based the measurements on the ball gown, but I see by your own dress that you have lost a little weight so some alteration may be required.'

'So you bought this dress specifically for me?'

'Well I didn't buy it for anyone else.' Calissa replied, turning and staring into the mirror as her skirt swirled around her. 'Come. Miss Taylor will see to you now. Oh wait, Taylor! And you are a seamstress! How ridiculous is that? Has anyone ever told you before?' Calissa snorted and laughed like a drain as the dressmaker pulled Violet's dress out of a long cover bag.

'No, ma'am.' She said wearily as she walked over to Violet 'No-one has ever pointed that out to me before. You are too funny.' She rolled her eyes as she showed Violet her dress. 'Shall I help you on with now this ma'am?'

*****

By the time Violet came back down the stairs she was exhausted, having been mentally and physically prodded and poked to within an inch of her life. The sun was already starting to set as she lay her bag down on the chaise longue and waited for Edie and Alfie to arrive, grateful for the few moments of silence before the barrage of questions that she knew was coming her way.

'Miss Yardley?' Violet turned at the sound of William Tremaine's voice.

'Dr Tremaine' Violet smiled.

'Please, call me William. I've been looking out for you.'

'Oh, something I can help you with?'

'I very much doubt it. I wonder if you could come with me please? You can leave your bag there. This will only take a couple of minutes.'

'Of course.' Violet made her way over to him, smiling as he held the door to the lounge open for her.

Inside, there was barely room to move. Old man Davenport stood alongside Mr Parnell who in turn stood next to Joseph. In front of them stood two police officers and a man in a black suit who was clearly attached to the constabulary in some way.

'Don't worry, Violet. You've done nothing wrong. The police have a few questions, that's all.' William put a reassuring hand on her arm.

'Miss Violet Yardley?' The man in the black suit made his way over to her.

'Yes.' Violet couldn't help but look around the room and the pairs of eyes that were on her now. All except Joseph's who stared not at her but at the hand that was still at her elbow.

'I just have a few questions for you. Same as I have asked all the others in the room so nothing to worry about.'

'Would you like to sit, Violet? Perhaps you'd like some tea?' William whispered in her ear. Violet shook her head timidly as Joseph walked over to the window, his back fixed firmly towards her.

'No, I'm good here, thank you, William.'

'Very well.' The detective cleared his throat. 'As I said, just a couple of questions. With regards to a Mr Charles Lewis. I believe you know him?'

'Of course.' Violet frowned. 'He's the local pharmacist. Why?'

'I believe he came to your home on Christmas night?'

'Briefly, yes. Most of the village did. We were having a yuletide celebration as we do every year.' The detective wrote something in his notebook with a small stubby pencil that looked as if it had seen its best days.

'And would you say Mr Lewis was in good spirits?'

'By 'in good spirits', I assume you mean was he drunk?' Violet shrugged. 'I honestly couldn't say. He certainly had a couple of drinks while he was with us, but I couldn't tell you if he'd had anything to drink before then. If he had he did not appear so drunk as to be incapacitated if that is what you are asking? He also said he was looking forward to a glass of port when he returned home, though I suspect that was an understatement.' Violet fixed her gaze on William as the detective furiously wrote additional notes in his pad.

'And aside from that, did he say what his plans were for the evening?'

'He said he had work to do. He said he was going back to the laboratory he has on the premises. He wanted to continue working on something for Mr Davenport. Joseph Davenport, that is.' Joseph turned at the sound of his name, confusion unfurling in his expression.

'I see. And can I ask what time that was?'

'I'm sorry, I have no idea.'

'I left you at about one in the morning.' William offered. 'And I assume a good couple of hours had passed between his leaving and mine.'

'That would seem sensible.' Violet agreed, trying to ignore the way that Joseph stared at her, all hardness and accusations. 'So, I would guess at around ten, possibly eleven, but that really is only a guess. Can I ask what this is about?' The detective closed his notebook and placed it back in his pocket.

'There was a fire at the pharmacy in the early hours of the morning. It started at the back of the shop. The pharmacy was gutted as was the butchers next door. Mercifully, Mr Rees, the butcher and his family escaped unharmed.'

'And Mr Lewis?' Violet was suddenly grateful for the hand that supported her.

'We found Mr Lewis a couple of hours ago.' The detective said. 'It would appear that he was trapped by falling timber. I'm sorry to be the bearer of bad tidings miss, but I'm afraid Mr Lewis is dead.'

Chapter thirty

'And there you have it, Dr Tremaine. That is everything you need to know.' Violet reached forward and re-aligned the small bottles of plant extracts in front of her, delicately turning them one by one between thumb and forefinger so that the labels all faced forwards. Better to stare at the phials than at her counterpart who sat opposite her, watching her intently as he wrote the last of her instructions into a small leather notebook, the nib of his fountain pen scratching the page and breaking the silence between them.

The library at Ty Mawr was nothing like as grand or light as the one she had visited in the university but that didn't mean she revered it any less. The walls were painted a deep mahogany and covered in large oil painted portraits. Of ancestors, Violet supposed. They were sat at a large oak table and on the opposite side of the room there was an old, cracked leather couch that was smothered in large, feather cushions. Bookcases made from the same wood were full of works of fiction and leather-bound encyclopaedia, though there were some conspicuous gaps which were haphazardly distributed across the shelves, most likely attributable to the stacks of books that were strewn around Joseph's room. For a fleeting moment, she wondered where he was and stopped herself mid-thought. It was none of her business, she reminded herself.

'This really has been most helpful.' William replaced the lid of his fountain pen, leaving the book open to allow the ink to dry. 'I have already placed the order for the bromine at a chemist in the next town from here, but just in case there is a delay in its delivery it is comforting to have an alternative solution. I shall ride out and collect what I need today.'

'I would be happy to help out in the meantime, if it's needed. It really is no bother.'

'Thank you, but, no.' William said awkwardly. 'Miss Parnell has paid me to take up this role so I feel obliged to honour that agreement. The gesture is greatly appreciated, though.'

'I understand. Well, let me know if you do need me.' Violet picked up her medicine chest and placed it on the table between them, picking up the small glass bottles one by one and delicately laying them in the velvet lined rack.

'I find myself envying you and this life of yours, Violet.' Violet glanced up at William as he looked out of the library window towards the mountains and the grey clouds that roiled above them. 'To live such a simple life, based on instinct and the world around you. I spend so much time seeking solutions to the most complex of problems and I often find that I am rewarded with greater doubts than I am satisfaction. There is always someone out there who has evidence that contradicts my own and which is every bit as compelling.' Violet closed the case and placed it on the floor by her feet.

'I have many questions for which I do not have solutions, William. Moreover, the answers which are handed me are oftentimes more unsettling than the dilemmas themselves. As for this peace you seek, I wonder if any life could be truly peaceful? None of us are ever truly satisfied, are we?'

'I would suggest you are closer than most.' William smiled. 'And certainly wiser. You are all honesty and goodness, Violet. If anyone deserves peace it is you.'

'It is kind of you to say so.' Violet smiled. 'Now, if only you could tell me how I might achieve it.' William leaned forward, his elbows coming to rest on the table as he rested his chin on his steepled fingers.

'That would depend on your dilemma. Perhaps I may be able to help.'

'Thank you, but in this instance, I think only time will provide the solutions I seek.'

'As you wish.' William regarded her thoughtfully as she sank back in her seat.

'Ah, there you are!' Joseph came bounding into the room, his smile stretching from ear to ear. He was wearing his thick black jumper, his trousers and boots covered in muck and straw. 'I just spotted Berkeley in the stables. Did you ride here alone?'

'Joe.' Violet smiled and bowed her head in greeting. 'No, I was accompanied here by Alfie and my mother. They've gone on to town in the cart. I believe Gwilym is escorting me home.'

'I am pleased. One can't be too careful.' Joseph smiled and Violet was instantly taken back to the night he had admonished her for being so foolish as to walk back to the camp alone, so soon after Aggy had lost her life only yards away. The same night they had… Heat flushed her cheeks as Joseph walked over to where Violet sat and took an apple from the fruit bowl that was only inches away from her, so close she could smell the coldness of winter on him. He dropped down into an armchair opposite her and oh, how every inch of his face said that he knew exactly what she was thinking. And how he relished in it. 'I've been with the farrier. I asked if he might re-shoe Berkeley while he is here. I hope that's alright?'

'Of course!' Violet replied. 'Let me know how much I need to reimburse you.'

'Nonsense. I should have had it done before I gave him to you.' Joseph took a bite of the apple. 'So, are you here for the final fitting?'

'I am, yes. I also popped over to speak to William beforehand. To talk through the homeopathic treatments that I prepared for you. William needed more information.'

'Did he?'

'I did, but your timing is most opportune.' William smiled at Joseph. 'Violet and I were just pondering life and it got me thinking about the future.'

'It did?' Joseph said suspiciously, looking between William and Violet.

'I was wondering if now might be the perfect opportunity to divulge our plans?'

'Oh! Of course!' Joseph placed the apple down onto a silver coaster and leant forward, resting his knees on his elbows. 'I can't particularly take the credit for this if I'm honest, Vi…'

'And in taking the credit, I have to admit to eavesdropping.' Violet frowned at William.

'Neither of you are making any sense.'

'Allow me to explain.' William got up from the table and began pacing the length of the room. 'When I came to the camp the other night, you'll recall you were talking to Mr Lewis when I arrived.'

'I was, yes. Why?'

'I confess, I was there for a short time before I introduced myself. At first, you were so engrossed in conversation you did not see me. I felt as though I would be intruding on something of a sensitive nature if I interrupted.'

'So, you listened in instead?'

'I'm ashamed to admit it, but yes, I listened in instead. It was only when my name was mentioned that I saw an opening to join the conversation.'

'I see. And why are we talking about this now?'

'Because I overheard you and Mr Lewis talking about a partnership.'

'Dr Tremaine mentioned it to me this morning at breakfast and in conclusion, we came up with a proposal.' Joseph interjected. 'What with the fire and poor Mr Lewis's passing. You know we need that facility in our town, Vi. We need somewhere residents can go to receive medical help and advice.'

'You're not thinking that I could take Mr Lewis's place surely? Violet looked between William and Joseph. 'Gentlemen, I am not qualified to hold such a position.'

'I am.' William suggested. 'I could take on the role of physician and run a surgery and you, Violet would run the pharmacy downstairs, with supervision, naturally. I think you would take to the role very quickly and you could still prepare your usual treatments. And you did say you were keen to advance your knowledge. Perhaps you could take classes at the university in Cardiff. Within no time I think you could find yourself with a very prosperous career. What do you think?'

'I think I am at a loss for words.' Violet said hesitantly.

'Mr Davenport and I popped down to town early this morning after breakfast. The damage to the current property is too great to consider re-establishing a business there any time soon but there are several vacant commercial buildings that we could make a start in almost immediately. Some of which have sufficient room for you to take up residence there should you wish to? I fancy I would look to purchasing one of the quaint little cottages nearer the river.'

'Move away from the camp?' Violet frowned.

'You said yourself the camp would likely move on at some point.' Joseph said quietly. 'You would need somewhere warm and secure and what could be better than to be under the roof of your own premises?'

'The camp is moving on?' William stopped pacing and turned to Violet. 'I apologise, Miss Yardley. When I suggested this, I was under the impression that your family had taken up a more permanent residence. It never occurred to me that I might be asking you to leave your family.'

'We are a nomadic folk.' Violet explained. 'We may not move far but it is in our blood to travel to new locations. Though nothing has been agreed yet.' She glowered at Joseph, all three of them turning towards the sound of heels striking against the wooden parquet floor in the hall and breaking the sudden silence.

'Dr Tremaine, are you finished with my friend now? The dressmaker is waiting on her arrival to finish the last-minute alterations and you are holding us all up.' Calissa stood in the doorway, her arms folded, her irritation barely masked. 'Joseph, you look a complete state! Why, you look like you belong in the camp with Miss Yardley!'

'This is my job, Calissa.' Joseph spoke slowly through gritted teeth. 'And there is nothing shameful in being associated with Violet or her family.'

'You are a landowner not a labourer! You must find someone to do it for you. I will not have my husband looking like…'

'Like what, Calissa?'

'Like a filthy beggar!' Calissa shrieked, her face turning puce as she stared Joseph down. 'I apologise, Miss Yardley. I was not criticising you, but you must understand, there are certain standards one must keep if one is to attain respect in society.'

'And I am not offended.' Violet said, her words even and measured in tone. 'Seeing as I am neither filthy, nor am I a beggar.'

'Sorry to interrupt. Dr Tremaine, your horse is ready.' Calissa turned back to the open doorway to find Gwilym stood behind her.

'Thank you, Gwilym. I need to get to town to collect the suits for tomorrow and fulfil the list that Violet has furnished me with.' William stood from his seat, bowing down to whisper in Violet's ear. 'And not a minute too soon if you ask me.' He picked up his notebook, blowing on the freshly inked pages before he closed it and placed it in the pocket of his jacket. 'I look forward to seeing you tomorrow, Violet'

'And I you, William.' Violet said as William made his way past Calissa, only minimally acknowledging her existence as he slipped through the door.

'Gather your things, Miss Yardley. I will see you upstairs.' Calissa fired a condescending glare at Joseph and disappeared from sight, her footsteps fading away as she retreated back to her room.

'Vi...' Joseph rose from his seat and held his hands out in front of him, a feeble attempt to appease the storm he knew was his heading his way

'You have created this deal with Dr Tremaine to keep me here. How dare you!' Violet hissed as Joseph moved towards her.

'No! I did it for you! Did you not say that he is the man you saw in the mirror? You said that this is the man you are fated to be with. If I cannot be with you, then I would at least see you happy.'

'Happy? You think that this is what would make me happy? My life is not yours to control, Joe!'

'I'm not trying to control you - I'm trying to help you!'

'You are lying, Joseph Davenport. It is written all over your face! Now, you remember this. I will decide where I live and who makes me happy and who I wish to spend my life with.' Violet shook her head. 'Put an end to this agreement Joe. If you don't, I will.' She grabbed her bag and stormed from the room. He would see her wed to someone else so easily? Even go as far as to create a situation that might put the wheels in motion? The thought left a bitter taste in her mouth, strengthened her resolve. She would see the wedding through tomorrow and then she would leave. There could be no other way.

*****

'You look perfect, Miss Yardley.'

Violet stared at herself in the mirror. The dress was indeed exquisite, identical in cut and shape to Calissa's, only the lack of floral decoration making them distinguishable from each other. She stood as still as a statue as the dressmaker made some final adjustments to the hem.

'It is a beautiful dress.' Violet admitted as she spun on her toes. 'And if feels so luxurious to wear.'

'Well, if one cannot be luxurious on one's wedding day, then, when can one?' Calissa smiled dreamily as she moved to the padded seat in front of her dressing table.

'Miss Parnell, I don't wish to offend you, but there is something I must ask.'

'You want to know why I have asked you to be bridesmaid?' Calissa twisted around on her seat. Violet chewed on her lip nervously.

'Yes. It's not that I'm not grateful…'

'Nonsense. I'm glad you raised the subject. I had intended to myself. The truth is, I did it for Amelia.'

271

'Amelia?'

'I fear she sees me as a cuckoo in the nest and I know she thinks very highly of you.'

'So, you want me there to what, exactly? Convince her otherwise? Not that I'm sure she thinks that way in the first place.' Calissa smiled knowingly.

'I think we both know that is not true. I know I would feel the same if a relative stranger came in and usurped me in my own home.'

'So, what do you want me to say?'

'Nothing specific.' Calissa turned back to the dressing table and lifted her tiara and veil from it, watching herself in the mirror as she delicately placed it on her head, the panels of lace flowing down to the floor around her. 'But if there's some way you can convince her that I'm not a complete ogre, I would be truly grateful.' She rose from her seat and stood behind Violet as the dressmaker got up and started to pack her bags. 'But enough of that. I sense that you hold Dr Tremaine in high regard. Am I correct?'

'He seems a good man,' Violet turned away from the full-length mirror and nervously paced to the centre of the room. 'but I cannot say I know him well enough to hold him in as high a regard as you seem to imply. Our interactions relate mostly to Joseph and his treatment and therefore I know little of his background, or his family. Save from snippets I have picked up in conversation.' Violet replied, thinking of William's interactions with her aunt at Christmas.

'Then allow me to indulge you a little if I may?' Calissa removed the veil and draped it across the bed, leaving it to the dressmaker to pick it up without a second thought. 'William Tremaine was still studying medicine when I met him. I had gone to a ball in the city. My first ball and I was very excited!

William was there with his Uncle and Aunt. From the moment they saw him my friends did not approve. They were convinced he was a wrong'un, you know. They were more concerned by his family rather than by the man himself'

'Why were they concerned by his family?'

'Because they had no wealth behind them. They lived comfortably, but they were not considered to be the sort of family that one would aspire to making connections with. I think my friends thought William a charlatan. Out to take my family for all we were worth. But I could see that William was a diamond in the ruff. I could see that he was a good man, even if they could not and I think that you see that too.'

'He is certainly easy to talk to and I find his love of literature and the sciences fascinating.' Violet admitted as she turned back to the mirror.

'I also see a particular fondness in William's regard.' Calissa smiled. 'I have known him long enough to recognise when he is distracted.'

'You are suggesting that he is distracted by me?' Violet laughed awkwardly. 'I think you must be mistaken.'

'No, I am never mistaken, Miss Yardley. All I ask if that you do not return his feelings, please do not indicate otherwise. William is a good friend and I would hate to lose him.' She walked over to stand behind Violet and began twisting her hair into the most elaborate chignon. 'But enough of this.' She smiled. 'Now that the dress is ready, how do you think we should do your hair? I think we should send for Winnie.'

*****

As dusk turned to night, Violet bid farewell to Calissa and hurriedly made her way back down the stairs, leaving Winnie to fuss around the bride-to-be. Recoiling at the sound of William's voice and Edwin's replying laughter she gingerly opened the door and dashed from the house, flying down the steps and quickly making her way to the stables, her head pounding, her nerves hanging by a single, rapidly fraying thread. Enough. This was too much. It was too much.

She ran into Berkeley's stall and dropped to the stone floor beneath her, slamming down onto her knees with a sickening crack, her chest thumping wildly as though her heart were trying to beat its way out of her chest. The wooden door slammed shut behind her as she reached up with trembling fingers, ripping out the pins that held her curls in place, the back of her neck hot and damp to touch, a stark contrast to the night air around her. Hysteria. An attack of nerves, she rationalised. She had seen her mother suffer similar, usually on the anniversary of her father's death. Her fists clenched, she pounded the stone floor, pain shooting through her hand and up her arm. Damn him. Damn her father for abandoning them. For breaking her mother's heart. Damn Joseph and his wedding and his plans for her. Damn Edwin for forcing this situation on them. Damn them all!

She inhaled sharply, pushing herself back onto her feet and reached up to wearily placed a calming hand on Berkeley who stood by unflinchingly. Soon. All of this would be over soon. And the camp would leave and she would be free. But that was the problem, wasn't it? That was why her mind and her body behaved as it did now. Because she didn't want to be free. This was not the life she would choose for herself. What was it Aggy had said? Want and need speak to different hearts. Standing in the stables as Berkeley rested his head on her shoulder, she wasn't sure if that was true. But then, it was what it was and no number of tantrums was going to change that. As the fluttering in her chest began to subside, she reached down and began fishing inside her bag for her cloak.

'Oh, no. No, no, no, no, no…' Violet pulled out the folded bundle of cloth from the bag. Not her cloak but the work clothes that she wore when she was labouring in the camp with the men. Her heart sank as she held the shirt and trousers up against the dim lamp light, and then it was though someone had lifted the veil from her eyes. She froze, casting her gaze between the stall where she stood and the house and when she was convinced she was alone she frantically began removing her gown. In seconds, the skirt and blouse were pooled in a heap on the floor and she was ripping off the corset that restricted her breathing and the petticoats that hindered her every move and she was slipping into her trousers. Made of black faded linen they were tight at the waist, billowing out to a wider cut at the hem. Enough material that they were not overly disclosive, little enough material that in certain circles they would most likely have been considered utterly scandalous. Oh, if the ladies of society could see her now. They would probably need smelling salts. Minutes later the top half of her outfit had been replaced by a linen shirt that offered no warmth but the freedom it gave in return was invaluable.

She removed her side saddle from Berkeley and grabbed Josephs instead, studiously strapping it to the mare and once she had stuffed her clothes into her bag she reached out and stole one of the carrots from the sack for the horse.

'How about we go for a proper ride?' She whispered as she slipped the reigns through her bag's straps and tied it in place and opened the gate to Berkeley's stable.

'Let's get out of here.' She walked the horse out and climbed on his back, resting the bag on her lap and gently steering him towards the main track that led from the house, the evening mist already turning to a light rain that she knew would soak her before she got home. Even that seemed appealing right now. Cleansing, even. She lifted her head towards the clouds, the simple sensation of rain on her face inviting her smile to return.

When Berkeley faltered she lowered her gaze and instinctively pulled on his reins, bringing him to a slow standstill. There was a lamp in the distance, the light from it strong enough to create a swirl of shadows below the trees. Not strong enough to reveal its keeper. Violet watched as the speck of light slowed and stopped, the hairs on the back of her neck starting to prickle. There would be no need for anyone to be hanging back so far from the house, especially not at this time of night.

'Violet, is that you?' A familiar voice broke through the mist that hung heavily under the trees.

'Joe? What on earth are you doing out here?' Violet exhaled through pursed lips, willed her heart to calm as she slowly made her way towards Joseph, her body swaying in the saddle. He was dressed more smartly now, as one would for dinner. In one hand, he held a storm lantern, in the other he carried a large bag.

'I'd recognise Berkeley's gait anywhere. And what do you mean, what am I doing? What are you doing out here on your own?'

'I was going to ride across the field. Go over the bridge close to the far side of the camp. It's safe enough that way. I was supposed to get Gil to escort me but, I just…I needed some time by myself.'

'Vi…' Joseph grimaced. 'Why will you not listen?'

'You didn't answer my question.' Violet ignored him. 'What are you doing out here? And where are you going with that bag?' Joseph scanned the track around him.

'There's no-one else here. I've just left the stables and it's deserted up there.'

'Very well. Here, take the bag for me.' Joseph passed the heavy canvas bag to Violet and took the reins from her before he started leading Berkeley down the track, the light from the lantern making the branches around them glisten. 'Rather than my telling you, perhaps it would be easier if I just show you.'

Chapter thirty-one

There was a companionable silence between Joseph and Violet as they slowly wandered away from the house towards the road that led into town, though Violet wondered how long it would last. There were so many things that needed to be said, none of them pleasant, but time was running out on them now. When they were only yards from the junction he tugged gently on the horse's reins, guiding them down a narrow track.

'This is the path to the grounds-keeper's lodge, isn't it?'

'It is.'

'I don't understand.' Violet hunched down to avoid the branches that hung over her head. 'Why are you needed here at this time of night?'

'I'm not. The property is empty.'

'I'm sorry, I'm not following.'

'Father thinks the groundsman is in residence, but the truth of the matter is, I've sent him back to his family for the winter. He hasn't been here for several weeks now.' They emerged from the tree-lined path into a wide-open field, any shelter from the rain now gone as Violet looked towards the simple stone structure in the distance and the warm yellow glow that emanated from its only window.

'There is clearly someone in there.'

'Not right now, there isn't.' When they reached the cottage, she climbed down from the horse as Joseph secured him to a nearby tree.

'I'm sorry boy, I won't be long I promise.' Violet reached out to smooth Berkeley's forehead. 'You will still get your run.'

'I hope you intend to keep that promise, because he will not forget.' Violet heard rather than saw Joseph smile.

'I never make a promise I cannot keep.' Violet replied, instantly regretting her tone. 'Sorry. That came out more harshly than I meant.'

'But no less harshly than I deserve. Come with me.' Violet followed close behind him, waiting silently as he made his way into the bungalow and held the door open for her. 'Please. Come in.'

The inside of the Grounds-keeper's cottage had seen better days. A roaring fire dominated the wall at the far end, the surrounding hearth blackened with soot and the stone floor was cracked in several places, some of it covered by a threadbare rug. The furniture, sparse as it was, looked like it was about to disintegrate at any moment. At the farthest end from the fireplace there was a poorly made bed and a side table on which stood an unlit candle and a small clock. There was a table along one wall which was covered in books and maps and near the door there was a small dresser that held a range of odd pieces of kitchen equipment, china and cutlery. Either side of the fireplace sat two high backed chairs with a small round table between them. Violet slowly made her way towards the dining table and leafed through the books on it. The books that she had seen in Joseph's room.

'Joe, are you living in here?'

'I retire here after dinner most nights.' Joseph leaned back against the door and watched nervously as Violet thumbed the pages of a medical encyclopaedia. 'I have for the last few weeks. I simply cannot bare to be in that house any longer than necessary. What with Calissa screaming at the staff for no discernible reason and Amelia barely talking to me. We haven't had a single polite conversation since the engagement was announced.'

'So, you hide in here?'

'Not hide, exactly.' The corners of his lips turned up into a grin as Violet turned to look at him disbelievingly. 'Alright, perhaps I am hiding here. But in all seriousness, can you blame me?'

'Not particularly.' Violet admitted. 'I take it you are doing the Grounds-Keeper's work?'

'What little work there is during the winter.'

'Which is why you were so muddy earlier.'

'Correct again.'

'But, Mr Davenport, you are the lord of the manor, not a filthy beggar!' Violet's hands flew to her mouth in mock indignation.

'Don't remind me.' Joseph sneered. He made his way to the small dresser, upending the contents of the bag on to the small makeshift counter.

'You smuggle food over here?' Violet laughed.

'I wait until cook has left for the day and then I raid the pantry.' He stacked the food parcels neatly. 'Would you like some mead?' Joseph held up a dark brown bottle that Violet instantly recognised.

'That's a bottle from the camp! You still have that?'

'It's the last one. I confess I have been drinking it sparingly. Gil finished off the ale a long time ago, as you can imagine. So, can I interest you in a cup? We don't stretch to anything as fancy as glasses out here.'

'A cup would do just fine, thank you.'

'Excellent.' Joseph moved around the smallholding like a whirlwind, all nerves and bad co-ordination as he pulled two chipped, faded teacups from hooks on the edge of the dresser and filled them with mead.

'Here, come sit by the fire and warm up.' Joseph placed the cups on the small table and waited behind one of the chairs as Violet walked towards him. 'Violet, what on earth are you wearing?'

'Oh.' Violet looked down at her outfit. 'These are my work clothes. I wasn't expecting to see another soul this evening. I thought they'd be more comfortable to ride in. I've borrowed your saddle by the way, I hope you don't mind.'

'But you're wearing trousers.'

'That's very astute of you, Joe. Tell me, are you also finding out for the first time that women have legs?' Violet said boldly, a vain attempt at masking her embarrassment as she sat down in the full glare of the fire, crossing one ankle over the other as was expected, but what use was such an attempt at etiquette when the material of her trousers was wrapped so tightly around her legs that they appeared to be no more than a second skin and the damp shirt she wore clung to her frame, the white material almost transparent where it grazed her flesh. Mortified, she glanced up at Joseph, his eyes wide as his gaze travelled the length of her. Only when she caught his eye did he have the courtesy to look away.

'Sarcasm does not become you, Violet Yardley.' Joseph cleared his throat as he handed her cup of mead and sat down in the chair opposite her and watched her thoughtfully. 'You do not look comfortable, perched there as you are.'

'That's because I'm not.' Violet snorted. 'You should try sitting with your back upright all the time and your ankles crossed. It really is very uncomfortable. If I were at home, I not be sitting like this, I can assure you.'

'Then relax, Violet! Pretend you are at home! For goodness sake, we are friends, aren't we? Good friends I hope, even with everything else going on. It's not as if I'm about to judge you for the way you sit, is it?' Violet took a long drink of her mead.

'Very well.' She reached down, untied her boots and kicked them off then swung her legs to one side, bringing both feet up onto the chair so that her knees were resting against her chest and the warmth of the fire licked at her toes.

'Does that feel better?'

'Much.' Violet all but purred at him. Joseph smiled as Violet took another sip of her mead, raising her cup in salutation as he did the same.

'I don't want to start an argument, Joe, but this is something that needs to be said. You know that I cannot stay, don't you?'

'I know.' Joseph said reluctantly. 'It's just, you said you were leaving and I panicked. And I know I had no right to do so, but I was scared that I was going to lose you and I saw a way that I might stop it from happening, as illogical as it was. Because I'm going to lose you anyway and that is my fault and my fault alone. I'll speak to William, persuade him to change his mind. I am sorry, Vi.'

'It is not your fault Joe. Circumstances have bought us to this place. We are not here by design. But thank you for offering to speak to William. I would hate to mislead him.'

'You didn't mislead him, Vi, I did. At least that is something I can put right.'

'I am sorry to hear about you and Amelia.' Joseph turned his gaze to the fire.

'What is there to say? She will not forgive me for the engagement. And why should she? I cannot forgive myself. Amelia and I used to talk about everything. It was only ever her, Gil and Aggy I knew I could trust. And you of course. She knew I intended to propose to you before you left.'

'You were planning to propose?' The words caught in Violet's throat as Joseph shifted uncomfortably, suddenly aware of the magnitude of his confession.

'And I told Amelia as much. When you returned, she was so overjoyed, she would talk of nothing else. You were the sister she'd always wanted. Now she feels I have taken that from her, giving her instead someone she cannot stand. She said I was turning into father. All business and no heart. My greatest fear is that I will never get her back. That she will never forgive me.'

'Perhaps if you explained?'

'Tell her that I am marrying someone I do not love in order to keep a roof over her head? No, it is not her burden to bear. I would not want that for her.'

'She has no idea how lucky she is.' Violet shook her head slowly. 'No idea at all.'

'I'm so glad I bumped into you on the road this evening.' Joseph sighed. 'I've missed talking to you. Over the past few weeks I've come to enjoy the silence to be found over here. But now that you are here, I find myself dreading the silence to come.'

'It is lovely in here Joe. It's so cosy.' Joseph nodded towards Ty Mawr.

'I would give all of that up tomorrow for this, if I could. I would buy a smallholding somewhere, where I might read and write.' Joe's face lit up as he spoke. 'I would have an atlas that I would consult and plan my travels from. I would explore the world, learn more about the people in it. Find out where I might be of best use.'

'That would be a noble mission indeed.'

'You would be with me of course.' Joseph said as if it were blindingly obvious.

'I would?'

'Naturally. We would be like Phileas Fogg and Passepartout.'

'You would have me be your servant?' Violet scowled as Joseph laughed.

'No! You would be my wife!'

'Joe…' Violet fired him a warning look as she took another sip from her glass.

'I know. I'm sorry. I shouldn't have said that. But it isn't wrong to dream, is it?'

'No, and it is a beautiful dream. But that is all it is. It is nothing but fantasy.'

'I have a question for you.' Joseph leapt from his chair and made his way over to a black dress jacket that had been slung over the foot of his bed. He grabbed a slip of paper out of the chest pocket and came back to face Violet.

'Violet Yardley, would you dance with me? I believe you owe me, let's see… at least half a dozen dances according to this card.'

'My dance card!' Violet took the card from him. 'You still have it?'

'I do. And I find that since the night of the ball I have been left wanting.'

'You have written your name in every entry.' Violet inspected the card closely and peered up at him through narrowed eyes.

'And yet you did not dance with me once. And before you say anything, I know, we didn't exactly have the opportunity. But we can make up for it now. If you say yes.'

'You want to dance here?'

'Why not?'

'Because there is nothing to dance to!' Violet chuckled. 'Besides which, there is barely enough room to swing a cat.'

'Then we will not attempt to swing any cats while we dance. As for music, we have our imaginations, don't we?' Joseph held out his hand. 'Please, Vi. Just one dance. It may be the only chance we get.'

We shouldn't get any chance.

Violet stared at Joseph's waiting hand. They shouldn't get a chance and yet here it was. Even as her mind screamed at her to say no she found herself placing her hand in his and rising to her feet anyway as if it were the most natural thing in the world. Because Joseph taking her by the hand was the most natural thing in the world.

'Very well. We will dance. One dance. Fool.' Violet laughed softly and allowed herself to be guided to the centre of the room and though she had danced a thousand times, she suddenly found herself a novice all over again, all arms and legs and no co-ordination as Joseph placed his hand on her waist. She brought her own hand up to rest on his shoulder and only once they had begun moving did she begin to feel some semblance of normality.

The dance was nothing you could put a name to. In fact, it wasn't really dancing at all, Violet thought, but they moved as one, every step of their feet, every twist and turn as synchronised as the rituals one saw in birds in spring.

'I could provide music if you like?' Joseph began to hum as they moved in small circles and Violet craned to listen to the soft melody that he had chosen for them.

'Is that Mozart you are attempting to murder?' Violet leaned back slightly to look at him.

'He's your favourite composer I believe? Besides which, I'm not murdering it. I'm offering my own interpretation.' Joseph reprimanded her in between softly breathed lilting notes.

'Is that so? I would suggest that you must hear something very different to the rest of us.'

'The correct version I think you'll find.' He smiled down at Violet and stopped humming. 'You are wearing the ring. Can I see it?'

'Of course. Let me just…'

'No, I'll do it.' Joseph unclasped his hand from hers and pulled the chain that was holding the ring out from the opened collar of Violet's shirt, holding the ring between his fingers.

'My mother told me the history of it.' Violet said. 'Turns out she knows as much about this ring as you do.'

'That doesn't surprise me. I expect my mother was having the same conversations with yours as she was with me. They always seemed to be conspiring about something, didn't they?'

'That is true.' Violet laughed softly at the memory.

'The amount of times she told me it was destined for you.'

'No.' Violet came to a standstill. 'Please do not say it was fate. I am so tired of hearing that word and everyone seems to be bandying it about at present. It is as though my life has been pre-destined and I have no control over anything.' Violet took a deep breath as she looked up at Joseph. 'Do you know what scares me most? What if it is true? What is everything was fated? What if your mother was right and I was supposed to wear this ring? If all of it was true and my fate has been taken from me, what do I have?'

'You will always have me, Vi.' Violet shook her head.

'You have said that before and whilst you may believe it, it was not true then and it is not true now. I will never have you, Joe. You are Calissa's now.'

'Never.' Joseph slowly reached behind Violet and unclasped the necklace. In one swift move, he dropped one end of the chain so that the ring slipped away from it, coming to rest in the palm of his hand.

'There is an alternative theory with regards to fate that suggests that there are two potential paths one might take. For the most part that is. I realise that in this instance there is a path that we must follow and so there is no second option, but in my mind, when I am alone, I see another path. In my mind, we are dancing, as we are at this very moment. Or were, at least.' He smiled crookedly as he slipped the chain into his pocket. 'Except there is music perhaps. But we are not in a crowded room, or at a ball. Truth be told, I don't know where we are. But we are outside and we are alone and we are staring at the stars as we dance and there is music, although that makes no sense because where would the music be coming from if we are outside and alone?' Joseph frowned and inhaled sharply, his chest shuddering as he exhaled through tightened lips. 'I'm procrastinating, sorry. I find myself nervous all of a sudden. Anyway, the point is, it is then that I produce the ring, and I tell you of my love for you and I try to prove that I am worthy of you and then when you finally agree I place the ring on your finger.' Unable to move, Violet watched as Joseph took her hand and slipped the ring onto her wedding finger. It fit perfectly.

'Joe, stop.'

'And it is just you and I.' Joseph looked from the ring to Violet. 'There is no-one to corrupt anything. No-one to take that moment from us. Because it is us who are fated to be together. It is us who are fated to spend every day of the rest of our lives together.'

'Joe, please.'

'And then, when I have placed the ring on your finger, only then do I kiss you.' Joseph leaned forward and softly brushed his lips against hers.

'Joe, you know that this is wrong.' Violet took a step backwards and looked at the floor, the walls, the fire, anywhere but directly at him.

'Wrong?' Joseph reached out and took her face in his hands. 'Violet Rose, this is the only thing that's right.'

'You are to be married tomorrow.'

'And you will find love with someone else.' Joseph closed his eyes. 'Do you have any idea how jealous I become when I see him touch you?'

'Dr Tremaine?'

'I swear, just seeing his hand on you.'

'There is nothing between William and I, and you know that. And besides, even if there was you would still have no right to be jealous. While you contemplate your future, have you ever stopped to think about the situation I find myself in? Tomorrow, in front of our friends and family, I must walk down the aisle behind the woman you are to marry. I have to stand there while you promise to love her and cherish her for the rest of your lives. How do you think that makes me feel? Shall I tell you? I am beyond jealous! And I am furious with myself for being so naive!' Violet stepped forward and slammed her opened hands into Joseph's chest. 'You have broken me, Joe. I swore I would never let you do this to me again and yet I have wandered into the same trap willingly. I must be the world's biggest fool.' Joseph sighed and wrapped his arms tightly around her.

'If anyone is a fool Vi, it is me. I have allowed myself to become a pawn in my father's games. I have been weak in defending my family, in defending my mother's memory and that weakness has led to the suffering of us all. So please, don't be angry at yourself. Your wrath should be directed at me. I am the one who deserves it.'

'No.' Violet shook her head wearily as she looked up at him. 'I know that everything you have done you have done to protect your sister, there is no shame in that. You are a good man, Joe.'

'And in being so I must lose the one person that I truly love?' He rested his lips on Violet's forehead.

'Yes.' Violet whispered. 'And so must I.'

'Had there been another path, had we followed it and I had offered you this ring, would you have accepted it?'

'With all my heart, Joseph Davenport.' Violet wrapped her fingers in the front of Joseph's shirt. 'I would have been honoured to be your wife.'

'My wife.' Joseph reached down and took Violet's hand in his own, the ring glistening between them. 'Can we not pretend then, for just one night, that we have taken the other path? Can we not just pretend that I am yours and you are mine and that nothing and no-one stands between us?'

Violet looked down at the ring and then back at Joseph. She should leave now. She knew she should. She should get out of the cottage and keep running until his touch, until the taste of him on her lips was no more than a distant memory. But the heart wants what the heart wants. How true her mother's words were. She took a deep breath and removed the ring from her finger and handed it back to him.

'Vi, no…' Joseph's eyes widened in panic as Violet held a finger to his lips and quietened him. She forced a smile, defying the tear that slipped from the corner of her eye.

'Ask me again.'

'Don't do that to me!' Joseph exclaimed as he breathed out shakily and glanced around the room. Seconds later was striding over to the fireplace, placing the ring in his pocket as he moved. With a sudden force, he grabbed the chairs and placed them flush against the walls then went back to the table hoisting it into the air and sending the cups of mead flying.

'Joe, what on earth are you doing?' Violet winced as the cups dropped onto the stone floor and shattered into smithereens.

'Damn!' He grabbed the dustpan and brush from the fireplace and swept up the broken crockery. When he was done, he inspected the tiles closely, squinting in the dim light. 'No, this won't do.' He grabbed Violet's boots and carried them over to her. 'Here, allow me.' His brow furrowed, he bent down and lifted her foot off the floor, gently easing it into the matching boot.

'Joe, have you lost your mind?'

'Quite possibly.' Joseph looked up at her and smiled as he lifted her other foot, sliding it into the remaining boot as delicately as he had the first. 'There.' He stood up and took her hand, walking her over to the fire.

'I will ask you again. No imaginary paths, no balls or music or fields with starlit skies. Just me, and you.' Violet bit her lip to keep from smiling, only mildly aware of the tears that ran down her cheeks as Joseph got down on one knee, retrieving the ring from his pocket and holding it between them with shaking fingers.

'Violet Rose Yardley, we are fated to be together, you and I. I know that I cannot be with you for an eternity as I would want to, though you will have my heart forever. And I know that tomorrow all of this will be nothing more than a memory, but just for tonight, will you be mine?'

'You know that I am already yours.' Violet ran her fingers under her eyes, wiping away the tears. 'The answer is yes, Joseph Davenport.' She held her hand out in front of him and watched as he placed the ring back on the finger before bringing his lips to rest against the back of her hand.

'Thank you.' He smiled as he looked up at her.

'You are supposed to kiss me now, I believe?' Violet giggled as Joseph got up from the floor.

'I believe I am, Mrs Davenport.' The smile dissolved from his lips as he took a step forwards and brought his lips down upon hers and smiled. 'I love you, Vi.' He whispered the words against her lips as Violet reached up to kiss him again, running her fingers through his hair as the kiss deepened, basking in his touch as he slowly ran his hands along the length of her body. His fingers slowly slid under the long shirt she wore until they came to rest against her waist and Violet gasped at the sensation of his touch against her bare skin as Joseph's lips moved in a steady line across her throat, his hands running the length of her back.

'Joe, stop.' She took a step away from him, her eyes never leaving his as she reached down and undid the buttons on her shirt, finally allowing the garment to slip to the floor.

'Violet Davenport, you are beautiful.' Joseph said, his voice barely a whisper as she moved towards him and silently removed his jacket and shirt, running her fingers over the scars on his back. The scars he had gotten defending her. There was no going back now, Violet realised. Though in truth, there had never been a way back. Not when it came to Joe. He kissed her again, more fervently now, claiming her completely, his touch igniting every nerve, turning them to flame as he caressed her, his fingers and then his mouth moving over her skin in slow languid circles.

'Take me to bed, Joe.' Violet looked down as Joseph stared at her in complete wonderment.

'You are sure?' Violet nodded as Joseph silently took her hand and walked her to the other end of the cottage. When they reached the bed, he picked her up and lay her down upon it, bringing himself up on the mattress alongside her.

'Tell me that you are mine.' Violet sighed against Joseph's mouth as he removed the last of the garments between them. He rested on one elbow, his other hand trailing the length of her body.

'I am yours, Violet Davenport.' Joseph said as he moved to lie on top of her. 'I will forever be yours.'

*****

'Mother?' Violet started as she slipped in through the gap in the canvas wall. 'You're still awake?'

Constance was stood by the fire, her hands clasped together in front of her, staring at a bucket of water that roiled with such a ferocity it was not hard to imagine the contents spilling onto the flames below and putting them out in an instant. She turned to look at Violet and smiled, though it was a sad smile, Violet thought. A smile she usually saved for the husband she had loved and lost.

'You didn't think that I would wait up until you returned? I'm preparing a bath for you. Come, it is nearly ready.' Constance said softly as Violet walked into the centre of the tent and glanced over at the sisters who were sound asleep. Or at least pretending to be. Her mother handed her a small glass that was filled with a milky liquid. 'It's Rue plant. You should drink it now.' Rue extract. To prevent unwanted pregnancies. Violet sat down on a chair besides that bath and stared at the glass before swallowing the contents in one mouthful without question. Guilt crawled into her bones.

'How did you know?'

'I went into town to pick up Alfie and Edie after they closed up at the market. I passed by Ty Mawr thinking I would save Gwilym the trip and I saw you and Joe. I'd say I'm surprised you didn't hear us but…It wasn't difficult to put the rest of the puzzle together.' She moved back to the fire to retrieve the pail, leaning heavily as she carried it back to the tub. 'As for the bath? No foretelling, I'm afraid. I heard Berkeley pounding up the track. I've actually been topping up the water for the last few hours. It is bitterly cold out there and I thought a bath might warm you before bed. That you might find it, soothing.' Constance quieted then, leaving the implications of her words hanging in the air.

'What have I done?' Violet looked to Constance as she poured the bucket of hot water into the bath.

'Oh, my dear girl. You have fallen in love.' Constance took her daughter's hand and led her to the bath, helping her undress before Violet climbed in and sank down into the warm water, lying back against the hard iron tub as Constance reached for the hairbrush and began to run it through Violet's hair.

'I'm sorry.' Violet whispered.

'Why are you sorry?'

'Because I've let you down. Everything you have ever taught me about right and wrong? I chose to ignore it all. I thought of myself and only myself. I was reckless and immoral with no thought for my reputation or anyone else's for that matter. You must be so disappointed in me and I cannot blame you. It is all my doing.' Violet ran the soap over her body, silently mourning the loss of Joe's scent on her skin as the perfume removed all traces of him. Constance put the hairbrush down and began sectioning Violet's hair as she had done since she was a small child. The ritual bought a strange comfort with it.

'You are my daughter. You could never let me down.' Constance sighed as she began to weave the sections together. 'People often say and do things that go against their nature for a variety of reasons Violet, but I believe love is the cruellest of masters.' Her mother reached for a scrap of ribbon in the pocket of her dress and tied it around the end of Violet's plaited hair. 'Old Man Davenport would not have lashed out the way he did had he not loved his wife so. Alfie would not have found Edie, had you not told him the truth, such was his love for you. I would not have considered leaving my family behind if I had not loved your father as I did.'

'You were going to leave Flossie and Ruby in the workhouse?' Violet turned to face her mother.

'It shames me to admit it, but yes. Mercifully, they were as welcome here as I was. Betrayal and infatuation often go hand in hand. Joseph would not have betrayed his fiancé if he did not love you as he does. And you? You have simply listened to your heart, allowed it to feel everything you were destined to feel with Joseph.'

'It is a beautiful sentiment but that does not excuse my behaviour or lessen my shame. Were my heart hardened I might allow myself some leeway. Might assure myself that Calissa Parnell is no friend. Not really. That she will never find out. But the fact that it will remain a secret does not lessen the guilt. I have wronged her and myself in the most awful way. There are rules that one must adhere to and I have flouted them so very badly.'

'Rules are not black and white. You must account for all the colours in-between.' Constance leaned towards Violet and wiped the tears from her face. 'I am sorry, Vi. You don't deserve this.'

Violet sank further down into the warm water and closed her eyes, calling to mind every kiss, every whisper, every touch, reliving each moment so that she might never forget. So she would always remember how she and Joseph had lain by the fire basking in the glow of each other. How he had cried her name as he had committed himself to her. But now it was over. That life was over. Violet stood silently as her mother wrapped a towel around her then handed her her nightgown.

'Where is the ring?' Constance looked from Violet's bare hands to her neck where the chain had once been.

'I left it behind.' Violet said. 'It's not right that I have it.'

'Perhaps you are right.' Constance conceded. 'Would you like to sleep in my bed with me tonight?'

'I'm not a child.' Violet forced a smile.

'You are a beautiful woman, Violet Rose. But you are still my child.'

'No, I want to sleep in my own bed. But thank you.' Violet said wearily. 'Do not allow me to sleep too late. We have a long day ahead of us. And thank you. For everything.' Violet hugged her mother and made her way to her bed, shivering as she slipped between the covers. Had he woken and found her gone yet? Found the ring? She imagined him lying tangled up in the sheets, sleeping peacefully, the way she had left him. There was no way she could have woken him. No way she could have said goodbye. Had he asked her again, she knew she wouldn't have had the strength to deny him.

'I know I joked about it before, but we could leave this place. Go somewhere they'd never find us. We could send for Amelia once we establish ourselves. She would not be homeless. We would ensure that she was safe and well cared for. What do you think?'

The suggestion had taken the wind out of her sails. That he would contemplate eloping, turn his back on his family, on his responsibilities, for her. And maybe, maybe if she had not loved her own family as she did, maybe then she might have said yes. Now, knowing that her mother decided differently, she couldn't help but question her own choice. Had fate thrown her a lifeline she'd chosen to discard? It didn't bear thinking about. She wrapped her arms around herself, aware of everything she had gained and lost within only a few short hours. Perhaps it was possible, she realised to die of a broken heart after all. Right now, such an option seemed almost favourable.

Chapter thirty-two

There was a flurry of activity in the courtyard with the house staff dashing around frantically making final preparations to the waiting carriages. Like a well-oiled machine they attended to the coaches in turn, cleaning the footplates, buffing the paintwork to a high sheen and attaching ornate bunches of winter flowering jasmine to the grab rails. The groomsmen were equally as frenetic, brushing the horses smoothly and methodically so that their coats shone in the pale morning light before they added the same blossoms to the horse's reins and as much as Violet begrudged the fact, everything was falling into place.

The skies over the valley had turned bright grey. Snow, she thought as she watched from a window at the top of the house. Today would bring the first real fall of the season. You could see it in the glow of the clouds. Save for the trees, it would turn the landscape to white, cleanse it of everything that had gone before. Like a blank slate. All memories erased, new ones waiting to be created. If only it were that easy. If only the heart could be wiped clean as easily as the ground beneath her feet.

From her vantage point she could see and hear everything. The men talking downstairs, Calissa barking final orders at whoever was nearby and the maids working flat out to make sure that the house was ready to receive the wedding party once the ceremony had finished. She jumped as the grandfather clock in the hallway struck the hour and watched as the staff scrambled back into the house before the chimes had even ceased. The first of the coachmen jumped up onto his carriage, his companion moving to wait by the door. One hour to go. Silence fell over the house as Edwin Davenport made his way out onto the drive, a thick grey coat covering his morning suit, his top hat perched neatly on his head. He slipped on a pair of black leather gloves as walked hurriedly towards the coach and removed his hat before he climbed in and sat down on the padded leather seat, peering impatiently back at the house.

'Joe…' Violet whispered, holding her breath as Joseph sauntered down the steps and across the drive towards the carriage, his pace unhurried, as though he had all the time in the world.

'Look at me. Just, turn around. Please.' She leaned against the wall, placing her hand on the cold glass, as if she could reach out and touch him, transfixed by his every step. When he arrived at the open carriage door he took off his hat and nodded his thanks to the footman and then he turned around, his eyes flying straight to the top window, finding her where she stood, as if he knew he was being watched. If he was angry that she had left without saying goodbye, he didn't show it now, his stare pinning her to the spot where she stood. He looked, defeated. A world away from the boy that had held her only a few hours ago when his eyes had shone, his smile as warm and as real as it had been on the day that they had met. Violet curtsied slowly, her eyes never leaving his, her heart faltering as he bowed in return. And then old man Davenport was leaning out of the carriage door and staring at the two of them, his gaze running back and forth before he beckoned Joseph into the carriage. Joseph regarded his father impassively before he looked up to Violet one last time and climbed in taking the seat opposite.

'Everyone seems to be hiding.' Violet whirled round to find Gwilym stood behind her. 'The main coach is to leave in about twenty minutes.'

'Amelia and I are both ready. Just the final touches being made to the bride now.'

'So I hear.' Gwilym glanced over towards the door of Calissa's room, through which the bride's screams could still be heard. He shook his head solemnly and walked over to the window to stand next to Violet, the two of them watching as the footman hurriedly closed the door behind Joseph and launched himself up to sit next to his companion. Barely a second had passed before the carriage was making its way around the circular drive and out towards the church, the first flakes of snow swirling in the air between them.

'I was just coming to find you.' Violet said.

'You were?' Gwilym eyed her suspiciously.

'I am to give you your favour.' She smirked, holding up a small corsage.

'Must I really wear that?' Gwilym grimaced.

'Do you want to incur her wrath? Today of all days?'

'Absolutely not.'

'Then you'll wear it.' She pulled the accompanying pin from the skirt of her dress. 'You didn't see that.' She murmured. 'I was petrified I'd lose it and she'd start screaming again.'

'Was there a point at which she stopped?' Violet looked towards Calissa's room and laughed quietly.

'No. There wasn't. Now come here.' Gwilym placed himself in front of Violet, holding out the lapel of his jacket as she held the favour into place.

'You look very smart, Gil.' Violet muttered, the pin wedged between her teeth.

'I feel like a penguin. You, on the other hand, look beautiful, Vi.'

'I look like a wraith.' Violet grumbled as she wove the pin around the corsage. 'I've already had Calissa interrogating me. Questioning whether I am well. She doesn't want me making *her* Joseph ill.' She closed her eyes and shook her head. 'I'm sorry, that was cruel of me.' Gwilym shrugged.

'If it's any consolation, Joe looks as though he hasn't slept either.' His cheeks instantly flushed bright red. 'I'm sorry, that was inappropriate. It's just, I came looking for you last night. Because I was supposed to escort you home. And I saw Berkeley outside the cottage. I need to stop talking now...'

'No matter.' Violet said dismissively, too tired to be anything but immune to the notion of being embarrassed. 'I know that there are no secrets between you and Joe. I'm glad he has your confidence.'

'As do you. If you ever need anything, Vi. Anything. I'll always be here for you. All you need do is ask.' Violet placed her hand against Gwilym's cheek and smiled.

'You are a good friend, Gil. Thank you.'

'I am also your companion to the church today.' He said. 'I'm to travel with you and Amelia. The bride and her father will follow behind. Amelia is waiting downstairs with your cape.'

'Well, then I suppose I had better let Miss Parnell know that we are leaving. I'll meet you downstairs in the hall.'

'You're going in there?' Gwilym looked wide-eyed towards Calissa's room and winced at the screaming that had reached fever pitch. 'I always thought you brave, Vi, but...'

'Now you just think me stupid?'

'I was going to say heroic.' Gwilym said dryly.

'If only I were a hero.' Violet laughed as she reached the door. 'Or a Greek goddess perhaps. I would be Nemesis, I think. And I would use my powers to render her mute. And wouldn't that be a blessed day for us all.'

*****

'Miss Yardley, you still look ever so pale.' Violet stretched her lips into a smile as Calissa eyed her from top to toe.

'As I said earlier, I didn't sleep very well.'.

'I believe it is because you are excited about today. Is that not the case? I know I barely closed my eyes last night.'

'Quite possibly.' Calissa beamed at Violet's false confession.

'You are so sweet, Miss Yardley. I realise that we have not known each other long but I am certain that we will be the firmest of friends.' Violet felt the heat rising in her cheeks.

'I just wanted to let you know that we'll be leaving now.'

'And you will be waiting at the church entrance for me? To arrange my dress?' For the first time since they had met Violet could detect doubt, weakness even, in Calissa's voice.

'I'll be there.' Violet turned to walk away and looked back. 'And Miss Parnell, can I just say you look absolutely beautiful.' She turned and made her way back to the door, her throat tightening, her hands beginning to tremble. When the door was firmly shut behind her, she leant against it, and took a deep breath.

'Ready?' Violet looked towards the stairs and found Gwilym still standing where she had left him, his arm held out for her to take. She walked over to stand next to him and peered over the balustrade at Amelia who was hovering in the doorway, Violet's cape hanging from a single finger.

'I am as ready as I'll ever be.' Violet glanced back up at Gwilym, tightly wrapping her hand around his arm. 'This is it, Gil. It's time to face the music.'

*****

The air was strangely still as the carriage made its way down the path that led towards the church, the snow turning from small white motes to thicker heavier flakes that were already beginning to settle on the grass verges around them. Gwilym sat on one side of the coach, spinning one of the wedding rings on his little finger as Violet and Amelia silently watched him from the seat opposite. With a blanket over their laps Amelia still shivered in the chill of the freezing air, snuggling up as best she could to Violet without causing their dresses to crease.

'I don't think the snow will settle on the roads. It has been too damp recently.' Gwilym pondered aloud as he glanced out of the window. Violet followed his line of sight, watching as the snow landed in the puddles on the track and instantly dissolved.

'No matter.' she said resignedly.

'No matter? You cannot be serious? The sooner we get home and back in the warm the better.' Amelia moaned. 'Having a wedding in January. I've never heard of anything so ridiculous.' She brushed her gloved hands over the blanket. 'But then this whole thing is ridiculous.' She looked over at Violet who stared studiously out of the window.

'Surely you know that this is a complete farce, Vi? Joe loves you, and you love him. It is as plain as the nose on your face. This should not be happening. It makes a mockery of marriage.'

'You are mistaken.' Violet said softly. 'Joe and I, we are good friends and I hope we always will be, but we will never be more than that.'

'I don't believe you.' Amelia scowled. 'You are lying, Violet Yardley.'

'It is the only answer I can give you, Amelia.' Violet said wearily. 'Don't question me further. Please.' Amelia looked to Gwilym who glared at her in disbelief and then back to Violet.

'You are right. I'm sorry. Please don't be angry with me.'

'I'm not angry with you, I promise.'

'You will not abandon me, will you? We will always be friends?' Amelia reached out and took Violet's hand in her own.

'Of course we will.' Violet smiled. 'Nothing will change that.' She looked out of the window as the carriage began to ascend the hill on which the church stood. *And I would not wish to abandon you, but in this I have no choice.* Violet looked at the girl who would have been her sister and held her tongue.

'Didn't Calissa want petals leading from the carriage to the church?' Violet looked down at the thick red velvet carpet that covered the path.

'Stuff and nonsense.' Gwilym protested. 'The ground is so cold and wet they'd have turned to brown mush within seconds of being laid. Joseph said he wasn't prepared to pay for something so ridiculous.'

'That's a brave thing to do.' Violet winced.

'Oh, she won't make a show of herself in public.' Gwilym said confidently. 'She'll bend his ear later though I'm sure. Poor bastard. Sorry.'

'I've heard worse.' Violet said as the footman opened the carriage door where the vicar stood waiting. He smiled broadly offering his hand as Amelia and Violet alighted from the carriage.

'Come wait in the vestibule, out of the chill.' He gestured towards the main entrance and then disappeared into a small side room closing the heavy wooden door behind him.

'I would be delighted to!' Amelia enthused. She reached down, gathering the hems of her dress and made for the small enclosure, turning back to look at Violet. 'Quick let's get in the warm, well, out of the cold, at least.'

'I'm right behind you, believe me.' Violet grabbed at her skirt and followed closely behind.

'I'll just wait here then, shall I?' Gwilym called out. Violet laughed.

'Someone has to take care of the guests.'

'Everyone is already here. Apart from the bride and her father.' Joseph walked down the nave leaving his father sat alone at the front of the church. He stopped when he reached the edge of the vestibule and leaned against the edge of the doorframe.

'Already here?' Amelia frowned and peered past him into the nave. 'But there are no more than half a dozen people here. Where is the rest of the family? Where are our friends?'

'I didn't invite them.' Joseph made his way into the vestibule and walked over to stand next to Violet, so close she could feel the warmth radiating from his body and it was all she could do to not wrap herself around him. 'You're going to freeze to death stood there in that.' Joseph cast his eye over her.

'As am I!' Amelia turned back from the main body of the church. 'And what I think you meant to say was 'you look heavenly, Violet.'

'Heavenly?' Violet laughed. 'I'm not sure about that, Amelia!'

'I would have said exquisite.' Joseph muttered under his breath, so quietly she was certain that only she would have heard him. She glanced up at him in surprise, heat rising in her cheeks as she watched his eyes taking in every inch of her as he had the night before, a coquettish grin slowly spreading across his face.

'Why are there no bells?' She flustered. 'It seems awfully quiet.'

'Master Davenport requested that the ringers stop.' The vicar reappeared, glancing over at Joseph. 'Didn't want the fuss.'

'That I can understand.' Amelia said under her breath. She turned to Joseph 'Are you ready, brother?' She said quietly. Joseph's face instantly lit up at softness of her tone and Violet felt her heart warm. Perhaps something good could come out of today after all.

'Ready for today? Never.' Joseph smiled weakly. 'I'm glad that you are here, Mimi.'

'Mimi? You haven't called me that in years!' Amelia giggled. 'And I wouldn't be anywhere else.' She walked over and wrapped her arms around him, holding him tightly. 'Unless I could be sat in front of a fire. Then I would most definitely choose to be there instead.' They froze at the sound of hooves in the distance.

'I must go back inside now.' Joseph grabbed hold of his sister's hand, squeezing it as he regarded Violet. 'And yet I find myself unable to move.'

'It's only natural to fret.' The vicar smiled at him. 'This is no small undertaking after all. One hour and it will all be over and you can relax and celebrate.'

One hour and it would all be over. Violet couldn't help but smile at the irony of the vicar's comments. Because it wouldn't be over. It was only just beginning. The sound of hooves grew louder.

'Mr Davenport, if you would. You and the best man, if you please? Bad luck to see the bride before and all that…' The vicar gestured towards the open door. Joseph let go of his sister's hand and made towards the door, closing it behind him without looking back.

*****

'Miss Yardley, is my dress arranged as it should be?'

Calissa twisted around to look at the hem of her gown. It was strange that you should be someone's bridesmaid, Violet thought and still not be on first name terms. It made the whole scenario seem like a complete facade. But then didn't she have as big a hand in creating that facade as the bride herself? She bent down to fan out Calissa's skirt, blocking out the thoughts that challenged her to turn and run.

'There.' Violet looked up, grateful for the veil that obscured Calissa's face which at least meant she didn't have to look the bride directly in the eye. 'Now it is perfect.' Calissa nodded and smiled nervously, taking her father's arm.

'Calissa, you look beautiful my darling daughter. I wish your mother could have been here to see this. She would have been so proud of you.'

'Would she? Have been proud of me?' Her father looked astonished.

'You are a beautiful, intelligent, accomplished young lady and I know she would have been bursting with joy to see you in such a prosperous union.'

Not a happy union. No mention of love or kinship, or fate, Violet noticed. This was clearly a marriage based on financial comparability and nothing more. That being the case, perhaps this union was forced on Calissa in the same way as it had been Joseph. And if that was true then surely they deserved all the luck they could get? The revelation made the guilt she already felt at her own indiscretion even worse. Only compounded her desire to leave the town as soon as she could.

'Well, let's get married, shall we?'

Calissa smiled at the vicar who turned and opened the door to the nave where Joseph and Gwilym stood waiting, Wagner's Bridal March filling the void around them. In slow, measured steps, Violet and Amelia made their way up the aisle behind Calissa and her father counting to keep their feet in time to the music.

Violet took a moment to glance around the near empty building. Amelia hadn't been exaggerating. There were a couple of women at the back of the church, Violet noticed, neither of which looked familiar. Acquaintances of Calissa's, she supposed, even though she had shown no interest in visiting her old friends since her return. They bowed their heads respectfully as Calissa and her father passed and Violet couldn't help but notice John Parnell's expression of surprise, as though the women were neither expected or invited. He looked back at Calissa and smiled briefly his face all bewilderment as he took a firmer grip on her arm and continued walking her forwards as the two women began to mutter behind his back. Violet looked to Amelia who shrugged subtly, her interest in them soon surpassed by her need to seek out her brother as they made their way down the aisle. And Amelia was right, Violet supposed. There were more important things to think about than petty gossip, even if it might lighten the burden.

Her mother and Alfie were sat a few rows from the altar, their faces seemingly turned to stone and Violet couldn't help but conclude that there were more people in on the deceit within the confines of the church than not. Only Dr Tremaine smiled, his eyes glowing as Violet passed him by. She fleetingly returned the gesture, her eyes pulled to the front of the church where she found Joseph, his hands behind his back watching her every move as she drew closer to him and even though she knew it was dangerous she allowed herself a moment to imagine. To imagine that she was walking in Calissa's shoes, heading to the altar as a bride, to marry the man that she loved, just as the fates had decreed. The notion left a bitter taste in her mouth as they came to a halt next to Joseph and Gwilym, Calissa reaching back to hand Violet her bouquet of white lilies as the vicar cleared his voice.

'Dearly beloved friends, we are gathered together here in the sight of God, and in the face of this congregation, to join together this man and this woman in holy matrimony.'

Violet raised her head, her gaze flickering between Calissa and Joseph as the light began to evaporate from the room, turning everything to black and suddenly she was no longer at a wedding. She was at a funeral. She was not rejoicing the union of Joseph and Calissa, she was mourning the death of her own fate, the scrying mirror shattering in her mind's eye all over again. Reality ripped through her, forcing the air from her lungs and turning her veins to ice. Was this how her mother felt when she thought about her father? No, Violet reasoned with herself. To lose someone in death, someone who you knew loved you as you loved them was a blessing in a macabre way, surely? But to know that the boy you love still walks the earth and you cannot walk alongside him because he is destined to hold the hand of another? The hand of someone he does not desire? Someone who was not worthy of his love?

The Vicar's voice began to blur and fade away and the room began to spin, the ground beneath her feet tilting and turning, stealing her balance from her. And then there was a hand holding hers, dragging her back to the surface. Amelia squeezed her fingers fiercely, forced her to breathe, grounded her back into reality. Back to where Joseph watched her with concern and where Calissa briefly turned to follow his line of sight, staring at Violet perplexedly before she turned back to the vicar.

'First, I am required to ask, if anyone present knows a reason why these persons may not lawfully marry, please declare it now.' Violet glanced at Amelia who stared back with wide, imploring eyes that were brimmed with tears. Violet shook her head subtly and Amelia turned away, though she did not let go of Violet's hand and Violet slowly realised that Amelia was not the only one who was crying. She glanced across at Old Man Davenport and caught his eye, his expression victorious in her defeat. She reached up and brushed a finger under her eyes, staring straight ahead at Joseph and Calissa. No, this would not do. He would not see her break. Not now. Not ever.

The rest of the service seemed to pass in a blur. There were no hymns as Joseph requested that there be none. There were a couple of prayers that Violet chose to ignore, not only because they clashed with her own beliefs but also because they both seemed aimed at damning her to hell. The vows were recited and whilst there was a hint of emotion in Calissa's voice Joseph was almost automated in his response, barely making eye contact with his bride, choosing instead to look anywhere in the church but at Calissa.

'Could I have the rings please?' Gwilym leaned forward, holding his hand out towards the vicar and whispered something in his ear. The vicar glanced over at Joseph and Calissa uncertainly.

'Am I to understand that there is now only one ring? For the bride?'

'That is correct.' Joseph nodded as Calissa opened her mouth to protest. 'There will only be one ring.' Calissa smiled at the vicar awkwardly.

'Very well. A slight change to procedures is required, but no matter. Joseph, take Calissa's hand and place the ring on her finger. Calissa, if you could repeat after me...Joseph, I receive this ring as a sign of our marriage. With my body, I honour you...' Violet frowned at Joseph who watched her cautiously as Calissa repeated the words aloud, promised to love and honour and obey him, to give herself only to him, to share all that she had, all that she was with him and him alone. She stopped mid-sentence and cleared her throat, gaining his attention for a sparse few seconds, his disinterest painfully obvious as his gaze flickered to her momentarily before he turned back to Violet. Violet's heart began to thump wildly.

He would not wear a ring? Would not make those same promises to Calissa as he had made to her as they lay together in front of the fire? As Calissa turned to glare at her a second time her face puce with rage, Violet stared down at the floor, desperate that their eyes did not meet. If only it were as easy to ignore the way that Amelia bounced on the balls of her feet as though she had finally found the excitement she sought, even if it led to the total and utter humiliation of Calissa.

'In the presence of God, and before this congregation, Joseph and Calissa have given their consent and made their marriage vows to each other. They have declared their marriage by the joining of hands and by the giving and receiving of a ring. I therefore proclaim that they are husband and wife. Those whom God has joined together let no one put asunder.' The vicar smiled at the newly-wedded couple. 'You may kiss the bride.'

Calissa smiled and lifted her veil, toying with it until it slipped into place. She took a tentative step forwards and leant forward into Joseph and Violet froze as he mirrored his bride's smile, gently placing his lips on her cheek, his eyes closed, blocking out her unspoken attempts to guide his lips towards hers. She took a step back, her joyful expression fracturing for a fleeting moment as he turned away, awkwardly shaking Gwilym's hand before he gestured towards the exit and then held out his arm for her to take. It was the simplest of gestures and yet it seemed to be enough for the warmth to return to her eyes.

'Congratulations, both. I thought the service was beautiful.' Violet handed back the bridal bouquet before they began the recessional walk. Calissa smiled but the sincerity in her expression was gone, her features pinched as though she had come face to face with the enemy. She took Joseph's arm allowing him to lead her from the church as the organist began playing Mozart's requiem. One of Violet's favourite pieces. It had to have been deliberate, Violet thought. A last unspoken message from Joe. She took her place behind the newlyweds, recalling Mozart's words when asked about the creation of the requiem.

'I fear I am writing a requiem for myself.'

It was a sentiment that Violet understood, only now it was as if the requiem was being used not to mourn the passing of a life, but the end of a friendship.

Chapter thirty-three

'Are you sure you are quite well?' Gwilym looked fixedly at Violet as the carriage made its way back to the house. 'You're still very pale. You're not suffering from any of the same symptoms as Joe, are you?' Violet waved her hand dismissively.

'I am well. Please, don't concern yourself, Gil. I was just feeling a little wobbly, that's all. I didn't get time to eat this morning.'

'Why would we not be concerned? I thought you were going to faint at the altar. You turned the most awful shade of grey, indeed you are still pale now.' Violet smiled thinly as Amelia took her hand and scrutinised her as a mother would her child, searching for tell-tale signs of something more grievous than lack of sustenance.

'I promise you, once I have eaten, I'll be just fine.' Amelia humphed in reply.

'Speak for yourself. Once we've eaten, I'll be heading back to my room. I refuse to participate in this charade for a moment longer than is necessary.'

'For Joe's sake, please, stay nearby a little while longer.'

'You will be staying too?' Amelia regarded her cynically.

'No.' Violet said, her voice barely a whisper. 'But then I'm not family. I wouldn't want to overstay my welcome.' Amelia snorted again.

'It isn't you that's overstayed their welcome, trust me.'

'Amelia.' Gwilym said admonishingly. 'We may not like the situation, but this is how it has to be. All we can do now is make the best of it and that includes rallying around your brother. He is going to need all the support he can get over the coming weeks and months. And you know he values your relationship above anything else.'

'So, you admit that this is a farce.' Amelia looked over to Gwilym, her expression a strange mix of triumph and vindication. 'And besides,' she glanced sideways at Violet. 'I can think of at least one person that he values more than me.'

'Amelia, please.'

'I know, I know, I'm sorry.' Amelia peered through the window of the coach and snarled. 'Can you believe the nerve of that woman? She's actually waiting to greet me as I enter my own home!' Amelia's cheeks reddened as they came to a stop in front of the steps and Violet leaned over her shoulder to gaze up the steps.

As a husband and wife would, Joseph and Calissa stood in the doorway awaiting their arrival, Joseph looking pensive while Calissa beamed at them.

'She's just putting on a show is all.' Gwilym said, glancing up at the newlyweds. 'This won't last more than a day, believe me. It'll be below her come morning.' He waited in place until the footman ran around the carriage and opened the door. 'Strange to be waited on, mind. I could get used to this.'

'It's yours.' Amelia grumbled as Gwilym helped her out of the carriage. 'You can take my place. I shall move up to the camp with Vi. I think I would find a more peaceful existence there.' Violet laughed and leaned over to whisper in Amelia's ear.

'It would be quieter certainly, and you would be most welcome. But I don't think the ruse would last for long. I can't imagine Gil turning up in one of your dresses for breakfast going unnoticed, can you?' Amelia cast her eyes over Gwilym who glared back with mock indignance.

'Perhaps you are right.' She conceded as they made their way up the steps. 'Maybe if he wore a bonnet.' She smiled at Violet as they reached the house. 'Thank you.' She whispered. 'Thank you for making things better. You always make things better.'

'If only that were true.' Violet smiled as she came to a stop, hovering on the step below Amelia, the snow swirling around them.

'Sister. Come and warm yourself.' Calissa smiled as she took Amelia's hands in her own. 'You must be frozen. I know I am!'

'Congratulations.' Violet called out over Amelia's shoulder, subtly prodding Amelia in the back.

'Oh, of course, forgive me. Congratulations.' Amelia forced a smile onto her face as she withdrew her hands from Calissa's and made her way into the house, closely followed by Gwilym who mumbled his own best wishes as he passed.

'I am so pleased for your both.' Violet said softly. 'Miss Parnell, you looked so beautiful. Sorry, I mean, Mrs…' The title stuck in her throat and Calissa laughed in reply.

'Do not fret, dear friend. I'm sure I'll make the same mistake many times over the coming months. Mrs Davenport…' She said dreamily. 'Can you imagine, darling?' She peered at Joseph over her shoulder. He smiled politely but said nothing. 'I wonder if you might wait here for a moment, Miss Yardley. I need someone to attend to my hair before we have our photographs taken.'

'You have a photographer?' Violet looked between Calissa and Joseph. Joseph grumbled something under his breath as he smiled and greeted the rest of the guests, Constance, Alfie and William filing past them extending their own congratulations. William stopped as he passed Violet.

'Duties successfully completed, Miss Yardley. You can relax now. And may I just say how utterly divine you look.'

'Thank you, William.' Violet felt herself blush, focusing on William rather than Joseph who glared behind him. 'Are you ready for the wedding breakfast?'

'I am always ready to dine.' He replied, leaning forward to whisper in her ear. 'Though I doubt this will be as enjoyable as the roasted chestnuts we shared in Cardiff.' Violet's eyes widened in astonishment as he winked slyly. 'I'll save you a seat.' Before she had a chance to respond, he made his way towards the dining room. Violet watched him disappear through the open door before she turned back to Joseph and Calissa.

'I'm sorry. What were you saying?'

'She was talking about the photographer.' Joseph said colourlessly. 'Why it is needed is beyond me.'

'Darling, I have asked Mr Varney to come all the way from London to take photographs because he is one of the best in his profession. It has cost a small fortune so I should at least be presentable my love. I promise you, we won't take a moment.'

'The fact that this has cost a small fortune is precisely my point. I don't understand why you need something so ridiculously extravagant.'

'Because this should be the happiest day of our lives. Surely you want something to remember it by?' Calissa's eyes began to glisten and Joseph glanced over at Violet who was looking anywhere but at them.

'Calissa.' Joseph took a deep breath, softened the tone of his voice. 'Everyone is waiting to eat. And you look fine. Can we not just get the photographs over and done with so we can sit down with our friends?' Calissa whirled round to face him.

'I do not want to look fine, Joseph! No bride wants to look just fine!' She grabbed Violet's hand and made her way towards the stairs dragging Violet behind her. 'This is supposed to be my day and yet you seem determined to spoil it. Come, Miss Yardley.' Violet turned to look at Joseph as she let go of Calissa's hand and took hold of the hem of her dress following swiftly up the stairs behind her, sadness overwhelming her. None of it, she realised, was for herself.

*****

'Take a seat at the bureau, we'll have your hair tidied in no time.'

'Now I see why you have no interest in William.' Calissa said to Violet with a clarity that instantly unnerved her. She quietly closed the door and turned to face Calissa who stood unwavering in the centre of the room.

'I'm sorry?'

'What is the connection between you and Joe?' Calissa rested her hands on her hips and waited expectantly. 'It's a simple enough question. Are you not able to answer?' Violet breathed in slowly, her eyes never leaving Calissa's as she drafted and modified her response until it was meticulous. Until she could be seen as nothing other than plausible.

'I don't understand what you're saying. Joe and I are friends. We have been friends for years.'

'No.' Calissa shook her head fervently 'Do you treat me like a fool, Miss Yardley. I saw the way he looked at you during the service. It is not the first time he has behaved that way towards you. I demand you tell me the truth. I will not be satisfied until you have answered me. Honestly.' Violet clasped her hands together in front of her.

'And what do you think that truth is?'

'That you love him. And he loves you. That my marriage is nothing but a farce!'

'Please Calissa, I'm sorry but you are so very wrong. There is nothing untoward between Joseph and me. What happened this morning in the church, I take full responsibility. I've had little sleep, I didn't get time to eat this morning and I felt a little faint. Joseph noticed, that's all. He was just being a concerned friend.'

'No. It is more than friendship. I see that between himself and his sister, though she is so cosseted she does not deserve it. The way he looks at you, it is not borne from simple affection. It runs far deeper than that. He looks at you the way he should look at me. He looks at you as though he would die for you.'

'Forgive me, but I think you are misinterpreting the situation. Joe is under a lot of pressure, as are you. As you have both been for the past few weeks. He is simply seeking familiarity and comfort as we all do in the face of uncertainty.'

'He should be seeking that with me!' Calissa's face reddened. 'Not with some dirty little gypsy girl that he has taken a shining to!'

'True friendship is not dictated by social ranking as you seem to imply it should be.' Violet said quietly. 'And at the same time, I would ask that you think about your own acquaintances. Is Joseph not as good a friend to me as Dr Tremaine is to you? He is in your employ yet you clearly view him as a social companion and your equal.' The comparison seemed to pull Calissa up short. She gazed around the room pensively, looking anywhere but directly at Violet as she considered. 'Joseph is my dear friend, but he is your husband, Calissa. And he is waiting downstairs for you.' Calissa's hand flew to her face.

'You are right.' Violet felt her shoulders slump as Calissa's face crumpled. 'Oh, heavens above, I'm sorry.' She ran her shaking fingers across her forehead and laughed nervously. 'I'm so sorry. I don't know what is happening to me.'

'As I said, you are under a great deal of pressure.'

'Nevertheless, I am behaving abominably. And I so dearly wanted us to be friends. I should not have called you such awful names. Will you forgive me, Violet?' Calissa looked at her pleadingly.

'You called me Violet.' Violet's eyes widened in surprise.

'I'm sorry. Miss Yardley.'

'I would prefer Violet.' Violet laughed gently. 'And you are already forgiven. Now shall we forget that this ever happened? I can still do your hair for you?' Calissa nodded and made her way over to her dresser without looking back. She seemed smaller. Frail, even. Violet watched her silently. Too close. There were too many lies too close to the surface, all of them waiting to be revealed. One mistimed look, one overly revealing word or sentiment would be the downfall of all of them. The sooner she was gone the better for everyone.

'Where did your friends go? I did not see them arrive at the house?'

'My friends?' Calissa looked up at Violet's reflection in the mirror. 'What friends?'

'The two ladies sat at the back of the church.'

'Oh.' Calissa preened the front of her hair as Violet tidied up the stray strands at the back of her neck. 'Yes, I knew they were visiting family in Bristol for Christmas, but I didn't think they'd be able to get here for the ceremony today. They'd already written to say as much. As for their not coming here for the breakfast, I assume they must need to return home sooner rather than later. Because of the snow perhaps. Either way, it was very kind of them to make the effort, don't you think? I hope we will meet up again soon. I must write to them and thank them for coming. It would have been lovely to speak with them for a while.' She lowered her hand to her lap. 'I do miss city life.'

'Indeed.' Violet agreed as she put the last of the hairpins back in place though in truth she couldn't imagine anything worse. Thankfully the camp rarely left the countryside but when they had Violet had truly felt like a fish out of water. The noise was continuous, the air smoky and bitter and the sheer volume of people...There was nothing about the city that enabled one to feel the slightest bit relaxed or at peace. She wondered how Joe would cope under the same pressure and promptly buried the thought away, hoping that she wouldn't be around to find out.

'All done. Shall we go find this photographer of yours?' Calissa finally smiled, a shy tentative smile.

'We shall. And you shall stand beside me.' She rose from her seat. 'And for what it is worth, I am truly sorry, Violet. You are a good person. You did not deserve the outburst I inflicted on you.'

'Why don't we just put it behind us?' Violet smiled as Calissa made her way towards the door, silently counting down the minutes until she could leave. Until she could finally breathe again.

*****

There was an impatient murmuring as Violet made her way into the dining room with the rest of the wedding party, the photography had taken longer than expected. Her cheeks aching Violet glanced around the room and spotted William subtly waving to get her attention. She made her way over to him, slipping into a seat between him and Alfie. Alfie screwed up his face as she sat down.

'Is it vital that we attend this?' Constance laughed under her breath and playfully smacked him on the leg.

'Of course it is, Alfie. You know it is!'

'But I feel so out of place.'

'We'll leave as soon as the breakfast is over. Believe me, you're not the only one dying to get out of here.' Violet leaned over and whispered in his ear, desperate not to be overheard. Not that anyone could be heard over Calissa's high pitched squealing as she moved to take her place, she and Joseph having been seated directly opposite Violet with Gwilym and Amelia filling the seats either side of them. If Joseph had wanted understated that was certainly what he had managed to achieve. As soon as he and Calissa were seated the waiting staff began pouring into the room. Joseph scowled.

'What is this?' He looked at the bowl that was placed in front of him. Calissa laughed.

'It's soup, darling.'

'I can see that it's soup. I thought we were just skipping straight to the main course? We looked at the menus and agreed them, didn't we?'

'I made a few changes. After corresponding with my friends in London we agreed that one can only be so provincial on one's wedding day. So, I asked cook to make some alterations to the menu.'

'What alterations?'

'Soup to start, turbot in lobster sauce as a second course, you still have your roast lamb as a third course, and then strawberries, jams and preserves, cake and madeira for dessert.'

'But we agreed…'

'This is our first attempt at entertaining darling. I want to make a good impression.' Calissa spoke in hushed tones behind her napkin, her head turned towards Joseph.

'And I would at least like to enjoy what is put in front of me, considering the cost.' Joseph countered, glaring at the bowl in front of him. 'And what is that infernal racket?' He looked up at the ceiling, wincing at the banging and crashing that rumbled over his head.

'I have asked the staff to move your writing desk into my room.' Calissa smiled. 'My suite is bigger than yours after all and I know how fond you are of that desk, even though it is a battered eyesore. Perhaps we will buy you a new one.' Joseph turned to look at Calissa.

'You have moved my desk to your room?'

'It means a great deal to you, so, yes.' Violet felt her stomach churning as Joseph's face paled. How had she not thought that far ahead? Not realised that the space she had occupied last night would be taken by Calissa from now on? He would lie with her every night, as her husband. It was Calissa he would talk to in the twilight hours. Calissa that he would wake with. And maybe one day they would have children and he would come to love her. The thought only exacerbated her nausea.

'Miss Yardley, please eat something, you are looking quite ill. I don't want to have to pull you out of the soup!' Violet looked up from her own bowl to where Calissa regarded her, her laughter a shrill blast of noise that made Violet wince behind gritted teeth.

'Of course.' Violet lifted her spoon as the others began eating. 'It sounds as though you have laid on a magnificent spread, Mrs Davenport.'

'I have certainly done my best. And I will be going a step further tomorrow morning.' Calissa lifted her spoon and ran it through her soup before she looked back at Violet. 'I have given the kitchen staff the day off. I intend to make breakfast for my new husband and family. I have been preparing the menu for weeks now.' Calissa smiled at Violet as Joseph looked to her disbelievingly.

'You look a little pale yourself, Mr Davenport. Might I suggest that it is because you can scarcely believe your luck? To have wedded such a beauty as Calissa?'

'William, you are too kind. Isn't he Joe?'

'Too kind.' Joseph glared at William who lifted his glass and proposed a toast to the happy couple, all humour and grace which seemed to enrage Joseph even further as much as he tried to mask it with a smile.

'But wait, I am neglecting my dinner companion.' William grabbed a basket of bread rolls from the centre of the table. 'Miss Yardley. Can I interest you in a bread roll to accompany your soup? By their appearance I would suggest that this is no plain bread roll?' He looked to Calissa for confirmation.

'You are correct. I have requested that they be made using a traditional French recipe.' William nodded, suitably impressed.

'So, there you have it, Miss Yardley. Can I interest you in a traditional French roll?' Violet watched as Calissa drifted off into another conversation and Joseph turned to talk with Constance before she turned her attention to William.

'What on earth are you doing?'

'I'm having a little fun, Miss Yardley!' William lifted his wine glass and finished off what was left of the contents before topping up his and Violet's glasses. 'Lord knows, we could do with it.'

'Still, you shouldn't be so rude!'

'You're enjoying it as much as I am and don't try to deny it.' William grabbed his knife and speared a curl of butter, lifting it from the plate that sat in front of him. 'Now, here, allow me to spread what is undoubtedly the best butter throughout the entire British empire on the finest French roll that was ever baked.'

The rest of the meal was mostly dominated Joseph's and Calissa's fathers as they talked business from each end of the table. There were sporadic periods where Constance would engage Calissa in conversation and Violet could see the way that everyone else relaxed when her mother's voice filled the room, the pressure lifted off them even if it were for the briefest of moments. It was something her mother was always good at, putting people at ease. It was why she was so good at her work. Why she kept so many close friends and why Violet loved her as she did. 'There has been no mention of a honeymoon?' Constance enquired. Gwilym cleared his throat.

'I was going to ask the same. Sir, you have made no plans for your absence. Who will run the business while you are away? Are there any extra chores you need me to pick up?'

'Just Joe, please Gil. And to answer your question…' Joseph began wearily before Calissa interrupted.

'We will not honeymoon until I can be assured Joe is well enough to take an extended trip.' She took a slow, lazy sip of madeira. 'But I fancy that we will travel and explore the far ends of the earth when he is ready to do so. Isn't that right darling?' Violet reached out for her own glass and consumed the contents in one mouthful, smiling appreciatively at William as he refilled it. 'We would be like Phileas Fogg and Passepartout.' Violet smiled at the memory. What had she said then? It was a beautiful dream, but that was all it would ever be. She glanced up at Joseph and found him staring back at her. Did he know what she was thinking? Of course he did. He always did.

'And what about you, Mrs Yardley?' Constance lowered the candied fruit that she was about to bite into.

'What about me, Mrs Davenport?' Calissa smiled at the sound of her new title.

'You are nomadic are you not? I wondered when you might next be travelling on to pastures new?'

'Please, I don't want you to think that you are not welcome.' Joseph said testily. Constance smiled, completely unaffected by Calissa's comment.

'I assure you I didn't perceive anything of the sort in Mrs Davenport's query. And to answer your question, Mrs Davenport, the matter has not yet been agreed. It very much depends on when we perceive there may be a need for our talents elsewhere. That could be tomorrow, it could be in a few weeks. We never really stay anywhere for prolonged periods of time.'

'A few weeks!' Amelia exclaimed. 'No, you cannot leave me!' Violet smiled sympathetically.

'I won't be very far away, I promise. I'll still be able to visit from time to time.'

'You'll be around more frequently than that I hope.' William took a sip of his madeira. 'After all, I'm going to need your expertise if we are to get this business off the ground.' Violet looked at William and then at Joseph who chose not to look at her but to play with his dessert fork, spinning it on one of its fronds on top of his plate. So, he had not cancelled the arrangement after everything she had said.

'What business is this?' Calissa's father interrupted.

'The local pharmacy. I would like to acquire it. And I would like Miss Yardley to be my partner.'

'This is the first that I've heard of this. Violet?' Violet smiled awkwardly at her mother and Alfie who watched in bemused silence.

'We are still in the first stages of negotiation.' Violet replied. 'There is a lot to be discussed before agreements are made.'

'I fancy you might be more than partners some day!' Calissa's father laughed, a raucous laugh that seemed to start from his boots and raised his glass to William, unaware of the eyes around the table that watched him or how Joseph scowled at him even as William smiled bashfully. 'Well, if you need any advice you know where to find it.'

'I do not wish to ruin the bearer of bad tidings, but the snow is getting much heavier. Mother, I think it might be wise to leave sooner rather than later. We may not get the cart home if we stay much longer.' Constance looked at Violet and then out of the window.

'Good lord you are right child.' She smiled at Calissa and Joseph. 'I'm sorry to leave so abruptly but I think we should depart as soon as possible.'

'Of course. I'll have your cart brought to the front of the house.' Joseph leapt from his seat.

'Darling there are staff to do that for us.' Violet couldn't help but smile as Gwilym caught her eye and Amelia began giggling behind her napkin. Well, that was that then. She hadn't even made it until morning. Unaware that she was the source of any humour, Calissa watched as Joseph moved round the table.

'We may have staff to attend to our needs, but these are our guests and I am happy to ensure that they have safe passage. Besides, a blast of fresh air would be most welcome.'

'Would you ask them to prepare my horse as well?' William finished the last of his madeira. 'I need to get to the post office before the snow cuts off the path.'

'Of course.' Joseph glanced over his shoulder as he walked out into the hall and called for the footmen before he ushered Violet, her mother and Alfie to the front door, stopping to help Violet into her coat. 'The weather can be a powerful ally.' Joseph mused. 'I used the very same excuse to clear the house so that I could ride to the camp on the first evening I heard of your return.'

'You did?' Violet turned to look at him.

'I did. Gil and I came to the camp on the evening of my birthday. Of our birthdays. You were sitting by the campfire. For a second I could have sworn that you saw me.'

'I didn't see you.' Violet took a step back, mesmerised. 'But I knew it. I knew that you were there. I told myself it was just wishful thinking.'

'The things I should have done differently.' Joseph mused.

'And I.' Violet lamented. 'I should have said yes last night, Joe. When you asked me to leave. We could have made it work.' She sighed. 'But it is too late now. What will be, will be.' She looked up at the falling snow. 'I must go.'

'You intend to leave here forever. And you will not stay nearby.' It was a statement, not a question. Joseph stared at her, the blood draining from his face.

'Violet, are you ready?'

'Yes.' Violet glanced over her shoulder at her mother then turned back to Joseph. 'Be happy.' She smiled and placed her hand on his cheek.

'I love you.' Joseph breathed the words against the palm of her hand. Violet let her hand drop, clenching it tight as though she could capture his words, her smile slowly dissolving.

'I love you. Goodbye, Joe.' She took a deep breath and looked at him one last time and walked away.

*****

'Violet, you look so beautiful!' Edie gushed as Violet made her way into the tent, her hands holding her skirts up and out of the snow.

'I don't feel it.' Violet mumbled as she made her way over to the small enclosure that was hers and hers alone. 'Come and help me untie this dress, will you Edie?'

'Of course!' Edie dutifully followed behind her, leaning up against her back and wrapping her arms around her as soon as they were out of sight. 'Was it very bad?'

'Worse.' Violet whispered. 'He is married, Edie. Married. It is over.'

'Or, is it just beginning?' Edie offered, and Violet couldn't help but smile, grateful for her friend's never-ending optimism.

'Do you think you could do something with this dress? I think you would make a wonderful bride in it. If you want it that is?' Edie's eyes lit up.

'You are giving it to me?'

'I can think of no-one worthier of something this beautiful.'

'Oh Vi, thank you! Thank you, a million times over!' Edie squeezed her tightly. 'I don't know what to say!'

'Yes is all you need say.' Violet removed herself from Edie's grasp and giggled. 'Someone should get something out of this wedding, after all.'

*****

Her mother was gathered together with Alfie and her sisters when Violet wandered back into the main enclosure. They huddled around the fire murmuring quietly amongst themselves, their voices falling away when they noted her arrival.

'Please, don't stop on my account.' Violet looked over to them as she walked past.

'Alfie has something for you.' Her mother called out, stopping Violet in her tracks.

'I'm sorry, Vi.' Alfie made his way towards her blushing furiously, a small brown package in his hand. 'Gil gave this to me when we were going into the church. Said the postman had given it to him and he just wanted someone to keep hold of it until after the ceremony. Why he didn't just throw it into his own carriage is beyond me, but I guess his head was all over the place, what with his being best man and all, so I just stuck it in the saddlebag. It's for Doctor Tremaine. He turned up at the ceremony just before you did but by the time he'd arrived, I'd completely forgotten about it. I hope it's nothing urgent.'

'Don't worry Alfie. I'm guessing this is the parcel that William just went to collect. It's medication for Joe. You can pop it over there in the morning. Really, it's fine.' She looked at the parcel and the neat script on it before she placed it down on the table and made her way over to the mirror, pulling the sheet from it so that the onyx pane reflected the light from within the tent, casting her in silhouette.

'Why do you go to the mirror now child?' Flossie called out as Violet dropped down in front of her muted reflection.

'I need answers, Aunt Flossie. Guidance, I don't know. Just something.'

'But you already have the answers you need. Think, child! Think!' Ruby leapt from her chair and moved to stand in front of her sister.

'Flossie, hold your tongue.'

'Oh hush, you silly old goat.' Flossie swept her arms out, brushing her sister aside.

'Floss, I'm warning you. It is not up to you to determine fate. You are over-stepping the boundaries!'

'The fates.' Flossie said bitterly, jabbing a finger at Ruby. 'I'm sick and tired of waiting for the fates to do the right thing and I will not stand by any longer waiting to see what kind of a hand the fates deal! There are too many people dying and the way we're going we're going to lose one of our own. This will not do Ruby! It will not do!' She pushed past Ruby and made her way over to Violet, grabbing the parcel off the table. 'I don't like William Tremaine child. I don't trust him.' Violet frowned as Flossie pulled a chair over to where Violet knelt and sat down beside her.

'I'm sorry, aunt. You're going to have to explain.'

'Do you not think it strange that Joseph has not fallen ill since Tremaine arrived?' Violet shook her head dismissively.

'You're confused. Doctor Tremaine is here to help. And truly, it is no surprise that Joe has not been taken ill. His condition is sporadic in nature. I will agree that like you, Mr Lewis had reservations. He too questioned the diagnosis of pleurisy and the use of bromine. But William explained his reasoning and I think Mr Lewis was greatly comforted after they talked.'

'Was he child? Or is that what you chose to hear? Besides, if he was so assured, why did he go back to the pharmacy and continue trying to find an alternative explanation? I mean, I can understand his concerns. The diagnosis and treatment suggested make no sense.'

'But Charles admitted himself that he had failed to investigate the obvious. William simply went back to basics at the library and Charles was mortified when he realised what he'd missed. And when it comes to treatments William was of the impression that Charles was just being old fashioned and that he needed to try more modern methods.'

'Maybe that's true. But that doesn't make Tremaine right when it comes to the cause or solution either. Besides, don't you think that old man Lewis had already investigated the obvious? His lifestyle may have been dubious, but that old man was as sharp as a tack.'

'So, what are you saying?' Flossie handed Violet the package.

'I'm saying open the parcel.'

'Floss!' Constance walked up behind her sister. 'That's against the law! You cannot ask Violet to engage in such acts!'

'So she'll just have to open it carefully.' Flossie answered simply. 'Carefully enough that we'll be able to re-seal it without there being any evidence of it having been tampered with.' Violet looked at the parcel, turning it over and over in her hands. 'Well, what are you waiting for child?' Flossie's voice pulled her out of her reverie.

'You really don't trust him?' Flossie shook her head, ignoring her sister's curses behind her.

'Very well.' Violet took the parcel and delicately untied the string that held the brown paper in place. Fold by fold she pulled the paper back, finally placing it on the table and staring at the plain white cardboard box in her hands.

'Open it.' Violet flipped up the lid and stared at the two smaller white boxes that were packed tightly together inside.

'No, it cannot be…'

'Is it bromine?' Flossie asked.

'It's arsenic. I, I don't understand.' Violet looked up from the package. 'Isn't arsenic also used in the treatment of pleurisy?'

'It is. So why does he feel the need to lie to you?'

'Oh, sister…' Constance sighed and dropped down into the chair next to the furnace as Ruby came to stand next to her, placing a calming hand on her shoulder.

'You should not have interfered with the fates. There will be consequences for this!'

'Hush, Ruby, for goodness sake!' Flossie retaliated, her eyes never leaving Violet. 'Now, what are you going to do, child? The fates are in your hands now.'

'You genuinely suspect that William is behind Joe's illness?' Flossie said nothing as Violet dropped the parcel on the table in front of her. 'But if that is truly the case, what does this mean for Mrs Davenport? She presented the same symptoms as Joe.' Flossie nodded approvingly.

'So, I'll ask you again child. The fates are in your hands now. What are you going to do?'

Chapter thirty-four

Violet perched on the edge of her bed and gazed into her hand mirror as she ran her fingers under her eyes, hopeful that the simple gesture could remove the dark circles that lay there. Even in the dim candlelight they stood out like a sore thumb. Perhaps tonight. Perhaps tonight she might finally rest. She placed the mirror down on the bed and stood to shake out the creases in her dress. After considering each of her outfits in turn she had decided to opt for the half mourning gown. After all, this was not merely a formal visit that she was making. This was a nod to the dead.

Aunt Ruby was sitting by the stove when she entered the main room. She was watching the kettle boil with vacant eyes, seemingly oblivious to the steam that spindled up from its spout, the vapours hissing as they fought to escape the confines of the vessel. Violet walked over and took the kettle from the flames, her appearance bringing Ruby back from wherever her imagination had taken her. She watched in silence as Violet poured the water into a waiting teapot and placed the kettle down on a cast iron trivet next to the fire.

'Will you help me arrange my dress, Aunt Ruby? I would appear to be all fingers and thumbs and lacking in patience this morning.'

'Hardly surprising child. You must be exhausted.' Ruby reached down and straightened the edges of the gown before she pushed herself to her feet to re-tie the laces in the corset. Taking a step back she cast her eye over the dress. 'You've chosen well. You look very smart, Violet Rose.'

'I don't feel smart. I feel tired and angry and more than anything else I feel like a gullible fool.' She toyed with the string on the re-wrapped parcel. 'So much is riding on this. What if I say or do the wrong thing?'

'You'll know what to do.' Ruby patted her arm and made her way over to the teapot, grabbing a spoon and swirling the leaves inside. Violet glanced over at aunt Flossie who still slept soundly, her back facing the centre of the room. The sight bought a smile to her lips.

'Clearly I am not the only one who is exhausted. I have not heard aunt Flossie snore once since I woke.'

'Pfft.' Ruby shook her head slowly. 'I warned her that there would be consequences.'

'What do you mean?'

'She interfered with the fates, child. She knew the price. A life for a life.' Ruby turned to look at Flossie. 'And she loved you more than life itself.'

'What? No!' Violet dashed over to where Flossie lay. She was as still as a statue. There was no rise and fall to her chest, the rosy complexion that had turned her cheeks to flame such a short time ago faded to ash. Violet reached out to touch her hand. She was as cold as stone. Violet whirled on Ruby.

'She did not die alone. I held her hand as she passed.'

'She's dead because of me?'

'No, she left this world for you. Not because of you.' Ruby stirred the contents of the teapot one final time, placed the strainer over her cup and began to pour as though it was the most normal thing in the world. As though her sister were not lying dead only a few feet from where she stood.

'We should wake mother.'

'No.' Ruby said firmly as she sat back down. 'Let your mother sleep a few minutes longer. Besides, they said their goodbyes last night. Flossie insisted your mother not stay up. She knew she'd be needed today.'

'You mean, you all knew what would happen?'

'Of course we did, child! You heard us warn her!'

'Yes, but I didn't think you meant…Why didn't you tell me?'

'What good would that have done?' Ruby took a sip of her tea and placed the cup and saucer in her lap.

'I could have stopped her!'

'Ha! You think you could have stopped her?'

'I would have tried!'

'And you would have failed.'

'Still, you should have told me.'

'And have you go to bed with that on your conscience? You'd have been lying there fretting and moping all night and not getting any rest and you wouldn't have been ready to do what you need to do today. Your aunt did this for a reason, so I suggest you concentrate on that for now.'

'But I didn't get to say goodbye.' Ruby reached round to grab Violet's cloak off the back of the chair where she sat. 'I know, pet.' She said softly. 'But there will be plenty of time to mourn. Now go. Go and make things right. Do not let your aunt's sacrifice be for nothing.' Violet nodded, wiping the tears from under her eyes. She leant over and kissed Flossie's frozen cheek, silently saying goodbye and walked over to take the cloak from Ruby, throwing it around her shoulders and swiftly fastening the button.

'Here.' Ruby placed her teacup on the table next to her. Standing up she delved into the pocket of her apron. 'Wear this.' She reached up and fixed a small cameo brooch to the collar of Violet's cloak. 'This belonged to Floss.

Take her with you. I think she's going to want to see this, don't you?' Ruby smiled softly as Violet leaned forward and pecked her on the cheek.

'Thank you.' Violet lifted her hat from the table and fixed it in place before she slipped on her black velvet gloves, using them to wipe away the last of her tears and turned to her aunt, her mind suddenly as clear as the ringing of a bell. It must have resonated in her face by the way her aunt smiled at her with a look of pride that was almost fierce in its nature.

'That's it. There's my girl.' Ruby returned to her seat and retrieved her cup from the table. 'Remember Violet Rose, the fates are with you. Now go.'

*****

Violet cursed as she stepped out of the tent and her feet sank into the snow. It was far too deep to take the carriage. But then maybe the carriage was a bad idea anyway. It would alert the staff in the house to her arrival. She turned back into the tent and grabbed Joseph's saddle and reins and made her way over to the ramshackle enclosure where Berkeley stood waiting for her, his breath a fountain of steam in the cold morning air. She pulled his blanket from his back, throwing it over the fence next to her and quickly tied the saddle and reins in place before she led him towards the edge of the camp.

'Looks as though you're going to get that run now, lad.' Violet whispered as she ran her hand down his nose. 'Just don't slip on the ice. For the love of god, don't slip.' She clambered on to Berkeley, cursing as her skirt wrapped around her legs.

'Stop, stop, stop. You'll tear the dress to ribbons the way you're going.' Alfie made his way out of his tent, lantern in hand and walked over to her. 'Let me help.'

'Thank you.' Violet sighed as Alfie rearranged her skirts so that she could move in the saddle.

'Are you ready?' He came to stand in front of Berkeley.

'I am.' Violet nodded assertively.

'I'll see you soon.' Alfie tousled Berkeley's main and looked up at Violet. 'Be careful, Vi.'

'I will, I promise.' Violet replied hurriedly. 'I must go.' She took one last glance at Alfie as he stood aside before she made her way out onto the narrow track that followed the river. After what felt like a lifetime they crossed the bridge that led them into wide open fields, the view almost as clear it would be in daylight, so great was the power of the moon against the frozen landscape. Berkeley began to wicker, stretching his neck forward and pinning his ears back.

'Oh, you know, don't you?' Violet smiled as she dug her heels into his flank. 'Go, Berkeley!' Violet grabbed onto the reins fiercely as the horse launched from a slow walk to a breath-taking gallop and for a brief few minutes nothing else mattered. It was just the icy wind that blasted across her face and the muffled sound of Berkeley's hooves, pounding the ground and kicking out the snow behind them as they traversed from field to field, Berkeley requiring no instruction whatsoever. But then he knew where he was going, Violet supposed. He knew he was going home.

The only lanterns still lit were those outside the main entrance and in the kitchen as Violet walked Berkeley back into his familiar old stall. In the distance, she could hear the dogs barking as they played, hear Gwilym commanding them with gentle blows of his whistle as he called the pack back together. They would be home soon. No matter. Gwilym had done his job. She heard the Grandfather clock in the hall strike six as she made her way along the side path and into the kitchen.

'There you are Ma'am.' Winnie was stood in front of the sink, deftly slicing carrots and throwing them into a pan of water. 'There's a cup of coffee keeping warm on the stove for you. I'm just getting things ready for lunch.' She said, her eyes never leaving the task at hand.

'Please, call me Violet,' Winnie smiled and nodded.

'As you wish, Violet.' She turned at that, her eyes widening. 'I take it you rode here?'

'Does it show?' Violet winced as Winnie giggled.

'A little.' She threw the last two chunks of carrot into the saucepan and dried her hands on the towel that was tied to her apron. 'Here, let me tidy your hair for you.'

'Thank you, Winnie.' She sat down at the table in the centre of the kitchen, smiling up appreciatively as Winnie removed her hat and began to fix her hair back in place.

'Gwilym said you would be here early but I couldn't make head nor tail as to the reason why.'

'It is unusual I know. But I have a parcel for Dr Tremaine and I need to ensure he gets it. I have to leave town for a few weeks and mother insists we depart as soon as the sun is up.'

'Oh, I see. Well, Mrs Davenport is due down in half an hour to prepare breakfast. I'm about to put out all the ingredients and the recipe cards for her now.' Winnie chuckled mischievously. 'Bless her cottons. I don't think she has a clue what to do in the kitchen. I had to run through all the different instructions with her time and time again so she could just get on with things this morning. Quite romantic really.'

'It is.' Violet said cheerily as Gwilym made his way into the kitchen.

'Was that you tearing across the fields?' He grinned as he made his way over to the fire and began rubbing his hands together vigorously.

'I can't imagine there are many people stupid enough to be out riding at this time of the morning, can you?' She thanked Winnie as the maid pinned her hat back in place and made her way back to the stove. 'Did you sleep well?'

'Not particularly. I was in the groundskeeper's cottage last night. We ran out of wood. It was freezing in there.'

'We?' Violet frowned.

'*We.*' Gwilym repeated more forcefully.

'Oh, I see.' Violet bit her lip to keep from smiling as she sipped her drink, revelling in its warmth.

'Exactly. Went down like a lead balloon that did.' He glanced over at Winnie who, though she had her back to them, was undoubtedly hanging on their every word. 'Perhaps I could find you somewhere more comfortable to wait? The library perhaps?'

'That would be wonderful, thank you Gil.' Violet put down her cup and followed Gwilym down the hall and into the library.

'I'll collect you when it's time.' Gwilym showed Violet to a seat next to the freshly lit fire and made his way back to the door. He turned as he made his way out. 'If you need me, call. I won't be far away.' He gently pulled the door shut leaving Violet alone with her thoughts.

Chapter thirty-five

'Good morning.' Amelia smiled wearily as she made her way into the dining room. She quietly slid down onto the seat next to Joseph, rubbing her fingers across her eyes and doing her best to stifle a yawn.

'Did you sleep well?' Joseph peered at her as he leant forward and grabbed his napkin from the table. He shook it out and laid it on his lap as Amelia rested her head on his upper arm.

'Once the screeching had stopped.' Amelia grumbled. 'She's your wife, can't you do something to placate her?' Joseph shrugged.

'No-one has managed it before. I don't know why you think I should be any different.'

'That much is true, I suppose.' His sister yawned again. 'As intelligent as you are, I confess I have never yet witnessed you performing miracles of any sort.'

'There, that is all of it.' Calissa burst into the room carrying a bowl of greyish looking kedgeree. She placed the dish in front of Joseph, smiling to herself as she made her way along the table, filling everyone's cups with fresh coffee.

'Amelia, I made you hot chocolate.' She placed a smaller pot in front of her new sister.

'That's lovely. Thank you.' Amelia smiled nervously and poured the thick liquid into her cup, her eyes widening as she took a sip. 'It's delicious!'

'My mother's recipe.' Calissa smiled. 'She used to make it for us when we were little.' She glanced up at Joe as she filled his cup with coffee and placed it back on its saucer. 'Did you sleep well darling?'

'Very well.' Joseph smiled. The truth was he was still cold to the bone, but it was worth it, he thought. It would never stop being worth it.

'I am pleased. Here, you must try this coffee. A friend of ours who has travelled to the Americas bought it back as a gift. It sounds like such a magnificent place. Perhaps one day we may even get to visit there ourselves?'

'Perhaps.' Joseph winced as he sipped the coffee.

'It is too strong for you.' Calissa pouted. 'I have ruined it.'

'No, it's just a little stronger than I'm used to.' Joseph smiled awkwardly as he took another sip. Calissa's face lit up in reply.

'Father is quite partial to this particular bean. He has been sulking ever since I told him I was saving the last bag for today, isn't that right father? Hence my decision to make two pots. One for each end of the table, because if I don't make you your own, father will probably drink the lot!' She snorted as her father downed the contents of his cup in one mouthful and raised the empty vessel to her. 'You have done a wonderful job here, Calissa. Simply wonderful.'

'Thank you, father. What do you think, Joe?' Joseph glanced over the table. There was everything from kedgeree to cold meats and devilled kidneys that looked more like bullets than anything edible. There was a bowl of bread at the far end of the table which looked like the most attractive option available and placed directly in front of him was a plate of scrambled eggs that he guessed might need slicing rather than spooning.

'I think you've worked really hard.' Joseph conceded, unable to ignore the guilt that gnawed at his bones. Because it wasn't that she was particularly awful. Well maybe she was, but more than that, she just wasn't Violet. He smiled softly and took another sip of his coffee as Calissa moved round the table to sit beside him.

'Please, tuck in. I wouldn't want everything to get cold.'

'God forbid.' Edwin muttered under his breath. Amelia and Joseph turned to look at their father as he glanced up from his empty plate and winked, the corner of his lip curling up as Amelia buried her laughter behind a napkin and Joseph found himself grinning, albeit awkwardly, at his father for the first time in as long as he could remember. This was why he had gone through with the wedding, he told himself. This was what mattered. Joseph reached forward and grabbed the plate of solidified eggs and passed them to his father.

'Perhaps you would like to serve?' Edwin Davenport scowled at him in reply but there was no malice in it, his eyes twinkling as he took the plate from his son.

'I'd be happy to.' His father whispered. 'If you would be as kind as to pass me the bread knife.' A sudden sharp knock at the door brought everything to a standstill.

'Sorry for interrupting, but you have a guest sir. I understand it's quite urgent.' Gwilym bowed towards Edwin and stood aside allowing Violet to make her way into the room.

'I'll be just outside if you need me.' Gwilym cleared his throat and closed the door behind him.

'Miss Yardley, what is the meaning of this? Do you have any idea what time it is?' Edwin bellowed from his seat. Violet cast her eyes over the table, watched in silence as the men belatedly took to their feet and bowed before she curtseyed stiffly in reply.

'Mr Davenport, I apologise for the intrusion at this early hour sir, I am leaving town for a few weeks visiting family and there were a few things I needed to tie up first.'

'Oh. I see.' Edwin didn't even attempt to mask his self-satisfied expression. 'Well in that case you had better come in. Please take a seat.' He gestured to the empty chair opposite Calissa.

'Thank you, sir. I won't take up too much of your time.' Violet moved across the room and hesitantly took a place at the table.

'Nonsense! It is a pleasure to see you, isn't it, Joe?' Calissa protectively placed her hand over Joseph's. 'Can I get you something to eat? Some coffee perhaps?' Violet shook her head.

'No, I am quite content thank you.'

'I wouldn't say no to a top-up.' Mr Parnell called from his seat. Calissa sighed wearily.

'Father, the pot is directly in front of you.'

'Please, allow me.' Violet got up from her seat and made her way over to Calissa's father as Calissa clasped her hands together and held them to her chest.

'What a darling friend you are! I have been run off my feet this morning and I am quite worn out!' Violet looked at food laid out on the table.

'I'm not surprised. Did you do all this this morning?'

'With my own fair hands!' Calissa beamed. 'But enough talk of food. Who are you here to see?'

'Not to see. I'm here with regards to a parcel that was delivered here yesterday evening. By Alfie.' Violet clarified. 'It belongs to William.'

'A parcel for William?' Calissa frowned. 'Oh! You must be referring to Joe's medicine! Well, now before you get to that, perhaps you can solve a mystery for us, Miss Yardley. We haven't seen hide nor hair of him since the wedding.' Violet glanced over at Joseph who watched her intently. She held his gaze for just long enough. Willed him to understand. *Whatever happens next, just, trust me.* Turning away from him, she smiled at Calissa and leaned forward, resting her hands on the table, the cuffs of her sleeves slipping away from her wrists.

'Vi, what are those bruises on your arms?' Joseph's face paled. 'What happened to you?' Violet looked down at her arms and back to Joseph.

'Oh, that's nothing. Do not concern yourself, Joe.' Joseph reached forward and grabbed her hand, turning her arm to inspect her wrist more closely.

'Do not concern myself? These are fingerprints. I'll ask you again. Who did this to you?' Violet pulled her arm back from his grasp, her eyes never leaving Calissa.

'I know, Calissa.' Violet smirked. 'I know everything.'

'What on earth are you talking about?' Calissa leaned back in her seat, all confidence melting away. 'Dearest friend, you sound as though you have gone quite mad.' Violet rose to her feet.

'I know about you and Tremaine. He has confessed everything. And you should know that the reason that you have not seen him since the wedding is that he is currently being held in the town jail.'

'What on earth is going on?' Edwin's face turned puce. 'How dare you march in here…'

'Please, sit down, Mr Davenport.' Violet cut him off. 'You have had your say, sir. Now I will have mine.'

'How dare you! Gwilym! Come and remove this witch from the room!' A split second later Gwilym appeared in the room. Ignoring his master's commands, he silently closed the door and turned around to lean against it.

'You need to hear what Miss Yardley has to say, sir.'

'Did you hear me lad?' Edwin rose to his feet. 'Get over here now, boy or you'll be out on your ear!'

'Enough!' Joseph bellowed, rising to face his father. 'Sit down, father! The least we can do is hear what Vi has to say.' He stayed standing as Edwin returned to his seat, silenced by his son's rare outburst.

'Joseph, darling don't be ridiculous! I appreciate that she is a close acquaintance of yours, but she has clearly lost all sense! I want her out of here! She is frightening me!' Calissa glared at Gwilym and back to Violet, her expression as cold as ice.

'No. We will hear what Vi has to say.' Joseph returned to his seat and looked over to Violet, returning her gaze. *I trust you.* 'Please, continue.' Violet nodded, a new wave of confidence surging through her as she regarded the silver jug of coffee placed on the table in front of Joseph.

'Coffee all the way from the Americas? Very expensive apparently. I know this because you told Gwilym so as you prepared it earlier this morning. Just before he switched the jugs.'

'What did you say?' Calissa paled.

'Perhaps I will have a cup after all.' Violet reached out and filled the cup in front of her then took a sip, her eyes never leaving Calissa. 'It is rather strong. Almost as if you were trying to hide something, don't you think?' She glanced at the pot at the other end of the table. 'Or was that the one you were hiding something in? The one your father has been drinking from? Hmmm…'

Violet considered the pot in front of her, tapping her fingers against its side. 'Well, I'm drinking from this one so I guess it must be that one.'

'Father…' Calissa looked to her father uncertainly.

'It is surprising, troubling even, when one realises how quickly a loved one's loyalty can waiver, especially when they are forced to consider the notion that the last time they'll see the sun will be as they walk to the gallows.'

'Where is William?' Calissa stood from her seat. 'What have you done to him?'

'I didn't do anything to him. I can't say the same for the Police.' Violet took another sip of her coffee. 'And as I stated before Mrs Tremaine…' Violet let the moniker hang in the air. 'He, is in jail. As is the cook who I believe you lined up for a position here. The same cook who has not only been in Mr Davenport's employ, but also in yours for the last three years.'

'That is a lie! Father, stop her!' Calissa's cheeks flushed bright red.

'Quiet, Calissa!' Joseph rose from his seat, silencing her instantly. 'What do you mean, Vi? Mrs Tremaine?'

'They've been married for just over a year now.' Violet turned to face Edwin. 'I'm sorry you should have to hear this from me in such a hideous fashion, but you must know the truth. Your wife was not taken by a curse, sir. There was no disease. No sickness. And Joseph has not been plagued by whatever ailed her. Your wife was poisoned. Joseph is being poisoned. Can I have the parcel please, Gil.' She reached her hand backwards, placing it flat so that Gwilym could place the small white box on her gloved palm and smiled her thanks.

'What is that?' Joseph squinted at the box, trying to read the label on the top.

Violet placed the box down on the table. 'I received this package yesterday. William was supposed to collect it from the post office, but the postman decided he would do him a favour and bring it to him, given that the weather looked to be worsening. He gave the parcel to Gwilym outside the church who then gave it to Alfie for safe keeping, but Alfie forgot to hand it over after the wedding.

'I thought it was Joseph's medication and I had intended to send Alfie here with it today. But then my aunt Flossie told me of her suspicions surrounding William. She suggested that I open the parcel. So, I opened it. Illegal I know, but William and I had been working on a cure together, had we not? I thought I knew enough of him to be able to gauge the goodness of his character. I have to say I thought I would prove her wrong. But I didn't find what I was expecting. And I knew I was the only one who could finally put this whole matter to rest. I was the only one who could make sure that the truth was told. So, I wrote to William.

'Alfie found him coming back from the post office. He passed on the note in which I asked to meet him at the proposed pharmacy under the pretence of wanting to discuss the new venture and informing him that I was in possession of the parcel. You can imagine his relief when he arrived, although it was relatively short-lived. He was certainly surprised to find the Police waiting for him I must say, but after some, persuasion, he was strangely keen to confess all his darkest secrets.' Violet gloated.

'When Alfie delivered this box to the house last night, his instructions were to leave it on William's dresser. And you knew it would be there waiting for you this morning, didn't you, Calissa? It had already been agreed that

William was to leave the wedding breakfast early and collect this from the post office, am I right? We were all here when he was preparing to leave. Once he had collected the package he was to come back here, place it exactly where you found it and then leave town to visit family. Or at least appear to. You were supposed to have found a letter from him saying just that weren't you? That he had gone to visit his parents as his mother was under the weather? I'm surprised you weren't a little more concerned when you didn't find a note. Or at least, you didn't appear to be by your tone earlier. Did you not worry that something had gone wrong and he might have been found out? He is your husband after all.'

'No, you're lying.' Calissa's voice was barely a whisper. Violet smiled and inspected the box more closely.

'It was most fortunate that it ended up in my hands. Or unfortunate I suppose, depending on your perspective. Because you see, what I had found was not the medication I was expecting but arsenic. And today was going to be the day that Joseph had a sudden and final attack of whatever mystery illness ailed him and his mother. And the miraculous Dr Tremaine wouldn't have been here to save him. You were in their sights too Mr Davenport. They were going to pass off your own death as a heart attack, brought on by grief. It would have been quite achievable too, after all, you would have had your own physician return to carry out the autopsies, am I right Calissa? Amelia was to be sent to boarding school and Calissa, the merry widow and her father would take this house and its lands for their own, where eventually she would find love with her physician.

'At least, that was the original plan. When the Parnells arrived here and learned of the accusations that had been levelled at my family they found a far more plausible story at their disposal. It was agreed that Dr Tremaine, who isn't actually a doctor by the way, would diagnose arsenic poisoning and it would be down to Calissa to inform the police of the recent problems between our families. The police would have found the evidence they needed as well wouldn't they Calissa?' Violet stared at the box. 'You see there are two of these packages. The other is with the police now, but the plan had been for William to stop by the camp, en-route to his family home, and plant the second box in my medicine chest. It would have been all the evidence the police needed to convict me and see me hung as a murderer. Either way, Mr Davenport, neither you or Joseph would have seen this day out.'

'Insolence! Edwin, have this girl removed from the house immediately before I summon the police!' Calissa's father leapt from his seat.

'Did I not explain that William, has already confessed, Mr Parnell? He also confessed to killing Aggy.' Violet turned to Joseph whose face had begun to pale. 'Aggy overheard a conversation between Calissa and William not long after his arrival. His first arrival. They'd been talking about how it wouldn't be long before you were dead and they could finally make it publicly known that they were married. Calissa realised that Aggy had heard everything when she saw Aggy running from the house. Aggy was on her way to the Police station when William found her and threatened her to remain silent. She refused. William panicked and he beat her to death. They agreed that he should stay away a while longer, in case the police waned to question him. William didn't think he would be able to hide his guilt. He eventually returned on the night of the ball.

'It was on his advice yesterday that the cook was also arrested. She too has already confessed her guilt in these matters. It was she who poisoned Josephine's food and she was doing to the same to you, Joe. And you, Mr Parnell, were paying her to do it, weren't you?' Violet gestured towards the coffee pot next to Calissa's father. 'But I would suggest that you have more important issues to deal with at this very moment. Not least the large amount of arsenic that you have consumed during the last half hour. At your own hand.'

'Father...' Calissa leapt from the table. 'Do something!'

'You are quite certain in your accusations, Miss Yardley? Edwin turned to Violet, his voice hardened, void of emotion. 'You could find yourself in an awful lot of trouble if you are not telling the truth. Perhaps *you are* the one responsible. Perhaps it is *you* who is creating the most elaborate of stories to escape the noose.'

'It was me that confronted William, sir. I was there when he confessed and I was at the police station until the early hours of the morning being interviewed as a witness to these matters. I assure you that every word I say is true.' Edwin nodded thoughtfully and fell back in his seat.

'John?' Is this true? You killed Josephine? I don't understand. She was your friend.'

'Friend? I loved her Edwin! She was never meant to be yours! None of this was ever meant to be yours!' John Parnell's face turned an ugly shade of red as he gripped onto the table fiercely. He was in pain, Violet realised. The arsenic was already beginning to take effect, stripping him of rational thought; of the ability to lie. Though maybe it was a truth he had been desperate to tell for a long time.

'I loved Josephine, Edwin. You *knew* how I felt about her and you took her for yourself anyway. You took everything from me! This house. The grounds. Everything that Josephine and I would have shared had we married. When the children's mother died, I begged Josephine to leave you and marry me. Unfortunately, she refused. God knows why but she was besotted by you. I'd contemplated killing you, but I knew that even if you were dead, she would never be mine. And I couldn't live, knowing that she was here, within these four walls with you and I would never be by her side. Better that she die and you suffer a lifetime of misery.'

'Oh my god, you killed Bea too, didn't you?' Edwin whispered, glancing at Calissa who gasped at the sound of her mother's name. 'You killed them both.'

'Bea's death was necessary. She was a complication that needed to be removed.' John said coldly.

'But, you loved mother.' Calissa frowned. 'You said that this was because he stole this land from you. That he had cheated you out of this house.' John Parnell scoffed at his daughter.

'And how do you think he did that? Are you really that stupid Calissa? As for your mother, she was nothing but a tupenny streetwalker.'

'No. You loved her.' Calissa said quietly, shaking her head.

'A male heir was all I wanted and what did I get? Three spoilt little brats who were nothing but a drain on my finances.' John Parnell doubled over, growling as he clutched at his stomach. 'You stupid bitch! You couldn't even get this right! No wonder your sisters disowned you. You are a disappointment to everyone you meet!'

'But your sisters are dead.' Violet frowned at Calissa.

'Who told you that?' Joseph got up and moved round the table to stand next to Violet. 'Her sisters were sat in the back of the church yesterday. I knew they'd had a falling out but…Calissa, I don't understand. Why? What did we ever do to hurt you that you would inflict this upon us?'

'We needed the money!' Calissa shrieked 'Grandpapa's estate has been running at a loss for years. We needed to do something before we lost it forever. We've already sold the house in Chepstow for a fraction of what it's worth. We were going to sell Ty Mawr and start again. And you!' Calissa pointed at her father. 'You said that this place was ours for the taking! You said it was ours in all but name!'

'You came to us for money? And the only reason I married you was because…I hope the irony isn't lost on you, father.' Joseph glanced at Edwin as his father slumped back in his chair, his eyes fixed on John as he staggered around the table. His skin was already becoming grey and clammy, his legs beginning to wobble as though he were drunk. He reached out to grab Calissa, cursing as Joseph lurched forward and wrapped his hand around John's arm. 'You paid to have my mother killed?'

'Get your hands off me!' John scowled 'Go back to your dirty little whore!'

'Murderer.'

'I said let go of me!' John threw his arms upwards forcing Joseph to release him and turned to walk away, his balance faltering as Joseph grabbed him by the shoulder spun him around and punched him, putting every ounce of his being behind a single blow to John's face. The sound of bone shattering filled the air as John Parnell fell to the floor, his eyes fluttering shut, blood trickling from the corner of his mouth. Violet took a step forward, gently took hold of Joseph's arm.

'You will get retribution. You can let them in now, Gil, don't you think?' Violet looked over to Gwilym who nodded and opened the door wide, allowing Constance, Alfie and six men in uniform to flood into the room. Violet watched in silence as Calissa and John were dragged from the room, their protests echoing throughout the house as they were carried away. Only when the police carriages disappeared from the end of the drive was the house finally silent. Even then, nobody moved.

Epilogue

'I don't know why you felt the need to use the summer carriage so early in the year. And to keep the roof down? It seems utterly nonsensical.' Joseph stepped from the courthouse and turned to his father, watching through hooded eyes as he slipped on his gloves and grumbled under his breath.

'We have been cooped up in that blasted house all winter. The air in there is so stuffy you can barely breathe. Besides, it is not that cold.' He waited for Edwin to join him and they made their way down the steps together, walking hurriedly from the gated courtyard and out onto the main street.

He was pretty certain that the last of the snow had fallen now. The sky was a deep blue, twists of white cloud streaming across it and in the distance, you could see that spring had come back to the mountains, the rusts of winter fading away once more, relenting to lush shades of vibrant green as though life itself was fighting back. He held open the large wooden gate, waiting for his father to pass through before he pulled it to behind them, closing it with a resounding thud.

Gwilym was exactly where he had left them. He glanced over in surprise as Edwin and Joseph made their way over to the carriage, shoving a large pasty back into its paper bag and dropping it onto the seat beside him as Edwin climbed into the rear of the carriage and Joseph jumped up to sit beside him.

'It's already over? I thought you'd be in there for hours.'

'First case of the day. Besides which, there was no possible defence they could have mounted that would have seemed plausible.' Joseph muttered as the carriage pulled away. The observation made it seem as though the trial had been a speedy one. Nothing could have been further from the truth. The change in season was testament to that fallacy. Three months they'd had to wait for the Assizes court to roll into town. Three months of purgatory. Three months of dreading having to reveal the family's most intimate secrets to complete strangers. But it was over now. He could almost feel the tension melting away, his mind finally giving his body permission to relax. Gwilym glanced over at Joseph and back to Edwin as the coach made its way out of the town.

'What was the verdict? If you don't mind my asking?'

'Only Calissa escaped the noose.' Edwin craned his neck to look at Gwilym. 'She got a life sentence. Screaming hysterically she was when the judge put his black cap on for sentencing. And John, I don't think he believed it was really happening. I think he thought his status would somehow get him out of the situation altogether. It was only Tremaine and the cook who seemed resigned to their fate. Calissa might see daylight in a decade or so, perhaps. But after solitary confinement for at least a year and hard labour afterwards? I don't think she'll survive it, if I'm honest.'

'The old man probably wishes the police had just let the arsenic do its job rather than this.' Gwilym smirked. 'The hangings. Do you know when?'

'No.' Joseph shook his head. 'And I have no desire to know. I've seen enough death to last a lifetime.'

'You are not pleased with the result?'

'What is there to be pleased about? This is not a victory, Gil. William Tremaine's family have lost a son, Cook's family have lost their breadwinner, so who knows what will become of them? Her children will probably end up in the workhouse which would be a tragedy. As for the Parnell family, they have lost a sister and a father. They may be adults, but they are orphaned now. So, I find more sympathy than I do satisfaction in the verdict.'

'At least now it is over.' Edwin reached back and patted Joseph on the shoulder. 'It is time for us all to move on. And it was good of your Violet to come back and give evidence, I thought. She didn't have to.'

'Violet's back?' Gwilym slowed the horse to look at Joseph. 'She came back for the trial?'

'The Police requested that she come back as a vital witness for the prosecution.'

'Not true at all.' Edwin declared. 'She could quite easily have provided a sworn statement but she demanded that she be back for the trial. Constance wrote to me a few days ago to assure me that she would be there to testify. Extremely magnanimous given the way I've treated them.'

'Did she look well?'

'She looked very well. She was every inch a fine young lady.' Edwin mused much to Joseph's surprise. 'And a brave one to boot.'

'Why didn't you tell me?' Gwilym squirmed in his seat as Joseph turned to face him. 'On the night of the wedding. When we were at the lodge. You knew that family had killed my mother and you never told me. You should have come straight to me, Gil.'

'Come straight to you?' Gwilym raised his eyebrows in disbelief. 'I think we all know how that would have worked out. You would have gone berserk and chased them out of town and they would never have received the punishment they deserved.' Gwilym laughed softly. 'You nearly did find out. You missed Alfie by a matter of seconds on your wedding night. When you came down to the gardener's lodge, he'd just left through the back entrance of the house. Once he'd dropped off the parcel we'd chatted in the kitchen and agreed that I would get the hounds out of the way so Violet could get into the house undetected.'

'Which is why you'd gotten up so early.'

'And why I insisted that you finish off the remainder of the mead. So you wouldn't.'

'You let her put herself in danger.'

'No, she was never in danger, Joe. Alfie got word to Tremaine to meet her at the new premises, said it was something to do with the lease and that Violet had a package for him, while Violet went to the Police with the arsenic. They escorted her to the shop and Alfie met them there with the shop owner, though I confess she insisted she be alone when she confronted him. The police hid themselves away in a side room.'

'Her arms were covered in bruises.'

'There was a brief scuffle, I'll admit. When he realised he'd been caught out he tried to escape through the back door. Violet held onto him until the Police could get him under control. The next morning, when Vi came to the house, I was outside the door listening to everything that was going on, as were the Police. It was vital that we got that confession. Which we did. And besides, you were in the room. You wouldn't have let anything happen to her.'

'True enough.' Joseph nodded in agreement. 'It doesn't matter how many times I try to process it all, it is still so surreal.'

'Some years after we were married, your mother told me that John had proposed to her, even though we were engaged by then.' Joseph spun round to face his father as he spoke. 'I understood then why he hadn't been able to make it to the wedding. When Josephine died, he was so troubled, but I naively thought that it was more that he was grieving again for his own wife. That your mother's death had somehow stirred the pain that still lived in him. I felt such pity for him because I knew how it felt. How much it eats you up on the inside. He was grieving, that is true, but I see now that guilt was the predominant reason for his reaction. Then of course he came up with the business proposal for the shooting grounds.

'I thought it was a good idea. That it would bring so much goodness into our lives. The marriage between you and Calissa almost seemed like the icing on the cake. And I knew I was on the way to wasting our fortune. I was desperate that Amelia get to stay in her home. If I had even imagined the hatred in his heart. And now I think of Josephine and Agnes and the way I treated the Yardleys. I threatened to destroy them. To say I am ashamed is an understatement.'

'These are all wrongs that can be righted, sir.' Gwilym glanced back at Edwin. The elder man smiled in return.

'You are right of course, Gwilym. In fact, I was thinking, could you stop at the crossroads please. Joe, perhaps you might like to walk up to the camp? There are some things that need rectifying sooner rather than later, don't you think?' He slipped his hand into his pocket and pulled out a small box. Joseph paled as he took the parcel, not needing to open the lid to know its contents.

'I found this in your room. I was not prying, I promise. I had come to apologise, but you were sound asleep. I spotted it on the table next to your bed.'

'I, I thought I had lost it.' Joseph stammered.

'But you couldn't ask for help in seeking it. Because you shouldn't have had it in the first place. You know, I can't believe you said nothing as I made the staff take the house apart looking for it.' Edwin smiled. 'You were right, of course. To hide it from me. But then you were right from the start. There is only one person that this belongs to. I think it is time that you put that right. Don't you?'

*****

'You know, you didn't have to work today.'

'Yes, I did.' Violet raked her hands over her face as the carriage pulled away from the market. 'I needed to get back to reality. I have been going insane for the past few weeks. Besides, I wanted to make sure you hadn't accidentally killed anyone while I was away.'

'That is totally uncalled for!' Alfie glared at her with mock indignation. 'Your aunt and I ran a very tight ship while you were gone! With Edie's help, of course. And no-one died.'

'I'm joking, Alfie!' Violet laughed. 'I'm grateful, truly I am and I'm sure you all did just as well without me.'

'I wouldn't go that far. The regulars were asking for you something rotten. Turns out you are much more sociable than Aunt Ruby. Though I doubt I'm the first person to have said something along those lines.'

'And I doubt you'll be the last.'

'So, how was it? The court case, I mean.'

'What is there to say? I helped a man sentence three people to death today. How do you think it was?'

'What on earth are you talking about? They chose to do what they did, Vi. They murdered four innocent people in cold blood. It was you who ensured that they got the justice they deserved. It was a very brave thing to do.'

'It was hardly brave.'

'You made sure that the truth was told. You put the safety of the camp, of the Davenports ahead of your own. If that's not brave, I don't know what is.'

'And Flossie lost her life in the process.'

'She died to ensure you could do what needed to be done.'

'That doesn't make it any easier.' Violet grabbed for the end of the blanket that covered her lap, toying with the tassels on the fringe. 'I know that Flossie saw no other way, but I can't help but think, if I hadn't been so blinded by Tremaine…'

'He is, was, a conman, Vi. He set out to fool you. It was his job to.'

'I was naive and gullible.'

'You were human. And you did nothing wrong.' Violet shook her head sadly. He would never understand. She wondered if anyone ever would. To have someone sacrifice their own life for yours. The burden still weighed heavily on her.

'You know you do her memory a disservice by mourning the way you do.' Alfie reached over, taking her hand in his.

'I know, I know.' She squeezed his fingers lightly. 'Change of subject. Tell me, do we have a date for your wedding?'

'Not yet.' Alfie groaned. 'Edie has refused to even consider dates. Said she wouldn't do anything of the sort while you were away.'

'You are not serious?'

'Couldn't be more so. And she frets day and night about that blasted dress! What will everyone think if I wear it, given where it came from? Will Violet be offended if I alter it? What if I ruin it? What if it ruins the wedding? Jinxes it somehow?' He let go of Violet's hand, raising his own and pinching thumb and forefinger together. 'I swear to the gods Vi, I am this close to burning the damned dress!'

'Oh, Alfie, I'm sorry!' Violet tried and failed to hide her laughter.

'I'm glad that my misery amuses you.' Alfie frowned at her. 'Actually, while we're alone, there is something I've been meaning to say.'

'Oh?'

'Just, thank you really I guess.'

'Well, you're welcome, Alfie. I mean, I don't know what I've done, but…'

'When you refused me, I was so angry. I thought you must be the stupidest girl in the world to throw something so easy away. But that was all it was, wasn't it? It was easy. It wasn't real and it never would have been. You made me realise that there was more.'

'And now you are happy?'

'More than you can imagine.'

'Then I am happy. And really, you do not need to thank me.' Violet smiled. She looked down the lane as the camp came into view. 'Do you have any other news for me?'

'No, I haven't seen him. Ow!' He flinched as Violet slapped his arm. 'Don't tell me that wasn't what you were asking Violet Yardley!'

'Maybe it was, maybe it wasn't.' Violet said, haughtily. 'But thank you for telling me all the same.'

They came to a stop at the edge of the camp. Everything looked the same as it had the day they'd left and yet it was all so different. Most of the men sat around a large table that they'd acquired from who knew where, playing cards and supping ale, the women pulling washing from a makeshift line as the fire was lit. Violet watched as two female customers left her tent, all smiles and ease. Whatever her aunt had said to them, it had been something they had clearly wanted to hear.

'We have visitors?' She squinted though the dusk at a caravan that was parked next to the tent. A row of gas lanterns drenched the traditional wagon in light, revealing its sage green exterior, the beading between each panel embellished in twists of gold. At the front, someone stood on a footstool, painting an arch of flowers over the entrance. Violets and dusky pink roses. Violet slowly climbed down from the carriage, watching as the man worked, each move of his brush smooth and methodical, his shirt covered in dirt and paint as he filled in the finer details of a flowering rose. Alfie smiled sneakily at Violet as she watched Joseph climb down from the stool.

'Oh, sorry, no I recall now. No, I've seen Joe several times over the past few months. Almost daily in fact. Turns out he's not just a pretty face, after all. Did you know he's really good at carpentry?'

'No, I didn't.'

'Well, he is. All the paintwork is his too. Insisted that he finish it alone, no matter how many times we offered to help. Looks as though he's finished in the nick of time as well.'

'What's going on?' Vi asked, her eyes never leaving Joseph as he stood back and cast an eye over his work.

'Not for me to say, Vi.'

'Vi!' Joseph turned round to look at her and bowed, his eyes never leaving hers as Edie ran across the camp and threw her arms around her. 'I'm so glad you are back! Are you well? You look well!'

'I am well, Edie.' Violet replied distantly, as Joseph turned to pick up the paints and brushes on the porch area of the wagon. 'Edie, what is this? Perhaps you can tell me whatever Alfie can't?'

'Not for me to say, Vi.' Violet looked at her friends and rolled her eyes. They already spoke as one? That was going to take some getting used to.

'Seriously, what is this?'

'Come to the tent and we'll talk.'

'Of course, but I need to say hello to Joe.'

'He'll wait for you, believe me. You need to see your mother first.' Edie grabbed her hand and dragged her across the campsite, removing any chance she had to protest. She glanced back at Joseph who was staring at her nervously and smiled a thin, apprehensive smile in reply as Edie pulled her into the tent.

*****

The enclosure seemed bigger, now that Flossie's bed had been removed. Only her chest of drawers and bedside table remained, covered in white lilies and bunches of lavender and rosemary to cleanse and bring balance back to the tent. Violet made her way over to aunt Ruby and hugged her fiercely. She seemed smaller, frailer, somehow though her eyes burned as brightly as she could ever recall.

'How are you, aunt?'

'Happier now that you are returned.' Ruby's eyes glistened. 'It's been awful quiet here. I hadn't realised how much I had gotten used to that daft mare snoring in the corner.'

'I hear you've been working on the stall?'

'And I have to say I've enjoyed it immensely. Although a few of the regulars might disagree. Prissy, stuck up creatures. Not everyone is keen to hear the truth, it would seem.'

'What do you mean, Aunt Ruby?'

'Ruby can tell you all about it later. Come, sit by me a moment.' Her mother called over to her from a seat next to the stove. 'There is to be a celebration of Flossie's life tonight, so we do not have long.' Violet slipped her arms from her aunt's waist and made her way over to her mother, taking a seat opposite her.

'The caravan outside. I assumed we have guests, but then I saw Joe painting it.' Violet said, knowing that whatever the truth was, her mother probably already knew it.

'I have been led to believe that the caravan is yours Vi.' Constance smiled.

'Mine? I don't understand?'

'Joseph bought it for you!' Edie said excitedly. 'He came by just a few days after you'd gone. Asked to borrow Berkeley and then we didn't see him for about a fortnight. When he showed up, he bought the caravan with him. Seems he was in Bristol on business with his father and there was someone selling it in the market there. He bought it on the spot apparently, had it transported back to his house and took Berkeley back to train him how to pull it properly. Then he turned up here, horse, wagon full of wood, boxes of paint and paintbrushes and he's been here pretty much every day since.'

'He's just been carrying out the finishing touches, I gather.' Constance smiled. 'He popped in for tea earlier and we had a chance to talk.'

'Oh? Did he say why he bought it? I mean, I don't know what I should say to him. I cannot accept a gift of such magnitude, surely?'

'You need to listen to what he has to say. I will not speak for him' Constance leaned forward and ran her fingers through the front of Violet's hair. 'He is a good man, Violet.'

'I know, mother.' Violet said distractedly, peering out through a gap in the canvas towards the caravan. Constance smiled.

'Good. Go change into something for Flossie's party. Joe is waiting for you. And remember. Follow your heart. Not your head.'

*****

The sky had turned to onyx as Violet made her way over to the caravan where Joseph sat on the porch, now wrapped in his familiar old black jumper. He smiled as she approached, bowing his head in greeting.

'Miss Yardley, I'm glad you could join me.'

Mr Davenport - it is good to see you, sir. Now if you would be good enough to explain what going on here, since no-one else seems able or willing to?'

'It would be my pleasure.' He turned to stand and reached a hand out to her, guiding her up the steps that led into the caravan and opening the door to let her in. 'Be careful, the paint around the door is not quite dry.' He stood to one side, watching her nervously as she made her way inside and followed her in, closing the door behind them.

'Oh, Joe it's beautiful!' Violet came to a standstill in the middle of the caravan, all thought, all her prepared speeches, melting into silence. On one side of the space there was a series of cupboards and work surfaces, a log stove burning between them, on the other a small sofa, next to it a tiny wooden table and a writer's bureau which was already covered in manuscript paper and bottles of ink and fountain pens. There was a raised dais at the end that was framed by curtains which were gathered back to reveal a bed covered in blankets and cushions, but it was the ceiling that caught violet's eye. Dark blue wallpaper covered in golden stars had been inset into wooden arches as though he had captured the night and made it hers.

'I've managed to acquire a new bottle of mead. Could I interest you in a cup? Still no fancy glasses I'm afraid.' Violet nodded wordlessly as Joseph moved around her and lifted two familiar chipped cups from a shelf. He grabbed the mead from the counter and filled the cups passing one to her.

'You approve?'

'Approve? Joe, it's breath-taking.'

'I'm glad you like it.' He took a sip of his mead. 'You were gone longer than I expected. I started to wonder whether you would return.'

'The trip ended up being far longer than we had anticipated.' Violet admitted. 'We went to visit cousin Charlotte. Flossie's daughter.'

'Flossie had a daughter?'

'When she was fifteen. She was adopted by a vicar and his wife. They couldn't have children of their own and Flossie saw a way of giving Charlotte everything she would never be able to give her herself.'

'That must have been a horrendous decision to make.'

'I'm sure it was' Violet agreed. 'Charlotte always knew that she was adopted though. We used to visit her all the time. It was the first place mother thought of when she made the decision to leave. We thought it would only be for a few days.'

'Why did you need to leave at all?' Joseph frowned.

'Because it seemed like the right thing to do. Crowds can be a fickle thing as you and I both know. We didn't want people to think that we took any kind of satisfaction in what happened. That we weren't gloating.'

'No-one would have thought that.'

'People look for scandal where there is none and we didn't want to make it worse, so mother thought it best if we left for a few days. Let the dust settle. But then of course, Flossie died in the night. So, rather than us just visiting we had to deliver the news of her death to Charlotte. It was only when we arrived we found out that her remaining adoptive parent had passed on very recently. She had planned to visit Flossie here, so when we told her the news, she was beside herself as you can imagine. We couldn't leave her on her own.'

'Of course.' Joe said sympathetically. 'Is she well now?'

'She is better, but I would not say she is well. She plans to tidy up her adoptive parent's affairs and visit the camp for a while. Learn more about Flossie's life. I think it will do her good.' Violet took a sip of her mead. 'If I could have come back sooner though, I would have. I can't imagine what you have been through. I'm sorry. I hate that I left you alone for so long.'

'Gil was around, but it wasn't the same.' Joseph admitted. 'But then, it's never right when you're not there.'

'How are things now?'

'The house has been strangely quiet. Although, perhaps that is because Calissa is no longer screaming the walls down.' He put his cup on the counter. 'Amelia has convinced father to sell the estate. There are too many memories there. They spend a lot of their time looking for a smaller house in town.'

'So, what does this mean for you?'

'It means I am free, Vi.' He smiled as the sound of voices and violins pierced the silence. 'Perfect timing.' He took Violet's cup from her hand, placing it next to his own. 'Perhaps you would be daring enough to dance with me a second time, Miss Yardley?'

'There is at least music this time, Mr Davenport. 'Though it is not necessarily appropriate I hope.' She smiled as she moved into his arms and they began to move. As though the past few months hadn't even happened.

'It's a beautiful melody.' Joseph mused.

'It's a tale of a lost love.' Violet said. 'Of a man who wakes to find that the love of his life has fled in the night.'

'You'll never flee again, will you, Vi? Promise me.'

'I won't leave again.' Violet said softly as Joseph looked up at the stars on the ceiling, pulling her closer.

'We have found the other path, I think. We are under the stars, dancing while the music plays.' He lifted his hand from her waist and placed it in his pocket, retrieving the ring that she had worn and left behind. 'It has taken a lifetime to get here and now that we are here, I am, again, lost for words.' He laughed nervously and took a deep breath as he stilled. 'I found this caravan and I knew it was the answer as soon as I saw it. I will need to visit my family from time to time I know, but travelling is in your blood. And wherever you want to be, I want to be too. So, I built us a home of our own. The only memories this place will hold will be the ones that we make. If you want.' He paused and cleared his throat. 'I spoke to your mother earlier. I wanted to do it properly this time. I asked her for your hand.'

'Oh? And what did she say?'

'She gave me her blessing. Your aunt on the other hand, said that if I ever wronged you, she would ensure I spent the rest of my life covered in hideous boils. I doubt very much that she has that ability, but I didn't question her.' Violet laughed.

'You are asking me to be your Passepartout?'

'I am, Miss Yardley.'

'There is nothing I'll ever want more. Yes, I will.' She held out her hand. 'So, you had better put that ring back, Mr Davenport.'

'It would be my pleasure.' He slid the ring back in place and kissed Violet's fingers.

'Thank you.' He looked up and smiled as she brought her lips to his.

*****

'Are you sure you do not want to dance?'

'Hmm?'

'Edie has been calling you for an age. If you want to go and dance…' Violet nestled further into Joseph's body, revelling in him and the warmth of the fire that raged only feet from them.

'I find myself far too comfortable, sir. I don't think I ever want to move again.' She smiled contentedly as Joseph laughed against her back.

'Very well. In that case, there is something I want to ask you.'

'You don't think you've asked me enough questions today?' Violet tilted her head to look up at him, instantly transfixed by the way his smile glowed in the light of the bonfire. 'Very well, you may ask me one more question.'

'It's something that's been preying on my mind for an age now.'

'You are worried about something?'

'Not worried, just, curious. Well, a little worried, perhaps.'

'What on earth is it? What do you want to ask me?' Joseph stared over at the flames.

'That first day, when I came to see you. You were by the pond. I heard you talking to someone. You said, and I think your exact words were, 'who was the man who was with you?' I'm assuming the man you were referring to Tremaine, given that he appeared during the scrying ritual, but who appeared with him, Vi?' Violet's breath hitched in her throat. She reluctantly sat up, turning to face Joseph on the hay bale they shared.

'I had meant to ask you sooner, but then with everything else that was going on, the time was never right. You left and I found myself thinking about it more and more. And then when I was at the market in Bristol, where I bought the caravan, there was a girl there offering to tell people's fortunes and my inquisitive nature got the better of me. I asked her about the scrying and she was absolute in her reply. She said that you either saw the face of the person you were to marry or you saw no-one at all. But you saw two people. And then I remembered how distraught you were.'

'I see.' She grabbed the edges of her cloak and wrapped it tightly around her, a bitter chill running down her spine.

'Who did you see, Vi? I've imagined that maybe there is a link between this world and others, a guide of some sorts. Perhaps that is the answer. But then I worry that you heard something that troubled you greatly. Saw something, even. Have I upset you?' Joseph watched her studiously.

'No, you have not upset me.' She regarded Joseph cautiously. So much had gone unsaid in the past and it had only ever led to pain and loss. Hidden truths were not an option anymore, even if those truths brought consequences that divided rather than united. 'Come with me.' She stood and took his hand, leading him back to her family's tent.

'Vi, what's going on?'

'There's something I need to show you. If I can. I don't know that it will work though.'

'The moon is new. It will work, child.' Violet glanced over at Ruby who lay in bed, one eye open.

'Aunt Ruby, I'm sorry, did we wake you?'

'No, that infernal racket outside has prevented me from getting one ounce of shuteye.' She smiled knowingly. 'I believe the mirror is waiting for you both.' She rolled over, turning her back to them. 'Just try not to destroy this one.'

'I did not destroy the last one.' Violet muttered under her breath.

'Who destroyed it?' Joseph asked, his eyes wide.

'I'll explain everything. I promise.' She took Joseph's hand and led him to the corner of the tent, guiding him to a stack of cushions on the floor as she pulled the sheet from the mirror. Without looking back, she moved around the tent, extinguishing all the candles, leaving only the two that stood either side of the mirror alight. She made her way back over to where Joe sat cross-legged on the floor, positioning herself in front of him.

'Before we begin, you need to clear your mind. That shouldn't be too difficult.' She glanced back and winked at him as he laughed nervously. 'Put your hands on my waist and close your eyes. As I breathe in, you breath in, as I exhale, you exhale.' Joseph nodded and placed his hands on her waist and closed his eyes. Violet leaned back and brushed her lips against his. 'I love

369

you.' He did not open his eyes, just replied with a smile, his fingers squeezing her waist gently. Violet took a deep breath. 'Let us begin.'

They sat in silence for what felt like the longest time, Violet listening to the pattern of Joseph's breathing. When she heard it slow, felt him calm as his fingers relaxed, she opened her eyes and gazed at their reflection. 'Look into the mirror, Joe.' She took a deep breath, exhaling through pursed lips and stared at the sheet of onyx unflinching.

'Mirror of souls, I call to thee,

Remove the veil that I might see,

Send spirits forth, reveal their light,

Let darkness fade within their sight.

Mother of souls I pray of thee,

Pull down the veil, confide in me,

My one truth path, my life revealed,

In stories told and silence sealed.

So mote it be.'

The candlelight instantly flickered, the temperature around them plunging.

'Vi…'

'Don't worry. Nothing can harm you here. Just, keep your eyes on the mirror.'

'I can smell Jasmine.' Joseph said tightly. 'My mother's perfume.' Violet couldn't help the smile that danced across her lips.

'You came back.'

'Came back? It was my mother that you saw?' Violet nodded.

'She looked so distressed. After Tremaine appeared, she showed herself. It was her that broke the mirror. We tried to ask her what was wrong, but it all happened so quickly. I wasn't sure if the two apparitions were related, if she was telling me to stay away from you, if she was perhaps trapped between two worlds somehow. When you saw me, I was trying to reach her and failing abysmally. When Aggy died, I came so close to telling you. I thought it might give you hope. The knowledge that there is another life after this one. But I was scared that you would think me crazy, or that your father was right after all. That I was indeed a witch.'

'But she was warning you. About Tremaine.'

'Turns out she was. She was still guiding fate, even from the grave.'

'Mother.' Joseph stood and walked to the mirror, gently placing his hand upon it as thousands of petals poured from within the black pane and cascaded down onto the floor at his feet.

'What is she saying?' Joseph stared at the petals in awe as they settled around him.

'Pink cyclamen.' Violet said sadly. 'It means she's saying goodbye.'

'What, no!'

'She is ready to pass, Joe. She's done what needs to be done here. It's time to let her go now. She will wait for you on the other side. You will see her again, I promise, but, for now, you must say goodbye. Let her know that you are ready. Let her know that she can leave in peace.' Joseph's head fell, his eyes closed tight, his hand still on the mirror.

'I miss you.' The words slipped from his lips, barely a whisper. 'Sleep in peace, mother. I promise I will see you on the other side.' The last of the petals slipped over Joseph's hand and drifted to the floor.

'And so now you know.' Violet stood and walked up behind Joseph, placing a hand on his arm, resting her forehead on his back. 'If you want to leave, I will not stop you. I will understand.'

'Why would I want to leave you?' Joseph turned to face her, his face panicked.

'Because you see me as the witch your father warned you about after all. Most folk would be running for the hills right now.' Joseph smiled, lifting her face so his eyes could meet hers.

'Vi, you are so wrong! You have been gifted with something I cannot even begin to fathom. I will never leave your side unless you tell me to and I do not think you a witch. Well, not a bad one anyway.' He grinned and wrapped his arms around, pulling her close. 'And besides which, we are fated to be together, you and I.' He took her hand and led her away from the mirror. 'Thank you for showing me. And for giving me the chance to say goodbye.'

'What happens now?' Violet smiled as they left the tent.

'We look to the future as it has always been intended.' Joseph smiled. 'But first, we dance.'

The end.

Printed in Great Britain
by Amazon